T0271656

The Witching Hour

The Dandy Gilver Series

After the Armistice Ball

The Burry Man's Day

Bury Her Deep

The Winter Ground

Dandy Gilver and the Proper Treatment of Bloodstains

Dandy Gilver and an Unsuitable Day for a Murder

Dandy Gilver and a Bothersome Number of Corpses

Dandy Gilver and a Deadly Measure of Brimstone

Dandy Gilver and the Reek of Red Herrings

Dandy Gilver and the Unpleasantness in the Ballroom

Dandy Gilver and a Most Misleading Habit

Dandy Gilver and a Spot of Toil and Trouble

A Step So Grave

The Turning Tide

The Mirror Dance

Standalones

In Place of Fear

Catriona McPherson

The Witching Hour

HODDER &
STOUGHTON

First published in Great Britain in 2024 by Hodder & Stoughton Limited
An Hachette UK company

1

A CIP catalogue record for this title is available from the British Library

Hardback ISBN 978 1 399 72039 7
Trade Paperback ISBN 978 1 399 72040 3
ebook ISBN 978 1 399 72041 0

Typeset in Plantin by Palimpsest Book Production Ltd, Falkirk, Stirlingshire

Printed and bound in Great Britain by Clays Ltd, Elcograf S.p.A.

Hodder & Stoughton policy is to use papers that are natural, renewable
and recyclable products and made from wood grown in sustainable forests.
The logging and manufacturing processes are expected to conform to the
environmental regulations of the country of origin.

Hodder & Stoughton Limited
Carmelite House
50 Victoria Embankment
London EC4Y 0DZ

www.hodder.co.uk

In memory of Gareth Hughes:
scientist, crime-fiction fan and friend

Prologue

The kirk in the village of Dirleton has no clock in its tower, and so there is no chime from above to accompany the earthy crack below when fragile skull meets solid rock. Nevertheless, the hour does strike on sundry other timepieces all around the village green and the lanes leading off it: an antique grandfather clock at the turn on a stone staircase; a grandmother clock above a Scotch dresser in a cosy dining room; a polished-gilt carriage clock under its dome in a back parlour; a large, plain wall clock behind a bar, meant to stop all arguments about last orders; a pretty, coloured clock, rumoured to be Limoges, sitting on a cottage chimney piece; a kitchen clock, sooty from the range below, fat and comforting like its reassuring tick; and a folding travel alarm, so small as to be inconvenient for any but a lady's fingers to wind, which takes up the corner of a writing desk. The strokes, whether marked by a solemn, deep gong or the tinniest little ring, echo it all almost perfectly: the shout, the trip, the gasp, the stumble, the stagger, the drop, the dull crack of bone, the helpless groan, the spasm of limbs, the final settling and, then, as the last note fades from all the clocks, the stillness.

Nowhere is more still than a village at night. Woods and moors have creatures abroad on their nocturnal round. Cities and towns are a-bustle with light and sound. But a village – a blameless, orderly, settled village such as Dirleton – is a portrait of peace. Nothing will disturb that peace till morning. Nothing will stir, once those who were watching have made themselves sure that life is extinguished and have done what they need to do.

Chapter 1

If Nanny Palmer could see me she would rap my knuckles with a hairbrush and send me straight to bed: she drilled me in posture, in table manners, in attentiveness to guests, and currently I was lolling like a rag doll in my dining chair, full to my clavicles with the first four courses of dinner and barely even pretending to listen to what my neighbour was saying. We were out of the habit of entertaining on this scale at Gilverton, truth be told, and I had dug into clear soup, poached fish, a terrine of pigeon and a sorbet, quite forgetting that there was still roasted meat, salad, pudding and cheese to go.

So I would have gone off to bed gratefully enough had Nanny sent me, throbbing knuckles or no, but there was no chance of escape tonight. It was Hugh's birthday, his sixtieth birthday to boot, and the entire Gilver family was determined to make it a gala occasion. I had gathered all of his dearest friends, with no thought for myself about whether they had wives to bring or if such wives as they did have were much of a treat. I had also let our cook, Mrs Tilling, wander off into the by-ways of Hugh's Victorian childhood and Edwardian youth as regards the menu, to wit the pigeons, and the suet still to come.

Moreover, I had lifted the blanket ban on war talk at the table. For one thing, it was pointless to expect the men to speak of anything else, since most of these friendships had been born in the army and stiffened to their current state either in Africa or in the Great War itself. Besides, for months now Hugh's conversational menu had consisted solely of news about Europe and predictions arising therefrom and was replaced by brooding silence when said news and predictions were vetoed by me. Brooding silences at a dinner party were not to be countenanced, and so for his birthday I had relented, even though as a result I had had to listen first to Major Someone on my left regaling me with anecdotes about Spion Kop and then to Colonel Someone Else on my right drooling over Spain's recent antics as only a childless bachelor, himself too old to fight, could do.

'Difficult month, May,' he said, poking the gooseberry ice as he had just poked the terrine. Such was my desire to turn away from Franco, I fell on this gambit like a shipwrecked sailor washing up on an island in a storm, feeling none of my usual disdain for anyone ill-mannered enough to remark on the food at another's table, beyond a murmur of 'how delicious' for form's sake. I launched into winter savoury, summer chicory, ducks stowed in the icehouse and even Gilverton's new electrical refrigerator, not caring that within moments he glazed over with a depth of boredom equal to mine from five minutes before.

Alec Osborne, on the other side of the table, caught my eye and twinkled at me, causing me immediately to finish my point and ask the colonel about barrack rations. Whereupon Alec, who knows me so well after seventeen years of detecting together, only twinkled more and leaned in close to Daisy Esslemont, his own neighbour, to whisper about me. Daisy smirked and shot me a look that was unchanged from the looks she used to shoot me across gallery floors in Paris while we were both at finishing school, whenever she manoeuvred Mademoiselle into expounding on the artistic merits of some fleshy nude in oils or rippling marble god.

I was happy to see her smiling. The only disappointment of the entire day was that her husband Silas was missing the party owing to a prior and unbreakable engagement. Daisy had been uncharacteristically sour about it when she had arrived alone.

'Such nonsense,' she had said, sitting at my dressing table and inspecting her face with a critical gaze. 'Regimental dinner, my eye. How long have he and Hugh been pals, Dandy?'

'Since short trousers and midnight feasts at Kingoldrum,' I said, leaning over her to dab at my hair with a brush, trying to fluff it up a bit and reduce the oil-slick effect my maid's attentions had produced. 'But Hugh doesn't mind. If it was the Black Watch instead of the Atholl Highlanders, he'd be there himself.'

'And we could have kedgeree on our laps in your sitting room, watching the babies roll about,' said Daisy.

'Hardly babies now,' I said. 'They pelt around like clock-work motor cars. Lavinia got herself stuck in that old apple tree in the corner of the cutting garden yesterday. Terrifyingly high up. The garden boy had to fetch a stepladder.'

'I still can't believe you're a grandmother,' said Daisy, opening her mouth in a silent scream to paint it.

Nor could I. Donald, my elder son, had married very young and set right to it, presenting us with a pair of sturdy twins before the year was out. And Mallory was pregnant again right now. A year ago, I might have raised an eyebrow:

she had proved herself all but incapable of dealing with two infants and the memory of Lavinia and Edward's early days was not one I expected soon to fade. Now, clutching at straws somewhat, I consoled myself with the thought that if conscription came, as Hugh said it must, there was a slight chance that single men would go first, that married men without children might be taken before fathers and even that fathers of three – or four, if Mallory's size was a reliable indicator – might be called up before fathers of two. In fact, it could all be over before Donald's name came to the head of the list. If it started. I was still clinging to "if", as were all mothers throughout the land.

'Throughout the continent, I daresay,' Alec had tried to claim once in quite the bitterest fight we had ever had. 'In Germany and Italy just the same.'

'Then they shouldn't have voted for monsters,' I shot back.

'I don't suppose all of them did,' Alec said. 'The Italian election was a travesty. And the boys who'll fight on the German side weren't of age when—'

'I can't listen,' I told him.

'What is it you say in these parts, Dandy? We're all Jock Tamson's bairns?'

'Sickening mawkishness,' I said.

'To remind ourselves that all of us are God's children?'

'I couldn't care less about anyone's "bairns" but my own at the moment. Really, Alec, I don't argue with you about the trenches. How dare you argue with me about a mother's feelings. Truly, how dare you have the gall.'

'Madam?' Grant, my maid, was in the room. I had not heard her enter and clearly had not heard more than one attempt to gain my attention either, for both she and Daisy were staring at me.

'Grant,' I said, starting and dropping the hairbrush.

'The others are starting to arrive,' she told me. 'There's a Mrs Keith in the hall, wearing a most peculiar garment. Becky tried to take it off her but it's not a cloak after all. It's a dress.'

'A dress I want to see!' said Daisy. 'Come on, Dan.'

As we were leaving my bedroom, I noticed Grant straightening the dropped hairbrush. Such was the kindness with which we were all treating one another as the clouds gathered. I had messed up my hair and Grant herself had declined to scold me.

'Weevils!' said the colonel, finishing his story about army food.

I shuddered politely and drew breath to make a reply, but evidently this was a rich seam of anecdote and he had barely scraped at it. He was off again, regaling me with a competition he and his fellow officers had held once to "guess the game". Another of the men joined in and together they relived happy days, recalling with a shout of laughter a time that the bottles of coffee essence and Worcestershire sauce got swapped by a native cook.

'Made not a blind bit of difference!' the colonel said, wheezing with mirth. 'That antelope was as high as a kite. Take more than coffee to put a dent in it.'

I let my attention wander and the long meal wore on.

I did not then, or later, pay much heed to the table itself, for Pallister had done himself and me proud. The silver glittered and the flowers, hours into the evening, looked as dewy as the moment they were picked. He had pressed me into buying terrifically expensive candles too – really quite jaw-droppingly expensive – but he was right. They burned with steady pale ovals of flame and there was not a drip to be seen. He had been sour about Becky and a village girl instead of footmen, of course, but at least he offered the beef while Becky wrangled the gravy boat; and the girl managed the vegetables nicely as far as I could see.

As the salad was cleared, I found my eyes drawn to Teddy, my younger son, whom I had placed beside his invited house guest, a girl by the name of Dolly Cartaright. He had met her at a Christmas party in an unlikely district of London, where one of his school chums had a studio or a printing press or some such thing, and had started dropping her name into conversation at Easter, before coming to my sitting room, quite solemn and unlike himself, to ask if she might be included in tonight's party.

'Family and old friends though, darling,' I had said.

'Well . . .' was all the reply he made, but I know my son and that was enough. I went straight to Hugh in his business room to pick over the news.

'Cartaright?' he said. 'Not Cartwright?'

'Nor Carter-Wright,' I assured him. 'Teddy wrote it down for me to address the envelope.'

'What address?'

'London,' I told him. 'A 3F, I'm afraid. A flat. But north of the river. It's so hard to tell these days. She could be anyone.'

'Dolly Cartaright,' said Hugh. 'She sounds like a barmaid.'

'I don't care if she *is* a barmaid,' I said. 'Or a chorus girl, or even a . . .' My imagination ran out.

'An artist's model,' said Hugh. 'Like What's-her-name.'

'I think she was a muse,' I reminded him. 'Although that might be the same thing, now I consider it at a distance. She *was* very . . . limber.'

Hugh rewarded me with a snort of laughter.

'And I mean it. I don't care. If she marries our son—'

'If marriage isn't too old-fashioned for her,' Hugh chipped in.

'And the call-up goes for single men first—'

'It won't or only very briefly.'

'—then she could pull pints of beer in the Atholl Arms for all our friends and I'd drive down at closing time and offer a lift home.'

'What friends of yours drink pints of beer in the Atholl Arms?' Hugh asked me.

I rewarded him with a little snort of my own. 'So I may invite her? To your birthday?'

'I look forward to it,' Hugh said. 'Saves booking a clown.'

How wrong we both were. When Miss Cartaright turned up and was presented to us over tea in the library, she was revealed to be the daughter of a minor but respectable branch of perfectly good Shropshire family, whose widowed mother had married an American and not only taken his name herself but also bestowed it upon her child. Dolly was short for Dahlia, my own middle name, a coincidence that sparked an instant affinity, by way of shared suffering.

At the current moment, as the pudding plates were cleared, she had half her attention on Teddy, but not owing to complacency or indifference, I thought, after watching a moment or two. Rather, it seemed they were automatically attuned to one another like a pair of radio transmitters, or I might mean one transmitter and its receiver: aware without concentrating, hearing without listening, answering without speaking. They were, in short, clearly in love. As I say, though, she was a nice girl of the sort I understood and the other half of her attention was politely trained on the general conversation being batted around that end of the table, not quite like the beach ball we had all been taught to emulate, since the topic was the League of Nations, but not quite beyond the pale of what passed, this spring, for normality.

I was not the only one noticing. Hugh caught my eye and, without moving a muscle in either his brow or his cheeks, still managed to convey a shared thought with me. We had been married such a long time, I reflected, that I could interpret the various absences of expression without any trouble at all. Donald does not share his father's poker face. He was waggling his brows and quirking his lips at me in a manner more suited to entertaining his toddlers than communing in public with his mother. I was glad when Mallory frowned at him across the cloth and thus persuaded him to check his exuberance a little. Her look to me was far more measured. She has an attractive way of pursing her lips that, while being the opposite of a smile, nevertheless manages to hint at smiling. She did it now. I smiled openly back at her, feeling a great surge of contentment suddenly. My husband was enjoying his party, my daughter-in-law was becoming a good friend, my prospective daughter-in-law looked as though she would slot into the family nicely, and my grandchildren were cosily ensconced in their father and uncle's old nursery for the night, out of earshot, making it no matter to me if an excess of cake at Grandpa's birthday tea had left them too boisterous for sleep.

Then, as quickly as the wave of happiness rose, it drained and, as though I had turned the dial on a kaleidoscope, I saw my family in quite a different arrangement: my husband too old to fight, granted, and my grandson too young, my daughters-in-law a source of companionship and succour besides, but my sons, my boys, gone; as lost to me now as they would be hence, since the path we were all on led one way, straight down, with no turnings. I felt a sob begin to build under my ribcage and it took all of Nanny Palmer's training to turn a visceral impulse to flee into something approaching conventional behaviour.

'Shall we, ladies?' I said, standing and dropping my napkin.

There was a moment of silence. Pallister, only just beginning to think about bringing the cheese in, stopped dead and frowned at me. All the gentlemen shot to their feet and got ready to help the women with their chairs. Daisy said, 'You've turned over two pages at once, Dan,' raising a titter. But Mallory, bless her, and Dolly too, bless her twice, dabbed their lips, rose smoothly and headed for the door.

Both Hugh and Alec followed my progress with concerned looks. Hugh's brow cleared when I stopped behind his chair, put a hand on his shoulder and said, 'Happy birthday, dear. And don't think for a minute that starting early means you don't get to finish late.'

Most of his chums met this evidence of wifely generosity with great good cheer, raising glasses to me and even murmuring praise. I heard a few 'Splendid woman's and 'Lucky blighter's and the like. Hugh placed his hand briefly on mine and patted it. Only Alec continued to watch me as I stalked away, and only Pallister spoke.

'Madam?' he said. 'Shall I . . . ?'

Poor Pallister. Apart from the village girl, tonight's dinner was a quite a return to the good old days for him. He had been polishing and bullying since the day before yesterday. And now I had spoiled it.

'Don't undo Mrs Tilling's lovely arrangements,' I said. I had seen the rounds of Stilton and the pyramids of dusky figs and I knew that dismantling the platters to send half of the bounty to the drawing room would break her heart. 'We'll be fine with coffee and some bonbons,' I assured him. 'And no rush even for those.'

Then at last I made my escape and managed not to go into a cupboard to howl before I dragged myself to the waiting ladies.

'Jolly good idea, I say,' Daisy greeted me, as I slipped into the room. 'I'm stuffed like a foie gras goose but I'm too greedy not to fall on nice cheese when I see it.'

'Good Lord,' I said. 'Mrs Commander, Mrs Keith, ladies: Mrs Esslemont here is a very old friend and you must excuse her.' Both the wives I addressed gave me tight smiles and turned to one another, apparently intending to speak tête-à-tête if there was such coarseness on offer in the wider company. For Daisy, I had to admit, was drunk. I regretted telling Pallister we could wait for coffee.

'Girls,' I said, joining Mallory and Dolly in a little grouping of chairs well away from the fire and the drinks tray. 'Thank you. The war talk suddenly felt unbearable. Mallory dear, please tell Dolly she hasn't fallen in with gypsies. I'm not usually so odd, I assure you.'

'Mrs Gilver,' said Dolly, pressing my hand between hers. 'The night before last I ate scrambled eggs right out of the pan with a spoon. Standing up. I've been thinking about my nanny all night to try to remember my manners. Please don't worry about me.'

I laughed and turned my hand to squeeze one of hers. 'My dear girl,' I said, 'if I had a pound for every time Nanny Palmer floats into *my* head . . .'

'Well then,' said Mallory. 'I'm not going to bother putting these back on.' She rolled her long white evening gloves into a ball and threw them over the headrest of her chair, then wiped her hands together as though declaring a job well done. I chucked mine after hers and I have to say it felt marvellous.

12

'I've left mine in the dining room,' said Dolly. 'They probably tumbled off my lap when I stood up. So I'm the gypsy if anyone is, wouldn't you say?'

'You are two very good girls,' I said. 'Now, I must go and look after Mrs Esslemont. She's . . .'

'Sauced,' said Mallory. 'It's not like her. My goodness look at her, Dandy! She's loosening her frock!'

Daisy was indeed grappling with the buttons down one side of her evening dress.

'If I can keep my belt knotted in this state,' Mallory said, patting the hummock at her middle, 'then anyone can. Oh, look at the colonel's wife! Talk about sucking lemons. What on earth's going on? Do you know?'

I hastened to Daisy's side to see if I could find out, leaving the girls giggling.

Of course, Pallister had ignored my permission to hold off on coffee and sweets and was already entering with an enormous silver tray, delicate china rattling since he moved rather more quickly than his usual stately glide. I guessed he wanted to get back to the dining room before Becky and her assistant could cause any havoc there. I gave him a grateful smile as I poured a cup for Daisy and bore down on where she was lolling on a chaise longue.

'Budge up, you sot,' I said. 'What's the matter with you?'

'Ugh,' she said, shifting to one end of the chaise so that at least her gaping buttons were hidden by the cushions. 'What's *ever* the matter, Dandy?'

I thought about this remark for a moment, while sipping at my own blistering cup of wicked black sobriety. (Ever since Mrs Tilling took up the habit herself she has become a reliable source of excellent coffee.) Daisy's life was comfortable enough as far as I could see. She had three daughters

13

– one just married, one engaged, and one still having fun – pots of money, an easily run house, and the kind of natural kindness and cheerfulness that meant she held on to her servants. There was really only one possible source of trouble.

But she had been married to Silas for a long time and had made her peace with his habits years ago. He had never embarrassed her and no one – whether spurned lover, angry husband, or determined child – had ever knocked on her door. I was at a loss as to what he might have done to upset her so, beyond missing tonight's party.

'I told you already,' I said to her, 'Hugh doesn't mind. And you're far too good a friend of the house to feel awkward about turning up alone, aren't you? It was a treat for Alec, apart from anything.'

'I got five minutes of Alec and two hours of the major,' Daisy said. 'Do you happen to know what regiment he's the major *of*, Dandy?'

'The Black Watch, I assume,' I said. 'Isn't that how he and Hugh know one another?'

'It is not,' Daisy said. 'Ugh, this coffee is like tarmacadam. It's flattened down all my lovely fuzz from the wine.'

'That was rather the idea,' I said. 'And I'm going to get you another cup. Perhaps you could attend to your frock?'

'What?' said Daisy. Then: 'Bloody hell!' She sat up straight and, while not quite slapping her cheeks with her palms, she nevertheless managed to pound some manner of decency back into herself. She always had this talent. She could scramble back into our rooms in Paris and look sober enough to convince Mam'zell she had merely been outside to look at the stars.

Now, all these years later, she had had more practice, and turned aside to rearrange herself as I made for the

14

coffee tray. The major's wife, as it happened, was there for a top-up too.

'Do help yourself to a bonbon,' I said. 'I must apologise for dragging you all away before the end of dinner. I hope you're not still peckish.'

'Not much chance of that,' she said. 'Delicious dinner, my dear. Quite a treat for us these days.' She leaned in close. 'Between you and me, I made sure to pack liver salts for Percy. Whenever he goes to a regimental dinner he comes home in quite some distress. *Anno domini*, he says. Getting old and losing form, as are we all.'

'And what regiment *is* that?' I said. It was rather a bald question but I could not think how to soften it. Besides, she was telling me about her husband's stomach and it seemed that we must be beyond the need for pussyfooting. 'Didn't he serve with Hugh?'

'Oh no, not the Watch,' said Mrs Major. 'It *is* the Watch for dear Hugh, isn't it? I seem to recall so. Percy is an Atholl Highlander.'

'But—' I said, before I caught myself.

'If Hugh said they "served" together,' she went on, 'he probably means on their tour. Europe, you know. Wild oats. Can-can dancers and what have you. A little joke. And all water under the bridge. Men will be boys.' She laughed at her own little joke and even went so far as to repeat it. 'Men will be boys indeed.' Then she leaned in even closer and dropped her voice to barely a mutter. 'You should perhaps help Daisy Esslemont to see it that way. Remind her of her many compensations.'

This remark would have mystified most people, but I thought I understood it. Silas had startled his friends and earned first their scorn and then their envy by starting up an insurance company of all things, years ago when the rest of us were still pretending we could live forever on our rents. Mrs Major evidently believed that a wife kept in furs and Paris fashions should not complain about even such renowned philanderings as those of Silas Esslemont.

I disagreed. I thought if Silas insisted on betraying his class by entering into business, he should be held to the morals of middle-class businessmen.

'Poor Daisy,' was all I said, however.

'Hmph,' said Mrs Major. 'Percy had a tough row to hoe with her at dinner. I overheard some actual grilling, don't you know? On the topic of . . . well, I'm not exactly sure what. The secrets of the officers' mess or something.'

'I shall take her more coffee and hope it helps,' I said, excusing myself and returning to Daisy.

'At least put some sugar in it,' she said, after the first sip. 'This is filthy stuff.'

'It's supposed to be,' I said. 'That's the mark of good coffee. Like olives and whisky. Now look, Daisy dear. I had a word with his wife and I must say I think you're being very silly. I'm quite sure that the major respects Silas and the rest of the regiment enormously, but he has been friends with Hugh since they were boys. You know what it's like when you have two invitations for the same day. I toss coins.'

'What are you talking about?' said Daisy. 'The major isn't skipping the mess to toast Hugh. He told me all about the feast they had at the *last* Atholl Highlanders' dinner, and it was a week and a half ago. While I was visiting my mother.'

'I don't—' I said.

'Which means wherever Silas is tonight, it is not where he said he was. He chucked Hugh's birthday, leaving me to come alone, and he lied about why. He has never done that before, Dandy.'

I paused to consider the machinations required to run a string of mistresses for upwards of twenty-five years without lying to one's wife, and paused further to feel grateful for Hugh's incapacities when it came to subterfuge, then I decided a brisk approach was best.

'Well then no doubt he is somewhere rather different from where we might expect. Perhaps he's organising a surprise for you. Or perhaps he wanted to visit a doctor for something embarrassing?'

To my regret, Daisy's face drained. 'Oh my heavens!' she said. 'That's it! He's ill. He might be *dying*!'

She shot to her feet and made a beeline for the tray of whisky and soda on the opposite sideboard from the coffee things. Rattling the decanter against the edge of a glass, she poured herself a gargantuan measure and, ignoring the siphon, drank it straight down. Then she poured another, even larger, which she brought back. Conversations all around had sunk to that murmur which allows for perfect eavesdropping.

Daisy sank down beside me. 'I've known there was some-thing wrong all winter, Dan,' she said, gasping rather – after another good glug. 'He's been preoccupied and peculiar. Of course, I thought some chit had got her claws in too deep for him to shake her off, but I think you're right.' She set her empty glass down and sat up very straight before declaiming, 'Silas is dying!'

'Oh for heaven's sake,' I said. I had only floated the notion to get her to shut up about the other possibility. Only now did it occur to me that presenting an inebriated woman with the means to indulge in melodrama had been misguided in the extreme.

'I need a drink,' Daisy declared, as though she had not just had four or five, masquerading as two. She got back to

17

her feet, with less alacrity now, and tacked towards the whisky, saying over her shoulder, 'My husband is dying, Dandy.'

'Don't be silly,' I said, not even caring that our conversation was enthralling the entire, now silent, drawing room. 'Why not go to bed, Daisy?' I urged. 'It will all look very different in the morning.'

I was right. It certainly did.

Chapter 2

Sunday, 14 May 1939

'Madam.' Grant has the perfect voice for a lady's maid, soft yet penetrating. She has never had to repeat her first salutation to wake me up in the morning and today was no exception, despite the fact that it was still dark and I had been up until well after eleven, first attempting to curb Daisy in the drawing room then, having failed, practically carrying her upstairs. I had not fallen gratefully into my bed until midnight, and had not finally got to sleep until nearer one.

'Mmmmm?' said Hugh, groggily, from the pillow beside me.

I opened one eye, hoping to catch Grant smirking, a coarseness I could never scold her for out loud but the knowledge of which, shared between us, would put me in moral credit for months. I should have known better. Grant's face, shining with night cream and topped by the kind of sleeping bonnet I thought had gone out with marcel waves, was solemn. Was, I thought as I opened the other eye, grave.

'What time is it?' I said. Even Bunty, my Dalmatian, had not stirred from her billet at the foot of the bed.

'Five,' said Grant. 'There's someone on the telephone.'

'Asking for *me*?'

'Urgently.'

Bunty accepted the unwelcome reality before I did. She roused herself like a reluctant shift worker and jumped down. She stretched her front legs by sticking her bottom high in the air and pressing her chest down, stretched her back legs by sticking her chest high in the air and pressing her bottom down, and finally shook herself all over until her ears rattled.

'Good girl,' said Grant. 'That's the ticket. Madam, where's your dressing gow— Oh! Where's your *night*gown?' she amended, as I threw back the blankets. I wriggled into both, shoved my feet into bedroom slippers and followed her downstairs.

I was rarely about at five in the morning, before even maids were stirring, and the stairs and halls of Gilverton seemed most unlike themselves, grey and ghostly, frowsy with a day and a night's dust and still redolent of tobacco and rich food from the evening before. My feet turned, without bidding, towards my sitting room, but I heard Pallister clear his throat and realised that he was standing, resplendent in a tartan dressing gown and showing peeps of what looked like silk pyjamas, holding the hall telephone.

'What's going on?' I asked him.

'I hardly—' Pallister began. It was most unlike him to dither but then I did not know how five in the morning usually finds him.

'Who am I speaking to?' I said, taking the instrument out of his hands instead of waiting any longer.

'Who's this?' said a voice, rather peremptorily in my opinion, given that whoever it was had telephoned my house at this ungodly hour of the morning.

'Mrs Gilver. And you are?' I said.

'Ah, Mrs Gilver,' said the voice. 'I was put on to you by—'

'I shan't ask again,' I said in the stiffest tone I could summon so many hours before breakfast and after such a late evening. 'Who are you?'

'This is the police,' said the voice, in an injured tone. I glanced at Pallister and mouthed, 'Police?' He nodded and I managed not to roll my eyes. Twenty years ago a telephone call from a policeman would have outwitted Pallister's sangfroid quite handily, but Alec and I have fallen in with them far too often for such squeamishness to be warranted these days.

'I'm ringing you from Haddington Police Station,' the voice went on. 'I was put onto you by the staff—'

'Haddington, Constable?' I said.

This slur finally jolted a name out of the man. 'I'm *Sgt* Dodgson,' he said. 'I was put onto you by the staff at Croys. They told me there's a Mrs Esslemont lodging there?'

'Lodging isn't quite—' I said, then abandoned it; it hardly mattered. 'Yes, Mrs Esslemont stayed here last night. What's going on?'

'And she was there all night?' Dodgson said.

'I find that a most extraordinary question, Sgt Dodgson,' I said. 'I'm afraid if you won't tell me what this is about I shall ring off and take it up with the chief constable at nine o'clock.'

This was bluster; I had only the haziest idea where Haddington was – somewhere south of Edinburgh – and not the faintest clue which constabulary it fell under, much less whether I knew the chief constable in question. It worked though.

'There's been an accident,' Dodgson said. 'A Mr Silas Esslemont has met with a misfortune.'

'Is he all right?'

'And there's a witness, see?'

'Is he badly hurt?'

'And all this witness can tell us is—'

'Which hospital has he been taken to?' I took the mouth-piece away and said to Grant, 'Make some tea and tell Drysdale to get the car ready.' She bustled off.

'He's not in a hospital,' Dodgson was saying as I returned my attention to him.

'Oh! Good,' I said. Then something about the quality of his silence made me shiver. 'Where is he?'

'Laid out on a board in the back room of a local pub.' Dodgson said this with rather too much relish for my liking.

'And what exactly makes you think this unfortunate individual is Mr Esslemont?' I said. 'He has no connection with Haddington, as far as I know.' What I was thinking was that Silas might have exhausted all the female company in Perthshire over the years, but even he was not such a Lothario that he would need to cast his net as far as that.

'It didn't happen at Haddington. Do you know Gullane?'

'Mr Esslemont had no reason to be in Gullane either,' I said. There was a golf course of some repute there but there are nearer and better at St Andrews.

'It wasn't Gullane,' said Dodgson. 'Gullane's just the nearest place you might have heard of. It was Dirleton.'

'Where?'

'The village of Dirleton. Charming wee place but off the beaten track. I was helping you situate yourself, Mrs Gilver.'

'But what makes you connect some poor chap who met with misfortune at Dirleton, by Gullane, near Haddington, with Mr Esslemont of Perthshire?'

'A letter in his pocket,' said Dodgson. 'And a signet ring. It's Mr Esslemont all right.'

I took a deep breath and let it go again slowly, alarmed to

22

hear how shaky it sounded. Silas, dead? *Silas?* He did wear rather a prominent ring on his little finger, as it happened. 'I shall fetch Mrs Esslemont,' I said. 'It might take a minute or two though. If you would give my butler here your telephone number, Sgt Dodgson, perhaps we can ring you back. In case the exchange cuts us off. They do tend to—' Then a thought struck me. 'Hold hard, though. Why did you ask me if Mrs Esslemont was here all night?'

Grant sidled back through the green baize door, looking worried.

'Well, as I tried to tell you, madam, the witness apprised us of the fact that the assailant—'

'Assailant?' I exclaimed. Grant boggled.

'Assailant, Mrs Gilver. The witness apprised us of the fact that the assailant was a woman.'

'Still rather a leap to—' I began.

'And then the letter too,' Dodgson said. 'We ascertained Mr Esslemont's name from the address on the envelope but we also perused the contents. As part of the investigation, you understand. All perfectly proper.'

'In this instance, I agree,' I said. 'Who was it from? Because whoever *that* is must surely be your leading suspect.'

'An excellent question and a sensible deduction, Mrs Gilver,' Dodgson said. 'But given the contents, it struck us all – the constable and the surgeon and myself – that Mrs Esslemont certainly had a motive.'

'Ah,' I said. 'How disappointing.'

'Interesting,' said Dodgson. 'You didn't expostulate, Mrs Gilver. You didn't give voice to any shock or incredulity.'

He made an excellent point and I kicked myself, not quite internally. At least, Grant noticed something and shot me a quizzical look.

'As I say, Sergeant,' I went on, trying for a breezy tone, 'Mrs Esslemont was here all night. And right now I need to go and tell her this dreadful news.'

'Or happy news,' said Dodgson. 'Given the letter.'

Odious man. 'Are you married, Sergeant?' I asked him.

'To my job,' he said, pompously in my opinion.

'Well, in case you ever do marry a woman rather than a job,' I said, 'you might be comforted to know in advance that your future widow will mourn you no matter what kind of hand you make at being a husband. I'll ring back shortly.'

I gave the telephone to Pallister and stamped off upstairs, almost angry enough to forget how dismayed I was. Bunty huddled close in at my heels that way she does when she senses all is not well, and Grant kept pace with both of us.

'I liked "future widow",' she said. 'Nicely put, madam.'

'You'll have gleaned that Silas Esslemont is dead,' I said. 'By the hand of a woman, according to some witness they claim to have drummed up. I'm afraid Mrs Esslemont is in for a time of it.'

We were at her door and, with a gentle knock, I entered. I had left her flat on her back in her petticoat, having removed her gown and jewels, and I expected to find her still lying there, or tumbled in a wreck of bedding after the kind of torrid night my sons tell me can sometimes follow such indulgence. To my surprise, however, the bed was empty.

'Daisy?' I said stepping over to the dressing room, although I did not see what would have taken her there. 'Grant, go and see if she's in the bathroom. She might be . . . unwell.'

'Yes, Becky told me,' Grant said, and disappeared.

While she was gone, I crossed to the curtains and, withdrawing them and turning to survey the room, I soon found myself hoping against hope that Grant would return with news of Daisy's misery and a request for a prairie oyster. For not only was my friend nowhere to be seen, but her dressing gown was hanging on the back of the bedroom door and her slippers were tidily tucked under the edge of her dressing table. The gown I had laid over a chair last night had, in contrast, vanished. Her satin shoes likewise were not where I had placed them.

'No sign,' said Grant, returning. 'And that's not all, I'm afraid. I should have told you immediately, but when I slipped out to ask Drysdale about the car . . .'

'What? Spit it out, Grant.'

'Well, madam, your Cowley's gone.'

We stared at one another. I broke the silence first. 'She probably got up early and went home,' I said.

'But her chauffeur's still here,' said Grant. 'He shared Drysdale's room last night. I had to whisper to Drysdale so as not to wake him.'

'Well, she's probably . . .' I said, giving it my best.

'Of course,' said Grant, giving it hers.

Neither one of us, though, was convincing the other nor herself. We stood and regarded one another glumly, trying to find a way to dismiss the facts: that Daisy was angry with Silas, and was drunk, and was gone. And someone had taken my motor car somewhere, in the middle of the night. And Silas had been killed. By a woman.

'It might not be him, madam,' Grant said at last. 'What's a letter? What's a ring? And Mrs Esslemont . . .' Then her voice ran dry.

'Would never . . .' I managed to add before mine did the same. I felt the horror of it suddenly threaten to overwhelm me and was grateful for Bunty's worried, wet nose nudging into my hand, forcing my clenched fist to open. 'Right then,' I said.

'Right then,' Grant agreed.

I had to muster all my acting ability for the good sergeant. I told him that Mrs Esslemont was prostrate with grief and not equal to speaking on the telephone. I suggested that I bring her to Dirleton as soon as she felt up to the journey and thanked him for his time.

'Very well,' he said. 'With any luck he'll be fit to view by then.'

'What?' I said. 'I certainly didn't mean to offer her up to fulfil that horrid task. Not a bit of it. I shall bring a friend of the family to take care of identifying Mr Esslemont. I only meant that I was sure you would want to speak to his wife. His widow. And so I shall drive her down there.' *As soon as I find her,* I added to myself.

He rumbled a little but, offered an escape from having to drive a police motor car all the way to Perthshire to pick up a widow with – as he believed – a solid alibi, he accepted.

'Best pack for overnight,' I said to Grant as Pallister took the telephone out of my hands. 'We need to find the baggage and get her down there before the sergeant starts to smell a rat. I'll stay with her till tomorrow and bring her back again.'

'And the friend of the family?' Grant said. 'Mr Gilver?'

'Mr Osborne,' I said. 'Mr Gilver has guests.'

Pallister cleared his throat. 'Yes, yes, I know. I have guests too. But Mallory is more than capable of what's required. And needs must.'

Just then we all turned at the sound of a soft footfall above us. Alec's head, tousled from sleep, appeared over the banister. 'What am I being volunteered to do?' he asked.

'What are you doing up?' I said.

'Telephone bell, hurried footsteps, muttered conversation. Apart from the fact that you're standing in the hall instead of sitting at your desk, Dandy, I would say there's a case in the offing. Is there?'

'I can't tell you now,' I said. 'I'll howl and wake all the guests. But get ready quickly and I'll tell every grim detail on the way. Come on, Bunty.'

By seven o'clock, with Hugh informed and taking the news bravely, Alec, Bunty and I were tucked into Alec's Daimler, the three of us, with warm rolls and a flask of coffee for the journey.

'Where are we going?' Alec said.

'Croys,' I told him. 'To fetch Daisy and take her to a little town in East Lothian. I hope.'

'Why? As a matter of interest. Not that it's not a lovely day for a long drive. But, you know.'

So, as the mild green morning flashed past the windows, I apprised Alec of events, managing to get through it without my voice cracking. It helped to be telling Alec of all people: high emotion could be driven off by dire embarrassment, it seemed.

He expressed a perfectly proper amount of shock and sorrow at the news of Silas's death. For it was true indeed that he, through Hugh and me, was a friend of the Esslemonts in the usual way of people with estates in the same county and with shared concerns about weather, crops, and tenants. Besides, Alec is a dear man. If one did not know one would never guess the dark underside of his connection to the Esslemonts, still there all these years later as how could it not be.

For, once upon a time, Alec had been engaged to a sweet girl called Cara Duffy, whom Silas had ruined when she was not much more than a child. She died at another's hand, owing to the scandal, and her death was Alec's introduction to me, the reason we embarked on our first case together as we tried to solve her murder. It was the very genesis of Gilver and Osborne. Understandably, we do not discuss any of this. Yet more understandably, there has never been love lost between the two men.

'Is there a suspect?' Alec asked.

'It was a woman who did it,' I said. 'Or so the police have been told.'

'Well, it would be,' Alec said. 'Or a husband of a woman.' He paused. '"Been told"? There was a witness then?'

'Apparently so.'

'And now poor Daisy has to go and collect his body from some godforsaken place in the middle of nowhere? How awful for her.'

'I certainly hope that that's all the awfulness she has in store.'

'What do you mean?' Alec said. He swung the motor car round a particularly vicious bend. The Gilverton road is a beast of thing. Not that the main road we were hurtling towards was much better.

'I mean, I certainly hope she's at Croys to be fetched.'

'Yes, I wondered about that,' said Alec. 'Why did she go home so early? Oh God, not sheep!' We had rounded another corner to be greeted by the sight of a woolly grey river filling the roadway before us. 'Why are they moving sheep, Dan? Lambing is done and there can't be a lowland field eaten down already. It's May. Is Hugh moving them up?'

'I neither know nor care,' I said, nodding at the shepherd as he passed the car, deep in his flock. I could not see how the man kept on his feet, carried along as he was by the solid mass of animals surrounding him. Alec winced as his paintwork took the brunt of a horn. The only happy soul was Bunty, standing with her head out of the back window and her whole body wagging from the joy of this entertainment. 'The thing is,' I said, 'the police at Dirleton or Gullane or Haddington rang Croys – as they would. Ugh, I will never get used to that smell. I'm sure English sheep don't pong so much. And whoever answered the telephone there said she was here. As *they* would too. Because she was. But the thing is . . . she borrowed my Cowley sometime in the night and took off. She must have slipped into her house without the staff there noticing.'

Alec was silent for a while and then he said, 'That's certainly one possibility.'

'Yes,' I said. 'She wasn't feeling very well at bedtime last night. And, with the prospect of not feeling very well again this morning, I assume she wanted to go home and sleep in her own bed.'

'I can't agree with you there,' said Alec. 'She seemed extremely well when I last saw her yesterday. Full of merriment.'

'Don't be cruel, Alec. That wasn't merriment. She was drowning her sorrows.'

'Good Lord, how many ewes *are* there? No wonder they've stripped whatever field they've been in. I don't approve of these enormous flocks. It's like something from Russia!'

It didn't help that the shepherd was now bellowing for his dog, apparently lost somewhere in the midst of its charges, nowhere to be seen.

'Anyway, what sorrows?' Alec said. 'She always seemed quite reconciled to Silas being Silas. What sorrows would cause her to steal a car and drive home, even though her own car and her own chauffeur were right there?'

I said nothing.

29

'While her husband's being put to death by an unknown woman?'

'At last!' I said, as the flock thinned and the last few ewes plodded past us. Despite my claim that I had no interest in Hugh's pursuits, I was glad to see that the stragglers straggled only because in any crowd someone has to be last, not because they were limping or gasping for breath. I do hate to see a creature struggle with its existence and Hugh has no time for such poor husbandry either. Even Alec looked with an interested eye and gave a satisfied nod.

'Fine beasts,' he said. 'They deserve a better dog, frankly.'

For the shepherd was still berating his missing helper at the top of his lungs.

'I've never heard Hugh mention it,' I said. 'And you know how he feels about ill-trained dogs. Not you, darling,' I said, reaching back to fondle Bunty's ears.

'But to return to Daisy,' said Alec. 'Be honest. If this were an ordinary case instead of a friend, you'd think the story far more simple. You wouldn't be trying so desperately to cast two parts: the missing woman and the female assailant. I'm not. I'm quite happy to conclude that Daisy had a very good reason not to take her own car and driver on her trip last night.'

I could not bring myself to pooh-pooh it. Instead I sat under a blanket of helpless misery and let it crush me. After a moment, though, a thought occurred. 'But, Alec, why on earth would Daisy choose an evening when she was in Perthshire and Silas was practically down at the English border, instead of one of the endless evenings they spend together at home?'

'Hardly endless,' Alec said. 'Which is rather the point of the matter, wouldn't you say?'

30

'She couldn't have made herself look more suspicious if she tried,' I persisted.

'Yes but she must have meant to get back here before the household was up,' said Alec. 'She's probably coming round the next bend, just about to crash into my bumper.'

He spoke in jest but I felt myself stiffening in my seat anyway and it was this that allowed me to see over the hedgerow hummock at the side of the lane, where a flash of black and white down the steep bank caught my eye.

'Hmph,' I said. 'That shepherd's dog has abandoned his post and gone rabbiting.'

'Doesn't sound like any sheepdog I know,' Alec said. 'Are you sure? Maybe it's injured.'

He is terribly sentimental about dogs, and he was slowing even as he spoke, pulling over to the edge of the lane and craning his neck to see.

'Oh my God, Dandy!' he said and wrenched open the door, throwing himself out and clambering over the lip of the bank, ignoring the brambles that tore at him and the thick mud that instantly caked his shoes.

'What the devil?' I said, getting out and standing on the running board to get a better view. A view that sent me scrambling after him.

It *was* the dog, a typical scrawny little Border collie, thin as a whip, and it was working harder than ever it had with a flock of sheep, I would wager. For it had seen or smelled or sensed something wrong as it passed this spot, and it was trying to right matters.

Far down the bank, almost at the burn that bubbled along the bottom of the cut, my little Morris Cowley sat with its crumpled nose hard against a sturdy beech tree and its wheels jammed up with mud and bracken from its long slide. The dog was digging its back legs in and tugging at something dark, just outside the open driver's door.

Alec, with no thought to his safety, launched himself down the bank, skidding and stumbling, and – arriving beside the dog – grabbed it by the scruff and hauled it away. Then I saw what it had been hiding from sight. It wasn't *all* dark, although most of it was soaked through and coated with mud. There was a pale arm, and a white face, and even the dress still showed some of the oyster-coloured silk among the smears of filth.

'She's breathing!' Alec shouted. 'Oh thank God! Dandy, she's alive! I thought the dog was— But he was rescuing her. Trying to.'

Beside me Bunty whined, confused and upset by this strange tableau. 'What should I do?' I called down. 'Can we haul her up together, between the two of us?'

'No chance!' Alec called back. 'Go to the house and telephone for help.'

'The— The doctor?'

'And the police,' Alec said.

'But—'

He turned away from her then and stared up at me, narrowing his eyes and shaking his head slightly, as though in disbelief. 'Look at the marks, Dandy. Look at the bank.'

I did not need to, for I had seen them immediately upon climbing out of the motor car. My Cowley was facing straight downhill, but it had left the lane a little further on than we had got to and had slid and tumbled on an unmistakably diagonal path to where it lay. Daisy had been returning to Gilverton.

'Right,' I said. 'Yes, of course.' I had no real choice in the matter, I reluctantly concluded. Besides, we could not hide an injured woman who had crashed a motor car, the way I had hoped to hide a missing woman who had merely borrowed one, no matter that Silas's murder would now be solved almost before the case was opened. Daisy, drunk and angry, had driven away in the night, committed an unspeakable crime, and tried to return without anyone knowing she had gone. She almost made it but for our treacherous road, or perhaps her exhaustion, or her shock at what she had done when she viewed it with dawn's sobriety. Now her life was over, as surely as was Silas's, and her daughters' lives too.

I made my sorry way back to the motor car to set in motion the saddest course of action I had ever known.

Chapter 3

Not to be callous, but one silver lining was the breaking up of our house party. Hugh's pals and their wives began to melt away immediately after breakfast, murmuring about this and that: prior engagements suddenly recalled; duties they had hoped to ignore that were pricking consciences after all; even a claim to be starting a cold, which came complete with a few desultory and unconvincing sniffles. No one was fooled but no one demurred. 'Of course,' I said. 'Lucky you remembered. Good of you to make the sacrifice. Best at home with a hot toddy.' Then, when the door closed on the last of them, I trailed to the library where Hugh and Alec sat sunk in gloom. Alec is no longer counted as a guest at Gilverton. When the company shrinks to just the three of us, we feel quite as though we are in the family circle.

Of course, this morning, the company also included Daisy, lying upstairs unconscious, a broken arm and a broken leg both hastily plastered, a grievous wound to the back of her head bathed and bandaged and left to chance, for there was nothing more than that to be done. So said the nurse summoned from the hospital at Perth, who was also swelling our number but so discreetly she did not intrude.

The household was completed by a doughty police matron, far less discreet, who had taken up her post inside the bedroom door, staring stonily at the patient and refusing all offers of tea, breakfast, or even a newspaper to while the time away. She had roused herself a little when I visited Daisy's bedside, as though I might abet some plan for escape and it was her job to foil me; not at all as though the prisoner was sleeping like a fairy-tale princess, oblivious of her plight and as likely to flee as was the feather bed in which she lay. I took Daisy's hand and gazed at her, but was not minded to speak to my old friend with the police matron listening. After a while, I conveyed thanks to the woman – who was, after all, only doing her duty – by means of a tight smile, and left them.

'Where's Ted?' I asked, dropping into an armchair and welcoming its embrace. Hugh's part of the house is not stylish, for he has resisted all attempts to redecorate these last twenty years at least, but he does himself very well for creature comforts, as all men do. Bunty laid her head on my lap and gave a long groan, which summed up the mood of the room beautifully.

'Gone to back to Benachally with Donald and Mallory,' said Hugh, sounding rather bleak. 'And taken Miss Cartaright with him.'

'Poor thing,' I said. 'I hope this doesn't put her off.' I imagined her writing or telephoning to her mother to report on the momentous occasion. *Oh yes, lovely people, Mummy. One of their friends is a murderess, but apart from that, you know.*

'She seemed quite sanguine about it all when she made her goodbyes,' said Hugh. 'Sensible girl.' It is his highest praise for any female and the thought seemed to have cheered him up a little. 'Mind you,' he went on. 'I would have said the same about Daisy before today.'

'I can't bring myself to believe it,' I said. 'I keep going over and over it, round and round. All I can come up with is that, if she did do it, it was only because she had some kind of brainstorm.'

Alec wrinkled his nose and gave a hefty sigh. 'The trouble with that,' he said, 'is that what she did – if she did it – was clearly premeditated.'

'How so?' said Hugh. 'I don't see that at all, old chap. She was stewing about yet another indiscretion, angry that he left her to walk into a party unaccompanied – which is shabby behaviour, in anyone's book.'

Despite my deep sadness and wretched exhaustion, that raised a smile in me. How typical of Hugh to find a lapse in manners shabbier than decades of infidelity.

'Then the major rubbed her nose in it. Oh yes, it's all come out, Dandy. She got as drunk as a lord and decided she'd had it.' Hugh huffed out a sigh. 'Or perhaps she only meant to confront him and things got out of hand. Do we know *how* he died?'

'The sergeant didn't say,' I told him. 'But we'll soon get a chance to ask him. He's on his way from Dirleton now, according to Pallister. Poor Pallister. Every time he thinks he has digested the worst that life will ever bring him, it serves up more.' I puffed out my cheeks and let a long breath go, hoping it would take some of the misery with it as it left me. 'But I must admit I don't follow either, Alec. What sets you against a "moment of madness"? Except for the two hours' drive.'

'More like three,' said Hugh. 'In that little motor car, in the dark.'

'Simply this,' Alec said. 'How did she know where to go?' He sat back and let the question sink into us, let us try and fail to find an answer. 'She said he was at a dinner for a Perthshire regiment. If she believed that, she would hardly have gone to Dirleton to find him. If she *didn't* believe it, then she chose to lie to you, Dandy. In either case, she laid a false scent quite deliberately. Do you see?'

'But wouldn't she have abandoned her plan when the major scuppered her story?' I said.

'Perhaps she did,' said Hugh. 'Then she got drunk in her disappointment or – let's be generous – relief, and the drink muddled her judgement until, not thinking clearly, she set off after all.'

It made depressingly good sense and it sent all three of us into renewed silent glumness. I do not know what thoughts filled the men's heads, but for myself I was borne back into the long ago, when Daisy and I were young, when life was fresh and plump and just about to fall into our outstretched hands, when the Great War already on the distant horizon had not entered our empty heads, much less another in its wake such as we were facing now. For one moment, I wondered if perhaps it would be best for Daisy to slip away and never face the shame and misery awaiting her should she recover. Then, as though to slap me back to common sense and simple kindness, came a loud rap on the front door.

'Copper's knock,' Alec said. 'Here we go then.'

If ever there was a sign that the East Lothian constabulary had Daisy and Daisy alone in its sights, it was surely the fact that not only was Sgt Dodgson ushered into the library moments later, but that he had with him a certain Captain Wicks, whom Hugh recognised with a flare of eye and nostril even before introductions had been made, for Captain Wicks was the chief constable of the county. They had abandoned the corpse, the scene of the crime, the witness already found and those who might still be in the offing, and had descended on Gilverton,

37

where lay the suspected, accused, tried and convicted Daisy, for the taking.

Pallister was dispatched to fetch the hospital nurse and, while we waited, we tried to glean what we could about the murder.

'Now then, my dear fellows,' Hugh said, with a great air of taking charge. 'What makes you think that the corpse you found is my old friend Silas Esslemont?'

Alec and I shared a guilty look. Was it possible that we had not told Hugh about the letter? It was.

'Letter in his pocket addressed to him,' said Sgt Dodgson, 'and his initials on his ring.'

'How exactly did he die?' I asked. Both men stared back at me with lips sealed. 'Unless it's grisly,' I added. 'He is an old friend and I'd rather not know the details if they're dreadful.'

Alec smirked. He knows me. These policemen did not.

'His head was bashed in,' said Sgt Dodgson, probably believing he was teaching me a valuable lesson: to wit, do not ask a question if the answer is going to be unwelcome.

'Have a care,' the chief constable put in mildly. He did not strike me as a thrusting sort.

'At Dirleton?' I said. 'Where? In someone's house? Surely not in a *public* place?' I had shaken out an answer with a display of feminine squeamishness he did not know was feigned. Now I hoped to do the same again, this time employing that distaste for spectacle, that yearning for respectability, by which the middle classes – including policemen – set such store.

'Right there on the village green for all the world to see,' the sergeant said. I was beginning to get the measure of him and I did not care for it greatly.

38

'I say,' was all the chief constable now offered.

'"The world" consisting of a single witness, I think you told me, Sergeant?' was what I said next.

'One witness is plenty,' came the reply, 'when we have a suspect in . . . Well, not custody but safely in hand.'

I gave him a cold stare. "Safely in hand" was an extremely unpleasant way to refer to the fact that poor Daisy was lying in her bed of pain with a police matron monitoring her every breath. 'Why on earth do you imagine that Mrs Esslemont would harm her husband?' I said.

'The letter in his pocket was short and to the point,' said Dodgson.

'I have no wish to hear—' I began.

And so of course he told me. If I had asked to hear he would have taken it to his grave. "Come to me," he said. 'That was the whole of the message. "Come to me". And it was signed "One you have wronged".'

'Strikes me you should be looking for whoever that is,' Alec said.

'Thank you very much, sir, but we don't need any assistance,' said Dodgson.

'Although we are a man down, as it happens,' Captain Wicks piped up. 'The inspector – a very capable fellow – is on his holiday. Fishing in the Dee, I believe. That's why I've stepped in in such an active capacity.'

His claim to be "active" was at such odds with the evidence before our eyes that it was hard not to snort. And I was sure Dodgson's jaw was clenched with resentment as he repeated, 'We don't need outside help. We have our suspect in hand.'

'In hand but in no fit state to be interviewed,' Alec said, addressing his remark to the chief constable. 'I hope that was made clear to you before you decided to drive all this way.'

'Oh, so you've been in her bedroom, have you?' said Dodgson.

Such a nasty remark shook a response that was almost forceful out of Captain Wicks. 'Now, now,' he said.

Hugh had been silent but, at this fresh outrage and in the absence of anything approaching discipline in the chain of command, he piped up. 'Keep a civil tongue in your head when referring to Mrs Esslemont, please. And when speaking in the presence of my wife, for that matter. There's a good chap.'

I would not have trusted myself to say anything, for there was a rage bubbling in me as though I were a cauldron over a fire. How dare this jumped-up little nobody of a sergeant insult Daisy, and Alec too for that matter, while lounging uninvited in my library. I had a good mind to tell Silas, I thought. He might be a bit of a Don Juan but he was as ready as the next man to defend his wife's honour and he would knock Dodgson's block off for that partic—

Then my roiling thoughts snagged on a sudden realisation of the dreadful new truth: the truth we would all have to live with, every day, for the rest of our lives. I felt tears – finally; hours after the first glimpse of the sheepdog! – begin to gather in my eyes.

'Please excuse me,' I said, rather huskily, and I hurried from the room.

Daisy lay exactly as she had lain all morning, her face as white as the bandage around her head, her broken arm slung from a length of tape thrown over the bed frame, her broken leg suspended from another and her breath coming in rasping groans from her sleep-slackened throat.

'Ah, Mrs Gilver,' said the police matron. 'The nurse is away to talk to the detectives.'

'Detectives!' I could not help exclaiming, although it was true that both men wore plain clothes. 'I didn't come to speak to the nurse anyway,' I added. In truth, I did not know why I had come.

'No, no, it's just I might need to step aside a minute,' she explained. 'If you would stay awhile?'

I am not cruel and so I nodded my assent. But I am only human and, unfairly – for it was her colleagues downstairs I was angry with – I refused to offer the information I felt sure her remark had been intended to shake out of me. Instead, I left her to wander the passageways in search of a lavatory, or a servant who would help her. Once she was gone, I sat down on the edge of Daisy's bed and picked up her hand. It was warm but otherwise utterly lifeless.

I remembered, however, what I had heard from one of the soldiers in the convalescent home during the war. I had played cards with him, quiet games of whist until he finished whittling himself a cribbage board and then contests more bitter than I had ever known in a bridge four. While the cards were dealt one day, he told me he had been unconscious for a week after the shelling but had heard every word spoken near him. 'I knew my legs were gone,' he told me. 'I knew my fiancée wept and wailed to her mother about the chore of taking care of me for the rest of my life, even though she put on an act for the doctors. I didn't miss a thing.'

'Ugh,' I said. 'What a good thing you found out her true colours.'

He shook his head and smiled ruefully as if to say he did not blame her. He did not need to; I blamed her enough for us both.

And I never forgot him. Now, sitting by Daisy's bed, I spoke to her because of what he had told me. It felt foolish and I was glad no one else was there to hear, but I did it just the same. 'Thank goodness Hugh wouldn't let me get rid of these old four-posters,' I said. 'This one has come in terrifically handy, hasn't it? For "traction", I seem to recall is its name. It looks awfully uncomfy though, darling. I do hope you're not getting pins and needles.'

Daisy breathed in and out.

'Now, I'm afraid you're going to have a couple of rather dreary guests any minute now,' I went on. 'A Sgt Dodgson – quite a rotter, if you ask me – and a soaking wet blanket of a so-called chief constable who must be someone's nephew; there's no other explanation for it. They're coming to see you unless the nurse heads them off. She seemed like a kind sort. I do hope so.'

I watched Daisy's chest rise and fall for a moment.

'Oh darling,' I said next. 'What on earth were you thinking? After all these years?'

I remembered Daisy and Silas's wedding as though it were yesterday: the tightness and scratchiness of my headdress; the interminable speeches; the way she gazed up at him in frank adoration; the amused look on his face as he glanced down at her. I was as innocent as she in those days. Now, I would know what it meant to see a bridegroom mildly entertained by his bride's devotion on the big day. If I had seen it on Donald's face I would have boxed his ears and told Mallory to run away. If I saw it on Teddy's during his engagement, I would take Dolly aside and suggest she keep looking. But Daisy, or so I thought, had accepted the facts of her life years ago. I was mystified, truly.

I was also apparently wool-gathering. At least, I jumped as if poked in the ribs at a sudden movement beside me. Daisy's eyes were open!

'Dan?' she said, in a rusty squeak.

'Darling!' I said. I shot to my feet, looking wildly about myself, even though I knew the nurse was downstairs with the policemen. I sat down again and took up her hand, rubbing it desperately. 'Lie still, Daisy,' I said. 'You've hurt your head. Oh my dear, I thought—'

'Hurts,' Daisy said. It came out like a growl.

'I know, I know,' I said. 'I'll get the nurse to give you some morphine. She won't be long.'

'Silas,' Daisy croaked.

'Ssshh,' I said. 'Don't try to speak any more just now. There's a good girl.'

'Want Silas,' said Daisy in a sort of fading whisper.

'Shush,' I said, hopelessly. I could not tell whether she was wailing in remorse and regret for what she had done or if the blow to her head had wiped out the memory of doing it, and I did not know which was worse. I closed my eyes, praying silently, although I knew not what for.

'Dandy.' My eyes flew open. Her voice was louder, with perhaps a little more strength behind it. 'Where is Silas?' she said, and then she let a long breath go, as though the effort to speak had exhausted her anew. Her eyelids fluttered but she screwed her face up and managed to keep looking at me.

I stared back. She had to be in tremendous pain, but her gaze was determined and her eyes looked clear and were focused upon me. I had experienced the unsettling sight of a man with one pupil enormous and one tiny. I had seen soldiers' faces blurred by their broken minds. Daisy looked exactly the same as her old self, except for the bandage.

'Darling,' I said. 'Silas died.' I felt the jerk as she gripped my hand in a sudden spasm. 'Darling,' I said again. 'They think you killed him. At Dirleton.'

I had thought her face was as white as milk already but upon hearing these words it paled yet further until she looked in tone and texture exactly like a tallow candle. And the shock of the news really had depleted whatever little store of strength she had managed to find. Her eyelids drifted down and her grip on my hand slackened. I watched, with held breath, until I saw her chest rise and fall in steady time once or twice, then I turned as the door began to open.

'Hirl—' Daisy said, the merest trace of a murmur, and the police matron was back in the room.

'The men are at my back,' she said. 'The nurse is bringing them.' It seemed she had gone on quite an expedition through my house then. I wished I had directed her to the nearest lavatory after all. I said nothing. I simply looked at Daisy and then back at the matron.

'I don't think Mrs Esslemont is equal to answering questions,' I said.

The police matron bristled. 'I'm perfectly well aware that the prisoner is unconscious, madam,' she said.

'There is no prisoner here, my good woman.'

'But naturally the sergeant and the chief constable need to see it for themselves.'

I opened my mouth to say more. I was not aware then nor could I make a statement under oath now regarding *what* I was about to say and, in any case, I was prevented. Subtly but undeniably, Daisy squeezed my hand. I glanced at her face and this I *could* swear to: there was the tiniest little frown line showing between her brows. I squeezed back and the line cleared as I watched it.

Then I patted her hand and stood. 'Very well,' I said. 'If two policemen find it worth their while to stand at the bedside of a patient in a coma, who am I to argue?'

44

I swept out. Halfway down the stairs, I met Dodgson and Wicks, tramping upwards still in their overcoats, although they had left their hats somewhere at least. The nurse brought up the rear and, although I would have said I have a pretty decent poker face, she grabbed my arm as I plodded past, and asked me softly: 'What is it?'

I boggled at her. 'What do you mean?'

'What's happened?'

'What's *happened*?' I echoed, reminding myself of my sons when they were small, playing for time when I had caught them in naughtiness. 'Well, my friend is at death's door and has just been made a widow. And my house is full of policemen.'

She let my arm go and I hoped I was imagining the shrewd look she gave me as she hurried away.

Back in the library, I considered sharing the news with both menfolk. The trouble is that Hugh, most sturdy and dependable Hugh, has a very straightforward view of some things, including the law of the land, which is not always helpful in the kinds of predicaments where Alec and I often find ourselves. Reasoning that Daisy was my only business here, I had just about decided to say nothing to him when a discreet cough in the library doorway announced the presence of his factor, estate manager and great friend.

'Hardly the moment, sir,' he said in that perfectly judged tone somewhere between business-like assertiveness and old-school deference, 'but we had a plan to discuss the Hendr—'

'Good Lord, the Hendrys!' said Hugh, leaping to his feet. 'Are they here?'

'Sitting in the estate office with all the paperwork in order.'

'If you'll excuse me, Dandy,' Hugh said giving me a slight bow. 'I'm doing no good lounging about and this business has been months in the preparation.'

45

I inclined my head and Hugh all but broke into a trot making his escape.

'*What's* going on with the Hendrys?' said Alec, when he was gone. He is just like Hugh sometimes, with a distressing tendency to care about the minutiae of tenants and policies.

'Do you know them?' I asked, rather brusquely perhaps.

'One of their older daughters is being trained up as a parlourmaid,' said Alec. 'Barrow tells me she's excellent.'

I smiled at him. He is nothing like Hugh, who just about knows Becky's name after all these years but is proof against all knowledge that maids are trained on the job.

'And now that we're alone . . .' said Alec, 'what is it you need to say, Dandy? You know, before you burst.'

'Don't be vulgar,' I said, annoyed to discover that Alec, like the nurse, had seen through my attempts to calm myself and appear normal. 'If you must know . . . Promise me I can speak in confidence, Alec.'

'As ever,' he said gravely. 'What's wrong?'

'Daisy woke up,' I said. 'That galumph went to visit the lav. And Daisy woke up and talked to me.'

'Good grief!' said Alec. 'Why did you let the coppers in? She should have a solicitor with her if she's awake again.'

'She's not,' I said. 'Well, that's to say, I think she is. But she closed her eyes when the police matron came back and she squeezed my hand to make me button my lip. She looks exactly the same as she did before. She'll be fine. Unless she sneezes, I suppose.'

'What did she say?' Alec asked. 'Did she confess? If she's faking unconsciousness, Dandy . . .'

'This is exactly why I wouldn't tell Hugh,' I said. 'Of course she didn't confess. Alec, that's the thing: she didn't know. She didn't know Silas is dead.'

'Are you sure? What did she say?

'Groans and moans at first. I think she's in great pain. It's heartbreaking. And then she called for Silas, several times.'

'What did you tell her?'

I put my hand over my mouth. 'I might never forgive myself for how I blurted it out. I told her Silas had died. And I *swear* she didn't know. It came as a complete shock. She blanched and almost swooned. She *didn't* know. I'm sure of it. And when I told her everyone thought she had done it, she . . .'

'She what?'

'She said something very indistinct. I think she was trying to tell me something.'

'Indistinct but sounding like what?' Alec said.

'I heard "hirl",' I told him. 'Or "earl", possibly. Very guttural.'

'Did either make sense in the context?'

I screwed my face up trying to remember. 'I had just said that Silas had died, at Dirleton, and everyone thought she did it.'

'Well, there you are then,' said Alec. 'She was repeating "Dirleton", or trying to. Dirleton *is* the most puzzling bit of the whole thing, when you think about it, Dandy. What's a tiny town in a distant county got to do with Silas Esslemont?'

'Well, there *you* are then,' I shot back, rudely I suppose. 'If Daisy did it, she'd hardly be surprised to hear where it was done, would she? She's far too ill to pull off an innocent act.'

'Just ill enough to pull off an even more ill act?' said Alec. 'Faking a coma?'

'Jolly sensible, if you ask me,' I told him. 'If she can keep it up, it gives us some time.'

'Us who?' said Alec. 'Us, Gilver and Osborne?'

47

'Who else?'

'It might have been us, the dear friends of Daisy and pals of Silas.' He gave me a very even stare.

'In which case you would leave it to me and take yourself off to deal with other concerns?'

'I'm only human,' Alec said. 'Even professionally, where I grant you my private feelings shouldn't come into it, if Silas were suspected of murdering Daisy, I shouldn't lift a finger. I hated the man, Dandy.'

I tried not to look startled. He had never said anything even approaching that in all the years since Cara died. 'As it stands though?' I asked him.

'Who's paying us?' said Alec, in a very different voice.

'Well, Daisy,' I said. 'Presumably. When she's better.'

'Ah,' said Alec. 'I don't believe we've ever presumed payment before, have we?'

'Come on, Alec,' I said.

'I'm teasing you,' he replied. 'I like Daisy and feel a great deal of sympathy for her, no matter what she's done. Of course I'll help.'

I stared at him. 'But Gilver and Osborne, darling,' I said. 'Servants of truth. Not agents of revenge.'

'We'll see,' said Alec mildly.

'Oh for God's sake!' I burst out. 'Stop being so wry and detached. I know you don't – can't possibly – care that Silas is dead. In fact, you should be glad *you've* got an alibi. But you said yourself you care about Daisy. And you care about justice, don't you?'

'That's a thought,' Alec said, with his eyes suddenly very wide. 'My alibi is that I was asleep alone in a room all night and I haven't touched a hair on his head all these years so far. Rather flimsy, which gives me good reason to sort this out.

Because I certainly care about my own neck.' He sighed. 'And Daisy's too.'

'Well, we'd better not leave it up to those policemen to save either.'

'I'm sorry, Dandy,' Alec told me. 'I'm not really detached, as you put it. Only, I find myself in the grip of a perfect maelstrom of unpleasant thoughts.'

'Feelings,' I said, knowing that this was immeasurably worse.

'Feelings,' Alec agreed sheepishly. 'Working hard on a case is the perfect distraction. To Dirleton we shall go!'

Chapter 4

Dirleton on any other day, on a visit for any other purpose, would have been quite charming. I had expected one of those straggling Scottish places that is no more than a single road clotting and clearing: from farm, to petrol pump, to smithy, to cottage, to shop, to bank, to pub, and then back to cottage, smithy, stable yard and finally farm again. Instead, Dirleton was almost English in its quaint and ordered prettiness, with a village green and clusters of chocolate-box cottages, their spring gardens bursting with mallow and cherry blossom, all behind clipped hedges and painted gates. One side of the green was even more romantic than that, formed as it was by the turreted and crenellated wall of a castle, right there in the village, a stone's throw from the inn at the far end.

'Presumably Silas came to see whoever lives there,' Alec said, nodding at the castle keep. 'I wonder who it is.'

'If it was an ordinary house visit,' I said. 'But he hid it from Daisy so that's far from a given. As to who lives there, I haven't a clue.'

We drove once all the way round the vaguely triangular perimeter road, passing – besides delightful cottages – a telephone kiosk, a pillar box, a tea room, a grocer's, a tiny sub-post office, an even tinier branch of the British Linen Bank, one out-of-place sort of brick building I thought might be a small factory, a butcher, and one of those indeterminate establishments – part haberdasher, part gift shop – where ladies while away the time buying and selling unneeded items, depending which side of the counter they happen to dally. Finally, in an offshoot from the main green, with a little grassy stretch of its own, we spied the school, the church, the village hall and, behind grand walls and tall yew hedging, the manse.

'Another possibility?' Alec said. 'Does Silas have many friends in the clergy?'

I snorted but, thinking we should perhaps suspend jokes about Silas's character for a while, did not reply.

When we had completed our circuit, Alec pulled up in an empty little space I supposed to be meant for parking motor cars and coaches, since there was a public lavatory set off to its one side. I have learned that, despite Scotland being so lavishly provided with castles, still wherever there happens to be one there are day trippers who will want to visit it. Indeed, there was a wooden sign hung on hooks outside the nearest gate in the castle wall, which I took to be a list of ticket prices.

'Did you see it?' Alec said, stopping the engine and taking out his pipe. It was a fine day, breezy and bright, and so I opened the door at my side. Alec's pipe in an enclosed motor car is not to be borne.

'Did I see what?' I said, squinting out of the windscreen. I do hate to be bested by him. He is insufferable when he gets the chance.

'The scene of the crime,' he said in an incredulous, and I might add insufferable, tone. 'The place Silas died. Promise you won't gawp, Dandy, because I'd rather not attract the attention of that bobby just yet, but look where I'm looking now.'

I had not even seen the bobby. Of course, at the merest sweep of a glance I spotted him now, standing in the shadow of the trees at the west side of the green, with his helmet pushed back and his hands clasped behind him. He was facing slightly away from us, as though his gaze was fixed where Alec's too now rested.

There, at the corner where the road led down to the church, hall, school and manse, a little patch of the smooth grass was covered with an expanse of sacking – held in place with what looked from here like giant hatpins but could not be.

'Oh, Alec,' I said. 'Poor Silas.'

'Indeed,' said Alec, politely. Then he smacked his hands on the steering wheel. 'Now then, shall we try for lodging at the unimaginatively named Castle Inn? What reason shall we give out for suddenly alighting here? We're going to look like ghouls unless we think of something.'

'Why don't we play a straight bat and say we're detectives? When those policemen get back from Gilverton we shall have to anyway.'

'But until then . . .' Alec said. 'And anyway we should wait to see in what esteem Dodgson and Whatsisname are held by the general populace before we align.'

'Wicks,' I said, then considered the problem. 'Might we be historians? Family historians? Scouring the kirkyard for Gilvers or Osbornes of yore?'

'That would be over by teatime,' said Alec. 'Speaking of which . . .' For it was getting close to being too late for luncheon and Alec cannot countenance a missed meal. 'We should really have stopped in town,' he said, not for the first time. 'Or along the coast somewhere.'

'I wish I had brought Bunty,' I said. 'She's the most marvellous ice-breaker. The perfect excuse to go a-wandering twice a day, apart from anything else.'

But Bunty, from the goodness of her heart, had taken up

a station at Daisy's bedside after the departure of the policemen earlier that day, and it would have needed more of a termagant than I to drag her away. Even Hugh had looked fondly at her when he popped his head round the door and saw her sitting bolt upright, staring at Daisy as though at a butcher's bone.

'She's rather prominent, mind you,' Alec said. 'She draws notice. Ah well, I daresay we'll think of something. And why should we be subjected to interrogation, after all?'

'Why indeed,' I agreed. No sooner had I spoken, though, than I caught sight of something moving towards us very low and fast and I turned, expecting to find a large dog or a small pony bearing down. To my astonishment it was a person, a girl, the impression of a long torso having been formed by the way a cloak streamed out behind her. Still, a girl should not look like a dog, but she was dressed all in ashy black and she was very short, really quite tiny, and seemed to scurry on legs bent almost at right angles besides. Such was her oddity that I felt myself stepping back and pressing against the side of the motor car.

'Who are you?' she demanded. Her voice was unremarkable, compared with the look of her: a nice and well-modulated Scottish voice such as one hears ten times a day in any town.

Alec and I each opened our mouths but nothing came forth from either.

'He's dead,' she hissed.

'Lizzy!' A shout rang out from somewhere behind us and we turned to see a tall man in a uniform I could not quite place, striding our way. Lizzy – if that was the name of the black-cloaked little person – took off like a crow on a gust of wind and, scuttling towards the nearest portion of the castle wall, seemed to disappear into it. If it were not for the fact that Alec and the uniformed man showed every sign of having seen the creature I would have thought I was dreaming.

'Well, you don't look like detectives,' the man said, drawing up beside us. He was younger than I had thought at first, his face having been hidden by the peak of the cap upon his head and his gait made crooked by a large canvas satchel slung over his chest. He carried, I noted, another of the enormous hatpins that were holding the sacking over the ugly place on the village green where Silas died.

'Are you—?' I said, squinting at his hat badge.

'Paddy Watson,' said the man. 'Postie by profession and parkie by dint of my tidy mind.' It was a postman's satchel, I now realised, and the badge was His Majesty's insignia. As to the hatpin: with the nudge of hearing that he was a park-keeper I now recognised it as one of those spikes used to pick up the sweet wrappers despoiling municipal lawns. Mr Watson, it seemed, had combined his duties into one sortie today.

'As I was saying,' he went on, 'you don't look like plods and you don't look like press.'

'We're neither,' said Alec. He had come around to my side of the motor car while the flapping black creature bore down upon us and he now stood close enough subtly to nudge me. I am a connoisseur of Alec's nudges after all these years. This one meant "Keep quiet and keep up". He had thought of something. 'We're researchers,' he said.

It was a better – not to mention vaguer – disguise than any I could have hit upon. But I did not have the chance to marvel at Alec's quick thinking, for I was immediately distracted by the tremendous effect his claim seemed to have had upon Mr Watson.

'Researchers?' he echoed faintly. 'You're . . . ? I don't understand . . .'

'You don't understand what there is here in your village to interest us?' said Alec. 'We're used to that.'

'Hardl—' said Mr Watson. Then he shook his head like a dog newly emerged from a pond and gave a short laugh. 'I see,' he said. 'Researchers. Well, you've come on a most inopportune morning, I must say.'

'Oh?' I said.

'It pains me greatly to say so but there's been a death.' He did not sound pained. He sounded arch, for some reason. 'I'm afraid a stranger at our gates was shown violence instead of welcome.'

'Violence?' I burst out, rather proud of remembering that this should be my reaction.

'Violence,' said Mr Watson. 'Sorry to upset you with such bald speech, but there was an attack in the dead of night.' He nodded down across the green towards the covered place.

'We were wondering about that,' Alec said.

'I think the idea is to wait for the fingerprint men to come and . . . dust it,' Watson said. 'If dusting is what fingerprint men do.'

'Dust the *grass*?' I asked. I knew these chaps were getting cleverer all the time but that seemed a leap into the realms of magic.

Mr Watson frowned. 'You haven't done much preparation for your trip then,' he said, fixing me with a stern look. 'What is it you're supposed to be researching, if anyone asks?'

I boggled at his rudeness, but Alec stepped in.

'All my fault,' he said. 'I believe that the muse can easily be chased away if one flaps a notebook too hard in her presence.

It was my express desire to let Dirleton speak to us and say whatever she would . . .' His voice trailed off.

Oh Lord, I thought to myself. Once before, Alec had taken on the role of an artistic sort – a painter in that case – and taken it on with great gusto. I now saw that he intended to bring the same zeal to his new turn.

'Well, I'd better get on,' said Mr Watson, the only sensible response to such drivel. Plucking a letter from his satchel, he read the address and strode off, spiking up a bus ticket with a twirling flourish of his stick as he went on his way, making a beeline for the inn and disappearing into its open gateway.

'Researchers then,' I said. 'And obviously there is something in Dirleton to be researched. But what, do you suppose?'

'Beats me,' said Alec, who is worse than my sons for picking up modern slang. 'What do you make of him saying "if anyone asks"? *He* was asking. Why didn't that count?'

'And what if it's researchers into church history or a special kind of frog only found in Dirleton's duckpond?' I went on, ignoring him. 'Your Oscar Wilde impersonation won't do at all in that instance.'

Alec stared at me as if I had landed a terrible blow. 'I don't know what you mean,' he said. 'But for what it's worth, my papa met poor old Oscar once and said he was a thoroughly sensible man and not nearly as tiresome as you'd imagine in private company.'

'You forgot to say "So there".'

'It was implied. Now for God's sake, let's stop wittering and get on with it.'

By this time, as might fairly be imagined, the police constable on duty guarding the sacking and hatpins – I could not seem to think of them any other way – was looking up at Alec and me with a great deal of interest. I could not tell if it was professional curiosity or the human sort, born of boredom. In either case, I waved to the fellow and he waved back, which I took as an invitation to stroll down there and annoy him. Alec sighed, probably about the luncheon he imagined dwindling into impossibility with every wasted moment, but a young constable struck me as far more biddable than "fingerprint men" and we needed to take this chance while it was going.

Good afternoons were dished out amongst the three of us and the constable lifted his helmet politely, showing us a head full of plastered-flat fair hair and a deep dent all around his jaw and temples where his chinstrap had been digging in.

'The postie said you're watching over a piece of evidence in a criminal matter,' I said, employing Scots like a native born, to set the chap at his ease. He was very young indeed and awkward-looking with it, rather shuffling about the feet and gulping about the throat.

'Till they all get here from Haddington,' he said. 'That's right.'

'Can we have a look?' said Alec.

This shocked the boy – he really was not much more than a boy – and he swallowed hard a couple of times before he spoke. 'I'm stationed to *stop* people looking, sir,' he said. 'And it's no sight for a lady.' He tipped his head towards me as if to remind Alec of either my presence or my sex.

'As a professional researcher,' Alec began, 'there is no experience too—'

'Ohhhh,' said the child, making quite a good few syllables out of it. 'You're *them*?' He looked back at me with quite a different expression upon his scrubbed and innocent face, less poleaxed than Mr Watson had been, but still interested. He was certainly less poleaxed than Alec and me. 'Well then,' he went on, 'you'll have seen worse I daresay.' He seemed to be softening. He poked his tongue into one cheek and rubbed a hand along his jaw, so inexpertly shaven that even this early in the day it rasped a little. 'Although,' he said.

'Although?' Alec prompted.

'Nobody's said it's anything to do with all that, you understand.'

'I do,' said Alec. I presumed he was lying. I certainly understood nothing.

'But then nobody's said it isn't, you see?'

'I do see,' said Alec, presumably fibbing again.

'It's a bit of a coincidence else,' said the constable.

'It is indeed,' said Alec. 'And we don't like coincidences in our line of work, any more than you do.'

This expression of fellow feeling bucked the young man up terrifically. I exhaled, making as little noise as I could; I had thought Alec was overplaying his hand, in trying to add substance to a conversation the topic of which he was entirely in the dark about. But he seemed to have got away with it.

'Just a quick look,' said the constable, then he stopped and checked around himself, twisting his head one way and then the other as though for eavesdroppers. There was no one abroad anywhere. Dirleton was quite remarkably empty. Granted, it was the Sabbath, too late for churchgoers and too early for the spilling out of children from Sunday school, but this far south surely there should have been a villager or two taking the air.

'Rest assured,' said Alec gravely, 'if you let us have a peek we won't breathe a word to your boss.'

'Or to her either,' the boy said. 'I'm Dirleton as well as police, you know. *She's* not to be told.'

58

'Certainly not,' Alec said. 'Heaven forfend.'

With that, the boy was convinced. He strode with more vigour than his conversational style had presaged towards the sacking and hatpins. It was only then that I noticed it was stretched over something that lay underneath far from flat. I felt my footsteps slow as I began to wonder what I had agreed to view.

Alec and the constable took one spike each and wrestled them out of the ground, then the constable, with great care, folded back the sheet of canvas – upon my closer inspection it had revealed itself to be much sturdier than a flattened sack after all – and displayed what lay beneath.

'Oh!' I said. There was a stone, either bun-shaped and resting on the surface of the ground or round and three-quarters submerged. In either case it protruded about a foot at the crest of its dome and was about two foot across. I should have said it was a very plain and unassuming thing, the sort of rock that sticks out of sheep fields and riverbanks all over this thin-soiled land, but it had been given prominence by a ring of cobbles set around it like a Tudor ruff, to mark it out and show it off. That was its second most notable feature. Its first was the dark spreading stain, close to black now, that was smeared all over the top and down most of one side. Silas's blood. I put a glove to my mouth and pressed hard to stop another sound escaping.

'Thank you,' said Alec. 'You should probably cover it back up.' He had had a good look, standing with his hands on his knees like a gardener inspecting seedlings, and he straightened with a groan. 'Now we must get to the Castle and secure our luncheon and our rooms.'

'You're staying with the Halliburtons?' said the constable. 'Are they back then?'

'I don't know the landlord's name,' said Alec, 'but there's only one—'

'Oh!' said the constable. 'Not the *castle*. The Castle *Inn*. Dirleton folk call it the inn to keep things straight usually.'

After making our goodbyes, Alec shepherded me away, murmuring at me not to say anything. We passed a row of large villas on the west side of the main green in silence and arrived at the sweep of the inn, where closed windows and open ground meant we could be sure of privacy.

'Alec, what was all that about?'

'I haven't the faintest clue. Who's "she"?'

'I don't mean what *he* said. I mean you! If there are researchers expected, we can't impersonate them. What if they turn up?'

'We'll claim a mix-up. The postman said that the proper business of the researchers had been interrupted by an un-related event, if you remember. So we shan't overlap.'

'That seems almost certain to cause trouble,' I said. 'What manner of mix-up would it be? And, since you mention it, how did the postman know what our interests are? And why was he so astonished that we were here, since he seemed to know we were coming?'

'Not the foggiest,' Alec said.

'Besides, that constable – wet behind the ears as he may be – thought rather differently and suspects a connection. Between what and what though?'

'A very good question, Dandy. I'm planning to prop up one end of the public bar from opening time until the last bell tonight and see if I can work out the answer on the strength of the inevitable gossip. At the very least, I should be able to find out who "she" is.'

'Yes that struck me too,' I said. 'We're looking for a

murderous "her", hoping it's not Daisy. And we're hearing about a "her" – she who must not be told – who surely can't be Daisy. That's a very good sign, if you ask me.'

'And we did say, before we even got here, that if Silas had been set upon there would be a "her" at the bottom of it, didn't we?'

'Speaking of gossip, though,' I said. 'Wouldn't you have thought the villagers would be out and about gossiping right now? Flitting between houses? Cramming into the tea shop? Where are they all?'

Alec took a quick glance a round and frowned a little. 'You make a good point,' he said in that way of his that always makes me feel like a dog being given a biscuit. 'Come to think of it, where's that postie cum parkie? He should be whistling his way round the village going in and out of every gate. But he merely popped up to head off that peculiar creature—'

'Lizzy,' I reminded him.

'—and then disappeared again.'

'And what was he doing delivering letters at this time of day anyway?' I said. 'Dirleton surely doesn't run to a second post on a Sunday? It's gone two o'clock.'

'It hasn't!' said Alec. 'Oh God, if the dining room is closed I shall blame you roundly, Dan. Come on and help me beg them for favours, won't you?'

He hared off and I followed him, wondering if I would be able to swallow a bite. The late night, early morning, poor Daisy, poor Silas for all his faults, and this peculiar little village had all unsettled me completely. Still, at least Alec seemed to be treating the matter as a case now. Perhaps he had packed his history with Silas away somehow, as even the best of men are always able to do.

61

I crunched over the gravel to where he held the inn's front door open and we entered a dark-panelled but not uninviting lobby done up in the Highland style, with mounted heads and tartan upholstery. An elderly-looking woman with faded hair scraped into a meagre bun looked up from where she was passing a quiet day on the reception desk by catching up on her mending and pulled down her glasses to inspect us.

'You'll be the writers then?' she said. 'The researchers. Paddy Watson popped in to say you'd arrived.' She was staring at us with a level of wonderment more suited to Hollywood stars or royal personages than a pair of researchers come to a village that had things to be researched.

'That's us,' said Alec, evidently in for a pound. I, in contrast, sensed us drifting towards rapids I could already hear. I felt we were bound to plunge off the edge unless we somehow managed to learn a few facts to support Alec's breezy claims, and soon at that. And even if we were lucky in that regard, we'd be in deeper trouble still once the real researchers turned up, not to mention beyond all hope of saving when the police arrived and revealed our true identities.

'I'm Miss Clarkson,' the woman said, jabbing her needle into her work and coming around the counter. Once again, as had been the case with the park-keeper, this new acquaintance grew younger-looking as she approached. Her skin was not age-mottled, but freckled, and her hair was not faded but simply naturally sandy. When she removed her little spectacles completely I judged her to be thirty, if that. 'Nessie Clarkson,' she said in a voice deep with some meaning that was lost on us. She was watching us most avidly too. 'And you've met Paddy Watson. And was that Lizzy Hogg greeting you?'

I should not have called it a greeting, but otherwise she had summed up most of our Dirleton acquaintance. 'And the young constable, whose name we didn't catch,' I said. I took my little notebook and propelling pencil out of my bag to jot these names down as they came.

Miss Clarkson made a curious gesture then, as though to dismiss the constable from consideration. 'Jimmy McLean,' she said. 'Now, I'm afraid there's no one about to show you to your rooms.'

'Can't you leave the desk?' I asked.

'Oh, I don't work here,' Miss Clarkson said. 'I'm a seamstress and dressmaker. I'm only helping out because there's been an unfortunate incident and the landlord is also the village joiner, you see.' I did not, but she swept on before I could say so. 'Miss Halliburton is busy at the moment too, but once she's done I shall send her to you with hot water, and when the landlord's back he'll bring up your bags. He'll have to leave off and get back here before opening, won't he? I mean, I try to be a good neighbour but I can't pull pints.'

'A coffin doesn't take much joinery,' said Alec, showing off that he had seen the connection between the unfortunate incident and the sudden busyness of the landlord.

'Is Miss Halliburton not a barmaid?' I asked, trying to form a taxonomy of villagers. What had the constable said about her?

'Good heavens no,' said Miss Clarkson. 'She's laying out the body.'

I dropped my pencil, snapping off a good chunk of its lead as it hit the tiled floor. I should not have been surprised. Silas died yards away from the inn and outside of villages with cottage hospitals, towns with hospitals proper, and cities with mortuaries, the local inn has always served as an ad hoc resting place for corpses as well as a venue for inquests and even an impromptu prison if push comes to shove. What is more, Sgt Dodgson had told me in the five o'clock telephone call exactly where Silas was.

I loathed to think of him still and cold in some back bedroom of the Castle Inn, as Daisy lay just as still though warm and living at Gilverton, with that police matron crouched beside her like a vulture and the sharp-eyed nurse no doubt just about to see through her act.

'You don't look well, madam,' said Miss Clarkson. 'I'm sorry I spoke so baldly. I assumed – what with the book you're writing – you wouldn't be easily . . . Why not sit down and have a cup of tea before you go up?'

'Bite to eat, please,' Alec said, the wretch. Unfortunately I did not have the wherewithal to scold him.

Chapter 5

Alec was in luck. The dining room of the Castle Inn was indeed closed, had closed at nine o'clock the previous evening and would not reopen until six today, but Miss Clarkson directed us to the bar parlour and within minutes she had brought tea in brown china teapots and a dazzling array of freshly cut sandwiches such as even Alec could not fault.

'So there's clearly someone in the kitchen,' he said, washing down a mouthful of bread, ham, and pickled something – I could not see it but the pungent waves were unmistakable. I sipped tea and nibbled a plain biscuit. 'Which begs the question why Mr Landlord had to draft Miss Seamstress to let us in or to oversee Miss Castle as she tends to Silas.'

'That's who she is!' I said. 'The constable said it was Halliburtons who own the castle, didn't he?'

'I must say, though,' Alec went on, 'I don't understand why a member of the great family *is* tending to Silas. No matter if he was on a visit there or tom-catting around in one of the cottages. Blasted man.'

'I wish *I* could be irritated at him and not keep getting swamped by grief,' I said.

Alec regarded me steadily and I changed the subject back again.

'Unless she was a nurse in the—' I said. 'Unless she was a nurse and she's kept it on as a sideline.'

'Sidelines being the Dirleton way,' said Alec. 'Aren't you going to eat your sandwich?'

'I shall wrap it in a damp napkin and have it later,' I said. 'If I have any appetite, that is. I wish I knew where Silas was, exactly. Before I settle in to my room, I mean.'

'Not like you to be . . .'

'Sentimental?' I said. 'Spooked? I know. And that's not irritation or *grief*. There's something about this place, Alec. Don't you think so?'

'The pub? No, I don't. It's so comfortable and pleasant it's barely Scottish.'

I rewarded him with a small smile. I well remembered his mourning period for the public houses of his youth, with their cheery barmaids, bright fires, and hunting prints. The spit-and-sawdust drinking dens of his and my new home did not meet the case at all.

'The village,' I said. 'The villagers. The . . . Oh, ignore me.'

He did not go quite that far, but he did wait on the landing a little later while I unlocked the door to my assigned bedroom. I peeked inside and saw cheerful print curtains, a snowy counterpane on a cosy bed, and even a jug of peonies on the dressing table.

'How very Milly-Molly-Mandy,' I said.

'Who?'

'Sickening stories for little girls,' I told him. 'Mallory bought them for Lavinia and I've read them so many times I know them off by heart.'

'I'd say it looks jolly comfy,' said Alec. 'And I'm just across the way. Looking out at the yard, without any daylight to speak of. 'Twas ever thus.'

I twisted my face up in apology, for it is true that we ladies do tend to get the best of the billets. I stepped inside my room and sat down on the plump edge of the agreeable bed. I even noticed a hint of lavender puffing up, a subtle trace of that sunshiny smell one only gets from bedding stretched over bushes to dry in the open air. It cannot be taken for granted in Scotland, with their weather. Our weather, I suppose I should say, after all these years.

Beyond the fluttering curtains – my bedroom window was open at the bottom in a way that would greatly please Nanny Palmer – I had a view of the entire top portion of the main green, the road stretching to the east and most of the castle wall as it curved gently away. There was a small turret at the closest thing the wall had to a corner and I could just glimpse some formal gardens inside the palisades. Much further back, only half visible through some sheltering trees, the castle itself rose up from an outcropping of rock, exactly like a black toad grown to monstrous size by some fairy-tale magic. I shivered. Then, stepping closer, I craned to see if the smaller toad, that strange little stone under its cover, was visible from here. I was relieved to find that it was not. I brushed my fingers over the pinks in my window box to release their fragrance and regarded myself in the looking glass over the fire.

'Come on, old girl,' I said. 'Think of Daisy. There's work to do.'

Sallying forth to find the bathroom I thought must be around somewhere, I even managed to call out a cheery greeting to the maid – I assumed – who appeared at the far end of the passageway as if I had summoned her by opening my door.

'Thank you for all your excellent work with the linens,' I said. 'My room is delightful.'

'How did you know I was a laundress?' the girl said to me. I felt my smile falter. Although she was a bonny creature, blowsy curls the colour of chestnuts and a neat uniform of striped cotton with cuffs pinned over her rolled-up sleeves, there was something about her gaze that unsettled me. Perhaps it was no more than the directness of the look she levelled at me to match her bold query, so different from the quick glance and then lowered eyes I came to expect from domestics in my formative years.

'Gosh, I've made an even luckier lucky guess than I was aiming for then,' I said with an attempt at brightness. 'I took you for the chambermaid.'

'Oh,' she said, holding up one finger as if struck by a sudden thought and pretty well ignoring what I had just said, 'are you one of these "writers"? Nessie Clarkson said you were here but I didn't believe her.'

Without Alec I felt unequal to the charade and said nothing.

'Have you seen her yet?' the girl went on.

'Yes, Miss Clarkson was downstairs on the desk when we arrived.'

She made an impatient gesture. 'Not *Nessie*,' she said. Then she raised her chin. 'Manie Halliburton.' She held out a hand to mine.

'Halliburton?' I said, suddenly realising who this was. I let her hand drop and shot a glance along the way she had come, to where the passage sank into darkness, like a throat. I shook that unbidden thought from my head. 'And you live at the castle?' I said. I was more puzzled than ever. A daughter of the great family clinging to her nursing was one thing, but a member of the Halliburton clan working in a laundry was something else again.

'Not me, missus,' she said. 'There's Halliburtons and Halliburtons in Dirleton. I thought you'd know that. I've a little cottage handy for my laundry. Does me. Fact, I need to be getting back. I've done him up the best I can, the poor soul. It was the least I could offer him.'

'The least . . . ?'

'A winding sheet and a posy of herbs,' she said. 'I'm not an undertaker. It's a black day for Dirleton this. And we didn't need another one. Well, I don't need to tell *you*.'

She bobbed a polite curtsy then and left me. As her footsteps faded on the stairs, ringing out like knocks on a door from her wooden pattens, I heard a latch and turned to see Alec's face peering out. 'What the dickens?' he said. 'I didn't see whoever that was, Dandy, but I heard her. There is something very odd going on around here. What on earth do you suppose these fabled writers are coming to *write*?'

'I haven't the faintest clue,' I said. 'And who's to say it matters? The point is, that's the second time someone's spoken of "her" and it would be perverse not to assume "she" is the killer.'

'Well then we must find her, wouldn't you say?'

'How?' I demanded. It came out like a howl, as it so easily does if one's tone of voice is not quite under one's command.

'The landlord's back,' Alec said. 'He just brought a coffin into the yard on a little cart. I saw him from my window.'

'Let's ask him who "she" is then,' I said. 'Better than asking Miss Clarkson.'

'Why's that?' said Alec.

It was not until I opened my mouth to answer him that I realised I did not know. Not for the first time since arriving in Dirleton, I shivered. I decided not to look around for open windows or doors ajar. I decided to believe there was a draught and not dislodge that belief by checking.

★ ★ ★

'I take it you mean Mither Gollane?' The landlord, with a little sawdust in his hair from his morning's task, stood behind the public bar, polishing away at a tankard as if he were readying brasses for a horse show. I nudged Alec discreetly. He had done it! And with no more than an 'I say, my good man, I don't suppose you could point us towards the lady in question, could you? In all of our researching we failed to take the simple step of finding out her address.'

Alec nudged me back, but quellingly if anything; as if to say we shouldn't be passing notes with our elbows, like schoolchildren. The landlord was peering at the shine on the pewter flank of his tankard and noticed nothing.

'That's her,' said Alec.

The landlord looked out of the open door towards the desk where Miss Clarkson was bent over her sewing. 'You're going through with it all to that extent then?'

I could not have summoned an answer but Alec was well away. 'Better had, since we've come,' he said.

The landlord inclined his head, signalling agreement. 'But wouldn't you have needed to be here yesterday?'

'What do you mean?' I asked.

'Oh, it's like that, is it?' the man said. He looked tired and rather white about the eyes but they twinkled as though he were teasing me. I could not begin to imagine what about. 'Aye well,' he went on, at last. 'It's nocht to do with me.' He spat on the tankard and reapplied his cloth.

'You're not familiar with the story then?' Alec said.

This time, his attempt to act in-the-know went badly. The landlord looked up again and his twinkle had hardened to a more calculating glint. 'I suppose when it's not you and it's not yours it might strike you as no more than that,' he said.

Alec, chastened, said nothing.

'We must seem very cold waltzing in here to poke around your home village,' I offered.

'The whole thing's daft if you ask me. But we're used to it. Only, take whatever she tells you with a pinch of salt, won't you?'

'Naturally,' said Alec.

I, with my propelling pencil poised over my open notebook, said, 'And what's her address?'

The landlord shook his head with something between a laugh and a snort. 'I wouldn't call it that. Through the gates at the top of the manse road and head for Archerfield. Past the links, you'll see it there in the trees.'

'So this would be opposite the sad place where . . .' I said.

'The *louping stane*, aye,' said the man, then drew in and let go an enormous gusting sigh. 'The sad place where, right enough.' Once again, he glanced out of the open door towards the reception desk. 'Black days again for Dirleton,' he said, in a lower voice. 'You caw canny, the pair of you.'

'You're very kind,' I murmured and, dragging Alec along, withdrew.

'You've got years of Scotch nonsense on me, Dan,' he said, as we stepped out of the hotel. 'What was all that about?'

'Well "caw canny" means be careful,' I told him. 'I suppose the landlord thinks the murderess might still be abroad – which is a thought actually, isn't it? If it wasn't Daisy, which I insist is the case, then I daresay she is.'

'But not just that,' Alec said. 'What about the rest of it? The dark days and the . . . what did he say?'

'Louping stane? A stane is a stone, obviously,' I said. 'And to *loup* is to jump. Like "leap", you see? So I'm guessing that the boulder sticking out of the ground where Silas met his

71

end is a stone that the Dirletonites jump from, or onto, or over. For some reason.'

'Some reason!' Alec scoffed. 'I think we could probably guess, don't you? Won't it be the usual?'

For Alec had been dumped neck-deep in the most torrid Scottish folklore during an early investigation of ours, when a nightmarish man – actually a perfectly ordinary man, but heavily disguised by the head-to-toe application of burdock seeds, so that he ended up looking like a Frankenstein's monster afflicted by fungus – had been put to death by poison. The Burry Man, as he is known, was indeed paraded around for "the usual" reasons: good luck, good harvests, good riddance to all evil.

'Rather unfair, darling,' I said. 'What about the green man in all those little English churches? Not to mention Morris dancers.'

'Oh, always best not to mention Morris dancers. I say, look, Dandy! The fingerprint boys are here.'

I looked up and saw that, right enough, there was a small huddle of men in identical mackintoshes and soft hats clustered around the stone. The constable was standing off to the side trying to look dignified while holding a hastily bundled-up armload of canvas. He gave us a miserable smile as we drew near.

'We should have lifted it up on sticks,' the constable said. 'To save from smearing everything. And that only if it came on to rain. Pegging it down tight's about the worst thing we could have done, short of setting to with a scrubbing brush.'

The nearest man twisted round from where he was kneeling over the stone with some kind of instrument – it looked like a hair curler but surely could not be – and said, 'Beggars belief there's a man on the force that doesn't know that. And who are *you*?'

72

'Oh no one,' said Alec. 'Passers-by.'

'Well, damn well pass by then,' said the fingerprint man. 'This doesn't concern you.'

Alec is slow to anger, but he got two spots of colour high on his cheekbones at this, clashing painfully with his usual colouring, which is half freckles and half weather.

'Come on,' I said. 'We seem to be somewhat surplus to requirements.' I shepherded him to the corner of the green, where lay a pair of open gates complete with a little lodge cottage.

'Bloody rude of him,' said Alec. 'I don't expect to be welcomed by the plods when we are flying under our own colours as detectives, but there was no need for that to be directed at perfectly ordinary strangers.'

'You've been blinded by the offence,' I said. 'That man was supposed to be concentrating on his job, carefully searching for prints to help solve a murder, but his hands were shaking.'

'A drunkard?'

'And his voice was shaking too,' I said. 'Not to mention that fact that he was drawn and haggard with it. Alec, I think he was terrified.'

Alec pushed his lips out and narrowed his eyes. 'Of what?'

'Exactly,' I said. 'It can't have been the blood or the fact of the murder. Not a man in his job. So what was it?'

Alec said nothing.

'I have no idea what we're looking for on this path, by the way,' I went on. 'So I suggest we look closely. You take the right and I'll take the left and we can swap if we get cricks in our necks. Agreed?'

'Typical!' said Alec. 'We were told it was "in the trees" so you take the side with all the trees.' It was true that there was more woodland on the left and it was not beneath me in the usual run of things to make sure I was the one who found what we sought. But in this instance the thought had not occurred to me. I rolled my eyes at him, stepped to the right and turned my face ostentatiously to the golf course lying beyond the hedgerow. Alec, often a sore winner, made a loud tutting sound and took himself to the left-hand edge of the path to search there.

In the end we both found it, since the smell of a cooking fire – woodsmoke and burning fat – alerted us before the fire itself and the rest of the encampment came into view. It was halfway up a sloping bank in a copse of rowan trees: a little structure somewhere between a lowly cottage and a superior shed, with a tin chimney sticking out and waxed paper in the windows. In front of it – wisely in my opinion, given the state of that chimney – the householder had decided to cook dinner en plein air. An iron tripod was suspended over a neat little fire with a piece of meat hanging from a hook, scenting the air with something not quite rank but certainly gamy.

'Who's there?' came a call, making both Alec and me jump, for there was no one to be seen. Then, as we watched, a portion of the landscape seemed to dislodge itself and reveal the shape of a person dressed in such perfect green and brown patchwork garments, with such a wrinkled nut-coloured face and such a drab nest of hair, that her whole attire amounted to camouflage. 'Come away up and let me see you,' she said, gesturing us towards her with a hand like a bundle of twigs, so dark and bony was it. 'Who are you?'

'We are writers,' Alec called. 'We are a pair of researchers come to see you.'

'The pair of researchers who're coming to see her are going to be livid with us when they get here,' I muttered.

74

'By which time we will have gleaned a great deal of useful information,' Alec muttered back. 'Anyway, if this interview proves that their concerns are not our concerns, we can rip away our disguise before bedtime. Come on, Dandy.'

'I wonder why the landlord thought they were arriving yesterday,' I said, but Alec had gone ahead and was not listening.

We picked our way through a thicket of brambles, just coming into blossom, and on past some gooseberry bushes, a couple of hollies and a decent patch of nettles – such was the selection of thorny, prickly and stinging vegetation that formed the entranceway to this creature's dwelling – and found ourselves standing in a neat clearing, with rows of vegetables laid out as strictly as any Victorian head gardener ever decreed, the beds edged with miniature willow hurdles, the beans, peas and a profusion of flowers growing up turrets of the same willow, which had been fashioned into such fantastical shapes that a simple vegetable patch had taken on the aspect of a topiary garden. The path leading through this haven to the shack was lined with pots of marigolds and geraniums, all pulsing with early colour. And there seemed to be a little spring at one side, bubbling merrily into a cocked jug before spilling into a wide, shallow bowl. There was a henhouse too – rather more sturdy than the human dwelling, made as it was with even sticks like a Wild West cowboy fort, and decorated with whimsical ladders and chutes like a helter-skelter. A proud-looking black cockerel strutted about and knocked at the ground as though he thought he were a bull, a couple of his fat wives waddling and clucking along beside him, searching for grubs.

In the middle of it all, the woodland creature sat on such a low stool that, tiny as she was, still her knees were around her ears. She was the most ancient-looking person I had ever seen in my life, her eyes yellowed and pink-rimmed, her hair thin at the scalp and broken at the ends, and her teeth, when she smiled, no more than dark stumps in her head. My surprise can well be imagined then, when she stood up to her full diminutive height without a trace of a hump in her back or a bow in her legs and shot out a hand to seize mine with a sturdy grip.

'Mither Gollane,' she said. 'But you knew that.'

'Of course,' I replied. 'I'm . . . Dandy Gilver and this is Alec Osborne.'

'Incognito, are you?' said the crone. 'I was telt the room at the inn was booked under a Dr Crabbie and a Dr McEwan.'

She was shaking Alec's hand now and I took the opportunity to jot these names down in my little notebook.

'I see,' said Alec. 'Well, what's in a name?'

She had been about to let go of his hand, but at his words, which struck me as anodyne enough, she gripped his fingers so hard that he winced.

'And you're here to interview me for your book?' she said.

'Quite correct,' Alec said. 'Shall we begin?'

I gathered my jaw from where it had landed after it dropped and looked around for somewhere to settle.

'Here, "Dr" Gilver,' she said, with a ready sarcasm. It was unsettling to hear one's attempt at disguise being treated with such derision. The fact that her words were accompanied by a kind gesture – inviting me to take her vacated seat – did not remove their sting. Nevertheless I accepted and settled myself onto what I now saw was a tree stump. Alec was offered an upturned bucket and the crone – Mither Gollane – sat upon the ground, waving away our protests.

'Who are you really though?' she then said, skewering us with a look.

'The more interesting question is "Who are you?"' said Alec. He has long held that everyone loves to talk and that a fresh audience is hard to resist. Right now, Mither Gollane had a choice: to keep on grilling us or to share her story with us. I waited with pencil poised.

She nodded, sucked those stumps of teeth once or twice, and, in her own good time, made her choice. 'Very well, if you want to go through with it,' she said, 'I'm exactly who I claim to be. No matter who you are.' Alec sat back. I hunched over my notebook. 'There are others who would grab my glory, but they cannot prove it and I can. If you look in the parish book right there in the kirk at the end of this very path, you will see. I was born right here in Dirleton in 1831, on the first day of November as midnight finished striking. And don't listen to any who says otherwise.'

Alec and I shared a frown. Granted, she was old; she looked older than any living woman or man I had ever seen. She looked exactly like what the boys and I had steeled ourselves to see when the archaeologist unwrapped Boris Karloff in that horrific picture they made me watch.

I am hopeless at mental arithmetic so it was Alec who spoke up. 'That would make you one hundred and seven years old,' he said.

'And six months and thirteen days,' said the crone. 'That is true. It's in the parish book, my mother's name and my father's name and mine. Written by Mr Stark in the last year of his ministry. I was confirmed by Mr Scott. That's in the parish book too. Married by Mr Logie, a few pages on, and I thought to be buried by Mr Kerr, but there he went and died with the old queen and so it'll like be Mr Wallace who sends me to my rest.'

'Remarkable,' I said, sure she was lying.

'I am,' she retorted, with a smirk. 'Or you wouldn't hardly be "writing a book" about me, would you?'

'Right then, Mrs Gollane,' Alec said.

She interrupted whatever he was planning to ask her. 'I'm not "Mrs Gollane". I was *Mrs* right enough for many a year. But I'm Mither Gollane now. I can step inside and get my papers to show you. Now, I do not have my birth paper. You'll need to go to the parish book for that, like I said. But I have my marriage lines and I have all the birth certificates that show my babes again and again and again once more. So they will have to do you.'

With that, she clamped her hands on her knees and, almost unbelievably, she rose from where she was seated on the ground without any struggle or even so much as the kind of groan Hugh emits and I try not to when rising from so much as a dining chair.

'Right, Dan,' Alec said, when she had stumped off to her shack, 'it seems we are scholars engaged upon an investigation of Scotland's, or perhaps Britain's, oldest living people. We might need to look in her mouth or bang her knees with a little hammer, to keep the story going. Can you fake that, with all your nursing?'

'I was a companion in a convalescent home,' I hissed back. 'I'll do the knees and you take the mouth, if you're sure it's necessary. Or better still, try and bring the conversation round to Silas. He's the only reason we're here and that old woman can't have done for him.'

'She's stronger than she looks,' Alec said, shaking his right hand as though his knuckles were still throbbing.

'Well then let's just go. And leave her to . . . Crabtree and Mc . . . when they get here.' Then I coughed ostentatiously as a moving shadow told us Miss Gollane, or whoever she was, was returning.

'I've never been a great reader,' she said, 'even when my eyes were a fair bit better than they are now, but *you'll* see easy enough.' She divided her little sheaf of yellowed papers between us, two for Alec and two for me, and sat back down.

I unfolded one with great anticipation but should have known better. It looked like a birth or marriage certificate right enough; it was the right size and shape and made of just the right kind of thick vellum, but apparently keeping it inside a shack in a wood had it done it no favours, for the ink had turned from script to blooms of damp and not a single word was decipherable. I looked at Alec and he shook his head. The crone was beaming at us, with every appearance of innocent sincerity.

'Very interesting, Mrs . . . Mither . . .' I said, folding the papers and returning them to her.

'Like I said,' she told me. 'I came Mither Gollane fifteen years back and I'm proud of it. So I should be. Although I'd live a sight easier than this else.'

Alec was nodding along with a most complacent look on his face. He probably thought I understood it all and would explain it later.

'Ten years and more ago,' Mither Gollane went on, 'I made up my mind to bide with trees and ferns and God's good sky. No matter what anyone tells you. I worked hard all my days. I brought up nine children hale and hearty.' She hesitated. 'God has a plan for us all and it's not for any of us to question Him.'

'Stirring and sensible,' I said. 'I couldn't agree more.' I closed my notebook with a smack and screwed the lead of my propelling pencil firmly back down.

'Oh, that's you done, is it? It's a long way to ask not much.'

'For now,' I said. 'It's been a very trying day for one thing and, for another, we wouldn't like to delay your supper.' Much less be asked to stay and eat it. 'I should think that rabbit is nicely done by now.'

'It's not a rabbit,' said Mither Gollane. I steeled myself not to look. If it was not a rabbit I did not care to amass any more information on the subject. 'Here's me thinking you'd want to hear all about my stane.'

'Your . . . stain?' I said, not caring at all for the notion.

'My louping stane,' she said.

'Oh!' said Alec, leaning forward so eagerly that his bucket threatened to tip. 'We most certainly do. We didn't know it was yours.'

The old woman gave him a contemptuous glance. 'And what's made today "trying" anyroad?' she said. She was tending the lump of meat hanging over her fire now, poking it with a skewer and releasing even more fat to drip onto the coals. I opened my mouth to breathe through it. I had always been told not to but these were special circumstances.

'But haven't you heard?' said Alec. 'Since you mentioned it, I thought you must know. There's been a murder there.'

'Never,' she said. 'At my louping stane? That wouldn't happen.'

'It certainly *has* happened,' I said.

'That's a darkness,' said Mither Gollane, musingly. 'That'll need to be seen to.' She squinted as though to sharpen her eyesight and demanded, 'Are you going to put that in your book then, are you?'

'I shouldn't have thought so,' I replied. 'It's a complete coincidence, or so most of the village thinks.'

'Although one chap did hint that our interests and the motive for Mr Esslemon—'

'What?' Mither Gollane froze with her skewer aloft, looking even more witch-like than ever. 'What did you just say?' she managed at last.

'A man called Silas Esslemont—' I began, but the howl she let out cut me off.

'Noooo!' she wailed. 'Oh no! Who's he killed? How many? Why didn't somebody stop him?'

'No, no, no – settle yourself,' I said, raising my voice to be heard above her. 'Silas Esslemont has *been* killed. Silas Esslemont has been murdered.'

'I don't believe you!' said Mither Gollane, although she sat back down and let out an enormous wavering breath as though profoundly relieved. 'That can't be the way of it. Someone is making mischief with you. Who would do such a thing as lay a hand on him? No one in Dirleton would dare to try.'

'I don't understand,' said Alec. 'What do you mean?'

She had a firm hold of herself again. 'Him – that man – that name you said. Dirleton folk know better than to harm him. Dirleton folk are not fools.'

'What are you talking about?' I said.

'So whatever poor soul has been done away with, it's not . . . him whose name you said. It can't be. He'll not be dead. Not him! He'll be well protected. He'll be safe from harm.'

'I see,' Alec said. 'I see. Well, this is all very interesting, Mither, and I hope we can revisit it when next we meet.' He stood and shook out the inevitable creases that were the wages of sitting hunched on a bucket all this while. 'Tell me, since you don't care to say his name,' he went on, 'how do you refer to him, if you need to?'

'I don't,' she said stoutly. 'I've no need ever to. And so I don't.'

81

'I see,' said Alec again, maddeningly. He stuck out a hand to haul me to my feet and then with a curt nod he set off towards the path again. I gave a sickly sort of smile and followed him.

Chapter 6

'Rather puts paid to the notion that there are two separate matters afoot,' I said. We were back on the track, and Alec was looking wistfully over the hedge at a gaggle of distant golfers trudging between tee and green. I knew they were not trudging between green and tee, because a golfer is always at least a little jaunty from the fresh hope of a new hole. These had that dejected set to their shoulders that comes from knowing that one has already mucked it up with the first drive but must see it through anyway. 'I'm sure you can rent clubs,' I told him. 'Perhaps not at Gullane – that would be rather like asking for a tuppenny towel at a lido in Cap D'Antibes – but here perhaps.'

'And leave you with all of this?' said Alec. 'I think not.'

'But all of what?' I asked him. 'That's the question.'

'And an excellent one,' Alec said, turning from the golfers, who were disappearing over a rise anyway. 'Mither Gollane is entering her second childhood. Overdue if she's really a hundred and seven.'

'Rather harsh,' I objected.

'Why else would someone live in a hovel not even half as commodious as the shelter she made for her chickens? Why would anyone who could fashion that garden not fashion herself a house too? Why would she think she owns a stone sticking up out of the grass on a village common?'

'Granted, she seems eccentric.'

'Oh come on, Dandy! Eccentric? She's stark raving mad and we can't possibly use her claims to direct our view of what happened here. She said she had nine children, for a start. But she only brought us four bits of ruined paper. One marriage certificate and then what? Are we supposed to believe she had three sets of triplets?'

'I didn't assume it was a complete set of documents,' I said. 'Rather, a representative selection.' In truth, I hadn't put the claim and the papers together at all but it does not do to give way to Alec when he starts getting lofty. 'What about her reaction to hearing Silas's name? Is *that* to be dismissed as the ravings of a madwoman?'

'Harder to say,' said Alec. 'She heard a name in connection with a murder and immediately cast the part of villain rather than victim. That was interesting, for a start. And, before we could put her right, she immediately asked how many he had slain. Rather than *whom* he had slain, do you see? Plurality was an odd assumption, don't you think? Finally she jumped to the somewhat strange conclusion that he was too "well protected" to be harmed.'

He paused and looked at me expectantly. I shrugged.

'Make an effort, Dan. Come on! She wouldn't say his name. And when I asked her what she would call him instead, she wouldn't answer.'

Another pause and another shrug ensued, only this time I was not being entirely honest, for an inkling of an idea was beginning to form.

Alec kept on pressing. 'Who is it that the Scots have such squeamish notions about naming? What individual is given more nicknames than any other? Someone no Dirletonite would dare to challenge? Someone invincible and well protected? Someone rather more likely to do the killing than to be killed?'

I was beginning to feel extremely uncomfortable.

'Say it,' said Alec. 'Surely you're not as superstitious as that old witch?'

'Hardly a witch,' I said.

'Born at the witching hour, as midnight on Halloween becomes All Soul's Day?' Alec said.

'Yes, I thought that was overegging it a bit too. And a witch would have said it gladly. I shall say it too. She thinks Silas Esslemont was the devil. Or one of his minions at least. Protected by him.'

'Wouldn't you say that makes this case a great deal more intriguing?'

'If your tastes run in that direction,' I admitted grudgingly.

'Especially when added to the quaking of the fingerprint man.'

'That might have been no more than superstition left over from boyhood,' I said. 'If he's local.'

'Although,' Alec said, 'put together with the letter, it's surprising that the stone should strike terror, isn't it?'

'Is it? What do you mean?'

'Think of what the letter said, Dandy. "Come to me". That's pretty vague, and yet Silas knew where to come. I think that suggests the stone was a trysting place.'

'It should be easy enough to find out,' I said. 'In fact, we really shouldn't have left before getting Mither Gollane to tell us a great deal more. But she was giving me the willies.'

'She put a rather more rational thought in my mind as well as all that though,' Alec said. 'With her insistence that the dead stranger was someone else. No one, as yet, has actually identified the corpse.'

We were back at the lodge and we passed through the gates in silence and contemplated the quiet green. The finger-print men were gone. The constable was gone. The stone lay uncovered in its ring of cobbles. Without discussion, we walked towards it and stood gazing.

'Of course it was Silas,' I said, at length, once I had had a good close look at the dark stain and the scrape marks left by the instruments of the policemen. 'Why would someone else have a letter addressed to him? And be wearing his ring? And where is he, if not dead? It's a ludicrous idea to suggest it was anyone but Silas. Almost as ludicrous as the notion that he was some kind of demon. I pity that poor old thing, living in her shack in the woods in such an enfee-bled state.'

'Whistling past the graveyard, Dandy?' Alec said, and I might have flushed just a little; it was true that I spoke to exhort myself to disbelief rather than from true conviction. 'I maintain that she's either crooked or mad, but she seemed in fine fettle physically. Except for her teeth, and even that is surely a cosmetic problem if she's really equal to consuming over-roasted squirrel for her next meal.'

'Ugh!' I said. 'Is that what it was?'

'But to return to the point,' he went on, 'of course, I don't mean to give the claim any credence. It's preposterous. But it has to mean something that she mounted the argument. For one thing, it means she's heard of Silas. It proves he had some connection to this place and some reason to be here.'

'Well, we know he had a reason to be here, because he was here.'

'*Another* reason,' Alec said. 'A different reason from the one we expected. *That* would have been clandestine. Mither Gollane would hardly know him because he had a mistress nearby.

86

Her outburst confirms that Alec's connections to Dirleton are of a most peculiar kind.'

'Confirms?'

Alec gave me a startled look. 'You said it,' he replied. 'I'm merely agreeing with you.'

'I have no idea what you're talking about and it's most aggravating.'

He gave a soft laugh. 'Look around, Dandy.' He threw his arms out wide, taking in the whole of the scene: the gate lodge behind us; the school, hall, church and manse before us; the row of large houses with the inn at the top end, the row of sweet little cottages stretching away to the main road; and the huge featureless bulk of the castle wall, with its one odd little turret halfway along.

'What am I looking at?' I said. 'There is absolutely nothing to see.'

'Exactly!' Alec said. 'Talk about the dog who didn't bark. Dandy, a murder was done at this spot a few short hours ago. Since the body was found there's been a bobby on guard duty and a sack thrown over the spot. Now at last here is a bloodstain gruesome enough to satisfy the most ghoulish of ghouls, and not a single villager is out gawping at it. Why not? Where are they all?'

'That might not be because it was Silas though,' I said. 'It might be because of . . . Well, whatever made Mither Gollane say no one would be murdered at the stone. And whatever upset the fingerprint man.'

I cast my eye around and was relieved to see Manie Halliburton making her way towards us from the Castle Inn, with a stout wooden bucket in one hand and a scrubbing brush in the other. I waved to her and said to Alec, 'Here's the local laundress – the girl you overheard me talking to earlier – and she's obviously not shying away.' I lifted my voice. 'Miss Halliburton! You're come to do the village a good deed, I see.'

'It's a lucky thing for Dirleton is that stane,' said Manie. 'We can't leave it in that state.'

'Lucky how?' Alec said. He gave me an arch look. 'Is it a trysting place?'

'Eh? Naw,' said Manie. 'It's a louping stane.'

'But what exactly is that?' I asked.

'The school weans all jump over it on their last day of lessons,' she said. 'In the old days there would be handfastings over it too.'

'Handfastings are weddings, aren't they?' said Alec. 'Sounds like a trysting place to me.'

'Who owns it?' I asked, rather more to the point, in my opinion.

Manie frowned. 'Owns? It's not owned. It's . . .'

Having got my answer, I took a couple of coins from my purse and tucked them into her apron pocket. 'Here. You're a good sensible girl. No qualms about the task, I'm glad to see.'

'I'm a laundress, madam,' she said. 'A wee tate of blood is nothing to me.'

I was much relieved to hear a return to this practicality. Then she ruined it.

'It's the Sabbath Day,' she said. 'No harm will come to me. I asked them and they told me so.'

'Asked whom?' I said.

'My family,' she said, smiling. She set the bucket down and dropped the brush in it, then she folded the front portion of her skirt and pinny hem into a thick pad for her knees and kneeled on the cobbles to set about her work.

Alec was not satisfied, though. 'Do you mean to say,' he asked, 'that, on any other day, you might avoid Silas Esslemont's—'

Manie Halliburton, who had been scrubbing away most diligently at the flank of the leaping stone, let out a shriek at his words, threw her brush from her and scrambled to her feet, kicking over the bucket in her haste and confusion.

'No!' she said. 'Say it's not. That's not . . . who you said . . . That's not who I've been washing and winding, is it? Say it isn't. That's not whose eyes I closed with my own hands! That's not his blood I'm—'

She stopped talking and I watched in a kind of horrid fascination, as her face paled and the fright dropped out of her expression as her mouth fell open and her eyelids closed. She began to crumple at the knees and Alec and I both darted forward, squelching and sliding in the puddle of soapy water. Alec beat me to it, caught her around the ribs, and laid her gently down on the grass as she fainted. I removed my coat, took one shameful second to consider the pinkish soap suds I was about to lay it on, then bundled it into a cushion for her head.

'Manie!' We both wheeled round. A young woman dressed in a severe black and grey costume was approaching us from the manse road. I cast my mind back over the few hours we had been in Dirleton, wondering vaguely if we had already seen her once before, and then she was upon us. 'Manie! Is she— What happened?'

She shoved rather rudely past Alec and me and kneeled beside the woman, who was already coming round. 'Manie, Manie, dear. Wake up. What happened?'

'She was washing the blood off the stone,' Alec said. 'And when she heard it was S—'

89

'Anyone would find it rather unnerving,' I said, cutting him off. If the murdered man's name had the power to knock out the doughty Miss Halliburton, then it was not news to share willy-nilly. 'She has already had a difficult day,' I went on. 'Laying out the body—'

'—of Silas Esslemont,' said the young woman. She was still attending to Manie and we could not judge the expression on her face. No more could I, at any rate, interpret her tone of voice. 'Ah, here she comes,' the woman said next. Now her tone was easier to understand. She sounded affectionate and almost cheerful as she patted Manie's cheek. 'Hello again, you silly goose. Have you had any dinner? Have you been overdoing things? You fainted, Manie. You actually fainted. Like a lady in an old-fashioned melodrama. Here, let's get you up. And you can come and dry off in my kitchen. I shall make you some tea.'

Manie struggled to her feet, helped by the young woman, who was evidently much stronger than her willowy frame would suggest. I shared a look with Alec before the two of them were righted and could witness it. Something very fishy was going on here.

'Is it far?' Alec said. 'Might I help?'

The young woman turned to him and gave him a quick sweep of a look up and down. 'I rather think you've done enough,' she said. Alec blinked. 'And it's just down there, at the schoolhouse. I'm the schoolmistress. Miss Marion Meek.'

She helped Manie away and we watched them out of earshot.

'Well,' said Alec, when they had passed arm in arm through the gate of a cottage tacked on to the side of the school and disappeared through the front door. 'There's a misnomer if ever I heard one. Miss Meek, indeed!'

90

I could not help laughing. We had encountered school-mistresses once before on a case – in fact, I had found myself impersonating one – but Miss Meek was certainly the fiercest I had ever seen.

'But once you've unruffled your feathers,' I said, 'you might turn your attention where it belongs.' Alec scowled. 'She knew the identity of the victim. That makes her a suspect in my book.'

'She might only have heard, based on the letter, though,' said Alec. 'She might be walking out with the constable, for instance.'

'Did *he* know?'

'Or the sergeant.'

'Oh I do hope not,' I said. 'She struck me as a young woman with a bit of spirit and Sgt Dodgson is awful.'

'Well, I like that,' Alec said. 'A bit of spirit indeed! She looked at me as if I'd been passing notes in her class. That's all it takes to recommend someone to you, is it?' He turned to look at the cottage, musing. 'Odd how she wanted to shut Manie up, didn't you think? As the poor thing came round, Miss Meek made sure Manie didn't blurt anything out in her semi-conscious state.'

'You're right,' I said. 'That *is* what lay behind the babbling. What do we make of that?'

'I make nothing just yet,' Alec said. 'What shall we do next? I must admit, as a writer and researcher, I'd rather like to look in these parish books. Find out if the old witch is really the one-hundred-and-seven-year-old woman who lived in a shoe.'

'Oh please let's not,' I said. 'I can't face the minister, frankly, if the schoolmistress, postman, landlord, laundress, seam-stress, witch and village idiot are anything to go by. I'd rather view the body.'

'The constable was all right,' said Alec. 'And don't write off the landlord just yet. I'm hoping I can scare up a brandy out of him. I know it's Sunday but we're residents and that has to count for something.'

I bent and lifted my jacket, gingerly, with two fingers and by one tiny corner of the collar. It was ruined.

'I hope we're still residents,' I said. 'If the real writers have turned up, I wouldn't be too sure.'

The landlord was where we had left him, still polishing assidu-ously in preparation for opening time, and seemed well disposed to bend the licensing laws for such old pals as Alec and me. 'You saw her? Mither Gollane?' he asked, setting two glasses on the bar before us.

'Hold hard for now,' I said, placing my hand over one. 'I think we might be in greater need of brandy in a little while.'

'You're made of stiff fibre if she hasn't left you gasping for a drink,' he said.

'The thing is, you see,' said Alec, 'we have just heard who it is who was killed here. And it's come as rather a shock.'

'A terrific blow,' I said. 'We knew him, you see?'

The landlord stared. 'You knew the man who's been killed?'

'It's a small world. Or at least, it's a small county from which we three all hail.'

'So you're saying you made a reservation to come and stay here, to find out things about Dirleton and write them down for your book. Then you got here the very day that a friend of yours was murdered?'

I am lucky enough to have a sallow complexion, which is slow to flush, but Alec with his fairness and his freckles turned a flaming deep pink. Such is the burden of that colouring.

'You need to get your story sorted out,' the landlord said. 'Or give it up completely.'

It was excruciating. I was ready to chuck in the towel and make a run for it there and then but Alec, despite his blushes, persevered. 'We were told that the local police have gone to seek the widow, break the news and bring her here to view the corpse, all based on no more than some very flimsy evidence. A letter in his pocket and so on. It occurred to us that, if we took a quick look at him, we could put the thing beyond doubt and save Mrs Esslemont an ordeal.'

The landlord dropped his cloth and set his hands square on the counter, fixing us with a glare. 'That's not a name to go bandying about,' he said.

'So we are learning,' Alec said. 'Forgive me.'

The landlord sniffed deeply. 'You want to look at the corpse. Why the devil not just say so? There's no need to spin a tale. Not for me.'

'We really do know him and we really are trying to help, Mr . . .' I said. 'I do beg your pardon, what's your name? I don't believe you said.'

'I did say,' the landlord replied. 'When I spoke to you on the telephone, madam. When you were making the reservation to come and stay here. When *was* that? Do you remember?'

I was struck dumb. Alec took his usual route out of difficulties and filled his pipe. The landlord shook his head and laughed mirthlessly. He picked up his cloth again and folded it into a neat square, as though he had finished with polishing at last. 'The keys are all behind the desk out yond,' he said, nodding towards the reception lobby. 'He's in number thirteen.'

'Is he, by God?' Alec said.

'Aye, you'll have heard all that from the old dear,' he said. 'I wouldn't go so far. But room thirteen is where you'll find him. It's a hard one to let.'

It felt illicit to slip behind the desk out in the lobby of the inn and pluck the numbered key from the board of little hooks. 'This place is beginning to give me the absolute colly-wobbles,' I said, as we made our way upstairs. 'Between Lizzy Hogg, the old witch, the fainting Miss Halliburton and now even our friendly landlord.'

'Collywobbles?' Alec replied. 'When all we're doing is going to room thirteen to view a corpse who might be the devil? Buck up, Dandy.'

I did not dignify him with a response.

Room thirteen was beyond mine, up a step and down two, as is the way of these ancient inns. We paused outside, then Alec took the key from my hand and unlocked the door. Inside, laid on a door between two trestles there was an unmistakably human form, wound neatly in a swathe of crisp white sheeting. Alec stepped inside but I stayed where I was, on the threshold.

'I can't,' I said. 'I'm sorry.'

'Don't worry,' said Alec. 'It doesn't need both of us. Go and telephone to Grant about your coat. She'll scold you back to normal.' He gave me a smile and closed the door.

Back down in the deserted lobby, I asked the exchange for Gilverton and steeled myself to deal with Pallister – or worse, Hugh – but it was Becky who answered.

'Oh it's you, madam,' she said. 'I happened to be passing in the front hall when the bell rang. But now I've picked the thing up I've not a clue how to send you to Mr Gilver in the library. What do I do?'

'It's as big a mystery to me,' I said. 'Hang up and please

ask Miss Grant to ring me at this number, would you? Dirleton 19.'

As I waited, I entertained myself by snooping around the reception desk. There were myriad penholders, inkstands, revolving calendars and blotters, all advertising some brewery or distillery. Even the spray of budding blossom that hinted at Miss Clarkson's influence was set in a pint tankard with "Guinness" written on the side. In pride of place lay the register and I am afraid to admit that I perused it shamelessly. There was my name and Alec's, in his hand. There was a party of McClintocks who had evidently come on a trip over Easter, a great many single men who all seemed to have spent the same single night here about two weeks previously – I guessed at a golfing party – and then, at the top of the current half-filled page, something that interested me exceedingly. There was a pencilled-in and hastily rubbed-out again entry. It had left a blank line in the otherwise orderly book. I squinted at it against the light and managed to make out "Crabbie & McEwan, 7 n, 12/14". I squinted even harder, bending down close to the book, and was able to make out the pencil marks under the ink pertaining to the golfing party and the Easter family, and I concluded that the staff of the inn were in the habit of using the register not just to record arrivals but also to keep track of expected guests. Clearly Crabbie and McEwan had cancelled their booking. This was very handy for Alec and me since they would not now be turning up and causing us difficulty, but it explained why the landlord, who had presumably handled the cancellation, did not give our disguise much credence.

The telephone bell pealing out right beside my ear made me jump and I fumbled it rather as I hastened to quiet the thing.

'Well, madam,' said Grant, when the girl had put us through, 'what a time we're having up here.'

'As am I,' I said. 'What's going on at your end?'

'Those police for a start,' Grant said. 'They asked Mr Gilver all manner of questions about Mr Esslemont. Most peculiar.'

'Oh dear.'

'Not that,' Grant assured me with rather more perspicacity than I cared for. 'Much stranger than that. Was he a *fencer*? Did he *garden*?'

'What?'

'And this is not fences in gardens, mind. They were asking about swords.'

'*What?*'

'I know. That's what I said to Mrs Tilling and she couldn't make sense of it either. Mr Gilver *certainly* couldn't think why Mr Esslemont's hobbies would matter.'

'Nor can I,' I said, ignoring the insinuation that my cook had sharper wits than my husband. 'Now, what of *Mrs* Esslemont?'

'Miss Cartaright has proved herself there,' said Grant. 'She's taking on all manner of tasks. A lady-in-waiting, is the only way I can think of to describe it.'

'Describe what?'

'And I'm pleasantly surprised, nay I'm astonished, at the nurse.'

'Grant, what are you talking about?'

'I thought you knew,' she said. 'Madam. Let me just . . .' I heard some fluffy rustling as Grant manipulated the speaking piece in some way. When she started again, her voice was muffled. 'Mrs Esslemont is awake and aware, but wisely choosing to keep that to herself. And Miss Cartaright. And me.'

'You know!' I squeaked. 'What about the nurse?'

'Oh, there's no fooling a nurse,' said Grant. 'But don't worry. That dreadful Alexandra has put her back up so far that nice Nurse Susan would probably tie bedsheets to make a rope if that's what Mrs Esslemont needed to evade her.'

I took a couple of deep breaths. 'So Daisy's act of unconsciousness has been . . .'

'Busted, yes.'

'Busted? Really, Grant!'

'It's Miss Cartaright's word. She's spent a lot of time in New York. What with the stepfather and everything.'

'What happened to . . . bust her?' I said. 'Did she get the giggles?' Daisy was always one for collapsing in mirth at the most inopportune moments. Classical statuary was her particular downfall, but solemn occasions were fraught with danger too. Certainly, I would never sit beside her at a funeral.

'Giggles?' said Grant. 'I should say not. Weeping, madam. She was lying there still as a— Well, perfectly still and breathing steadily, but the tears kept pouring down her face. Freshets of them, no stopping it. And Nurse Susan knows you don't cry in a coma. Apparently.'

'But you're still hiding it from . . . ? Who is Alexandra?'

'Did you ever hear a more pretentious name? For a police matron? We are, yes. Miss Cartaright, Nurse Susan and I have persuaded Her Imperial Majesty of the Dunkeld Jailhouse that she can't be expected to sit vigil hour after uncomfortable hour when there are so many of us willing to take a turn. She's more or less popping in now. The rest of the time, she's in the kitchen working her way through the biscuit tins. Mrs Tilling is not best pleased but I've explained.'

'Mrs *Tilling* knows?' I said. 'That we are harbouring a murder suspect under false pretences? Good Lord, Grant.'

'And I imagine she'll have told Becky. So we'll handle the night shift very easily. Mrs Esslemont will need to be made comfortable after all. She has been sipping some clear soup and nibbling toast, you see. We can't ask Miss Cartaright to deal with a pot.'

'Grant, for heaven's sake!' Then a thought struck me. 'What about Mallory?'

'Oh don't worry,' said Grant. 'I'm not as green as I'm cabbage-looking.'

For my daughter-in-law was one of life's helpless innocents: she could not lie for toffee and nor could she act. She had reduced many a game of charades to a nonsense and I would be very surprised if my grandchildren managed to retain a belief in Father Christmas much longer.

'Good,' I said. 'Although the details are rather alarming, it's a relief to hear things are stable there. If you can keep Daisy out of the law's clutches until Mr Osborne and I get to the bottom of things down here, I'm sure it will all work out.'

'Have you seen Mr Esslemont, madam?' she asked. 'Can I tell Mrs Esslemont he's peaceful? She's breaking her heart crying.'

'Mr Osborne is viewing the body now,' I said. Then I raised my stock a little by adding, 'I *have* seen about a pint of his spilled blood. There's definitely something peculiar going on here, Grant.'

'Oh I wish I was there,' said Grant, the ghoul. 'I do so enjoy peculiarities. And spilled blood too.'

'Funny you should mention that,' I said. 'I happened to use my light wool coat – the one I travelled in – as a— Hang on, here he comes.'

Alec's feet, trousers, waistcoat and eventually face emerged out of the shadows on the staircase. He was rather pale and he used the banister to steady himself as he descended.

'It's him, Dandy,' he said. 'And no matter what I thought

of the man, no one deserves to die like that. I am so very glad you didn't stay and look at him.'

Grant was squawking in my ear. 'What's he saying? I didn't catch it. Who deserves what?'

'It's Mr Esslemont beyond a doubt,' I told her. 'And now I must go. Give my very best to Daisy when it's safe to do so and please be careful.'

I replaced the earpiece and set the telephone back where I had found it.

'Brandy?' I said.

Alec did not appear to have heard me. 'I never thought to see that look on a man's face again as long as I live,' he said. 'I had forgotten it. That expression of utter despair and terror mixed. I saw it every day, you know. Stretchering them back from the front line. Oh, Dandy. How can we possibly be about to do it all again?'

Chapter 7

It took several stiff whiskies, served in contravention of all licensing laws, before Alec was himself again. I made do with a cup of tea, judging that one of us should be sober in case of unexpected developments. Both orders were delivered by a broad but comely woman in her thirties, whose capacious white apron and striped dress suggested to me that she was a cook, perhaps the source of the earlier sandwiches.

'I assumed the Halliburton girl would have done something about his face,' Alec said, after knocking back the first glassful. 'Smoothed it. Shut his mouth, at least.'

'She claimed to have closed his eyes.'

'Not with any skill,' Alec said. 'They're open again now.'

'Thank the Lord it wasn't Daisy having to look at him,' I said.

'I suppose so,' said Alec, with a wry look, which I deserved, I suppose, for implying that his distress was nothing. He shook his head and looked around himself. 'Speaking of ladies' tender feelings, do you want to move through to the parlour, Dan? You shouldn't be sitting in the public bar just because I've got the heebie-jeebies.'

'Oh, writers don't mind where they sit,' I told him. 'There's some good news on the writers front, by the way. The real ones aren't coming. They've cancelled and been rubbed out of the hotel register. Hence the landlord scoffing at us but, on the bright side, there's no need to worry about bumping into them.'

'Do you think it's related?' Alec said. 'Do you suppose they abandoned their plan to come to Dirleton because they heard about the murder?'

'Possibly,' I replied. 'If the news is out. But we haven't seen any press lurking. On the other hand, they *were* coming to speak to Mither Gollane and she certainly knows something about Silas. Even if it can't be what she thinks it is.'

'But then Manie Halliburton threw her scrubbing brush halfway over the green when she discovered his identity. And the good doctors Crabbie and McEwan weren't coming to interview a laundress in her . . . twenties?'

'Thirties.'

'Or not about the secret of a long life anyway.' Alec paused and shook his head. 'Contrast, if you will, Miss Meek, who knew who'd been murdered and didn't seem perturbed in the slightest.'

'Pretty much everyone else except the constable is convinced that the two matters – the book and the murder – are unrelated. Paddy Watson, Nessie Clarkson, our name-less host—'

Alec shushed me, but too late.

'Call me Tom,' the landlord said, appearing suddenly at our little table. 'I've been sent out to tell you there's barley stew and a baked apple coming later. And to ask if you'd like it in the dining room, the bar parlour or off a tray upstairs.'

'How have you got apples in May?' I said. I disgust myself with my domesticity sometimes.

'Ah, you've not seen the castle garden yet, have you?' said Tom. 'She closed today as a mark of respect to the dead but she'll be open tomorrow.'

'She?' I said, my nose quivering at news of another "she" as does a gun dog's at the sight of a pheasant falling.

'Miss Maggie Goodfellow,' said Tom, with an oddly bitter tone for one who was serving up the garden's bounty on his menu.

'And who is Miss Maggie Goodfellow?' I asked.

'*They* closed, I should say,' Tom said. 'The Halliburtons. It's their garden, but it's our Miss Maggie who calls the shots.'

'Ah,' said Alec. 'The castle Halliburtons. As distinct from the laundry Halliburtons.'

Tom's face darkened.

'And about this garden,' I said hastily, wishing I were close enough to kick Alec under the table. We could not afford to annoy friendly witnesses, even if we did not know where the offence arose. 'Yes, regarding this garden, did Mr Esslemont have a connection to it?'

Alec, who had not yet heard the odd questions being asked at Gilverton, looked at me as though I had lost my mind. 'Why do you think that?' he said.

'I'd like to know too,' said Tom. His expression had not lightened any. 'You who's here to look into the life and times of Mither Gollane, even if you *have* happened to arrive when an old friend's been murdered, here of all places.'

'Or can you shed any light on a possible connection between Mr Esslemont and Mither Gollane?' I said, toughing out the way he had mocked us with our lie.

He put on an expression of wide-eyed innocence. 'You know him, so you tell me. And you're the experts on *her*, so you tell me again.'

For a moment, the three of us remained at a perfect impasse. Then Alec looked at me, enquiringly, and I gave him the faintest nod. 'Touché,' he said. 'Yes, all right. We are not writing a treatise on Dirleton's oldest and strangest inhabitant. Congratulations.' He fixed Tom with his most serious look. 'Are you willing to help us keep the subterfuge going? Will you trust that we are working in good faith at an honourable task?'

'I take folk as I find them,' Tom said, which was rather too cryptic for me.

'We are trying to solve the murder,' I said. 'To find the culprit. *Now* will you help us?'

Tom regarded us, one after the other, with a steady gaze, then threw his glass cloth over his shoulder and opened his hands wide. 'I can hardly refuse, can I?' he said. After consulting his pocket watch, he went on, 'There's twenty minutes till opening, so have at it.' Then he drew up a chair and sat down backwards on it, resting his arms along its rail and continuing to bestow that calm look upon us, one that seemed to suggest he had nothing to hide and nothing to share.

'For a start,' he said, 'it's the ladies of the village garden club that look after the castle gardens.'

I smiled. I have met many a garden club lady, not to mention a flower guilder, and I could easily believe him. 'Led by Miss Goodfellow?' I asked.

'Ha!' said Tom. 'Hardly. That's a joke, that is. No, indeed, Miss Maggie is not a garden club lady. Nothing like. She just tells them what to do.'

'Well how nice,' I said. 'What a friendly little village Dirleton is. Everyone pitching in. You've offered to help us. Miss Halliburton has been marvellous all day and Miss Meek stepped up to help her when it all got a little overwhelming.'

But at this Tom turned stony-faced again.

'Not to mention your giving over that room,' Alec said.

'The Haddington coppers should have been here long since and removed . . .'

'The police have certainly not been much in evidence,' I said. 'In fact, Dirleton has been like a ghost town all day. Which is one thing we would like to ask you about. Is it a very religious place? Have we been scandalising onlookers by traipsing about on the Sabbath?'

'Dirleton,' said the landlord, 'has a long, long history with a great deal of religion in it.'

Alec and I managed not to glance at one another, but I was sure we were both thinking the same: what a peculiar thing to say.

'Well, if it's nothing to do with gardening,' I asked him next, 'have you any idea why Mr Esslemont *was* in Dirleton?'

He shook his head. 'Golf?'

'Is there a fencing club nearby?'

'Fencing? Swords, you mean? In those white costumes? Not that I've ever heard of. Why?' He twisted his head to one side and narrowed his eyes. 'You're having me on, aren't you?' he said. He turned to Alec. 'What's she up to?'

'No idea, my good man,' Alec said. 'Ladies are a mystery to me.'

'Me too, and I've been married fifteen years.'

'I've a much easier question . . . Tom,' said Alec. 'I must say, I don't like calling you "Tom". You're the landlord, not the potman.'

Tom lifted one shoulder and said nothing.

'Do you know where Mr Esslemont was staying?' Alec asked. 'We assumed the castle.'

'Did you?' Tom laughed. 'The rich man in his castle, the poor man at his gate, eh? Sounds to me like you would be happy to call me whatever you want, *sir*.'

104

'And another easy one,' Alec said, ignoring the mockery. 'Had he ever been here before?'

Tom shrugged. 'I didn't see the corpse as they carried it in. I was in the cellar at my barrels. So I wouldn't know.'

'How about this then,' I said. 'Do you know who it was who witnessed the attack?'

He frowned. 'Did somebody? News to me and I've no idea.' He considered it a moment. 'There's not so very many houses look over the louping stane, tucked away like that.'

My admiration for this man's intellect was growing. 'And the stone brings us back to Mither Gollane again,' I said. 'I suppose you know she reckons it belongs to her.'

'Aye, she'll be out cleaning it tonight, more'n probably.'

'Miss Halliburton has already cleaned it,' Alec said, although he could not possibly know any more than did I whether much of the spilled water went over the stone.

'Manie did?' Tom looked briefly astonished, then nodded. 'Ah, right. No, I didn't mean that kind of cleaning.'

I should have pressed him on this but I shied away for reasons I did not examine. 'So *does* she own it?' I asked instead.

'Aye well, it's the oldest thing in the village and, like you said, she's the "oldest resident".' He shook his head and laughed. 'You've found out that much, eh?'

'But now that we've admitted we're in the dark overall, what else can you tell us about her?'

'Not a thing,' said Tom. 'I keep well away from her. Like she keeps well away from . . . everyone these days. She was the very same when she still lived in her house. Not in the woods like she does now. She locked her doors and pulled her curtains and ignored all callers till they left.'

'Good for her,' I said. 'I know the feeling.' I had often

wondered how the task was achieved with people who had no servant to claim they were not at home.

Tom was beginning to shift in his seat and look over his shoulder. I guessed he had yet more preparatory work to do before opening time and I suggested he go and take care of it, assuring him that he had been a great help and we were in his debt.

'Has he?' said Alec, when we were once again on our own.

'Who knows,' I replied. 'It will take all night to sort through what we've learned already and even at that none of it seems . . . to the point. None of the hints and snippets we've laid our hands on are . . .'

'I daresay it's all grist to the mill,' said Alec. 'What was all that about gardens and fencing?'

'Ah, yes,' I said. 'The policemen asked Hugh if those were interests of Silas's. I was puzzled too but perhaps you could shed light.'

Alec raised his eyebrows.

'Because the only thing I could think of to connect swordsmanship and horticulture is that both might lead to . . . abrasions. How much of Silas did you actually see, darling?'

'Abrasions?' said Alec.

'When our gardener has been pruning the roses he looks like . . . which king was it?'

'Do you mean St Sebastian?' Alec said. 'Anyway, fencers have quillions. Those basket thingummies. Besides, Silas's hands were folded, holding a nosegay, and not a mark upon them.' He shuddered at the memory.

'Shall we change for dinner?' I said, to distract him. 'I'm not sure when it's barley stew in a pub.'

'You'd be more comfortable in one of those nighties you

106

call a frock than in your tweeds,' Alec said. 'But I've nothing to change into even if I wanted to. I'll pop upstairs and wash at least.'

Dirleton's impersonation of a ghost town persisted throughout the evening: we were the only guests in the chilly dining room when we re-met there for supper half an hour later and there was no murmur of voices from the bar parlour or babble of voices from the public to suggest that other parts of the inn were any busier.

We were served by the comely, black-haired woman, who *was* the cook, as I had surmised. She brought deep bowls of stew and more of the excellent bread and asked us, most solicitously, if we preferred the raisins in our baked apples to be soaked in sherry or in whisky, and to tell her right then if we didn't fancy ice cream with a hot pudding because she just had time to whisk up an egg custard if she got right to it. Alec practically purred.

'Sherry and ice cream for me, please,' I said.

'The same, the same,' said Alec. 'I don't want to be any trouble.' She believed him. *I* knew he was building up credit in hopes of treats in store.

'Are you a Dirleton native, Mrs . . . ?' I asked, as she was setting out the plates.

'Bella,' she told us. 'I married in. Been here more than ten years. They'll thaw to me by the time of my wake. You know what these places are like. Or if you don't then you're fortunate.' I smiled. 'Ach, but it's a nice wee place. There's a bowling club and a reading room and a good school for the bairns. My youngest had an awfy time with her letters and Miss Marion took no end of trouble. Miss Meek, I should call her, only she was such a slip of a thing when she first came.'

'We've met her,' Alec said. 'She's far from a slip of a thing now. Rather terrifying, I thought.'

The cook drew a breath as though to say more, but in the end she merely nodded at the table. 'While it's hot,' she said and left us.

'Exactly, Dandy,' Alec said. 'What sort of idiot starts a chat with the cook when the food is on the cloth, rapidly cooling.'

'The detecting sort of idiot,' I reminded him. 'The sort who is casting around desperately for any kind of toehold in this case.'

'Oh I don't know,' Alec said, then he took a spoonful of the broth from around the stew, closed his eyes in ecstasy, and started ripping off chunks of bread.

'Well I do! Are you going to dip that—? You are. Thank God there's no one else here. Even Little Edward doesn't dunk bread in his soup anymore and he's not four yet.'

'What about Lavinia?' Alec said, with a sly smile. He has seen my delightfully robust granddaughter at table.

I ignored him. 'To return to toeholds,' I said, 'we have been here all day and we have no idea what Silas was doing here, why someone might have killed him, where Daisy was going when she left Gilverton this morning, who it was who witnessed the attack—' I broke off. 'What's wrong?' Alec was squirming in his seat like Donald and Teddy used to when taken to see elderly relatives; the combination of short trousers and horse-hair sofas was always a trial to them and they never learned that squirming only made it itchier.

'Wrong?' said Alec, unconvincingly. 'It's just you saying we don't know why Silas was here. I thought we had more or less decided we could hazard a guess.'

'Yes, I'd stick a tenner on it,' I said. 'He was here to see a woman.'

'That's another good reason to go to the castle tomorrow,' Alec said. 'This "*Miss* Maggie Goodfellow", whose name was given such odd emphasis by Tom earlier, must be a possibility.'

'And, while I take your point about . . . what did you call them? . . . . a castle still seems the most likely place to find swords too.'

'Quillions,' said Alec. 'Yes, it's worth checking.'

'Only, if that's the explanation, God knows why he made such a fuss about it this time of all the times he'd gone to see a woman in his lifetime. A regimental dinner indeed!'

'Quite,' said Alec. 'But the thing is, I was wondering if perhaps we already had a contender.' I waited. 'Miss Meek.'

'Miss Meek the schoolmistress?' I said. 'That poker in her grey serge? Are you mad?'

'Do you happen to know Silas's usual—' Alec began but he remembered a bit of decency and did not finish the question.

'And apart from that, a schoolmistress of all people has to be scrupulous about her reputation, Alec. A breath of scandal and she would find herself out on her ear, without a reference, like an Edwardian parlourmaid.'

'You never turned out a parlourmaid!'

'Well, no. I sent one to the nuns and then got her a new situation and Hugh made the lad marry another one and gave them a cottage. But don't change the subject. What could possibly make you consider Miss Meek as Silas's Dirleton paramour?'

'Just this,' Alec said, then most annoyingly he broke off to deal with a choking mouthful of stew, including a piece of lamb that would have made a whole chop if there had been a bone in it. 'When we met her earlier,' he went on at last, 'I got the idea I had seen her before.'

I laid down my spoon. 'Now, it's funny you should say that. I thought the same thing. At least I found myself casting my mind back and wondering if we had encountered her earlier in the day. I concluded that we had not, because there was hardly a crowd for her to be lost amongst, was there?'

'Hm,' said Alec. 'If you think you recognised her too then I might be wrong. She mayn't be Silas's bit of fluff after all.'

I snorted at the ludicrous phrase. Then a thought struck me. 'Hang on,' I said. 'What do you mean? You thought you recognised her and so she might be Silas's latest dalliance, but not if I recognised her too?'

There was a momentary flare of panic in Alec's eyes and he started patting his pockets for his pipe. Now I knew for sure he was avoiding my eye and trying to get himself a little thinking time. For there were two good spoonfuls of stew left on his plate, and spoonfuls with rich glossy chunks of meat at that – Alec, like my sons, always saved the best for last when he was eating.

I pointed. 'You've never left uneaten stew in your life,' I said. 'You've never left uneaten porridge, come to that. When you were a child I expect you never left uneaten gruel. So put all that gubbins down, look me in the eye and tell me what you mean, please.'

Alec dropped his pipe and baccy on the table and took up his spoon again. 'Don't be like that, Dan,' he said.

'By which am I to take it that you have met some of Silas's mistresses?' I said. 'Am I to take it that it's all very open and easy between the— between the men in his set? I almost said "gentlemen".'

'This isn't like you.'

'Indeed? Am I thought of as a good sort? Not the sort to make a fuss and spoil all the grubby fun? I had no idea you ranked us. I never considered that you discussed us. In your . . . clubs . . . or wherever.'

'Speakeasies?' said Alec. He was laughing at me.

'Did Silas get to know *your* friends?' I said. 'The ones you'd baulk at introducing to me? Even though I'm such a good sort?'

'Hardly,' Alec said, which was not as reassuring as he might have thought, not by a long chalk.

'And what about Hugh? Is he one of this . . . brotherhood?'

'*Hugh*?' Alec had finally taken a mouthful and he spluttered as he laughed through it. 'Hardly,' he said again.

That should have mollified me. I cannot account in any way for the fact that it made me angrier than ever.

'There's no club, you goose,' Alec said. 'There's no brother-hood. I just happened to recognise Miss Meek, was unable to place her and so wondered if perhaps she had been at some house party or something over the years. If so, then Silas was the obvious point of connection.'

'What do you mean "hardly"?' I said, ignoring, somewhat unfairly I admit, the reasonable explanation he had just proffered.

'Which one?'

I might not blush outwardly but that does not mean I feel no discomfort. The truth was I had meant the first one. It seemed that I cared more about what Alec got up to without me than whatever men like he and Silas thought of Hugh. I got to my feet and stalked out of the dining room, upset and ruffled and wishing Grant and Bunty were there to make bedtime the soothing process it usually is at home.

I was halfway up the stairs, valiantly trying to direct my thoughts towards the case again, when some of my own earlier words came back to me. I stopped so abruptly that I had to grab the banister to steady myself. Then I turned and made my way back down.

111

Alec was finishing my plate, having polished off his own, and that simple sight added to the sheepish look he gave me had the power to make me smile again.

'Sorry,' he said.

I waved it off. 'I said we didn't know what Silas was doing here,' I said. 'Or who the witness was. Or where Daisy was going. Or why someone wanted to kill him.'

Alec gave me the wide-eyed look that usually means he has no idea what I am getting at and I should carry on and deliver it fully.

'What, who, where, why,' I said. 'We are missing something.'

'How?' said Alec. 'We know how. His head was bashed in.'

'I forgot about how,' I said. 'But there's another one.'

'When!' said Alec.

'When,' I agreed.

'Sorry to sound churlish but so what?'

'Simply this,' I said. 'I began trying to make Daisy go to bed in Perthshire at ten o'clock last night. Gosh, was it really only last night? I got her settled by eleven. It is quite a task to undress a drunk, you know. And we found her back in Perthshire at seven o'clock this morning. Say the fastest she could possibly have got to Dirleton in my little Morris Cowley is three hours, as Hugh believes. And more than that on the outward trip, if I'm honest, since she would have had to drive with one eye shut to help her stay in focus She really was sauced. So that takes us to two in the morning at the top end and four at the bottom end. That's the . . .'

'Window of opportunity,' said Alec.

'What a marvellous phrase. Yes, exactly. And the thing is that that doesn't seem at all likely to me. Between two in the morning and four in the morning is, for a start, a very improbable time to be out on a village green in suit and tie

112

with a letter in one's pocket. That's when people get murdered in their beds. Or shot over a game of cards in a smoky back room somewhere.'

'Unless he'd got up out of his bed to leave and the person he was leaving took agin the decision and followed him to the leaping stone.'

'And for another thing,' I said, 'between two and four in the morning is an even more improbable time for any witness to be up and about looking out of a window and saying, "Dearie me. Who's that out on the village green being knocked over at this time of night?"'

'Nightwatchman, baker, milkman,' Alec said.

'Too early for a milkman to be anywhere but at the dairy,' I said. 'Far too early for him to be in the village. And *is* there a bakery in Dirleton?'

'There might be a *baker* in Dirleton who has to get up even earlier if the bakery itself is in Gullane,' said Alec.

'But you're forgetting it was Saturday becoming Sunday, so no milkman and no baker. As for a nightwatchman, what would he be watching?' I said, gesturing out of the window. 'Miss Halliburton's laundry?'

'It could have been a doctor called out to a confinement, or a new mother walking a squalling bundle up and down. Or a dyspeptic individual up in search of liver salts, or a—'

'I still think it's far more likely that someone saw Silas being attacked late on Saturday evening or early this morning,' I said. 'Just exactly when Daisy couldn't have done it. So we need to telephone to Gilverton and ask one of those dreadful policemen when it happened.'

'They won't tell us.'

'True. The constable might. Or we could find this witness and ask *him*. And, if Daisy is proven innocent, then I for one shall be very happy to leave the search for the real villain up to the police. I want to go home and forget I ever heard of Dirleton.'

'Why, Dan?' said Alec. 'You sound quite rattled. What's up?'

'I don't know,' I said. 'And that bothers me too. It might be no more than knowing Silas's body is lying in the room up there. Or it might be what we said: how deserted it is. How empty it's been all day.'

'We've met our fair share of locals,' Alec said. 'Tom, Bella, the schoolmistress, the constable as mentioned, Mr Watson, Miss Clarkson, Miss Halliburton, Mither Gollane.'

'Meeting Mither Gollane is hardly something to recommend Dirleton as a good spot to linger. And you forgot someone, Alec. Remember Lizzy? This morning. That little person dressed in black, flitting about like a bat? I don't think I've been quite at peace since the minute I clapped eyes on *her*, actually.'

'Go to bed, Dandy,' Alec said. 'In the morning we can relay a question to Daisy via . . . Well, Grant, I suppose . . . about when she left and when she got back and where she was—'

'I won't entertain the possibility that Daisy killed him,' I said. 'You weren't there when she found out he had died. And I won't interrogate her about what she *did* do. It's beneath us to want to and it would be beneath her to let us.'

'All right,' said Alec, with enormous patience. 'Very well. Then go to bed, Dandy, and in the morning we shall track down this witness or find out in some other way when the deed was done and, if you are correct, we will know that Daisy is innocent and we can point that out to those bumbling plods who're clustered round her bedside like so many vultures, and then they'll come back here and get on with solving this thing and we can go. If you're really so very determined not to encounter that peculiar little person, Lizzy, again.'

So it was Alec's fault, really, that I dreamed about her. If, in fact, it was a dream.

Chapter 8

My bed was comfortable and someone had been in with a flask of warm milk and a plate of biscuits during the evening. Besides those, I found a little shelf of books tucked into one of the eaves and I selected a familiar volume to send me off to sleep. Victorians rampaging around lonely moors was exactly what I needed to put the oddness of Dirleton into some kind of perspective.

Once asleep, however, the torrid opening chapters of Miss Brontë's melodrama began to combine with Alec's misguided teasing of me in the matter of the little black bat, his report of Silas's terror-struck face, my memories of the newsreels from the last war and my dread of what was coming in the next. I found myself thrashing my way through a tangle of holly and something that was not rowan, although my dream self called it by that name. There was, as ever, somewhere I had to be but I was impeded by a black cloak of some brittle material, spined all around with spokes so that it felt as though I were wearing an umbrella. I was plunging down a steep bank, the skeleton of my peculiar garment catching on twigs and thorns, and yet I was clambering up a dizzying slope, with the flapping wings of my cloak dragging me backwards, and yet I was hauling myself across a yawning flat expanse of ground towards a stone, round and veined like a human skull, with a crack in its side that was bleeding.

I started awake, gasping and sobbing in the perfect darkness of my bedroom, then trying to find a lamp, my heart hammering at the strange shapes and shadows that emerged as the blackness faded. The wardrobe was a hulking stranger looming over me and my own reflection in the glass of the dressing table was a distant ghost. And what on earth was *that*? It had to be a figure. Surely no accidental confluence of doors and coombs could produce so perfect a human outline in an empty room. With a shaking hand, I cast about the table for my candle, for at last I had remembered the solitary electric-light switch inside the door, the stark bulb hanging from the middle of the ceiling. Exhaling thankfully, I felt the cold brass under my fingertips, grasped it, struck a match and touched it to the wick, squeezing my eyes shut to save from seeing how the flickering flame would make the shadows leap and judder.

When I smelled the warming tallow and knew I had a steady light, I opened my eyes again and tried to breathe calmly.

The door to the hall was just closing.

A draught, I told myself, sinking back onto my pillows. Probably my door banging in a draught was what had brought the nightmare.

It wasn't moving now though, I noticed. It had closed over and there it stayed. And an even worse realisation was beginning to dawn on me. I had touched the candle with my groping fingers. Then I had struck a match. Only now did I see that the matches should not have been there in my other hand suddenly. Only now did it dawn on me that someone had passed them to me.

I leapt out of bed, shoved my feet halfway into my slippers and, grabbing my dressing gown from the hook but not pausing to put it on, I bounded out of my room, banged on Alec's door and threw myself down the stairs.

The front door, which I had heard being locked and bolted at ten, was now hanging slightly open and was not quite still, speaking of a hasty exit seconds before. I heard Alec's tread on the floor above and it spurred me to boldness. I swept my dressing gown on, swirling it like the cloak of a matador, then I belted it securely and plunged out into the night.

At first glance, all was at peace. The green was bathed in ghostly moonlight but the trees around the edge, the hedges, and the high walls of the castle keep made the blackest of shadows. If something was moving in those shadows I should never know. I stood holding my breath, waiting for a figure to break for the open, or for the glint of an eye to show in the darkness. I saw nothing. Then Alec was beside me, belting the cord of his own dressing gown and attempting to sweep his hair back where it belonged.

'Not that it's not a fine night for a stroll, Dan,' he said.

'Sssshhhh,' I breathed. 'Someone was in my room.'

'Are you sure?'

'No, but listen.'

He did not hold his breath as I was trying to, and so I could hear him panting his way back to calm after the rude awakening. The other sound was, however, definitely there. In autumn, it might have been a crunch and rustle. In winter, the crack of frost would have helped us be sure. Now, in May, it was much easier to move quietly over soft grass and past green stems of ferns, but no one can move silently. We could both hear, if we strained our ears, the pad of footfall and the whisper of cloth as someone's garments moved with their tread.

'Going towards the church,' Alec said, close to my ear. 'Let's follow.'

We, who had nothing to hide, stepped from under the tall tree at the inn gateway and struck out for the top of the

118

manse road. We had not gone quite twenty paces when Alec grabbed my arm and raised his other hand, pointing ahead.

'Is it my imagination,' he said, 'or is that stone—?'

I clutched him and might have let out a small cry. I had not been looking at the leaping stone; my eyes had still been trained on the shadows where I was sure our quarry was passing along, hugging the trees and hedges for cover. Even a glance at the thing made it clear, though. It was too big by far. It was higher than it should be and longer too, and it was dark and soft-looking, soaking up the moonlight instead of sending it back in reflection as a smooth stone ought to.

'Oh my God,' I said, breaking into a trot. 'There's another one.'

As we drew closer, we saw it more clearly, much too clearly to allow for denial. The figure was draped over the stone, his head on the grass at one side and his feet on the grass at the other. His arms were splayed out to either side. And he lay more still than any living thing can lie.

'Who is it?' Alec said, and reached out to the broad-brimmed hat that had slipped backwards on the poor unfortunate's head, hiding hair and face completely.

'Should you touch him though?' I asked.

'In case he's breathing,' said Alec. He took hold of the hat and lifted it clear, then fell back, uttering an oath I had never heard him use before, scrabbling away like a crab.

'No,' I said, feeling my throat thicken, for there was no head under the hat. There was nothing at all except the shining rim of cobbles, gleaming in the moonlight.

'Oh God,' said Alec. 'Look away, Dandy. Don't look at his feet!'

Of course I looked exactly there and I saw that not only had the head been removed but also one of the feet lay a good two inches clear of the trouser hem. I edged to the side to check the other and stopped dead.

Something about the way the body lay over the rock snagged at a memory. The oddly bulging arms and legs sticking out too straight and too weightless from the draped coat made me think of something I could not quite bring to mind. And the hands in their gloves, like starfish, fingers like sausages . . . I found myself remembering two beds in a night nursery and smothered giggles from behind a cupboard door.

'Oh good Lord!' I pushed the thing with the toe of my slipper. It rolled off the stone and began to disintegrate on the cobbles. The other shoe fell clear and one of the gloves dropped away from the coat cuff.

'Oh God oh God oh God,' Alec moaned.

'It's not real,' I told him. 'It's a stuffed bundle of clothes, Alec. It's a scarecrow. An effigy. It's a rotten trick but it's not a body.'

Alec picked himself up and came forward, still clutching the hat. 'What a shabby thing to do,' he said. Still, it took a few more deep breaths before he said any more. 'More fool the trickster, though,' he went on at last. 'These clothes are all going straight to the police station. Someone will recognise whose wardrobe they came from, wouldn't you say?'

'It might not be a Dirletonite,' I said. 'A villager, I mean. They're very good quality.' I was picking the guy apart, sorting the garments into two piles. They seemed to be a mixture of men's and women's: the outline of the dummy made from suit trousers and a coat, along with leather driving gloves and a pair of brogues, as well as the hat Alec was currently wringing in his hands. The stuffing was made of jerseys and summer skirts, even underclothes. I pulled stockings out of the gloves, watching the sausage fingers flatten.

120

'Where do you suppose that young constable lives?' Alec said. 'We should fetch him.'

'Should we?' I said. 'I agree that it's pointed and untimely, but it's a pointed and untimely piece of mischief and surely mischief can wait until morning.'

Then we both started violently at the sound of a voice nearby.

'That's bad luck, is that,' said a sibilant voice. 'That's black luck for you making fun of the louping stane. And when it's only just clean again.'

'Lizzy?' I said. It was the little flitting figure we had seen when we arrived. She was standing, still dressed all in black and with a black hat on her head too, staring at the stone with a rapt look. Her face seemed to shine like the moon, and was as white and as round too. When it split into a toothy grin I looked away.

'The only thing that ever goes on the stane is the nettles,' she said. Her voice sounded quite normal now and, when I glanced back at her, her face had lost its disconcerting leer too. 'And that's midsummer.'

'Lizzy,' I said again. 'You know a lot about the village, don't you? You were born here?'

'I was born far, far away,' she said. 'But I've lived here all my life.'

'But you know where Constable McLean lives?'

'I know,' she agreed.

'Can you go and knock on his door and fetch him?'

'Again?' she said. 'Oh all right then.'

She had turned to leave when her words struck me. 'Wait!' I said. 'What do you mean, again? When did you fetch the constable before?'

She was grinning again, more widely than ever. 'Last night. When he was real. When I saw what I saw. When she did

121

what she did. I ran and banged on his door and said, "Help, police!" "Murder, help!" That's what I did.'

We had found our witness.

'Lizzy,' Alec said. 'Are you sure it was a woman? How close were you?'

'I was looking out of my little window,' she said. 'It was a bad, bad woman in a long black dress. She killed him.'

Daisy was wearing a dress of opalescent satin that could not have looked black inside a coalmine. I shared a glance with Alec and he nodded, telling me to ask the question.

'What time was this?' I felt my fingers twitch, as if to cross them and stop the dreaded answer coming.

'The witching hour,' Lizzy said. 'It was the witching hour, of course.' Then she turned with a rustle of her peculiar garment and flitted away towards the long row of cottages opposite the castle walls, passing in and out of sight with the pattern of moonlight and shadow.

'Midnight!' I said, settling back onto my heels. 'Midnight, Alec! It wasn't Daisy. Oh those stupid policemen. Why didn't they ask me? Why on earth are they still up at Gilverton, crowded around Daisy's sickbed? It wasn't her. It couldn't be.'

There was a bench not far off from the stone, the round kind that circles the trunk of a tree and offers shady seating for ten people, although it poses rather a challenge when it comes to group conversations. Alec and I walked over to it now and settled in to wait for Constable McLean to be awoken, to dress, and to arrive.

'So we leave in the morning?' Alec said. 'I certainly don't care who killed the b— who killed Silas, as long as Daisy's in the clear.'

'Don't be a hypocrite, darling,' I murmured. I did not look, but I felt him turn to stare at me. 'You said yourself no one

122

gets to meet your dalliances. "Hardly" was how you put it, if you remember. And all Silas did was dally, after all.'

I could hear Alec breathing with great vehemence, but it took him a while to speak. 'There is no comparison,' he said at last. 'I am not married and Silas did not restrict himself to women of enough age and experience to accept or reject him. Cara was a *girl*!'

I let his words wash over me. As much as I had ever thought about it – and I tried not to – I had always assumed Alec was too chivalrous, too proper, for indiscretions. The news that he considered mature and worldly women fair game left me sunk in a perfect storm of rage and misery; one that I determined never to examine closely.

'I don't care who the murderess is either,' I managed to say, at long last. Then, after another silence, 'I really do think she was in my room.'

'What?' Alec clutched at me.

'Young Lizzy, I mean. Not the villain. Good grief. I was having a nightmare – or so I thought – but when I woke up I'm pretty sure she was there. I think she led me out here to find the dummy.'

'Which she put there?'

I shrugged. 'Does she have the . . . I mean, she's definitely not . . . Wouldn't you say she's at least simple?'

'She's odd,' Alec said. 'There's something slightly off about almost everything she says. "Born far, far away" indeed! I shouldn't think that's true. And when she reported her actions from last night, she sounded like . . . Do you know who she sounded like? Lavinia, announcing proudly that she'd achieved some milestone of a task. Remember that, Dandy?'

'Oh Lord, do I remember! "I potty!" "I sick up!" "I wet again!" Mortifying. She's such a little hoyden.'

'I suppose we'll know whether Lizzy did this, if her parents look through their wardrobes and discover all their clobber missing.'

'Except, I can't imagine her parents wearing this clobber,' I said. 'I don't suppose there's a label inside that hatband, is there?'

Alec turned the thing up and tilted it to catch the moonlight. 'D'you know? I think there is. A length of name tape anyway. Can you hold it while I strike a match, Dandy?'

The flame flared and settled and then Alec held it so close to the brim I feared it catching. He whistled, long and low. 'J.M. Crabbie,' he said.

'Who's—?' I began and then I whistled too. 'Crabbie of Crabbie and McEwan, the missing writers?'

'I don't understand,' Alec said, then stopped. Lizzy was returning, with the constable in tow. He was shrugging into his tunic as he made his way across the green towards us, his buttons winking in the moonlight.

'What's to do?' he asked, when he drew near. I was glad to see he had a powerful torch, which he now turned on.

'A trick of some kind,' Alec said. 'Someone made a sort of Guy Fawkes out of clothes and placed it on the stone. We thought it was another body until we touched it.'

'Queer sort of thing to do,' said McLean. 'I wonder whose clothes they are.'

'We found a label in the hatband,' Alec said. 'Suggesting that it, at least, belongs to a Mr Crabbie – Dr Crabbie, I should say – who was expected at the inn until he cancelled his booking.'

'He must be here somewhere, though,' said Constable. 'If all his clothes are.' He was sorting through them now by torchlight. 'Who is he?'

'Well, he put it out that he was coming to interview Mither Gollane with a view to writing a book,' I said.

I noticed Lizzy fidgeting just beyond the pool of light, but could not tell what bit of my report had troubled her.

'*More* writers,' said the constable with a disgusted look at Alec and me.

Lizzy Hogg was practically doing pirouettes now, so discomfited was she. I turned to her, hoping to gain something from her defenceless state.

'Lizzy?' I said. 'Were you in my room?'

'I don't know where you live,' she said. She accompanied it with a small giggle but I did not think it was the impertinence it seemed to be. She was simply a very odd sort of girl.

'I meant my room at the inn, dear,' I said. 'Tonight. Just before we all met here.'

'I— I was in the church,' she said. 'I came from that way.' She pointed and, right enough, when we had heard her approaching it *had* been up the manse road with the church at the far end.

'Do you have any evidence to support that accusation?' the constable said. He was still kneeling by the bundles of clothes, which was not a position of great authority, but he spoke in a sterner voice than I had heard heretofore.

I waved a placatory hand at him. 'I might have been dreaming,' I said. 'I have no quarrel with Miss Hogg, certainly. She has done us the great favour of exonorat—' Alec dug me so hard in the ribs that I staggered to the side to regain my balance. 'Oh!' I said. I had just been about to refer to Daisy, spreading news of our true identity further through the town. I paused, then made a bold decision.

'We are *not* writers,' I announced. 'It suited our purposes to slip into the space waiting for two writers to arrive, you see. But the truth of the matter is that we are friends of Mr Esslemont's wife. We're detectives.'

Lizzy fled. I glanced at Alec, whose eyes gleamed bright enough in the moonlight and torchlight for me to see their expression change. 'Interesting,' he said. 'Miss Hogg seems less keen to consort with detectives than with book authors, wouldn't you say.'

'Detectives?' said the constable. 'What force? Undercover, you mean, sir? And who's the lady?'

'Private detectives,' I said.

'But who's sent for you? Who's gone and went that far?' In his upset the constable's grammar appeared to have deserted him.

'We're not in the habit of breaking our clients' confidences,' Alec said, grandly.

'Well, see what you've got for it!' the constable burst out. 'You've landed yourself in the worst day Dirleton's had in three hundred years nearly. Who's took it all that way?'

'Mrs Esslemont, the widow of the victim, is a friend of ours,' I told him. 'It's my house, in Perthshire where she was staying, when her husband died. My house where your superiors have gone racketing off to. And so we came here to prove her innocence.'

'Which it was no trouble at all to do, I might add,' Alec said. 'Young Lizzy there confirmed it.'

'Lizzy isn't what anyone would call—' the constable began to object.

But there we had him and I went in for the kill.

'If Miss Hogg's evidence that the murderer was a woman is enough to send two policemen, including a chief constable, racing off to Perthshire to arrest Mrs Esslemont,' I said. 'Then Miss Hogg's evidence that the deed was done at midnight should be enough to bring them back again with their tails between their legs, full of apology and ready to hunt down the real culprit.'

'Midnight?' said the constable. 'Are you sure? That's not what she told us.'

'The witching hour,' Alec said. 'We asked and that's what she said. Very definite about it, wasn't she, Dandy?'

'But that's not midnight,' said the constable. 'The witching hour is three until four. Right now, in fact. It's just gone half past three, by my reckoning.'

'Rot!' I said.

'Although,' said Alec, 'I did have a troubling sort of a half of an idea when you said that, Dan—' He stopped short. 'Oh.'

'Yes,' I said. 'Oh, indeed.'

For I had only decided to come clean about our identity because Daisy was in the clear. If matters stood as they now seemed to, then we – I, to be fair to Alec – had revealed ourselves to have a deep interest in her innocence while such innocence was far from established. Was anything but!

'I'm not at all convinced,' I said. 'I bet if you asked a hundred people, if you asked the man on the Clapham omnibus, ninety-five of them would say midnight.'

'But if you asked ten people who knew what they were talking about, like Lizzy Hogg and me,' said the constable, 'they'd say three till four.'

None of us had noticed another person approaching.

'Jim? Is that you? What on earth are you doing?'

'Mr Wallace,' said the constable, scrambling to his feet. 'There's been a bit of nastiness again tonight. Well, not— A bit of silliness, I should say.'

'Are these the miscreants?' said the stranger. I shaded my eyes from the glare of the constable's torch, and could see a set of gleaming teeth and a matching gleaming band hovering in the darkness a few inches below. It was a dog collar. This then was the minister, wafting about the village in full battle-dress in the small hours of the morning. Did no one in this benighted place ever go to bed?

'No, no. No suggestion of that, Mr Wallace,' said the constable. 'These people . . . Well, I don't exactly know what brought them abroad.'

'Lizzy Hogg,' I said, for I did not believe her claim to have been nowhere near my bedroom.

'And how about you, sir?' said Alec. 'Are you summoned to a bedside?' It is seldom that a priest, like a doctor, is out in the night for any cheerful reason.

'I caught sight of you all busy at the stane, Jim,' said the minister, 'and thought I'd make the most of the opportunity. Since you were up anyway and almost on the spot.'

'The spot?' said the constable.

'The thing is, someone's been in the church.'

'Lizzy Hogg, I think,' the constable said.

'And ordinarily I'd be happy that anyone – Lizzy included – sought succour and found it, but tonight, with the body of that poor chap lying at rest, you see . . .'

'Is he?' I said. 'They've moved him?'

'After you'd gone up,' Alec said.

'And still the church was left unlocked?' I said.

'Oh no, but there are lots of keys about,' the minister said. 'Locked or unlocked is much of a muchness really. So, J— Well, Constable, I suppose I should call you if I'm asking for official help, but you'll always be Jim to me, lad. In any case, might you slip down and see what's what for me?'

McLean glanced at the bundles of clothes and then back at the minister.

'We can take those into safe keeping,' Alec said.

'Not if we're going to the church to see that all's well with Silas,' I said, rather more stoutly than I felt inside.

'We have this in hand, dear lady,' the minister said. 'The constable and I.'

With that, Alec and I took our leave and, laden with bundles of clothes, plodded back to the inn with the sort of weariness that only comes from sudden exertion after retiring for the night.

'It *was* a dream then,' Alec said. 'If someone was in the church right enough and Lizzy said she'd been there, then she can't have been in your room too.'

'I'm very much hoping that all of this makes a lot more sense in the light of day,' I said. 'And I do realise that I've nailed our colours to the mast, rather. Detectives, not writers, you know. But it will certainly make it easier to ask what we need to ask and not fuss on about a lot of guff we don't care about.'

'I suppose so,' Alec said. 'But police don't take kindly to private detectives grilling them, in my experience and yours too. One can't hope that the young constable continues to be quite so indiscreet indefinitely.'

I had no idea what he meant and no intention of giving him the satisfaction of saying so. Unfortunately, my busy silence while I scrabbled for enlightenment told him anyway.

'Cast your mind back,' he said irritatingly. 'Can you remember what Constable McLean said when he found out who we were?'

'Something about hundreds of years?' I said.

'That too, but first he said words along the lines of "Look what you got for coming digging around in Dirleton. You've arrived on a terrible day".'

'So?' I said. We were back at the inn now. 'Is your motor car locked?' I asked. 'Let's dump all this stuff in the boot until the morning, shall we?'

'So?' said Alec. '*So?* Think, Dandy. If he believed we had come to solve a murder he would hardly commiserate with us for turning up after a murder had been done.'

'Nor he would,' I said. We had arrived at the back of the inn and Alec struggled to get the boot of the Daimler open. 'Yes, you're right. He thinks, if we're detectives, we must have come to look into something else. He thinks the thing the writers keep sniffing round is the sort of thing a detective would bother with. That's interesting.' I dumped my bundle of clothes and tucked the trailing edges in.

'And then indeed there's the other bit,' said Alec, shedding his own load and balancing the hat on top. 'He didn't say hundreds of years. And he certainly didn't say "donkey's years" or "ages" or anything general.' He closed the boot and, taking his key from his pocket, he locked it. 'No, Constable McLean said it was the worst day in Dirleton for . . .'

'Three hundred years,' I finished. 'Do you think it's been three hundred years since the last murder? Is that what he meant?'

'If so it's the sort of thing we should be able to find out, isn't it?' Then he yawned an enormous groaning yawn like the roar of a lion after eating an antelope.

'Let's go to bed,' I said. 'Tomorrow is bound to be somewhat wearisome.'

My talent for understatement had never had such an outing.

Chapter 9

Monday, 15 May 1939

Breakfast at the Castle Inn was everything Alec could have hoped for as he bounded downstairs knotting his tie well before eight o'clock the next morning. There were kippers, kedgeree, and marmalade so dark and bitter it was almost the same colour as the coffee and one could scarcely believe there was ever an orange involved in its creation. He put away quite half a cottage loaf slathered in the stuff. I enjoyed the dainty challenge of deboning a small fish and sipped one cup of the coffee, then in unison we pushed our plates away.

'Still for the castle?' I said, as we stood and left the bar parlour, which doubled as a breakfast room.

Alec knitted his brow, as he rummaged for his baccy. 'What were we going for again?'

'The gardens, with their thorns, the possibility of swords – although granted it's a faint one – and Miss Maggie Goodfellow, whom I still think might have been known to Silas, as she seems to be known to Tom, our hospitable land-lord. Gosh, but it all seems most unlikely by the light of day.'

'Shall we instead go back to Mither Gollane and try to discover *her* history with Silas?' Alec said.

'She can't have killed him, darling,' I protested. 'She's too old and too tiny.'

'Manie then?'

'She can't have killed him either. I would swear that she didn't know who he was until we told her.'

'One can kill a stranger and find out who he was afterwards,' Alec said. 'That might make me faint too.'

I considered this for one second and then discounted it as beyond plausibility. 'You're saying she knows Silas and fears him, kills a stranger for no reason and then just happens to discover . . .'

Alec pulled a face in acknowledgement of how nonsensical that was. 'This case is terribly baggy, isn't it?' he said. 'More trailing threads than a . . .'

I could not apply myself to the search for a simile, though, because Miss Clarkson was bearing down on us. She wore her hat and coat, and had clearly come from outside where it seemed that at least a shower of rain if not a downpour was in progress. She shook out her umbrella and shot it into the stand.

'Glad I caught you!' she said. 'I've heard the news.'

Alec busied himself with his pipe and avoided her eye, leaving it to me to navigate this vagueness.

'I daresay,' I selected. 'There's nowhere like a village.'

'Detectives!' she exclaimed. 'And famous detectives at that.'

I murmured something in the self-deprecation line, pointing out that we were hardly Holmes and Poirot.

'Don't be modest,' she said. 'And now here you are in Dirleton, turning your attention to *our* little puzzle.'

'Not so little,' I said, more to avoid a silence than out of true offence at Silas's death being summed up in that way. 'Thank you for not being cross, Miss Clarkson. After we gave out that we were expected guests.'

'You forget that I don't work here,' she said. 'If Tom doesn't mind that bit of confusion, what's it to me? And since you are who you are,' she went on, with a slight show of hesitation, 'I've decided to do my duty and tell what I know.'

Of course, that changed matters for Alec. He abandoned his pipe unlit in his mouth – how he can bear the taste of the thing, plugged up with cold tobacco, I shall never be able to understand; it's bad enough when it's burning – and nodded at me to get out my notebook. 'Do, madam,' he said. 'Tell all and tell also why you haven't told the police before now.'

'Well,' said Miss Clarkson, smoothing the skirt of her mackintosh and preening under this attention. 'I didn't want to get anyone into trouble.'

'For murder?' I could not help the outburst.

'But I didn't see the murder,' she replied. 'I saw someone making his way to where the murder happened. Creeping along. Looking over his shoulder.'

'His?' Alec interjected.

'I thought it was a poacher, or perhaps a burglar. If I had heard, the next day, of anyone missing a bicycle from a shed . . .'

'You heard that someone had been murdered!' I said.

'By a woman at three o'clock,' said Miss Clarkson. 'And so a man at not quite two went right out of my mind.'

'What brought him back in again?' I said.

'No one had told me it was Lizzy claiming to have seen the murderess,' said Miss Clarkson. 'And so there's been a day wasted looking for a woman when it was a man all along.'

'I take it that, in your opinion, Miss Hogg is not reliable?'

'Lizzy is harmless but not quite . . . Well, she's been told many times about roaming around when she should be tucked up in bed. She's been warned that if she can't behave she might have to go and live somewhere else. Usually it's a lot of nonsense that amounts to nothing, but telling fibs to a sergeant of police when there's a murder on the go! That's another matter entirely.' She sighed. 'If the inspector wasn't away on his holidays it would never . . . Captain Wicks isn't . . .'

'We've met him,' I said, which won me a smile. 'Thank you for the information, Miss Clarkson,' I went on. 'But did you not consider that the man you saw creeping towards the scene of a murder might have been the victim?'

Miss Clarkson stared at me. *Glared* at me. 'He was too tall,' she said after a lengthy pause.

'Oh?' I said. 'You've seen Silas Esslemont's body?'

She squeaked.

'You met him when he was alive?'

'I saw the coffin,' she said. 'It wasn't unusually long.'

'They always look quite small though, don't they?' Alec said. I had no idea which coffin from his past he was thinking of; for my part it was my father's, and he was right. Well I remembered the shock of seeing what a small coffin contained such a huge person as he had always seemed.

Miss Clarkson was quite determined though. She shook her head vehemently and repeated her claim in more forceful terms. 'The man I saw creeping along on Saturday night was tremendously tall and unusually thin. He looked quite unnerving.'

I could not think what to ask next, but Alec came to my rescue. 'Why were *you* up at two in the morning?' he said.

'I have a very delicate stomach,' she said with a little moue of dainty embarrassment.

'Ah,' said Alec. 'Dear me. But weren't your bedroom curtains closed?'

Miss Clarkson gave him a disapproving stare. 'Of course my bedroom curtains were closed! I draw them at dusk! But

I went downstairs and took a glass of warm water with a little bicarb in it and there's a round window at the turn on my stairs, which hasn't had curtains on it in my lifetime.'

'Have you lived in the same cottage all your life then?' I said. My thought was to placate her but, for reasons beyond my comprehension, I had made matters even worse. She drew down her brows and looked daggers at me.

'I moved in when I was sixteen,' she said.

'So practically your whole life then,' I said. I had no idea what was wrong with the woman, but this latest remark of mine helped not one jot.

'And you'll be telling all this to the sergeant when he gets back?' Alec said. 'He'll ask why you didn't tell him yesterday too, I should warn you.'

He lifted his hat as Miss Clarkson stalked wordlessly away.

'Something fishy here, Dan,' he said, when she was out of earshot. 'Miss Clarkson is peddling the tale that no one who knew Lizzy Hogg at all well would trust her version of events. And that she – Miss Clarkson – has only just found out it was Lizzy who gave witness. Two problems with that story.'

I nodded to let him regale me.

'According to Lizzy,' he said, 'it was Constable McLean she fetched on the night of the murder. And he has presumably known her all her life. Also how is Miss Clarkson supposed suddenly to have found out, between yesterday and today, that it was Lizzy? It's not even nine o'clock yet.'

'I would say the village grapevine,' I said. 'But by that token she should have known all along.'

Alec groaned. 'Look, let's go to the castle to ask these shadowy Halliburtons if Silas was staying there. They might even know why he went out wandering.'

'It's open, at any rate,' I said, as we emerged into the last of the drizzle. I pointed across the green, where the doorway beside the ticket sign stood ajar.

'Let's pay our shilling and marvel at the roses then, shall we?' said Alec. 'Perhaps a garden club lady will oblige with some gossip.'

'Can I have a minute to marvel at the humdrum everyday scene first?' I said. 'It's awfully good to see children going to school and women with shopping baskets.'

'I agree,' Alec said. 'Whatever Dirleton's other oddnesses, at least we know that it was only the Sabbath keeping everyone out of sight yesterday.'

At a booth just inside the castle wall, a woman sat knitting. 'Sixpence each,' she said. 'Or tenpence with clock golf included.' We agreed that we could do without the clock golf, paid her, took our tickets and strolled into the grounds proper. The roses *were* marvellous, as a matter of fact, all the more so beaded with tiny raindrops, and we took our time strolling through them. Beyond was a lawn I took to be a bowling green, or at any rate an enormous swathe of grass edged with a steep kerb like a tea tray. It looked, after the rain, like a velvet dress sprinkled with crystal sequins.

I had described the castle itself as a toad when viewing it from across the green, but, as we stood in its lee while it yawned above us, it was more like an ogre, lumpen and looming, making me dizzy as I leaned backwards to take it all in.

'Some pile,' Alec said. 'How do you propose we go from admiring the blooms to asking the residents if one of their house guests was murdered?'

'We could claim to be visiting Miss Goodfellow,' I said. 'Could you spirit up a knotty question about propagation or something?'

'We don't even know who Miss Goodfellow is, Dandy,' Alec pointed out. 'She might be a maiden aunt. Or a housekeeper.'

'I don't think so, from the way Tom spoke about her,' I said. 'A maiden aunt is halfway to a garden club lady, isn't she? And a housekeeper wouldn't cause such . . . asperity.'

'*Is* it too fanciful to wonder if she was Silas's particular friend?' Alec said. 'If her loose morals are what made Tom spit the word "Miss" out so bitterly?'

'I wonder if Daisy would know anything,' I said. 'I wonder if Daisy is equal to being asked.'

'*I* wonder if being asked about a Miss Goodfellow would set Daisy back from whatever recovery she might have made,' said Alec. 'Let's try to find out for ourselves, shall we?'

'If only we had *his* excuse for banging on people's doors,' I said, pointing: Mr Watson the postman was barrelling towards us along a gravel path, with his head down. When at last he raised his eyes and caught sight of Alec and me, I would swear he feinted to the side as though to dart behind the nearest yew and hide himself from view. Realising that this would raise every suspicion in us, however, he steeled himself and with no more than a hitch in his step he came onwards.

'No one home,' he said. 'If you're on business and not here as trippers. I've had to leave a catalogue on the doorstep.'

'I hope it's dry,' I said, with a glance behind him.

He gulped a little. 'Indeed, indeed, indeed,' he said and only just stopped himself from saying it a fourth time. He swept his arms wide and drove us back the way we had come like a stockman getting a sow onto a cart. I had seen this manoeuvre once at Gilverton Mains and marvelled at it. This morning was the first time I had been subject to it personally.

Back out on the green, the schoolchildren had disappeared at the clanging of the bell, but at the bus stop there had formed a short queue of women, wearing headsquares and carrying baskets, and Manie Halliburton was pushing a tin cart along the far side, presumably collecting washing from the cottages there.

'I'll leave you to it then,' said Mr Watson and went trotting off across the grass. He had almost reached Miss Halliburton when he stopped short, turned on his heel as though trained in a parade ground and marched back again.

'Have you heard it was a man?' he said.

'We've heard various things from various people,' I said. 'But yes, that's the latest.'

'No one knew it was Lizzy Hogg saying otherwise, see?'

'Poor Lizzy,' I said.

'Ach she's harmless,' said Watson.

'But when you say "no one" knew, Mr Watson,' said Alec, 'what do you mean? Three policemen knew.'

'Um,' said Watson. 'The thing is . . .'

'Did you see him too?' said Alec. 'Miss Clarkson caught a glimpse, apparently.'

'Not I, not I,' said Mr Watson. 'And that's not all. That's what I wanted to tell you. I've no alibi.'

Despite the drizzle, which had just started up again, Alec lifted his hat and scratched his head. 'Do you need one?'

'More so than I did when it was a woman,' Watson replied. 'But I haven't got one to give. So there's an end to it.'

'But you are not much more than average height,' I said. 'And you are not a thin man.'

'What?' he said.

'We've been given quite a detailed description of the chap,' Alec said. 'I take it you haven't.'

Mr Watson said nothing. He departed with a sort of bow and cut along the side of the castle wall towards the nearest cottages in that direction, already rummaging in his satchel for the first household's budget of letters. Miss Halliburton watched his progress and seemed to call out to him when he drew near her. He answered by waving his arm, and she followed the gesture until her eyes found Alec and me. She regarded us for a good few seconds, then she let drop the barrow handles of her little cart and advanced.

'What now, for the love of God?' Alec said. But he moved to meet her, with me scurrying at his heels.

'Morning,' she said. 'Miserable morning.'

'I trust you're fully recovered,' Alec said. He has had less practice than I in conversing with Scottish women on Mondays.

'Not much drying to be had,' I said, which worked like a charm.

'I've a warm room with slats in the windows,' she said. 'I heard something about you. Is it true?'

'I expect so,' said Alec.

'Well then I've got something to say.' The following silence indicated otherwise, however.

'We'll treat anything you tell us with the greatest possible confidence,' I assured her. It was a meaningless assurance but it had worked before and it worked on Manie now.

She gave a firm nod and said, 'I saw the man that killed that other man.'

'Silas Esslemont,' Alec said.

Manie gulped and nodded.

'Did you tell the police?' I asked.

'I . . . No,' she said. 'On account of how everyone thought it was a woman done it. So it didn't matter what man I saw.

But then it turns out that was just Lizzy. She's harmless, Lizzy. Usually.'

'So we've been led to believe,' I said, not adding the rest of my thought, which was that we had been led to believe it in more or less exactly the same words. These three – Miss Clarkson, Mr Watson and now Miss Halliburton – were beginning to seem like actors in an over-rehearsed play.

'I saw a tall thin man hurrying along the road at about half past two. He passed my house, you know.' She pointed at the little lodge sitting by the gate to Archerfield, the golf links and Mither Gollane's campsite.

'Oh that's yours?' I said, wondering how a laundress could afford the rent on such a snug little place. It was the equal of any cottage in the village.

'Why were you up?' Alec said.

'To go over and check the copper,' said Manie. 'I had left it well stoked to soak a boiling overnight but I set my alarm to check on it.'

'And you happened to see a man making his way towards the stone?' I said.

'A tall thin one,' said Manie. 'I never thought anything of it. Because of the manse, you know? Same road. And so I would have thought he was going for the minister if I'd thought at all.'

'And did you glance down that way again, once you were out and about?' said Alec. 'Did you hear anything?'

'I didn't *go* out,' Manie said. 'I changed my mind. Leastways, I looked over and saw the chimney smoking away nicely and I reckoned the copper was fine till the morning. So I went back to bed.'

'Over?' I said.

Manie pointed to the brick building I had taken for a small factory or works of some kind.

'Quite an operation,' said Alec. He looked from laundry to cottage a couple of times with an interest I found unaccountable, although I too had found what she had just claimed somewhat notable.

'How long have you been a laundress?' I asked. She was a young woman but it was the sort of occupation that started early in life.

'Twelve years,' Manie said. 'Why?'

'Oh, just general nosiness,' I assured her.

'Right,' she said. Then, with a glance over at where her cart lay abandoned, she added, 'I better get back to it.'

Alec lifted his hat once again as she departed. 'Not that I'm disputing you being extremely nosy, Dan,' he said. 'But why do you care how long Miss Halliburton has been plying the starch for the good folk of Dirleton?'

'For a start,' I told him, 'I can't believe she doesn't know how to stoke up a fire to burn under a copper all night without her getting up in the small hours. Not after twelve years of doing it. And for another I don't believe she was boiling linens on a Saturday night. In a Scottish village? And one that keeps the Sabbath as assiduously as we saw Dirleton do yesterday? For shame! There's no way she would have hung out a boiling of sheets, towels and pillowcases on a Sunday. If she works at all on a Sunday it would be behind closed doors: ironing pleated frills or laying woolly jerseys out on racks. So either she's lying about why she was up or she's lying about being up at all.'

Alec nodded sagely. 'She's certainly lying about one thing,' he said. 'You can't see that chimney from the gate lodge.'

'I shall take your word for it,' I said.

'We could look for the house with the little round window,' Alec said. 'And check it for curtains. Why don't you do that, Dan? Or ring Grant and ask after Daisy, as you suggested. Or I tell you what: how's the notebook going? Are you getting the chance to write it all down as we go?'

It was an old bugbear, one we had been wrangling over since the start of Gilver and Osborne: Alec scorned my little notebook and my beloved propelling pencil, but ended up relying on its contents every time.

'I spent quite half an hour on it over early tea this morning,' I assured him. 'It's all ready and waiting for you.' Alec lifted one side of his mouth in a smirk. Our arguments are dear to us both these days. 'Why are you trying to get rid of me, darling?'

'Just that I've realised there's another thread to pull,' he said. 'I was planning to go down to the church and see what's what after last night.'

'Why am I banished from the church?' I said.

'Because Silas is there,' Alec said.

'He's in a coffin,' I said. 'That's quite a different matter from being wound in a sheet, next door to my bedroom. I think I'm equal to a coffin, Alec. Good God.'

Alec inclined his head and we made our way across the green, past Miss Halliburton's little lodge house, past the leaping stone and down the manse road towards the church at the end. Inside the school, the children were singing a hymn to start off their day and the sound of piping voices drifting out of the open windows was quite charming.

Dirleton Kirk was charming too in a haphazard sort of way, having a squat tower with Gothic pinnacles, a neoclassical bit – which looked jolly like a side chapel from outside, but surely couldn't be in these Presbyterian parts – and a startlingly modern stained-glass window.

'These elusive Halliburtons take an interest then,' said Alec, making me smile. Indeed Dirleton Kirk did remind one of a grand house upon which generations of wealthy individuals had lavished their attentions.

Inside, it was all very much more seemly. The "lady chapel" was nothing of the sort, but merely a bit of extra space with a memorial to some great family on the wall. The rest of the décor was dark boards, white paint, uncomfortable seats and bundles of parish leaflets, with the only point of interest the coffin lying across two trestles just below the steps to the pulpit.

The sight of the minister, Mr Wallace, sitting with bowed head in the front row was perhaps somewhat surprising, priests of every sort usually being about their pastoral business on a Monday morning, rather than praying.

We waited a moment or two, shuffling our feet and clearing our throats, and then we moved towards him. Halfway down the aisle, when he still had not raised his head in response to the sound of Alec's large shoes and my tipped heels, I was seized with a sudden dreadful notion. I grabbed Alec's elbow in fright.

'Is he dead?' I hissed, the church acoustics helping no end.

'No, not dead,' said the minister, flooding me with relief and mortification mixed together. 'Merely dismayed. World-weary.'

It was not at all the mood one expects from a minister of cloth praying beside a coffin. 'Sure and certain hope' is much more the order of the day.

Alec, walking slightly ahead of me, had just come up beside the man when I saw him start violently and seem to assault the minister, grabbing at him in a bewildering but very determined fashion.

The next few minutes were chaos. Alec grappled the minister out of the pew and got close to pinning him on the steps leading to the altar, before the other man regrouped and swept Alec's legs out from under him, sending him crashing down. The minister scrambled up waving his hanky – most oddly – above his head, but Alec lunged for his ankles and brought him to the floor. Then the minister scuttled awkwardly away to the side on both feet and one hand while Alec continued to jab and clutch for the other hand and whatever it held, draped in cloth and half hidden.

'Alec! What the hell?' I said, when I had recovered the power of speech.

'Don't touch it!' yelled the priest, after a particularly sharp lunge from Alec and a cry of triumph.

'Are you hurt?' he asked. 'Dandy, go and find a doctor.'

'I'm fine, you idiot,' the minister said, clambering to his feet and beginning to dust himself down. 'Stop pawing it, for heaven's sake!'

Then I managed to see what had been at the centre of the grappling match. A long, thin and wicked-looking knife, which the minister had valiantly been attempting to keep out of Alec's reach, but which Alec had finally managed to twist out of the man's grip. Panting, he stepped away, holding the thing behind his back.

The minister straightened up and spread his hands wide. He was still holding the large pocket handkerchief that had hidden the knife. It added a touch of stage magician to his appearance, despite the cassock.

'I was trying to preserve fingerprints,' he said.

Alec brought his hands around to the front and regarded the knife in his grip. 'Ah,' he said. He held it out and the minister, with a wry look, took a hold of it through the cloth, then, to my surprise, laid it on Silas's coffin.

'I say,' I put in. 'I don't think that's quite—'

He beckoned me close and pointed to the lid. I could not help gasping when I saw, all over the smooth finish of the pine boards, a series of little nicks as though . . .

'. . . someone came and slashed at his coffin lid with a knife?' said Alec.

'It was sticking up out of the wood when I arrived this morning,' the minister said. 'I was in the process of gathering the . . . stomach, I suppose . . . to go and report the outrage when you came and found me. One assumes it's the same knife.'

'The same knife as what, Father Wallace?' Alec said.

'*Mr* Wallace, if you don't mind.'

'Sorry,' said Alec. 'Early training down south, you know. But the same knife as what?'

'You haven't heard that particular nasty detail then?' was all the answer Mr Wallace made, not minded to be gracious to Alec, who had suspected him of the sin of suicide, had ruined some evidence in a murder case, and had confessed to high Anglicanism – or worse – all in the course of five minutes.

'Which nasty detail?' I asked.

'That poor Silas—' said Wallace. 'I should really call him Esslemont, for I never met in him in life, but he is in my care now. And I would hesitate to tell a lady, no matter what I call him. Who are you anyway? I was too flustered last night to wonder.'

'I think I know the detail without being told,' I said, as illumination broke over me. 'At least, the police who came to interrogate Silas's wife asked if he had been gardening. Or if he fenced. So we were right in assuming he had wounds on his body? We're friends of the family, by the way.'

'Tiny wounds the police told me,' said Wallace. 'Scratches. Less than scratches.'

145

'As though he might have been pruning and caught himself on thorns,' Alec said. 'My God, I hope there's a print or two left despite me being such a bloody fool. I do apologise.'

'Well, we shall see,' said Mr Wallace. 'The police will do what they can and I daresay whoever it was wore gloves anyway.'

I glanced at Alec. 'Whoever it was?' I said. 'You know who it was. At least, you know who claimed to be in the church last night.'

'Lizzy Hogg?' said Mr Wallace. 'No, no, no. The thing about Lizzy, you see, is that she's . . .'

'Harmless?' said Alec. 'Most of the villagers seem to have settled on that.'

'I was going to say that she's rather a stranger to plain facts simply told. She lives in a world of her own and tends towards stories. Simply because she claimed she was in the church, I wouldn't conclude she was anywhere near the place.'

Alec opened his mouth to argue but I found myself nodding. 'Yes, I thought all along that she blurted the tale of being in the church last night to divert attention from the fact that she was flitting about the inn. One does wonder why she was flitting anywhere, mind you. Where are her parents? Why isn't she better looked after? How old is she?'

'Um, fifteen or sixteen? And there are no parents, I'm afraid,' the minister said. 'She's a Halliburton ward.'

'Manie Halliburton is known to us,' I said. 'She should take better care of the girl.'

To my surprise the minister looked more grim at the mention of this name than he had at the suggestion of him committing suicide in his church or at the sight of knife marks in a coffin lid.

'Not her,' he said, through gritted teeth. 'Not *Manie* Halliburton! That shared name is the most unfortunate coincidence. Lizzy is a ward of the *other* Halliburtons. She spends most of her time at the castle.'

'Really?' said Alec.

'Ah,' I said. Perhaps I am growing cynical but I have seen it often enough that it is no longer a surprise. Behaviour that would see a pauper under lock and key in an asylum is winked at and excused in the great and the wealthy. Hugh's Uncle Nelson, for instance, roamed around the Highlands as mad as a hatter for years and the worst that ever befell him was a heavy cold when he did it naked.

'And the thing about castles these days,' the minister went on, thankfully misunderstanding me, 'is that they are terribly . . . porous. No such thing as raising the drawbridge in modern times. She's proving rather difficult to contain.'

'Mr Wallace?' I had not heard another person approaching and the voice from the dim rear of the church startled me. I turned to see an elderly man dressed in a neat town suit, but wearing a Fair Isle jersey underneath and a brown knitted tie.

'Ah, Mr Curr!' said the minister. 'My session clerk,' he offered to Alec and me. 'Jamie, I wonder if I could trouble you to sit with Mr Esslemont for a while. I need to take care of a bit of business and I don't want to leave him alone.'

Mr Curr's eyebrows met above his little round spectacles. Clearly the minister suggesting anything like a wake or a vigil was far too high to be borne in a Church of Scotland such as this.

'I shall draw up a proper rota as soon as I get the chance,' said Mr Wallace, 'but for now, unless you're busy . . .'

'Well,' said Mr Curr, 'I just put my head in for a minute

to make sure the cleaner had been, and the thing is . . . there's been a break-in.'

'Yes, we kno— Hang on. Do you mean in the vestry? How can you tell?'

'The cupboard,' said Mr Curr. 'The lock is lying twisted off in two mangled bits and the wood is splintered.'

Mr Wallace was on his feet, but beyond that he did not seem able to propel himself anywhere very decisively. 'The communion cup?' he said. 'The candlesticks?'

'Not that cupboard,' said Mr Curr. 'The bookcase. There's at least one volume missing.'

'A Bible?' Alec said. 'Have you a terribly rare one?'

That shocked poor Mr Curr even more profoundly, I thought. The notion of a Bible as a treasure was too much for him. 'Nay,' he said. 'Not the word of God. The doings of men. Some of our records have been taken away.'

The two men bustled off to investigate, leaving Silas forgotten and leaving Alec and me gaping at one another.

'A parish book stolen?' I said. 'How very interesting, wouldn't you say?'

'I rather think we know who took it,' Alec replied. 'Although I cannot imagine why.'

Chapter 10

'Hello, darling!' I sang out down the telephone, when Hugh had been summoned to the instrument. I was ringing for news of my dear friend in her invalid state and her new grief, of course, but also in hopes of gleaning information about our murder victim. We still believed the castle to be Silas's most obvious object in coming to Dirleton, and I thought surely I could ask a few gentle questions of his widow before making another foray. 'Hugh? Can you hear me?' I added when no reply came.

The silence continued. 'Hugh?'

'They're not here, Dandy,' he said at last. 'They can't overhear you. So whatever that was, you needn't trouble yourself with it.'

'And how are the boys?' I said. I was not, in fact, acting the part of a cheerful, loving wife in case of bat-eared policemen at the Gilverton end; I was making sure no one in the Castle Inn divined my true purpose. There did not seem to be a telephone for guests in a handy little cubicle anywhere, so it was either the one on the desk in the lobby or a trip to the post office, Mr Watson's domain. And, while there was no particular reason to believe that a Dirletonite would report Daisy's consciousness, it seemed wise to use caution.

Hugh sighed so heavily he outwitted the connection and we both had to wait for the buzzes and rumbles to settle again.

'They're full steam ahead,' he said. 'They've promised not to do anything until you're back but after that there will be no stopping them.'

'No stopping them what?' I asked. Then I realised. 'Oh. Joining up.' My voice suddenly felt dry and rather small, all thoughts gone of what the landlord might overhear. Alec frowned quickly and embarked on that infuriating set of mimes and whispers whereby the hearer of one end of a telephone conversation attempts to insert himself into the entire thing.

'Who?' he hissed. 'Donald? Teddy? Oh God, both? When?'

I turned my back on him. 'Thank you,' I said to Hugh. 'They've both promised?'

'And they are young men of honour who neither break promises nor shirk their duty,' said Hugh.

'In that case,' I said, 'I shall spin it out like billy-o.'

'Got to be faced, old girl,' Hugh said. 'Haven't you seen a paper or heard the radio today?'

I had grabbed this case – which was not quite a case – expressly to *forget* what radio broadcasts and newspaper editorials were trying to tell me about the wider world, so it should not have irked me so much to have Hugh refer to the policy.

'Might I speak to Grant, please?' I said, crisply. 'Since the conversation can be had in private. Since the three stooges aren't breathing down your neck.'

'Three what?' said Hugh, who has never been inside a picture palace since he wore short trousers. 'Oh, the policemen? I told you, Dandy: they've left.'

'Left?' I said, turning back to Alec. 'I thought you meant they weren't in the room.' Alec mouthed something at me, which I think was "coppers". 'Are they on their way back here? Have they decided Daisy's innocent after all?'

'They've gone to Croys,' Hugh said. 'Heaven knows why. They wouldn't tell me. As to Daisy, they've decided that since her coma seems to be deepening by the hour they're wasting their time. That terrifying police matron has gone back to her dungeon too. It's just Grant and the nurse now. I'll see if Grant can be spared, even so. Two ticks, Dandy.'

'Madam,' said Grant a moment or two later. 'How can I help you?'

It was as I thought, I reflected to myself. Somehow or another, in winkling out the police matron, Grant had grown even more bumptious than ever. She spoke with the air of a busy professional woman forced to interrupt her day to deal with an annoyance.

'Let's hear it then,' I said. 'What have you done?'

'What have I not done!' said Grant. 'I saw off those two men. I got rid of poor Alexandra and I've got Susan even more committed to playing for our team.'

'Who's Sus— Oh, the nurse. What do you mean?'

'She coached Mrs Esslemont very successfully.'

'In what? How?' I said, sounding plaintive even to myself.

'A short lesson in physical acting,' said Grant, 'helping her look less as though she's having a nap and more as though she's slipping away. It's mostly about softening the oesophagus and letting the breath appear to be a struggle. And various other . . . indignities . . . that the small-minded wouldn't believe a lady would deliberately choose. But Mrs Esslemont was absolutely game.'

'I'll bet,' I said. 'Considering the alternative. *Don't* tell me the details.'

'And then I worked on Alexandra to get her ruffled about being left babysitting instead of . . . oh now, what did I say . . .

151

instead of participating fully in the essential duties of the constabulary at such a critical time.'

'Grant!' I said. 'You turned the clouds of war to account?'

'"Considering the alternative" as you put it,' said Grant. 'Yes, I did.'

'And what exactly are the police *doing* at Croys?'

'Well,' she began, which was alarming in itself. Grant usually delivers the most astonishing enormities without so much as clearing her throat. For her to be pushed as far as uttering a "well" meant that something beyond belief was coming. 'You know how rich the Esslemonts have been getting? I hinted at financial improprieties and shadowy alliances. Mounting efforts to escape accountability. Marked increase in anxiety, just lately. That sort of thing.'

'You told two members of the East Lothian Constabulary that Silas Esslemont was a traitor to his king and country?' Alec's eyes grew so round I could see a complete circumference of white.

'Not in so many words,' said Grant. 'And not exactly. They've gone off unsure whether he's a spy or just a carpetbagger.'

'Oh well then!' I said.

'But they'll be busy with his papers for a while either way. Meantime, Mrs Esslemont was set free to breathe normally and help us work out what actually happened.'

'And has she?' I said. 'Why didn't you ring up and say so? Or send a telegram? Why wait for me to ring you?'

'Not yet,' Grant said. 'She can't remember anything very useful after leaving the dining room. It's quite common after a bump on the head, Susan tells me. And . . .'

'And she was pickled like an onion,' I supplied. 'She remembers nothing? Not even where she was going when she veered off the road?'

152

'Oh yes, she remembers that,' said Grant. 'She was going to find Mr Esslemont and give him a piece of her mind.'

'But she didn't know where he was!'

'She worked it out,' Grant said. 'She was too angry to go to sleep and while she was tossing and turning she worked out where he was and set off to give him what for.'

'How?' I said. 'Worked it out *how*? I do think some of this would have been well worth the cost of a telegram, I must say.'

Alec was now whispering and flapping around at my elbow like some kind of combined moth and bee. 'Daisy worked out Silas was in Dirleton,' I told him, hoping he would subside. Of course, instead, he became even more animated, and I had to put up a hand to stop him grabbing the telephone and taking over.

'Oh no!' said Grant. 'Not at all, madam. When I say she worked it out, I mean she dreamed up a theory of where he was and what he was up to and set off to box his ears. She had no idea where he actually was. She thought he had got rid of her with this tale of a dinner and he was luxuriating at Croys with . . . whoever . . . while she was out of the way. Like a mouse.'

'Mouse?'

'While the cat's away,' said Grant. 'You know.'

'That doesn't seem at all likely,' I said. 'What about the servants? Why on earth would Silas . . . ?'

'Well, as you said yourself, madam,' said Grant. 'About pickled onions.' We shared a tut and a sigh. 'Do *you* have anything to report?' she went on presently. 'Any messages to pass along?'

'Indeed I do,' I said. 'If you think Mrs Esslemont is equal to it – but only if; don't plunge in and upset her – ask if she knows a family by the name of Halliburton, please, or a young – no don't say "young" – woman. Actually, don't say "woman" either. Ask if Mr Esslemont knew anyone by the name of Goodfellow. You might ask Mr Gilver too, in case the acquaintance sprang from schooldays or the county.' I supplied her with more details than she could possibly need, then made my goodbyes and rang off to regale Alec with it all.

'You can't deny she's effective,' he said. 'If the coppers don't find any evidence of wrongdoing when they search Croys, well then: no harm done. Silas himself is beyond being damaged by the allegations.'

'Daisy isn't,' I reminded him. 'Nor the girls. Lord, the girls, Alec! Selfish as it sounds I'm glad I'm down here doing this rather than up there, dealing with them. I do wonder how they were told though.'

'One of them's engaged, isn't she?' Alec said. 'Do you think the fiancé will bolt?'

'Surely not!' I said, more from hope than conviction.

'If Silas had stayed at home and looked after his estates like everyone else,' Alec said, with rather unseemly relish, 'he wouldn't be such . . . low-hanging fruit.'

I said nothing. I understood that Silas's philandering and, in particular, his seduction of Alec's fiancée, even years before she *was* Alec's fiancée, had left a bitter taste in his mouth, but sneering at the man for starting a business and staying rich while the rest of us clung on and began to sink . . . That was nothing but sour grapes. Or do I mean dog in the manger? Nothing very edifying, anyway.

As we walked over the green to the castle again, I found myself terribly aware of how open it was and how completely

154

ringed around with cottages. I felt quite like a hare sitting up in a field, nose quivering, suspecting the guns were there but unable to see them. 'Do you know, Alec?' I said. 'This village is not at all suited to subterfuge. There's no cover. The only exception, actually—'

'Exactly,' said Alec. 'I've been thinking about that too. If Silas was anywhere out here on the green itself, he'd have been in full view of a dozen cottage windows. As he turned into the manse road, Miss Halliburton would have been able to see him from her little lodge and Miss Clarkson can apparently see a great deal from her landing window, wherever it is. If he had got a bit further *down* the manse road, he would have been visible from the schoolhouse, the manse itself through the trees, and the upstairs windows of that big house up there.'

'Although, at three o'clock in the morning, he'd be unlucky to be seen at all no matter what,' I pointed out.

'But where he actually died,' Alec went on, waving me to silence, 'that exact spot, the leaping stone, is quite unusually secluded. Look, we're just about in line with it now, and— No, in fact, this is too important: come down and stand by it. See if you agree.'

Trying not to sigh out loud, I turned my feet and followed him to the corner of the green and the little ring of cobbles surrounding the stone.

'Now look,' he said. 'Stand right beside it and look in all directions.'

I disobeyed him. Instead, I bent over it and stared downwards. 'It's been cleaned,' I said. 'Look, darling.'

Indeed, the stone was washed and gleaming, with not a trace of a bloodstain.

'And with plain old soap and water too,' I said. 'No matter Manie's odd hints.'

'Bleach actually,' Alec said. 'It's killed the moss between the cobbles. Manie must have returned. But as I was saying, Dandy: look all around.'

This time, I did as I was told. 'Hm,' I said. 'Well, the manse is hidden behind its hedges, and the cenotaph cuts off the view from the schoolhouse. All those windows I can see belong to the school and the village hall, don't you agree? And there are no windows in the gable end of that place.' I waved a hand at the end of the two of cottages leading out of the village to the north. 'I *would* have said that big house – farmhouse, do you think? Or a dower house maybe? It's quite a size anyway – I would have said, before we came and tried it out, that it looked right down this way but there's a curve in the road where the pub sticks out and actually I can't see more than the tiniest corner of wall. Certainly not a window. Not even an attic dormer.'

'The only window with a sight line to this spot in the whole village is that one,' Alec said.

I followed where he was pointing and squinted. At the curve of the castle wall there was that curious little turret and indeed it did have an arched and latticed window facing this way.

'But that's surely a folly,' I said. 'Or a garden shed. It must be centuries since watchmen patrolled the walls, actually watching.'

'Agreed,' Alec said. 'This spot, where the stone is, is not overlooked by anyone.'

'But what does that tell us? If Silas fell over and hit his head on a stone, then of course it happened where a stone is.'

'He didn't fall,' Alec said.

'Yes, but even if he was pushed of course he was pushed where the stone is. Otherwise he would have fallen harmlessly on the grass and stood up again.'

'Think, Dandy,' Alec said. 'Think about all the little nicks and scratches there must be on his body to make the police think of fencing or pruning, to make Mr Wallace say "the same knife".'

'I can't bear to.'

'Have you ever seen a picture of a bear baiting?'

'Oh, Alec, don't! It's too awful to be borne.' Because of course as soon as he put the picture into my mind it was impossible to think of anything else but Silas, walking backwards with his hands up in front of him, trying to defend himself from the jab-jab-jab of a thin knife driving him towards his fate.

'Almost as though,' Alec said, 'it mattered that he died where he did. With his blood on that stone. It was so terribly risky. To drive him either up from the manse in view of umpteen houses, or down from the green in view of umpteen others.'

'But witnesses have told us they saw the murderer making his way to the spot all alone, skulking in the shadows. Not driving Silas backwards with a knife.'

'Exactly,' said Alec.

I managed to suppress the sigh he deserved. 'Stop teasing me,' I said. 'Tell me what you've thought of and let's put our heads together.'

'My theory is as follows,' Alec said. 'To avoid being seen, all the jabs from the knife must have happened *actually* here. Not *en route* to here.'

'If we trust the witnesses,' I agreed. 'But so what?'

'So why didn't he turn and run? Why didn't he come into view of Miss Clarkson or even Miss Halliburton before she went to bed again? Why did he hang around within jabbing distance long enough to be cut however many times?'

157

'That,' I said, 'is a very good question. I can see it if he'd been cornered, but he could have made off in any direction. Why didn't he?'

'Why indeed,' Alec said.

'Was he fighting back?' I said. 'Trying to wrest the knife out of his assailant's grasp?'

'But why?' Alec said. '*Why* was he fighting back? Unarmed against a knife. Instead of running.'

'Perhaps . . . he was . . . remonstrating?'

'Bargaining, pleading, cajoling, threatening . . .' said Alec. 'And what does that tell us?'

'That he knew the person who attacked him,' I said. 'Is that what you mean? But we knew that already. Because he was summoned by letter to a place that didn't need any spelling out.'

'Knew him, yes,' Alec said. 'And was unwilling to end the meeting even when it had taken such an unspeakably odd turn as to involve a knife. But here's what I'm pondering, Dandy. And I'd like you to ponder it with me.'

'I'd like you to ponder it for me,' I suggested.

'Very well. Silas comes down to Dirleton to meet someone—'

'A man?'

'One thing at a time,' Alec said. 'They meet at a place known to both of them, a place that needs no directions. They talk, matters deteriorate sharply, and a knife appears. Silas, however, doesn't give up on the rendezvous and run away. Nor does he call for help. He allows himself to be cut, multiple times, and he keeps on trying. Think about it, Dandy. That is not just someone Silas "knew". That is someone Silas . . .'

'Loved, hated or feared,' I said. 'Deeply.'

'Which brings us to the second problem,' Alec said. 'Imagine the scene again.'

'Do I have to?'

'Silas is remonstrating or what have you with his assailant. His assailant is jabbing at him with a knife.'

'Will the doctor who looked at his body be able to tell if it's the same knife that turned up on the coffin lid?'

'You're supposed to be picturing the scene,' Alec said. 'Jab, jab, shuffle, shuffle. What happens next?'

'He loses his footing and trips,' I said. 'Falls over and cracks his head on the stone.'

'Think, Dandy!' He waited and then heaved an enormous sigh. 'Very well. One last clue. Trips over what?'

'The st— Hang on,' I said.

'Hallelujah!' said Alec. 'Exactly. No one who trips over a stone also hits his head on it.'

'So what happened?'

'I suggest that he tripped on the stone and then his head was bashed in with something else once he was on the ground.'

'But his blood was all over it.'

'Because once he was dead he was draped over the thing. Still bleeding.'

'So you're saying, in the teeth of all the evidence I have to point out, that even though we've got a knife and a boulder we should be looking for a third murder weapon?'

'Not that we should look,' said Alec. 'Just that we shouldn't faint if one appears.'

'So why not look?'

'Because we already have enough avenues to keep us running around like clockwork mice until Christmas and I for one can't face it.'

'Hardly the spirit,' I pointed out. 'And actually why *not* the knife? Jab, jab, jab – it does feel jolly ghoulish to put it that way, I must say – stumble, stumble, stumble and then why *not* just plunge the knife into him?'

'I don't know,' Alec said. 'It's one of a long list of things I don't know. Why was he here? Why did hearing his name send Mither Gollane into such a tizzy? Why did two perfectly decent witnesses keep quiet until they found out who the original witness was?'

'Why did Mither Gollane steal the parish book?' I added. 'We do both agree it was her, don't we? She boasts about her entries in it and then, suddenly, on the same night, it's gone.'

'Yes, but I rather think that's the other matter,' Alec said. 'We keep hearing it, don't we? That the writers were coming and the murder got in the way of the story they were chasing. It bothers me that she took vapours upon hearing his name, of course, but she can't have killed him; it's even less possible if he was struck with a heavy object. And I don't see how there could be a connection between Silas and a woman of over a hundred. Do you?'

'Well, not the usual sort,' I said. 'Of course, Manie had exactly the same reaction to hearing his name and she *is* in his age range – just – but even Silas has never taken up with a laundress.'

'You know what else?' Alec said. 'When Lizzy took to her heels last night, we both assumed it was finding out we were detectives that had done for her. But do you remember the other thing you'd just said?'

I shook my head.

'That we were friends of the Esslemonts.'

'Yes, but Lizzy Hogg couldn't have been Silas's object. Alec, she's a child! Honestly, the more I hear of gentlemen's private affairs, the less I care to.'

'All right, all right, have it your own way,' Alec said. 'There are two unrelated matters here. Two people broke into the same church on the same night. One to put a knife in a coffin lid and one to steal a parish book.'

'That can't be right,' I said, grudgingly. 'That's an affront to old Whatsisname, the barber.'

'Barber?' said Alec. 'Do you mean Occam's razor? Yes, I agree.'

For the want of anywhere else to rest, I sat down on the stone then, and put my chin into my hands, staring at Alec as I have stared at him so many times before over the years, waiting for murky waters to clear, waiting for a missing pip of information or crumb of memory to be revealed, waiting for that wonderful moment when an impossible tangle becomes a long straight thread and an unholy mess becomes a neatly completed puzzle with every piece tightly in place.

'How do you think the Dirletonites would take to a grown man sitting on the grass?' Alec said.

'They put up with Lizzy Hogg flitting about like a witch,' I said. 'Try it and see if anyone comes out with a broom to shoo you away.'

Alec, looking thirty years older than his age, let himself down with a creak and a groan. 'Oof,' he said. 'It's not very comfort—'

'Oh Lord!' I said, laughing and pointing behind him. 'I call that service!' For no sooner had his posterior touched the grass than a police motor car came into view, crossing the top of the green towards the Castle Inn. It turned slightly our way as it drew up and then, with a small spray of gravel, it set off again heading straight for us.

Alec leapt to his feet, staggering a little, and I hauled myself up too, offering an arm to stop him from stumbling, so that we were both standing to attention when the motor car reached us and Captain Wicks, followed by Sgt Dodgson, stepped down.

161

'Enjoying the view?' Dodgson said.

'I'm glad to see you, Sergeant,' I said. 'Both of you.'

'I wish I could say the same,' said Dodgson. 'If you've been causing mischief at the scene of the crime, I'll not be best pleased.'

'Now, now, Sergeant,' said Captain Wicks, as milquetoast as ever. 'Still, dear lady, I must agree. We shall take a dim view of any untoward interference.' He paused as if trying to think of something else to say and settled on: 'A very dim view.'

'Bad enough that you came down here and lied about who you were,' said Sgt Dodgson. 'Oh yes, we've had a report from Constable McLean.'

'I say,' said Captain Wicks. '"Lied", Dodgson. Come now. Unparliamentary language and all that.'

To my surprise, Alec was leaving it entirely up to me to deal with this pair. His head hung and he was scuffing his toe like a schoolboy hauled up before the head.

'We didn't lie about anything,' I said. 'We arrived. People assumed we were a pair of writers they were expecting and we said nothing one way or the other.' I was not sure that was true but I was in no mood to prostrate myself. Dodgson was being pointlessly fussy.

'You what?' he said, looking round at his superior officer, although whether for guidance or in disbelief it was impossible to say. His tone made Alec raise his head, at last.

'I say,' said Captain Wicks. 'All we heard from McLean was that you'd put it about you were some kind of writer chappies and then reluctantly admitted you were private detectives. He didn't say you'd impersonated Crabbie and McEwan. I say!'

I could not decide which bit of this to tackle first. It was odd that Crabbie and McEwan were known to the local police, odder still that the police minded our little fib amidst so many more serious worries. But, as well as that, I did not care at all for the suggestion that Alec and I had "admitted" anything, less so that we had done it "reluctantly". That sort of charge carries real weight with police on the scene and a crime on the go.

'We practised some harmless subterfuge while there was an unfounded suspicion about Mrs Esslemont,' I said. 'The better to clear her name, don't you know. But one surmises, from the fact you've all left Gilverton, that you've come to your senses and realised, by yourselves, that she is innocent.'

I was very proud of this. Of course, I knew they had only abandoned Daisy because they thought – thanks to Grant's coaching – she was in a deep coma. I also knew that when they had quit Gilverton they had merely gone up the road snuffling after the scent Grant had laid for them about Silas's shady dealings. The thing is, I should not know any of that and I had just made a magnificent fist of pretending so.

'Innocent and Esslemont are not two words that I'd put together,' said Sgt Dodgson.

'Unless you were writing a ditty for the music halls,' said Alec, earning himself a scowl.

'We've uncovered what you were no doubt sent here to bury,' said Dodgson. 'Silas Esslemont's connection to Dirleton, no less.'

I made a valiant attempt to take this news without any outward sign of surprise.

'But we shall have to leave that for another day,' Dodgson continued. 'Since we've now got ourselves a triple homicide to solve.'

'Trip—?' said Alec.

163

'Getting rather ahead of yourself there, Dodgson,' said Captain Wicks.

'We found their car,' Dodgson said. 'It had run off the road. Or *been* run off the road.'

'Whose car?' I asked.

'And some of their possessions.'

'Whose possessions?' Alec put in.

'But by no means *all* of their possessions.'

I could feel a cold trickle of a feeling, like a melting ice cube slipped under my collar.

'So,' Dodgson said, 'we don't have time to be standing around. I'll go and ask at the Castle Inn if the missing items fetched up there somehow, since they had rooms booked. And you, sir? Could you find Constable McLean and send him to the Mains to see if Will Simpson's new tractor can help us pull the car back up the bank?'

Evidently the chief constable was not to be trusted with the task itself, I noticed.

'I might just slip down and have a word with Mr Wallace,' said Captain Wicks. 'See if there's room for another two coffins in the church or if we're going to have to get a van to come from Haddington. And I'll ring up the doc and see about a PM.'

'So Mr Crabbie and Miss McEwan's motor car has been found,' said Alec. 'But the lady and gentleman themselves haven't been seen? What makes you call it murder then?'

I could not have found my voice to utter a single word. All I could think of was the bundle of clothes locked in Alec's boot and the absolute impossibility of explaining why we had put them there, much less left them there. That and the fact that every passing minute before we told Wicks about it made it all the more peculiar that we had not done so.

'Well, I'm no private detective like you,' said Dodgson, witheringly, 'but the blood inside the thing is what got me thinking initially. And the two bloody handprints on the rear bumper from the murderer shoving the car into a ditch out of the way. There was that too.'

'But no bodies, I take it?' Alec said.

'We've got every man out combing the woods,' said Dodgson. 'But no one could survive the loss of all that blood. There was a lake of it. A lake.'

'Gentlemen,' I said. 'Wouldn't you agree that nothing else matters but finding those two, in case one or both of them is still alive?'

'Not a chance,' said Dodgson. 'You could paddle in the blood like a bairn at the seaside.'

'Yes, all right, Sergeant,' said Captain Wicks. 'You've painted a picture. Everyone understands.' He gestured to me, the lady, but it was he who was looking green about the gills.

'Well then, wouldn't you say that nothing matters except the solving of these terrible murders as soon as trained police, private sleuths and witnesses together can do so?'

Alec laid a hand on my arm and squeezed. 'What Mrs Gilver is trying to tell you,' he said, 'is that we shan't hold you back, but we do have evidence to share whenever it's convenient for you to summon us for an interview.'

'Oho,' said Dodgson. 'Very good of you! How accommodating!'

'Still and all,' said Wicks. 'We had better press on, Sergeant.'

With a sheepish half-grin and a cold stare respectively, Wicks and Dodgson left us there. We were reeling, but I expect they were too, since country places as quiet as Dirleton cannot see such events as these with any regularity. They did not notice my pallor or Alec's rapid breathing as they marched away.

165

Chapter 11

'Let go, Alec,' I said, once they were out of earshot. 'I shall have a bruise tomorrow from the way you're digging your fingers into me. I haven't been pinched like that since I was in my nursery. Mavis was a perfect little lobster when she was a child.'

'I found something,' Alec said. 'But those coppers were so hoity-toity that I decided not to share it with them. I'd rather keep my own counsel and solve the thing under their noses.'

'They're bound to find out about the clothes though, darling,' I said. 'Lizzy, the minister and the constable know we took them apart from anything else.'

'We can tell them ourselves,' Alec said. 'Once we've had a chance to sort it all through.'

'Fat chance of that,' I said. 'I've never known a more incident-packed and yet completely impenetrable case in all our years.'

'Well, you're going to hate this then,' Alec said. 'Sit back down on your tuffet, please, and try to look as if you're not paying any particular attention.'

'To what?'

Alec looked around him, checking for witnesses – he could not have appeared any more suspicious if he had twiddled his moustaches and cackled – then he bent as though to tie his shoelace and pointed to something near his foot.

'Look, Dandy.'

I peered dutifully at the grass and saw a small grey object. It shone as Alec moved the grass blades with his toe. 'What is it?'

'I thought it was a pebble,' Alec said. 'Well, I thought the one I sat down and chipped my tailbone on was a pebble. I knew the one I tripped over as I stood up wasn't lying on the ground. It was rooted somehow, otherwise I'd have dislodged it.'

'Ahhhh,' I said. 'You were checking for more? I thought you were hanging your head in shame at being scolded.'

'By Wicks?' said Alec, sneering in a rather unpleasant way, to my mind. 'I think I could withstand *his* worst with head held high. How does a man like that come to head up a county constabulary, Dandy?'

I shrugged, barely listening since my attention was taken up searching for more of the little shining grey lumps in the grass. I spotted one and then another one, a third and, faster now that I knew what I was looking for, a fourth and a fifth. I did not crane to check behind me. I was sure enough without any such contortions.

'What are they?' I said. I was fascinated.

'Cleats,' Alec said. 'Eyes, I think.'

My shoulders slumped. 'You goose,' I said. 'They were there holding the tarpaulin in place until the fingerprint man and photographer came.'

'No, Dandy,' Alec said. 'That sacking was much skimpier than the circumference of this ring and those were park-keeper's spikes. We saw Mr Watson with another the same. Is anyone watching?'

'No one's walking by or standing at the bus stop,' I said. 'And we decided for ourselves that none of the houses over-look this spot, didn't we?'

'Right then.' He hunched down even lower. Anyone who *was* watching would have been forced to conclude that his shoelace was the most grievously unravelled specimen in the history of brogues. He spirited a little penknife out of some pocket and selected a tool I could not name. I saw him jab it hard at the grass and then, looking rather like Mrs Tilling when she guts a rabbit, he drew out a long thin spike, smeared with mud but still gleaming here and there.

'Tent peg,' he said. 'You see what this means, don't you?'

'I'm groping towards an understanding,' I said. 'But I would welcome your help. Would you like to drop that into my bag? It looks sharp enough to do harm to your trouserings if you pocket it.'

Alec did so, refolded his penknife and took out a hand-kerchief to wipe his fingers.

'This was no crime of passion,' he said. 'Nor even the work of a moment. Whoever asked Alec to meet him here, whoever drove him towards the stone with jabs of a knife, that person had been here in advance, pounding in a ring of tent pegs and stringing a wire around them.'

'So that he tripped and hit his head on the stone!'

'Precisely.'

'But why didn't the killer take them away?'

'He took the catgut or piano wire or whatever it was,' Alec said. 'That was a quick enough job. But pulling out a dozen to a score of tent pegs all firmly hammered in would take quite a while. More time than I'd be happy to spend skulking about where I'd just done a murder.'

'And why didn't the police notice them? Why didn't Constable Clarkson or someone else trip over one?'

'Perhaps they did and felt foolish,' Alec said.

'Why didn't that fingerprint man find them?' I tried next. 'He was all over the place on his hands and knees.'

'He was desperate to be done with it and escape, if you remember.'

'For reasons we haven't finally decided upon,' I said. 'A matter we should really address sometime.'

Alec ignored me. 'Besides, *I* wouldn't have thought anything of it if I hadn't just sat on one. And the police and doctor and what have you were, presumably, clustered around the body. Not however many feet away.'

'Six,' I said. 'Six feet. Isn't that what we're saying?'

'Of course,' said Alec. 'And then there's the fact that they can't have been pounded in this deep on Saturday night. If I cast my mind back to the booby traps we set at prep school – horrid little monsters that we were – I seem to remember that about five inches is ideal to make sure the wire is high enough to catch a chap no matter his gait but low enough to topple him.'

'Meaning that the murderer stamped them in hard after the killing and must have meant to come back and remove them later, but couldn't? Changed his mind for some reason? Who's been skulking about, as you put it?'

'Besides us?' Alec said. 'We're the most likely culprits for everything, I should say. We knew him. We've interfered. We pretended to be writers . . . But also, Lizzy Hogg, the constable, Manie Halliburton and whoever put the clothes here.'

'Even more reason to tell the police where the missing clothes are before Constable McLean gets the chance to,' I said. 'Thank heaven we blurted out to him that we'd found a label. That surely points to our innocence.'

'You do that bit,' Alec said. 'Find Dodgson and tell all. Then meet me back here afterwards. At the bench under the tree. But, Dandy? Try to spin it out if you can. I need a bit of time for what I've got planned.'

'Oh?'

'I'm going to get on to Barrow and ask him to get on to his pal whose sister works at Croys, find out what the coppers think they discovered about Silas's ties to this place.'

'Will the pal whose sister works at Croys know, do you think?'

'Oh Dandy, you're such an innocent in some ways. Haven't you learned by now that servants know everything that happens in the house? Barrow's pal – I think his name's Bamber, of all things – is a bigger gossip even than Barrow himself.'

'*Does* Barrow gossip?'

'Barrow told me Mallory was pregnant!' said Alec. 'He got it from one of the women who comes in at my place, who's a cousin of Mallory's maid. I knew before you, Dandy.'

'Good Lord, why didn't you tell me?'

'Because I'm the other sort,' Alec said. 'Not a gossip. I'm like Pallister. A vault.'

'Pallister!' I said. 'Golly, now that *is* a nasty thought. The things that Pallister could tell if he were the type.'

'His is a much cannier tactic. Making oneself unsackable by dint of knowing too much ever to be let go.'

'Sack Pallister?' I said. 'The walls of Gilverton would crumble.' I shook myself to drive away the thought of such an enormity and then fixed Alec with a glare. 'I'll take the clothes *and* accept my inevitable scolding but, since you bruised my elbow sending me the message not to speak up just now, I do feel it's your job to furnish me with an excuse. They're going to think it's very odd otherwise.'

Alec rubbed his nose and cleared his throat. 'I've got the perfect excuse,' he said. 'But I doubt you'll agree.'

'Try me.'

'Well, how about if you say it took you until just now to realise the items they referred to so mysteriously were probably the clothes we found. Say the revelation hit you and you came straight to tell them.'

'They'll think I'm an imbecile,' I said. 'And Constable McLean will confirm it.'

'That is the danger, yes.'

'And why didn't you with your manly intellect solve the riddle even while it outfoxed me and my fluffy little brain?'

'They won't wonder about that if I'm not there,' Alec said. 'Because they are the true imbeciles in the vicinity. Dodgson is like a little terrier, scampering around kicking up so much dust that the rat strolls away unseen. And Wicks is Wicks.'

'Very well,' I said. 'I shall take your word for it.'

'And don't forget that I actually referred to fresh evidence and Ramsay was too snooty to take me up on it. They'll be embarrassed about that too, if they've enough sense.'

'So you did,' I said. 'Well, I'll pass them along if you're wrong about their imbecility. In this instance, I mean. It's inarguable, generally speaking. Right. You grab a plum and I pick up a toad.'

'What plum?' Alec said. 'Ringing up Barrow? And being harangued about every speck of domestic misfortune that's befallen the household since I dared to leave? I don't think you know how easy you've got it with Grant and Pallister and Mrs T – Gilverton hums along like a top.'

Drat him, he was right.

Sgt Dodgson, whom I ran into on the Castle Inn's front doorstep, was pushed beyond what head-scratching, scoffing and appeals to the Almighty could afford him when I revealed

171

the whereabouts of Crabbie and McEwan's clothes. In the end, he merely raised his arms as though inviting an imaginary audience to marvel at me and then let his hands fall to his sides with a soft clap.

'There's no harm done,' I said. 'The clothes have been safely locked up in a clean, watertight place overnight and both Lizzy Hogg and your very own constable can confirm what I'm saying. I should rather think we've done you a favour, Mr Osborne and me.'

'Accidentally, coincidentally, and not at all by design, you just might have,' Dodgson said. 'But I'm reeling at the thought of what else you know and haven't piped up about. What else you've gone trampling into and made a mess of. What else you've heard and forgotten to pass on.'

'Nothing!' I said. I did not, of course, mention the fact that Daisy was awake, nor the fact that a crucial tool in the murder was right now lying in my bag wrapped in a hanky, nor that Mither Gollane was mixed up in this case in some way that made no sense to me, a stranger, but might well unravel the entire mystery for Dodgson, nor that Manie Halliburton had all but fainted when she heard Silas's name, nor even that Lizzy had fled. 'Well,' I said. 'That's not strictly true. There is the fact that someone rubbed out their names from the hotel register.'

Dodgson shook his head and rolled his eyes. Then he waved me towards the back of the hotel where, I assumed, there was a door leading to the stable yard and the treasure to be found in Alec's Daimler.

It was a gloomy spot, hardly less so this morning than when we had deposited our bundles. I plied Alec's little key and lifted the boot to let Sgt Dodgson feast his eyes and become more disgusted than ever. He stirred the piles of clothes, then

172

went off into a nearby shed, emerging after a few moments with some sacks, into which he stuffed the garments, most unceremoniously. 'It *would* be Lizzy Hogg,' he grumbled as he stuffed. 'It just would be. If we get any sense out of her, it'll be a nice change. I suppose you know she made up the tale of seeing a woman and lost us a whole day.'

'She's . . .' I said.

'Ach, she's a poor soul,' said Dodgson. 'She's had a hard life and she's making the best of it.'

'Where does she live?' I said. 'Surely not alone. She's very young for one thing and . . .'

'Oh no, they're good to her,' Dodgson said. 'Set her up in her own wee place and made sure she's looked after.'

'The parish?' I said. 'The Church? Or is it a benevolent society?' I rather wondered that whoever it might be looking after Miss Hogg had set her up here in Dirleton. I rather wondered, if it came to that, that none of the residents of this trim little village had kicked up a fuss about her being billeted here.

'No, none of that,' said Dodgson. 'It's the Halliburtons that took her in.'

'Oh yes, so I heard. The castle Halluburtons, rather than the laundry Halliburtons.'

'Oh, you've heard about *that*, have you?' Dodgson said. 'Aye well. They've given her house room and the rest of them all look after her together.'

The rest of whom? I asked myself. The other Halliburtons? And what was the "that" Dodgson wrongly assumed I knew? 'She certainly doesn't want for friends,' I said. 'In the last two days we've seen both Mr Watson and Miss Meek come galloping to her aid. No, hang on, sorry. It was Manie that Miss Meek rushed out to help.'

'Aye,' said Dodgson, 'it would be. You've nearly met them all then.'

The sacks were stuffed full and he took a little skein of string from his uniform pocket to tie the necks tightly shut. I was beginning to warm to Dodgson, in spite of everything. He seemed less egregious when separated from Wicks and there is always something irresistible about a man who saves useful lengths of string. It suggests that he has not quite done with boyhood, and I am predisposed to think kindly of boys.

The sergeant straightened from his task and looked beyond me towards the back of the inn. 'Speak of the devil,' he said.

For one dreadful moment, I felt my pulse quicken. Turning, however, I was relieved to see the outline of Miss Meek – who, right enough, I *had* mentioned a moment ago. She was hesitating in the gloom of the passageway as though summoning the courage to come forward.

'What can I do for you, miss?' Dodgson said.

'I can do something for *you*,' she said. Her voice sounded odd: less dainty than yesterday and rather lower too. I watched her with interest and then, as she moved out of the shade and into the daylight, I was aware of a sort of vertigo washing over me. This was not Miss Meek after all. Not only was the voice different but this woman was softer in line, dressed in garments the schoolmistress would surely eschew, and she held my gaze with an expression made up of a peculiar admixture of wryness, languor and some trepidation. I had never seen such a strange look upon anyone's face before. I expect mine was giving her something to ponder too, because for all the plain evidence that this was a stranger before me, a woman I was meeting for the first time, I could not shake off the ghost of my early impression.

174

'Are you here to see me officially?' Dodgson said. 'We can go to the station or if Mrs Gilver here would excuse us . . .'

'Of course, of course,' I said and took a step towards the gate to hurry off along the lane and leave them their privacy.

'No!' said the woman. 'Sorry, but, please don't go rushing off. I need to say it now before I lose my nerve and it would better if there's a witness, wouldn't it, Sandy?'

'Usually,' said Sgt Dodgson. 'But that's more for confessions.'

'This isn't quite that,' the woman said. She pasted a brave smile on her face and turned to me, offering her hand. 'You're the famous Mrs Gilver,' she said. 'Well, at least I know you're used to startling tales. Maggie Goodfellow.'

The equally famous, I thought. Or at least the hotly anticipated, by Alec and me.

While Miss Goodfellow was introducing herself, Sgt Dodgson had extracted his notebook and pencil from a pocket and I rather wished I could fish out my own. If the tremor in the woman's voice and the slight sheen on her face were anything to go by, she was preparing to say something well worth paying attention to.

'I heard that Lizzy had made a silly mistake,' she said. 'That it wasn't a woman after all who killed that man on the green the other night. Sorry, I've forgotten his name; I did hear it.'

'Esslemont,' said Sgt Dodgson.

'Esslemont, that's it. Anyway, it would seem therefore that it's *men* without alibis who're in a sticky spot,' she went on. 'And so, you see, it struck me as the right thing to do to come clean and reassure you that one man in particular *does* have an alibi even though he wouldn't say so, if his life— Well, which it does.'

Sgt Dodgson had stopped jotting things down and was frowning at her as though he did not follow. I not only followed; I was ahead of her.

'The thing is, you see,' she said, 'Paddy was with me.'

'Paddy Watson?' said Dodgson.

'Was with me, that night. All night.' She took a deep breath as if to say more, but in the end she merely turned on her heels and dashed back the way she'd come.

'Paddy Watson the postie and Miss Maggie Goodfellow?' Sgt Dodgson said once her footsteps had died away. 'Well, stone the crows.'

'Was he under particular suspicion?' I said. 'If not, I rather think Miss Goodfellow has jumped the gun. Who is she?' I added, getting the question in while the sergeant was reeling.

'Lives at the castle,' he said, which we already knew. 'She's a Halliburton, more or less,' he went on. 'Distant relation anyway.'

At last, I thought to myself. If she was a member of the great family, no matter what side of the blanket she was born on, here finally was a plausible reason for Silas to have made the journey to Dirleton: a pretty woman, of his own class or near enough, one of loose enough morals for Silas's usual purpose, one who had just volunteered to put herself into the middle of his murder. I chose not to say any of this to the good sergeant.

'They're certainly hospitable,' I offered instead. 'Taking in all and sundry. I'd like to meet them.'

'Not much chance of that,' said Sgt Dodgson. 'They're getting on in years and they live abroad most of the time. Come and go very quietly. There as many of us in this village have never even met them.'

I nodded. There were many in our set who were happy to take their rents and hand out a box at Christmas time but

176

would not dream of rubbing shoulders with the peasantry. I felt a rare surge of affection for Hugh, who knows all the names and gets as close to fussing as he ever has when misfortune befalls a tenant of his. 'If they're as lofty as all that, they don't sound likely to take Miss Goodfellow's liaison in their stride,' I said. 'In fact, elderly relatives of all sorts take a dim view of romping with postmen, I've found.'

'Have you now?' said Dodgson, with unnecessary crudeness. I withered him with a look and left him to get on with the rest of his day.

As I made my way back across the green, I turned over in my mind the silliness of the girl. It was all very well to be alarmed when suspicion switched from the women of the village to the men, but to demolish one's reputation the way Miss Goodfellow had just done was surely the last resort, and ought only have been turned to as Mr Watson was dragged off in irons. Moreover, we had already established that Mr Watson bore no resemblance to the tall, thin stranger Miss Clarkson had seen creeping around. And Miss Goodfellow did not, what is even more, strike me as at all careless about the matter. She had been white and strained as she delivered the alibi.

An alibi, I reckoned, that was not merely daft but also most suspect. If she was Silas's mistress, would she be carrying on with the postman too? Did she write the letter? Did she persuade her new lover to kill his rival? All in all, her blurted confession had raised suspicion rather than allaying it.

My thoughts were interrupted by the clang of the school bell and the instant monkey chatter of all the children pouring out to disperse among the cottages, or go bicycling off up and down the lanes to more far-flung homes. Two little girls, with black pigtails, disappeared hand in hand through the

177

front door of the public house, which was rather odd, but overall the pupils were a credit to Miss Meek: managing to sort themselves out without jostling or tears, the bigger girls dawdling hand in hand with the tinies rather than dragging them, which is always nice to see.

Of Alec there was no sign and I did not particularly want to sit like a good girl waiting for him, but what else could I do? As I gazed around, the idea struck me to go to the church in search of Mr Wallace. I could tell him it was more than likely Mither Gollane who pinched his parish book, ask him if he knew why, and also perhaps find out what Wicks might have let slip about the missing, bleeding writers.

There was no one around at the church, however. The front door was bolted and a quick circumnavigation told me that both the other doors, to the vestry and the coal shed, were locked up tight too. I peered out at the gate to see if there was any sign of Alec yet, then beat a hasty path across the front of the school and schoolhouse, heading for the manse. I told myself it was my imagination that I could feel Miss Meek's eyes upon me from behind one or other of the many windows. Still, it was with a great sigh of thankfulness that I gained the imposing gateposts at the foot of the drive and let the avenue of brooding yews envelop me.

Mrs Wallace was thrown into a domestic tizzy by my arrival, a fact I should have predicted, since I had watched two dozen schoolchildren scatter for their dinner minutes previously. 'Please, please, forgive my thoughtless intrusion,' I said, as she stood before me in the hallway, trying to pretend they had not started luncheon even though she had a cotton napkin clutched in one hand.

'I'll just get Mary to lay an extra place for you, Mrs Gilver. We've not even had our sherry yet.' This, with the unmistakable smell of mutton wafting out of a half-open door behind her and the unmistakable sound of someone laying down serving forks with a quiet clink.

'Mrs Wallace,' I said, 'forgive me speaking plainly to you but you should give it up as a bad job. I stand before you not Mrs Hugh Gilver of Gilverton, but Dandy Gilver of Gilver and Osborne, engaged on behalf of Mrs Esslemont to clear her name in the matter of her husband's murder. I'm a person today, and I've disturbed your luncheon. I would love to come back as a lady and have tea. Or I could bring Mr Osborne, who is a marvellous addition to any party, and we could have dinner. But for now, why not shove me into the minister's study with a cup of coffee and I'll talk to him when he's done?'

She had struck me as an entirely conventional woman, standing there in her tweeds and pearls, but at my words she gave a sudden wicked grin and waved me to an open door across the hall. I heard the minister chortling in the dining room too.

After a pleasant interlude, studying the minister's bookcases – and wondering what the parishioners made of D.H. Lawrence and Mary Wollstonecraft – the man himself joined me, carrying a tray of coffee and followed by his wife, who bore a plate of shortbread broken into petticoat tails and glistening with sugar. Alec must never hear of that, I decided.

'Did Captain Wicks catch you?' I began.

Mr Wallace shook his head. 'I can't have three coffins in the church,' he said. 'The two new ones will be off to the cellar of the cottage hospital at Gullane when they turn up and Silas Esslemont is going too. I don't like locking the place – succour, you know – but we can't have a repeat of this morning's uproar.'

Mrs Wallace tutted and shook her head.

'That was what I really wanted to ask about,' I said. 'Mr Osborne and I wondered if Mither Gollane might have taken the parish book.'

'Books, plural,' said Mr Wallace. 'And I shouldn't think so. She's an odd woman, increasingly so as the years accrue, but she's scrupulously . . .' He looked to his wife for help.

'Adherent to the way things should be done,' Mrs Wallace supplied.

'I see,' I said, more or less lying. The woman lived in a shack in the woods. 'Well then, the other possibility that struck us was that the theft of your parish books, plural, points to the murderer being someone with history at Dirleton. To there being something in the books he doesn't want known?'

'The murderer stole them?' Wallace said. 'It makes sense, but what a horrid idea.'

'It doesn't make sense to *me*,' Mrs Wallace said. 'What do you mean, Mrs Gilver?'

I took a hearty bite of shortbread to gain some thinking time. 'My word, this is delicious,' I said. 'I thought my cook made the best Scotch shortbread but this is a poem. Would your cook share her recipe?'

'Surely,' said Mr Wallace, looking amused for some reason. 'She most certainly would.'

'I most certainly will,' said Mrs Wallace. 'It's a simple three, six, nine like any other shortbread. We don't employ a cook on a minister's stipend.'

I gave a small laugh to cover my embarrassment. It was *my* embarrassment alone too. It is nothing these days for a lady to make all the food that comes out of her kitchen, with her own roughened hand. It is an egregious slip for a lady to forget the fact, though. I decided to return to my profession.

'It's something I've learned over years of detecting,' I said. 'One becomes sceptical of coincidences and it would be the most enormous coincidence for two different people to get up to mischief in the church on the same night. It would be an even bigger one for the same person to commit two acts of unrelated mischief. And so, one is forced to conclude that the murderer returned to the church, that the knife in the coffin lid was the knife used during the murder, and the theft of the parish books relates to those two facts somehow. Find the books, I say, and one has found the killer.'

Both Wallaces were gaping at me.

'In fact, if it were anyone else but a very old woman who had both made a point of mentioning the books just before they were stolen *and* reacted with violent distress to the sound of the victim's name, I should think her a very strong suspect.'

'Why?' said Mrs Wallace. 'What would her motive be?'

'That would remain a mystery,' I admitted. 'Besides, she *is* a very old woman and Mr Esslemont was a man in his prime. I can't believe she'd have the strength for it.'

'I don't think we need to consider Mither Gollane's strength or lack of it,' Mr Wallace said. 'Forgive me, I don't mean to take issue with the general rule regarding coincidences that you have formed over years of observation, Mrs Gilver. But there really is a better explanation nearer to hand in this particular case.'

'Oh?' I said. 'What would that be?'

To my great surprise, however, Mr and Mrs Wallace both looked rather . . . the word that sprang to mind was shifty. Mr Wallace even went so far as to clear his throat and cast a spaniel-ish look towards his wife. I knew that look very well. Hugh has been casting it at me for decades, I have seen Donald aim it in Mallory's direction once or twice already and there was no way someone as gormless as Teddy was going to make it to his wedding day without falling back on it too.

'It's up to you then, Mrs Wallace,' I said, earning another flash of that wicked little grin.

'Indeed,' she said. 'Well, Mrs Gilver, the thing is that my husband is a very kind man. He cares a great deal more about people than he does about the rules and regulations of the church, you see.'

'Good for him,' I said. Then, turning: 'Good for you.'

'And he has, over the years, christened many a baby that other ministers wouldn't have. For instance, he doesn't care much about whether a marriage certificate can be produced, do you, dear?'

'Nor would our Lord,' said Mr Wallace, which was even more startling than his wife's revelations. Church of Scotland minsters go in for casual references to the Lord even less than do Church of England vicars and *that* body of men certainly hold to the view that, while He is necessary, He is never to be flaunted.

'And, so you see, there are entries in the parish books that would attract unwelcome interest if anyone were to study them.'

'I *think* I see.'

'And so, if Dirleton were to be catapulted into sudden prominence and the press were to descend, then there might be consequences.'

'But why on earth,' I said, 'would the press – they do descend, I grant you – but why on earth would the press go poking about in the parish books because of a murder?'

'But the prominence we feared wasn't murder,' she said. 'Well, it is now, because of the murder. Or murders. One can hardly believe it! But no, it was the scholars. The writers or whatever they were supposed to be. Last time they were sociologists. They'd have been at the parish books like mice in a corn bin, wouldn't they?'

'The people who were coming to interview the oldest resident?' I said. 'Mither Gollane? I suppose so.'

'Is that what *they* told *her* or what someone told *you*?' said Mrs Wallace and I noticed the minister moving his foot a little to one side and nudging his wife's with it. She dropped her head and took a sip of her coffee.

I regarded both of them. 'I don't suppose there's any chance you'd just tell me what's going on?' I asked.

'If we knew, we most certainly would,' said Mr Wallace.

'Not with Silas's murder,' I said. 'The rest of it.' I waited but they stared back at me implacably. 'Or at least tell me this: have *you* hidden the parish books, Mr Wallace? To keep them out of harm's way?'

'Keep whom?' said Mr Wallace. 'I have no idea who you think might need my protection.'

Mrs Wallace let out a small squeak.

'I meant the books, sir,' I said. 'I meant keep the books out of harm's way. But *what* an interesting assumption on your part, I must say.'

Chapter 12

Alec was so full of his own news that I had not the faintest hope of sharing mine. And mine was the sort of news that had to be shared with the greatest urgency, in that it was not news at all. It was not a fact newly discovered nor an individual finally identified; it was a most delicate and elusive matter, a soap bubble, a trace of scented smoke, to be studied and digested while it lasted, for it was soon to be lost forever and once lost the chances of working out the brand of soap or cigarette were laughable.

Mr Wallace had slipped in his efforts not to tell me something. The slip itself was plain to see, but the hidden thing, the elusive thing, the identity of the "whom" that made Mrs Wallace squeak, that was something I was still carrying across the green like a sleeping baby or a ticking bomb when I saw Alec approaching.

'Dandy!' he shouted, and broke into a trot. 'You won't believe this. Barrow's pal's sister came through for us. I must send her a bunch of— or a box of— or . . . Does one still gives maids lengths of dress fabric?'

'One never did if one had a heart,' I said. 'Just as one never gave quinces or rhubarb from one's garden. I think Barrow's pal's sister would rather have a fiver. She's beginning to sound like Robert Poste's child, by the way. Doesn't she have a name?'

'Do stop wittering.'

'You started it. And I agree. I need to get something off my chest before it vanishes. Help me make sense of this, darling.'

'All in good time,' Alec said. 'I've got news. I found out Silas's connection to Dirleton! Robert Poste's child risked the wrath of the Croys housekeeper and went for a rummage in the business room. Apparently the policemen did most of *their* rummaging in there yesterday.'

'Alec, I've really got something I need to talk you about before I forget it. The Wallaces let something slip.'

'I'll give you three guesses. Come and sit down and apply your brain, Dandy.'

He turned and made for the circular bench under the spreading tree. I followed him, noting, as I plodded along, that the last few wisps of my notion were drifting off into the air above my head.

'Well?' I said, as I joined him.

'Three guesses,' said Alec, again.

'Mistress,' I said first.

'Amazingly, no.'

'Paramour of some other sort,' I guessed next.

Alec snorted.

'Something related to his business?' was my last attempt.

'Not directly,' said Alec. 'Although, without his business, I'm sure it would have proved impractical.'

I considered that at some length. What sort of thing would be made more practical by dint of owning an insurance company? 'Has he been burning down struggling enterprises?' I said.

'What? Good God, Dandy.'

'They do it all the time in Chicago. Well, in pictures about Chicago. Nightclubs burst into flames almost as soon as the

185

accounts book slips into the red. Usually with a plucky cigarette girl trapped inside somewhere.'

'I didn't mean it so literally,' Alec said. 'Merely that, without all the money sloshing around, he wouldn't have been able to manage it so discreetly. Since you've squandered your three guesses, I shall now tell you what it is.'

I waited. Alec filled his pipe, got it lit, sucked and sucked on it until he was all but invisible inside a blue plume, then took it out of his mouth and pointed the stem across the green towards the far corner, jabbing at the gateposts we had walked through to get to Mither Gollane.

'The police and then Flora Poste found the deeds for that,' he said.

'The Archerfield estate?'

'The lodge,' Alec said. 'The lodge where Manie Halliburton lives. It's on the deed as East Gate Cottage. Then there was a deed for another one that I think must be on the green somewhere, since its name is Castle View. And a third that could be anywhere, called Lilac Cottage. And the deed for the post office building as well as the little cottage behind it. And the school. The entire school, Dandy. It's not run by the county council. It's a private enterprise run as a charity by the Halliburtons and managed by Silas.'

'So he was here on a matter of business,' I said. I felt somewhat deflated by this dull news after the big build-up.

'Not the firm, Dandy. Not Silas the boss of an insurance company. Silas the man. He was acting in a personal capacity for the Halliburtons. Or in partnership with them. Even in guise as them.'

'Guise?' I said.

'And guess what else he ran for them.'

'I've had my three guesses,' I said.

186

'This is a new round.'

'The Castle Inn.'

Alec seemed to stiffen and then relax again as I spoke. 'No, well yes, but that's not what I meant,' he said.

'The laundry.'

'That goes without saying.'

Why had he gone so stiff his shoes had squeaked and then relaxed so much his breath had come out in a sigh? I wondered. I took a moment to look around in all directions. There was nothing else down the manse road except the church and no family could own a church and have a friend manage it for them. Although it did occur to me that it might explain the Wallaces being mixed up in all of this somehow. I looked straight ahead and let my eyes travel up the row of houses opposite where we sat. It would not be another cottage, held back to be rolled out like some grand finale. If it was not the pub there was not a great deal left. I looked to the left and let out a cry. 'The castle! Not the Castle Inn. The *castle*!'

'Silas was in possession of the deeds for Dirleton Castle,' said Alec, nodding. For one wild moment, I thought again about Miss Goodfellow. I had heard of gentlemen setting girls up in little flats in London . . . But then I remembered that she was the ward of the Halliburton family. When I started paying attention again, Alec was talking about them too.

'Silas was in a position of great trust with the Halliburtons and had been for almost thirty years, going by the dates on the lawyers' letters. You know how lawyers' letters follow deeds around like chicks after a mother hen.'

'I wonder if Daisy knew.' I cast my mind back to the dim morning in my guest bedroom when Daisy's eyes fluttered open and I told her Silas was dead. 'She said "irl", after all.

Not "Silas" or "dead". She said "irl". We always thought it might have been "Dirleton".'

'And that's how she knew where to set off to, to have it out with him?'

'I suppose so,' I said. 'Although she denies it. She told Grant she thought he was at home.'

Alec opened his mouth to argue but in the end simply stuck his pipe back in and clamped his lips down, nodding. 'Quite right,' he said. 'Let's not allow this monumental discovery simply to lead us back to poor Daisy.'

'Monumental,' I repeated.

I said no more but his shoulders drooped. 'Right again,' he said. 'Our new information tells us nothing about why he died.'

'That's hardly the spirit!' I said. 'Let's at least try. Let's knock on the door of Castle View and find Lilac Cottage and ask the tenants . . . oh I don't know. But find out who they are anyway.'

Alec suddenly sat up very straight. 'I don't think we'll have to ask them anything,' he said. 'I think they will fall into place as soon as we see them.' I frowned, completely puzzled by this. 'Because so far we've got Manie at the lodge and laundry, Miss Meek at the school, Patrick Watson at the post office . . .'

'And Miss Goodfellow at the castle,' I added. 'You're onto something here. Miss Meek knew who the victim was before anyone else. Manie washed him and had a fit when she found out who he was. Patrick Watson reckoned he needed an alibi and Miss Goodfellow, who is not a housekeeper it turns out, nor a maiden aunt within the meaning of the act, but a comely Halliburton ward, just *provided* said alibi, quite off her own bat.'

'Golly,' Alec said. 'To Lilac Cottage then. But first, what was it *you* wanted to talk about, Dandy?'

'Oh, is it time for me now?' I said. 'We're quite done with your news? Very well then: both the Wallaces know more than they should about something or other. They let slip that they know certain individuals who might need protecting. It came up in relation to the missing parish books. There are two missing, by the way.'

'Good grief, the parish books!' Alec said. 'I quite forgot about them. What on earth is going on here, Dandy? Where are the missing writers – or their bodies? Why did someone steal their clothes? And put them on the stone? Why did someone put a knife in the lid of a coffin? That's so ghoulish it's almost ridiculous.'

'And if Lizzy Hogg wasn't in my room, who was? Or, if she was in the church, did she see the man with the knife? Did *he* steal the parish books? Is he connected to Mither Gollane, who is after all the only person apart from the minister and the beadle who seems to care about them?'

'Also why is Silas the villain of the village, the devil incarnate, if all he's doing is taking care of things for these Halliburtons?' Alec added.

'And why on earth would a girl like Maggie Goodfellow blurt out that she spent a night of passion with the postman?'

'*What?*' Alec said.

'Oh yes,' I told him. 'That was the alibi. The one he didn't even need.'

Alec shook his head as though he had water in his ears from diving. 'One thing at a time,' he said. 'Or we shall lose track of all of it.'

'Shouldn't we at least tell the police about the tent pegs?'

Alec did not reply. He had stood and was staring up the green towards the castle, squinting against the pipe smoke. 'Do you know what, Dan?' he said. 'I'm not so sure that little

189

turret is a folly after all. I'm sure I just saw someone moving behind the window.'

'We really must get into the castle soon,' I said. 'I don't understand why these Halliburtons aren't more in evidence. Their business manager is murdered practically on their doorstep and they don't seem to care.'

'The police must have pinned them down, surely, and asked what they needed to ask them.'

'When?' I shot back. 'They discovered the crashed motor car en route home from Croys and we heard where they each went when they got here. One to a farm to fetch a tractor. The other to the minister to see about squeezing more coffins into the church.'

'Perhaps they telephoned,' Alec said. 'Or sent some other man. From Haddingotn.'

'Wicks wouldn't even send a sergeant to the manse,' I reminded him. 'He certainly wouldn't send a common bobby to a castle.'

We stared at one another for a moment or two hoping that one of us would think up a reason to breach the castle wall right now, then both of us gave up with a sigh.

'Right then,' Alec said. 'Lilac Cottage and Castle View.'

'I think we'll find Lizzy Hogg in one or the other,' I said. 'Sgt Dodgson said the Halliburtons had set her up with her own place.'

'Why not let's start right here on this nearest corner?' said Alec. 'Castle View must be in this row and the names are on the gates, which is very obliging.'

It was indeed, and right enough Castle View was halfway along, after Chimneys, Redroofs, and the Laurels, an adorable little dwelling with a round window between its dormers that looked exactly like the button nose on a teddy bear. We entered the gate and crunched up a path of broken shells between neat pocket-handkerchief lawns edged around by bedding and with a standard rose in the centre.

'No way this is Lizzy Hogg's place,' I said, following him.

Alec rattled the polished knocker without pausing. I hoped he had an idea what to say if someone answered, for I had none.

When the door opened, however, we had no need to introduce ourselves, for the person revealed was none other than Nessie Clarkson, dressed in carpet slippers and an apron, with a waft of sweet air from an afternoon's baking billowing out around her.

'Mrs Gilver, Mr Osborne,' she said. 'What brings you to my humble abode? Would you like to come in and have some tea?'

'No, we shan't keep you back,' I said. I could see Alec's face fall, out of the corner of my eye, but I did not turn his way. 'We wanted to talk to you about your landlord. Or his manager anyway. Your tenancy,' I went on. 'Here at Castle View.'

'My tenancy?' said Miss Clarkson. 'I thought you were detectives. Has the factor sent you? My rent's up to date no matter what he might have said.'

'Who *is* the factor?' said Alec. I nodded. If she meant Silas it was most odd of her to refer to him as though he had not just been murdered. If it was some other man, then we needed to hear his name. He would know more of Silas's Dirleton doings than anyone barring the Halliburtons themselves.

'But don't you know?' said Miss Clarkson. 'If you're asking questions on his behalf?'

'Not his behalf,' Alec said next. 'The Halliburtons' behalf.'

'The Halliburtons?' said Miss Clarkson. 'But they don't

concern themselves with small fry like my cottage rent. Why would they?'

'The truth is,' I said, feeling Nanny Palmer turn in her grave, 'that we've taken to Dirleton, haven't we Alec? And we heard there was a chance of some nice little lots coming vacant. Not this place, necessarily, but in general. Is Dirleton the kind of place where freeholds come up for sale often? Do you happen to know?'

Miss Clarkson frowned in evident puzzlement. 'You've "taken" to Dirleton?' she said. 'Yesterday and today?'

'To invest, Miss Clarkson,' Alec said. 'Not to live here.'

This affronted the Dirleton resident as much as anything so offensive might be expected to, but she tried to hide her umbrage under a deluge of information.

'I wouldn't have thought so,' she said. 'You'd better off in town if you're looking for anything like that. Not but what you could probably buy a field or two from a farmer and start up yet another golf course. There doesn't seem to be any limit on them. It's not like rival tea shops, so it seems. But no, Dirleton's never been a place that's attracted . . . speculators. I'm at a loss as to why you would ever think so.'

'Well, I can't say I'm not disappointed,' I said. 'But I suppose it was rather a lot to hope for. Why would a place like Dirleton have the capacity to soak up a lot of incomers?'

At that – which was no more than an inane remark intended to ease the transition between the conversation proper and the start of our goodbyes – I noticed a very curious thing. Miss Clarkson stuck out her bottom lip and extended it over her top one. At the same time, she laid one of her forefingers across her brow and drew it upwards towards the row of flat curls that paraded along her hairline. Miss Clarkson, in other words, had suddenly broken out in a fit of perspiration. Interesting.

'Well, we'd better be off,' I said, ignoring Alec's murderous look. 'We have an appointment at Lilac Cottage. Would you point us in the right direction?'

Miss Clarkson gave a startled look and waved us vaguely east with one hand while with the other she all but slammed the door.

'What the devil?' Alec hissed at me as we were halfway back down the path. 'Didn't you smell the baking?'

'Didn't *you* see her trying to hide the fact that she had broken out in a muck sweat?' I retorted.

'No but that's another reason we should have stayed and tried to winkle out what we could.'

'About incomers,' I said. 'It always makes people irritable but doesn't usually discommode them to that extent. It's very odd. I wonder if it's anything to do with the nameless "them" that the Wallaces let slip.'

'Wondering will have to do you,' said Alec, 'since you've left the field.'

'Oh for heaven's sake,' I shot back. 'I'll buy you a bun at the tea shop en route to Lilac Cottage. Will that do *you*? Although how you can want anything else more than you want to find the last piece to complete the puzzle, I have no idea.'

'If you're going to rush off like that without even speaking to whoever it is,' Alec grumbled. 'The puzzle isn't ever going to *be* complete.'

'We didn't need to speak to her any more, Alec. We confirmed, by merely looking at her, that yet another Dirletonite behaving very oddly is a Halliburton tenant. If you remember our last encounter with Nessie Clarkson before this one, she couldn't say enough about the creeping stranger she's supposed to have spotted on Saturday night, the one she failed to mention until she found out the victim's name.'

'Wasn't it when she found out the witness's name?' Alec said. 'When she found it was only Lizzy Hogg who pinned the time of death?

'Now we discover,' I went on, ignoring him, 'that she doesn't know the name of her own cottage's *factor*, if you believe that.'

'And that's not all,' Alec said, forgetting about buns, for a wonder. 'Her eyes flashed when you said "Lilac Cottage". You're right, Dandy. We need to get there right now.'

Unfortunately for Alec's sweet tooth and unfillable middle, we did not make it as far as the tea shop, for a little farther along the same street, just as the green ended, we passed Poppy Cottage, Primrose Cottage and Snowdrop Cottage one after the other, putting us in high hopes of Lilac too. With another step, we were upon it. The sign on the gate picked out the name in pokerwork and I supposed that the bunches of grapes at each corner of the plaque were in fact supposed to be lilacs. There were certainly lilac bushes on either side of the gateposts, neglected and straggling although still putting out a fair display of blooms. I drank in their sweetness as I brushed past them on my way to the door.

The little garden was overgrown with groundsel and couch grass, the patches of lawn choked with dandelions. And the cottage windows stared blankly at us, devoid of curtains, clouded over with dust and cobwebs. I lifted the knocker but did not hold out much hope when I heard the sound echo through what was surely an empty house behind the front door.

'Lizzy Hogg, do we think?' I said.

'I don't,' Alec said. 'And Silas, or whoever takes over from him, needs a kick in the trousers. This is a perfectly nice little cottage and it has clearly been lying empty for months.'

194

'Telling me!' The voice made both of us jump and we turned in time to see the nearest section of hedge shake and rustle and eventually produce a short woman of advanced years peering through at us from the garden next door. 'But it's not months, let me tell you!' she went on. 'It's well over a decade since she was putten out, the last one, and it's lain there empty all this time, weed seeds blowing over to my Bert's pride and joy of a cabbage patch round the back and they creeping weeds slinking under this hedge to ruin my flowers. You've made my day if you're moving in, the pair of you.' She gave us a look up and down and nodded. 'You look respectable enough and too old for screaming bairns. So, as long as you've no gramophone, and you keep the common chimney swept and *you* don't come in with a skinful and start shouting the odds on a Friday night, mister, I daresay we'll all get on fine. I'm not one for having neighbours in and out but I won't see you short if you've a true need for anything.'

With one last speculative look and another firm nod, she withdrew, just as Alec and I each lost control of our expressions and began to laugh as silently as we could manage with hands clamped to mouths.

'Oh dear, oh dear,' I said at last. 'I don't know whether to be flattered or appalled.'

'I'm appalled on your behalf,' said Alec. 'Too old for screaming bairns indeed! And you don't look at all like the kind of slattern who would let her chimney clog up with creosote until it caught fire.'

'No more do you look the sort to come rolling in at closing time and knock me about by way of a nightcap,' I assured him. Then I nudged him as the hedge started to rustle again.

'Are you going to stand there all day?' the head in the hedge demanded. 'This is a respectable row. None of us stands gossiping out the front for all the world to see. There's a back garden and a gate to the lane. You've no need to be making a show of us all.'

'We ahhh . . . we don't have the key, Mrs . . .' I said. 'We came to get the lie of the land before we committed ourselves as far as a formal viewing.'

'Spring,' said the head. 'Mr and Mrs Albert Spring. And never mind the mess, for it'll soon be swept and scrubbed. You don't look a stranger to hard work, missus. Or I can give you a hand if you provide the soap. Just as quick as my Bert can lend you tools till you've got the garden sorted, mister. You'll not have been used to a garden wherever it is you've come from. Here.'

Her head disappeared and in its place came a work-weathered reddish fist clutching a large key with a bit of pink tape tied to it to make a handle.

Alec looked at me, I shrugged, and he stepped forward to take the offered gift.

Once we were inside, we let the laughter go again. 'What is it about us that says we've only ever run to a flat?' I said. 'I'd jolly well like to know why Mrs Spring is so sure you don't have your own fork and spade!'

'I'd like to know what you think we're going to learn about the dead agent of a philanthropic landlord from looking around an empty house,' Alec said.

'Beyond the puzzle of why it's empty?' I said. 'It would be snapped up at Gilverton.'

'And Dunelgar.'

For it was indeed a snug little place. The front door opened straight into the only living room and the staircase led off this chamber too, but it was a large square place and would be light if its window were washed. The kitchen behind was just as big, with a small range and a commodious sink too, since there seemed to be no scullery. The window here looked out over a back garden so long I could not see its far end.

The mystery of the evicted tenant grew as we peered about the place. For while there was thick dust and grime over everything, even mouse droppings here and there, it was obvious that there had been no neglect while the cottage was lived in. The dust brushed off the range at a breath, showing burnished metal and polished blacking underneath, and the sturdy china sink was free of all stains although choked with cobwebs these days.

Upstairs there were two bedrooms tucked into the eaves, the big one to the front showing a scrape on its wallpaper where a headboard had sat when the place was furnished, and the small back bedroom still containing a row of three beds that made me think of Goldilocks, since one was full-sized though narrow, one was short and low to the ground and one was no more than a crib with side railings and a painting of a lamb on the footboard.

'Good heavens,' I said. 'I don't like to think that Silas had a hand in putting a family out into the cold.'

'When they'd been used to rather a snug little life,' Alec said. 'This is a bathroom in here, Dandy. A bathroom with running water.'

I popped my head around the door and marvelled at the little bathtub on its fat legs and the deep basin with its dusty taps. Alec went right inside and stood at the sink, staring out of the window. He half-turned and beckoned me to stand beside him.

I scoured a clean patch in the dust on the window and looked out at the wreckage of what must once have been a neat cottage garden, but was now overgrown with ivy and brambles, the various benches and barrows no more than hummocks under the vegetation. I glanced at Alec to see what was consuming him so about this scene and that was when, out of the corner of my eye, I saw it too.

'Is that what it looks like?' I said. 'There? And there?'

'I think so,' Alec said. 'Let's go down and see.'

Chapter 13

One could be forgiven for shuddering a little in a graveyard at midnight but there is nothing inherently spooky about an overgrown garden on a spring afternoon, so I was disappointed with myself when I felt my legs tremble upon opening the back door out of the kitchen and battling my way along the choked path into the belly of the garden at Lilac Cottage.

'They look a little too real for my liking,' Alec said. 'In fact, this whole place is giving me the willies.'

'But we're right, aren't we?' I said. I buttoned my glove tightly around my coat cuff and, thus proof against the thorns to some extent, plunged my hand into the thickest part of an unearthly lump looking for all the world like a woman in a hooded cape. Sure enough, under all the brambles and briars, there was a framework of woven willow.

'These little walls aren't walls either,' Alec said, kicking at a sort of kerb and then struggling to free his trousers from the clutch of the rose runners that snagged him. 'They are those midget hurdles. All round the beds, just like she's got at the new place. And look!'

I raised my head and followed his finger. It had been hidden from upstairs by the shade of a big old apple tree but now we could see at the foot of the garden another of the elaborate henhouses, complete with stairways and ramps all around it.

'So this was Mither Gollane's cottage,' I said.

'No doubt about it.'

'From which Silas put her out. And now she lives in a hovel. And he didn't even re-let it. No wonder she thinks he's the devil.'

'And so she killed him?' said Alec. 'Stronger than she looks perhaps?'

'Which would mean the case is closed,' I said.

'Hardly,' Alec said. 'What about McEwan and Crabbie?'

'They were coming to see her.'

'To add to the fame she enjoys. Why would she kill *them*?'

'Again though, rather her than anyone else. And remember, Alec, she knew right away that we were not the writers, didn't she? If she'd killed them, that makes perfect sense.'

'Yes, that was the work of a sharp mind. And wreaking revenge on Silas for chucking her out of her house is rather sane,' Alec said. 'Doing it the way she did, with the tent pegs and the wire, is the work of a meticulous planner. In contrast, the story of being over a hundred with nine children is quite mad.'

'And so she steals the parish books that would prove she's lying about it,' I said. 'Look, I know there are things we can't account for but Mither Gollane has a motive for Silas, a motive for the theft and at the very least a connection to the writers, which is more than we can say for anyone else.'

'But it was a man who killed Silas. Remember that, Dandy.'

'It was a woman first,' I reminded him. 'According to Lizzy Hogg. Then it was a man according to Miss Clarkson and Manie. It might change back again if we're lucky.'

'Let's at least confirm with Mrs Spring next door that Mither Gollane lived here,' Alec said. 'Perhaps these outlandish garden fixtures are a local tradition. How many gardens have we seen here after all?'

He had a point and so we made our way back through the house, down the path, up the next, and knocked.

'We would like to speak to the last tenant,' Alec said. 'To ask about the chimney and the boiler and suchlike.'

'Jessie Laird?' said Mrs Spring. 'You'll have a job.'

'The last tenant was Jessie Laird?' said Alec, seemingly stricken by the swift collapse of our new theory. He must have liked it more than he had let on.

'Aye, what of it?' said Mrs Spring.

'Nothing at all,' Alec said, recovering quickly enough. 'We thought we recognised the . . . willow work. But if it was this Mrs Laird who did it . . .'

'Oh no, that's not her handiwork,' Mrs Spring said. 'That would be too heavy a job for Jessie even when she lived here. That was somebody else did that. I don't just mind who now. One of them or the other.'

'One of whom?' I asked.

The neighbour's face stilled until it looked like a sculpture in bas relief. Then, as suddenly as the look had appeared, it vanished. 'I'm not one to gossip,' she said and slammed the door. We had had all we were going to get from her. My shoulders slumped, as I daresay Alec's did too.

'That keeps happening,' I said, staring at the door. 'The most innocuous question or mild remark keeps making people faint, or flounce off, or start ranting about the devil.'

'Once,' Alec said, 'it was us claiming to be a pair of writers come to town. No, not Mither Gollane refusing to believe it, before you shout me down. This was someone else poleaxed by our announcement.'

'You're right,' I said. 'There *was* someone. But who? Who was it who looked just about ready to swallow his tongue when we said we were writers?'

Alec squeezed his eyes shut and held his breath for so long I quite expected him to change colour as Donald and Teddy did when they were small and went through a phase of finding it the greatest fun. 'No idea,' he said. 'Can't remember. This case is maddening.'

'Uff,' I said. 'Perhaps the police have solved the whole thing without us. And we can go home.'

They had not. If anything, the case had twisted itself even tighter. And the constabulary had swelled to full strength: to wit, Inspector Ramsay was back from his holidays, still in his fishing hat and oilskin coat and rather redolent of the river. He, Constable McLean, Sgt Dodgson and Captain Wicks were all waiting for us in the bar parlour at the inn; Wicks looking gormless, the sergeant looking uncomfortable, the inspector looking beside himself with fury, and Constable McLean doing his best to look invisible.

'We need to talk to you both about this nonsense with the clothes,' Ramsay said, shooting a filthy look at Dodgson, presumably for taking them back from me and not arresting me on the spot. 'And the trick you pulled about who you were.'

'Steady on,' said Captain Wicks. 'Although actually, yes we do need to have a bit of a chat, it's true. We don't quite have a handle on exactly what's happening. Yet,' he added, as the inspector glared in his direction.

'Have you found the bodies?' Alec said. 'Do you need our fingerprints? I assure you we had nothing to do with the murder. Either murder. Any murder.'

'Bodies!' Ramsay spat. 'Murder!'

'You sound oddly scathing, Inspector,' I said.

'There *are* no bodies,' he told me through clenched teeth.

'There was no murder. There are no such people as Crabbie and McEwan, as you two clowns well know.'

'My good man!' said Wicks.

'What are you talking about?' Alec said.

'It was pig's blood,' said Captain Wicks. 'George McAdams, the butcher from Gullane, reported a break-in in his back shop and the theft of two buckets of pig's blood he meant to use for black pudding.'

'And Mrs Keith from Marmion reported the theft of her car,' added Sgt Dodgson.

'And Mr and Mrs Curr,' piped up Constable McLean, not to be left out of things. 'They reported that a great quantity of their clothes had been spirited away from the attic where they were packed in two suitcases, seeing as they were out of season.'

'But there was a name tag,' Alec said.

'In one hat!' cried Ramsay. 'And it was not a name tag. It was no more than a piece of tape with a name printed in ordinary ink. The work of a moment. Only a fool would fall for it.' The look he turned on Dodgson would have felled a lesser man.

'You're in good company, Sergeant,' Alec said. 'It fooled Mrs Gilver and me.'

'Did it?' said Ramsay. 'Did it indeed?'

I could tell he meant to make some very sharp point but it was lost on me. 'Can we help you with something, Inspector?' I said. I have often found that very innocent phrasing and a light tone can cause the already furious to become quite gratifyingly enraged and such was the case now. Inspector Ramsay turned mottled as well as purple and when he spoke he reminded me a little of a spluttering kettle left on the hob to boil dry and explode.

'Help? Help, she says! I should blo— dam— dashed well think you *can* help. Because here you are. You turn up. You're not who you pretend to be. You're here, there and everywhere doing God— hel— goodness knows what for a night and a day. Up and about in the wee small hours by your own admission – thinking you're so clever-clever. And what do you know? There's cars and clothes and buckets of blood going missing like never before in Dirleton, when you two hadn't set foot here.'

I did not set out specifically to rile the man but this was a preposterous suggestion and I am only human, so I am afraid that I exploded with laughter, which set Alec off too. 'Oh my dear inspector,' he said, when he had caught his breath, 'let us know *when* the blood was pinched and the car snatched and the clothes purloined and I'm sure Mrs Gilver and I can furnish you with an alibi for at least some of the shenanigans. As you say yourself, we've been getting about a bit since we arrived and there are plenty of witnesses to our movements. Dear me, how you do entertain yourself here in Dirleton.'

With that, we made an enemy for life. The inspector stood, righted his coat with a few sharp tugs and marched out, banging the door behind him. Dodgson lifted his eyebrows and explored his cheek with the tip of his tongue and Captain Wicks nodded gravely and let an enormous breath go. Constable McLean was doing his level best not to laugh.

'The thing is, you see,' Wicks said, 'this is all rather Dickson Carr for East Lothian and we are stumped. Of course, what we should do is call for help from Edinburgh. Or even Glasgow.' He paused to let that settle without capsizing his little ship. 'But I rather wondered if perhaps . . . Well, not to put too fine a point on it, if you two were to . . . I mean, I take it Mrs Esslemont hasn't formally employed you since she's unconscious, so it's not as if you'd be serving two masters. And then you wouldn't be the sort to tell any of the press johnnies or anything. Or perhaps we could decide to *agree* on that even.'

Dodgson was regarding his superior officer with a detached interest, rather as one watches a wasp trying to clamber back out of a jam jar, sticky and hopeless. Alec's face was stony. He was determined to listen to the poor man ramble for as long as he might need to, to reach the point. I, in contrast, took pity.

'You mean, you'd like us to act as consultants to the constabulary and quietly solve the murder, Captain Wicks? On the understanding that we keep it under wraps and let the inspector take the credit?'

'There might be a stipend,' Wicks said. 'I'd have to get my secretary to look into whether there's a budget we can bend to that sort of ad-hoc kind of a short-term understanding.'

'No need, sir,' I said. 'Mr Osborne and I were drafted as special constables during the strike of 1926 and our orders were never rescinded. We don't need to be consultants bothering any of your budgets. We can be seconded from Edinburgh for the usual daily wage.'

'What *is* the usual daily wage?' Alec said.

'It wouldn't keep you in port,' said Sgt Dodgson. Then, at a look from Wicks, he muttered a hasty apology.

'Right then,' I said. I get terribly hearty sometimes when there is much to be done. My mother would faint if she could hear me. 'We have a great deal of disorganised information to sort through and are in dire need of a plan of attack.'

'But first we must brief you,' said Wicks.

'Well,' said Alec. 'We know who died and when and how. And we know about the car and the clothes and the blood.

We know about the stuffed dummy on the stone and the knife in the coffin lid. We know at least one man who lives alone has an alibi. And we know about the booby trap over which Silas tripped to hit the stone. Now I come to think of it, I don't believe *you* knew about that, did you?'

Dodgson shook his head and Wicks simply looked bewildered.

'We also have a suspect,' Alec said. 'One we thought fitted Silas's murder nicely and did not fit Crabbie and McEwan very well at all. With them cut out of the picture, we might have a solution.'

'What we still don't know is why Silas would have rushed down here when summoned by that suspect,' I said. 'The letter was rather cryptic.'

'And also,' Alec added, 'that suspect had nothing to gain from the rigmarole with the blood and the clothes.'

'Alibi?' I said. 'Misdirection? Warning? Who can say?'

'Not I,' said Wicks. 'I'm barely keeping up with the summary. I'm not much of a one for puzzles, to be frank. I'm better on the parade ground. Isn't that right, Dodgson?'

'I wouldn't like to— Yes,' Dodgson said, with an air of being so far off the usual track that it made no odds anymore.

'Fear not, Captain Wicks,' I said. 'And thank you for your trust. I think we can take it from here. We would like to *see* the letter, however, if it can be arranged.'

'Ah, the letter,' said Wicks. 'We ah . . . Well, the thing is, you see, that we ah . . . brought it with us, didn't we, Sergeant. To . . . Well, as a . . .'

'To wave in front of our noses like a cloth at a drag hunt?' Alec said.

'Couldn't put it better myself, Osborne,' Wicks said. 'Constable?'

McLean was rummaging in his uniform pocket and he soon produced an envelope and handed it to Alec. 'It's been dusted,' he said. 'All manner of prints. I think every postie from here to Perth must have handled it.'

'Excellent,' Wicks said. 'Sgt Dodgson, I'll leave it for Constable McLean and you to soothe the Currs, Mrs Keith and the butcher. And Inspector Ramsay can busy himself with the missing parish books or take over that bit of poaching at Archerfield, as he sees fit.'

'I think the parish books fall under our remit, Wicks,' said Alec.

'Poachers it is, for Ramsay then,' he said. 'And I'd better hurry off too.' He stood, bowed to me, did an odd sort of semi-salute to Alec and left the room.

'He's got a tee-time, I bet,' said Sgt Dodgson. 'Only reason he took the job, or so I've heard.'

'Oh is that how it is, now that we're fellow officers?' I said. 'Gossip about the bosses, is it?' This earned another smile and eased us into our goodbyes and our separate tracks to our allotted tasks.

At least, Alec and I got as far as stepping outside onto the gravel and then paused for pipe and cigarette, both of us much in need of bolstering.

'You know what keeps tripping me up in this case, Dandy?' Alec said, from inside a blue cloud, once he had got the thing going. 'The question of who knows what. And how they find out what they know. I can't see the . . . connections. It was what you said about fellow officers gossiping that got the problem to the front of my mind. Do you understand what I'm getting at?'

'I do,' I said. 'I do and I agree. Yes, there are police, villagers overall, workers in the inn, church people . . . as one would

207

expect. But I keep getting the sense of . . . oh it's impossible to describe. I really do know though.'

'And another thing,' Alec said. 'We're used to people hiding what they know. That's inevitable around a murder. But, this time, people seem to know what they should not, or know odd scraps without knowing the whole. Or they don't seem to know what they know.'

'Oh well, that's Scotland for you, isn't it?' I said. 'It's worked very nicely for a thousand years. That way of knowing without quite knowing. It allows the likes of Mither Gollane to live a stone's throw from the church without Mr Wallace feeling the need to scold her.'

'And speaking of Mither Gollane then,' Alec said.

'Indeed,' I answered, suppressing a sigh. I dropped my cigarette and stubbed it out with my toe. 'She's neck-deep in this somehow or another. She mentions parish books and pouf! Parish books disappear. She mentions writers coming to interview her and pouf! Outlandish nonsense concerning said writers. And even if Silas didn't evict her he must have done something. Don't forget she called him the devil.'

'Not quite,' said Alec. 'If you remember. And besides, Manie Halliburton fainted and Lizzy Hogg didn't take news of him in her stride either. Mither Gollane has slipped down the rankings for me. I can't disregard her age and stature.'

'One doesn't have to be tall to hit a man on the head once he's tripped over your booby trap and is lying on the ground,' I said. Alec did not answer. 'What do *you* think is our next task then?'

Still he said nothing. Instead, he took the letter out of its envelope and unfolded it. 'Come to me,' he read. 'One you have wronged.'

I walked over to see the thing for myself. 'That doesn't look like the hand of an ancient person,' I said. 'It's not spidery enough. The handwriting of the elderly is never so . . .'

'Muscular,' Alec said.

'Confident, anyway.'

'Well then, I'm for the castle, at long last,' Alec said. I gave him an enquiring look. 'Because I've just thought of something. We already agreed that "one you have wronged" would most likely be a girl, didn't we? And we can't deny that "come to me" would bring Silas running to a girl as to no one else.' I nodded. 'And you concluded separately that Miss Goodfellow was the most likely recipient of Silas's affections.'

'More or less,' I said. 'More after I'd met her. She's rather lovely.'

'Well consider this,' Alec said. 'Perhaps Miss Goodfellow didn't claim the tryst with the postman to give *him* an alibi. Perhaps she did it to cover her own doings. That would be a very "confident" move, would it not?'

'Do we believe in graphology now?' I said. 'Isn't it as discredited as phrenology in these modern days?'

Alec shrugged and, as his shoulders dropped, his nose screwed up. 'Besides,' he said, 'I'm reminded yet again that the murderer is a man.'

'No, Alec,' I said. 'We can't simply swallow that bit of the tale. Miss Clarkson and Manie Halliburton say they saw a man skulking about. Only Lizzy Hogg claims to have witnessed the murder itself. And we know there was a man skulking about, don't we? Silas was skulking about. It makes much more sense that Manie and Nessie saw Silas and Lizzy did indeed see the woman who killed him.'

'But the man they saw was taller and thinner than Silas,' Alec said. 'Don't forget that Manie actually laid him out, Dan.'

I shook my head. 'I'm not sure I believe in the tallness

209

and thinness,' I said. 'It was the willow figures in the garden that suddenly made me question it. They looked squat and dumpy, viewed from the bathroom window, but enormous on the ground.'

'I don't follow,' Alec said.

'Similarly – well, in sharp contrast, actually – a man seen from afar on a moonlit night, with his shadow thrown onto the ground and yawning out behind him . . . Wouldn't he inevitably look like a daddy-long-legs?'

'Hm,' was all Alec said. He makes much shorter shrift of my theories than I of his.

'What?' I asked, crossly.

'Well, our objection to Miss Goodfellow giving Mr Watson an alibi holds good for an alibi of her own,' Alec said. 'That ostentatious tale of a night with the postman raised suspicion rather than allaying it. If she spent the night with Silas, all she had to do was keep her mouth shut and we would never have given her a moment's thought.'

'And anyway,' I said, 'could Silas really have fallen so far from decent behaviour that he would seduce Halliburton's ward? A man who trusted him so completely?'

'Fallen?' Alec said. 'Might I remind you how many years back it was that he seduced a young girl who was a guest in his own house? He had nowhere to fall. He only had to keep going along at the level he'd already sunk to.'

'Ugh,' I said. 'Well, let's go to the castle and have you meet the girl anyway. Besides, I want to look at some flowers. I need some respite from all this darkness and debauchery.'

Cloaked in the rectitude of Wicks's blessing, for no one else needed to know we were only feeling nosy, we left the inn and made our way for the third time to the gate in the castle walls.

There was a much better view of it all today, in the fine weather. We took the other path, away from the bowling green and the roses, past a pair of impressive herbaceous borders flanking a long lawn, with a gravel path around the edge, encroached upon by yet more determined-looking planting.

'I must divide my irises soon,' Alec said.

'It pains me to hear you speak that way,' I said. 'You are still a young man. You shouldn't know how to propagate rhizomes.'

Alec chose a path leading to a gloomy stand of cypresses, which shadowed a little knot garden, no doubt making the gardeners' lives a burden every spring. This year at least they had gone for those monstrous fleshy begonias, briefly acceptable this early in the season until the greenfly struck, after which they would be revolting. Skirting them and the bowling club clubhouse, and passing a few more scattered trees, we were brought inexorably to the castle itself, looking less like a toad or an ogre from this corner, from where we could see that it was well kitted out with the usual array of towers and the like.

'Where's the door?' Alec said, for the castle grew up out of such a rugged outcropping of solid rock that the lowest course of builder's stone was quite twenty feet above our heads. We set out clockwise around it, slogging our way past centuries' worth of new wings and ranges and then on past a courtyard until finally, almost back where we had started and almost five minutes later, we found ourselves on a natural rise that met one end of a drawbridge. It had been buttressed and made permanent with a substructure like that of a pier, and so practically begged us to walk over.

'Do these tickets buy us entry to the hall and battlements, do you suppose?' Alec said.

211

'One way to find out,' I replied. I set off across the bridge and in under an imposing arch leading to the keep. Most of the place was in ruins; that was clear immediately. There was, however, a section straight ahead where the windows were glazed and the doors were painted and smoke puffed cheerily out of a high chimney. If our sixpenny tickets entitled us to tramp around anywhere it was most assuredly not there. Accordingly we turned our feet towards the ancient remains.

'Should we have bought a leaflet?' Alec said. 'It's rather hard to make head or tail of it without help.'

'Speak for yourself,' I said. 'Between all my years in Scotland and the boys' enthusiasms when they were little, I have not the slightest trouble in tracing the history of the place from the stones that are left. Weren't you mad for castles when you were small?'

'Ships,' said Alec. 'I could get work as a guide on board the *Victory*. But search me about all this lot.'

'Ahem,' said a voice from behind us. We wheeled around to see Miss Maggie Goodfellow, dressed in a skirt and jersey, with a tea towel tucked into her waistband, and carrying an enamel bowl full of potato peelings on one hip.

'Mrs Gilver,' she said. 'What can I do for you today?' She gave me an arch look and carried on. 'If it's eggs you're after then your timing is impeccable. I'm just taking these scraps to the hens, so I can easily have a rootle while I'm there.'

Alec held up his ticket.

'Ah,' Miss Goodfellow said. 'I see. I take it you're the famous Mr Osborne? Well, you know. Wars, sieges, Cromwell, taxes, ruin. Have you seen the doocot? It *is* interesting. You should definitely stop off there on the way out. There aren't pigeons these days so you needn't fear for your hat.'

'Why don't you keep pigeons if you're so well served for a dovecote?' I said.

'I can't bring myself to wring their necks,' said Miss Goodfellow. 'They are such cosy, homely little birds, burbling away like old ladies at a tea. It's all I can do to put a chicken in the pot when it stops laying and they are the devil's own fiends.' She looked down at her basin. 'Speaking of which.'

'Miss Goodfellow,' I said. 'One minute, if your flock can wait for their peelings.'

She raised her chin as if to say, do your worst.

'We heard almost as soon as we arrived that the Halliburtons own this place. The castle, I mean. And you were referred to as their ward.'

'Was I indeed?' she said. 'How did that come up if it's not too forward of me to ask?'

I was determined not to flush. Of course it was monstrous cheek to have told her we had gossiped about her but we had a job to do and, by volunteering Paddy Watson's alibi, she had put herself in our sights. 'Mr Wallace mentioned it. I would very much like to meet them.'

'The Wallaces?' she said. 'They should be at the manse or out about the parish. Yesterday I would have said try the church.'

I was almost sure she was being disingenuous.

'The Halliburtons,' Alec said gently.

'Ah,' said Miss Goodfellow. 'I'm afraid the Halliburtons aren't at home at the moment. They're very rarely at home, in fact.'

'Will they be back this evening?'

'Oh! No. That's not what— They're in . . . Florence.'

'They'd better think about coming back,' I said. 'Or at least getting themselves to France.'

Miss Goodfellow frowned at me and then raised her eyebrows until her brow wrinkled like a ploughed field. She let a noisy breath go. 'I suppose so,' she said. 'Perhaps they'd better go to London. Or America. They've never been to America.'

Alec was frowning as hard as was I, now. She spoke as if she had the command of them, these people who had taken her in and still provided her with a comfortable home. 'So it's a Mr and Mrs Halliburton?' he said.

'My godfather and godmother,' she agreed. 'Although I was brought up by my nanny and didn't see much of them. They are great travellers.'

'So it seems,' I said. 'And you think they might journey to America in advance of what's coming?' Of course, they would not be alone. A number of our friends had started making noises. 'Might we have an address for them to catch them before they go?'

'Why?' she said, sharply.

'We would like to ask them about Mr Esslemont.'

Miss Goodfellow stilled and regarded Alec for a good long while before she answered. 'The murdered man? What would make you think he knew the Halliburtons?'

'Some documentary evidence has come to light,' I said. 'Rather a strange business arrangement.'

'And as well as that,' said Alec, 'we are at a loss otherwise to account for what he was doing here. There aren't any other people he could have come to stay with.'

Miss Goodfellow gave a twist of a smile at that. 'There are hundreds of people in this village, Mr Osborne. Cottages and farmhouses.'

Alec refused to rise to the bait. 'Are you saying Mr Esslemont subscribed to the philosophy that we're all

Jock Tamson's bairns? Or that *you* do and think he ought?' His tone was teasing, but the question was a sensible one.

'I?' she said, pressing her free hand against her chest. 'Do you suspect me of Bolshevism, Mr Osborne?'

'Bolshevism?' said Alec.

'Because we don't get much of that in Dirleton. You could try Haddington perhaps.'

Alec gave a guffaw that was made up of as much surprise as amusement. Miss Goodfellow kept a good poker face, hitched the basin of scraps higher on her hip and walked away. 'But truly,' she said over one shoulder, 'do take a minute to look at the doocot. We're very proud of it.'

Alec watched her go and I found myself following her with my eyes too: the swing of her everyday skirt, the confident way she planted her sturdily shod feet down on the uneven ground, the set of her head on her long neck. If the basin of scraps had been a little dog or a basket of flowers she would have looked quite the picture.

'Shall we then?' Alec said. 'Should we?'

I shrugged, then followed him back over the drawbridge and gazed about.

'Is that it?' Alec said, pointing at the little round tower set into the castle wall. It had an outside staircase leading up from the garden and a door that stood open.

'I suppose so,' I said. 'I can't imagine what's so special about it but perhaps, if we think about something else for a while, enlightenment will come.'

Accordingly, we made our way down the gravel walk at the edge of the herbaceous borders until we arrived at the base of the turret. It seemed to be made of two rooms, one on top of the other, and had more arched and leaded windows looking over the garden besides the one facing the leaping stone.

'Shall we go in?' Alec said. 'We did spend sixpence each.'

I led the way up the wooden stairs and along a little balcony to enter by the top door. Then I stopped. 'Oh!' I said. For what lay inside the door was not a dovecote at all, or if it ever had been then it was long ago. These days it was a tiny round cottage room, with a fireplace, a divan and a writing desk.

'I think someone lives here, Alec,' I said. 'There's a nightie peeping from under that pillow.'

Alec was exploring the far side of the round oom where, behind a false wall, a staircase led to the room below. He went down a few steps. 'Yes,' he said. 'That's a kitchen and the fire's lit.'

Turning, I faced out of the window we had seen and, as suspected, was granted a full view of the stone.

'I bet this is Lizzy Hogg's,' I said. 'Dodgson told me the Halliburtons had given her "a little place of her own" and Mr Wallace said she spent most of her time at the castle. And then she *did* claim to have seen Silas's murder. It would make sense if it was this window she saw it out of.'

'I don't see Miss Hogg as being in need of a writing desk though,' Alec said walking over to it. 'Or reading enormous volumes of—' His silence crackled and I turned to see what had struck him dumb. He was holding open one of two large calf- and buckram-bound books, staring at it.

'What—?' I said, then the light dawned upon me. 'Oh my good Lord! The parish books? Are those the missing parish books, Alec?'

'The very same,' he said. 'Of course. Of course they are. She said she was in the church the night they went missing, so of course she took them!'

'And what exactly did she take?' I asked. 'Two at random,

216

or the one Mither Gollane bade us look in to confirm her century?'

'Ummm,' Alec said, peering at the lettering on the bindings. 'This one is . . . it's rather faded. Huh, 1599 to 1653. Good grief. And this other one is 1915— It's the one that's still being filled. Make sense of that if you can.'

'I can't,' I said. 'It looks as if she simply grabbed a pair.'

'They make a fair old armload,' Alec said, picking them up and juggling them in a leaden sort of way, trying to discover how best to carry them. 'They weigh a ton, Dandy.'

'I'll take one if you can manage the other and the doors,' I said. 'Straight back to the church? Or over to the boys in blue?'

'Neither,' Alec said. 'Or rater, we *are* the boys in blue and I think we should keep them.'

'Alec, we have a murder to solve!'

'And these books were mentioned several times by an old woman who definitely knows something about the victim, and stolen by a young woman who claims to have witnessed him being killed.'

'When you put it like that,' I said. I looked around myself. 'But dare we?'

In answer, Alec stepped over to the window facing the green and looked in either direction. 'Nice and quiet,' he said. 'Good. Your room or mine?'

Chapter 14

We left the little round room looking just about as conspicuous as we could, with our cumbersome burdens. 'Oh look,' I said, from the vantage point conferred by standing on the balcony, 'a dovecote.'

It was there on the hill beyond the castle, an enormous thing the shape of a beehive.

'Miss Goodfellow might have waved an arm in that general direction,' Alec said. 'That would have been helpful.' He paused. 'I say, Dan.'

'Indeed,' I agreed. 'Did she, in fact, wave an arm in *this* general direction? I'm trying to remember. Did she mean us to mistake this place for the dovecote and come here? Did she mean us to find the stolen books?'

'She was pretty insistent that we take the time for a visit,' Alec said. 'And one does have to ask, what could be so exciting about a great big henhouse, when you get right down to it?'

'Let's go,' I said. 'Whether Miss Goodfellow meant us to pinch these back or not, Lizzy Hogg could return at any minute and find us in her house. We'd better skedaddle.'

I have never felt so much like a black bear crossing a snowy plain as I did while we strolled back over the green bearing those volumes. Mine grew heavier with every step and it was giving off that unmistakable musty odour of all old books as well as staining the sleeve of my coat with the crumbled dust of its leather binding, as bright as lily pollen and, I suspected, as stubborn.

We made it, however. It was the slack tide of the afternoon: deliveries complete; children at their lessons; women in their kitchens; and, fortunately for us, no one at the desk of the Castle Inn to see us passing as we scuttled for the stairs.

'Did you express a preference?' asked Alec on the landing, alluding once again to his firmly held belief that I always get a nicer room than he does, in whatever public house, private home, small hotel, or sleeper carriage we find ourselves. He is right, but it is no less annoying always to be reminded of it.

'Oh come along, Cousin Charlotte,' I said. 'As if it's going to kill you to be plainly billeted for a couple of nights. I shall let you sit on my comfortable chair.'

I opened my door and ushered him inside, wishing that the maid had not put a fresh posy on my dressing table.

Alec tutted so roundly he made himself snort. 'It's not one night though, is it?' he said. 'It's a lifetime. Have you even seen the bachelors' bedrooms at Gilverton? Army barracks, Dandy. Only colder and with thinner mattresses.'

'Of course I have,' I said, hoping I did not sound too guilty. The truth is I had looked over the upper storey of that wing of the house just once, shortly after I returned from honey-moon, and then put it out of my mind. 'It's only places like Chatsworth and Blenheim where the chatelaine never gets round the place in her lifetime.'

'Ring for tea and I'll forgive you,' Alec said. 'Ask about cake and I'll never mention it again. I had no luncheon to speak of.'

'China tea and something sweet, please,' I asked Bella when she answered my ring. 'Mr Osborne missed luncheon.'

'Mr Osborne had a ham and egg pie and half a jar of piccalilli,' the cook said. 'But there's a raisin loaf in the kitchen.'

By the time the tea tray arrived, Alec was already poring over one of the volumes.

'How shall we tackle it?' I said. 'Work back? Work forward?'

'This one's lavishly filthy,' he said. 'The really ancient one. You dig into the new one – surely it can't be quite so dusty – and sing out if you find anything.'

'Like what?'

'I'm assuming we'll know it when we see it.'

'Would you like a scrap of paper and a pencil, to make notes?' I asked him. He waggled his eyebrows. 'Of course not. When you say "sing out" you mean *you'll* sing out and *I'll* take dictation. Again.'

'What a lovely view you have,' Alec said. 'I look over the pig bin.'

'You promised never to complain again if I got cake for you!'

'Raisin loaf, Dandy,' said Alec. 'Be fair.'

I settled myself at the dressing table, pushing aside the offending posy and laying a patchwork of handkerchiefs on the painted surface in case the dust of crumbled calfskin did indeed stain. Then I opened the volume.

It began on the 5th of April 1915 with the birth of a Miss Mary Phail, to a farmworker and his wife. I took a moment to feel thankful that the minister had such a neat hand and the memory rose in me of Mither Gollane recounting the various reverends of her long life.

'I say, Alec,' I began, meaning to point out that this volume certainly could not contain the birth date she might want to hide.

He raised his head. 'I can't chat, Dandy. I'm trying to decipher a devilishly crabbed old script in this one.'

I applied myself to my own task. I should have realised what I was going to see. I could not then and cannot now account for my blindness, but as I read down the page of entries the shock of it hit me like a thunderclap. There, in the minister's regular, legible writing, were recorded death after death of the young men of Dirleton village: Logan, Burnside, Wardrop, McNeill . . . they marched down the page together as they had marched off to war. After their names came "Somme" and "Ypres" and "Gallipoli" and, heartbreakingly, "Atlantic sea" and "unknown, France" too. My eyes blurred and I lifted my head to look out of the window and across the green to the road stretching away, seized with a deep desire to grab Alec's keys and drive home to Gilverton without stopping, to gather Donald and Teddy to me, to lock them up like fairy-tale princesses if I had to, to cast spells on them both to make them sleep for a hundred years.

'Early success?' Alec said. He had noticed that I was not reading.

'I can't bear it,' I said. 'I can't read these, Alec. And I can't expect you to read them either.'

'Oh Lord!' Alec said. 'You've got 1915? It never occurred to me. But of course I can do it. Good grief, a list of names in a book? I've seen them all on the cenotaph already.'

'Not with their ages,' I said. 'Not with the names of the battles.'

'Surely not!'

'The names of the towns. Towns that only mean "battle" now. That only say carnage and horror. And is it all to happen again? Are there to be more towns in Germany and France and Italy that will never again be known as a place with a pretty church or a place where they make such and such a wine, but only the place where so-and-so many died? Or

221

the place where this many killed that many? I can't bear it, Alec. You don't—' I was just about to commit one of the great transgressions, until I managed to stop myself.

Unfortunately, Alec knows me far too well for the tactic of not saying something to mean he does not hear it. 'You're right,' he replied. 'I *don't* know how you feel. I cannot imagine what it would mean to send those boys off to war. And it's time I did something about it instead of dabbling endlessly and never getting anywhere. If Cara—' He stopped.

Because *I* know *him* so well, I filled in the speech he chose not to deliver. If Cara, his fiancée, had not died in 1922, he might have a daughter thinking about her season, a yearly bill for a handful of sons away at school and still a few left in the nursery. I decided to answer the bit he *had* delivered.

'I shouldn't imagine that will offer much of a challenge,' I said. 'And I shall throw rice like anything.'

'In the meantime,' Alec said, 'do you want to swap? This one is quite interesting once you get your eye in. There are names you would recognise from today – here's a Curr, for instance – and the jobs are fascinating: tanner, wheelwright, thresher . . .'

'I thought a thresher was a machine,' I said.

'Not in 1599 it wasn't,' said Alec. 'I say, here's a Halliburton. A Jessamine Halliburton.'

'Jessamine!' I said. 'I take it she is of the castle Halliburtons, and not the laundry branch of the family.'

'Might all have been the same back then,' Alec said. 'Fortunes rise and fortunes fall. This Miss Halliburton was born to the landlord of a place called the Four Feathers.'

'Keep reading,' I said. 'She'll probably die of a chill on the next page.'

'Let's agree to believe she'll get married in five pages' time,' Alec said. 'But I won't notice, because we're not whiling away the time here, Dandy. We're searching. And, as I say, I'll cope with the young lads at the front if you trawl through these Tudors. *They'd* all be dead now anyway. Dandy? Are you listening?'

'Sorry,' I said. 'Yes, indeed. Sharp focus on our goal, darling. Only, I just found the birth of Paddy Watson, the postie. Or *a* Paddy Watson, anyway: 1915, to the laird of Dirleton Castle: a son, Patrick.'

'It can't be him, unless the great family *were* Watsons then and the Halliburtons came later.'

'Even so, how would the scion become a postman?' I asked.

'Fortune falling sharply?' Alec said. 'Family out of the castle and son into a job?'

I said nothing for a moment, thinking furiously. Presently, I cleared my throat to attract Alec's attention. He looked up with a small sigh, keeping one finger on his place. 'Listen to this,' I said. 'And tell me if it doesn't make sense of something Mr Wallace said to me. About kindness and rule-breaking. I thought he meant he had no hesitation in christening babies born on the wrong side of the blanket but if this entry is anything to go by it's much more than that.'

'What are you talking about?'

'Our Mr Wallace is quite the radical in his quiet way. He not only christened this little Patrick Watson, but he declined to put the disgraced Miss Watson's name in the book for all to read. Far from it, he put the father's name in the book – or as good as – "laird of Dirleton Castle". Good grief, Alec, the minister held up the rascal of a father and put his responsibility down there in ink, while keeping the mother quite out of it.'

'Well, well, well,' Alec said. 'What an outrage.'

I bristled.

'In the eyes of the straitlaced and blinkered, I mean. Personally, I'm filled with a sneaking sense of awe for the good minister.'

'Me too,' I admitted.

'Can you keep on with that volume after all then?' Alec said. 'And let me crack on with mine? I don't want to look away from the script too long in case I lose the knack again. It's terribly ornate. Like modern German with all its twiddles and tassels.'

At the mention of modern Germany, I found that it was suddenly a relief to go back to perusing the parish records of twenty-odd years ago. Awful as things were, at least we knew the worst of it.

'Here's Maggie Goodfellow,' I said. 'With her Sunday name, of course. Margaret Goodfellow, born to . . . Heavens, born to the laird of Dirleton Castle! Gosh.'

'She did say she was a ward,' Alec reminded me. 'And that's what that word always used to mean. I wonder why *she* lives in the castle and not a cottage? What put her head and shoulders above poor little Paddy?'

'Her mother's station, no doubt,' I said. 'Miss Goodfellow senior must be gentry. Must have been gentry, rather.'

'Have you found her death?' Alec said.

'Oh no,' I told him. 'Just that, if she's been taken in by the father's family, presumably her mother wasn't there to look after her. Just a guess.'

Alec grunted. 'She could have gone to an aunt or a cousin surely,' he said. 'The Goodfellow family has deep roots in Dirleton, it seems. I'm looking at another Margaret Goodfellow born here in 1602.'

'Any Hoggs?' I asked. 'Because if you say yes then I'll have to conclude that there's some sort of strange *droit de seigneur* going on. I've found our Manie to your Jessamine and I've found our strange little Lizzy. Elizabeth Hogg, daughters both of guess who?'

'The laird of Dirleton Castle?'

'Except he's been promoted. He's down as "laird of Dirleton" now. The very same. Thirty-first day of October, 1922 for Lizzy.'

'You're up to 1922 already?' Alec said. 'Well, I suppose it's easier to read the modern writing. What?' he added, at what I presumed must have been a flash of guilt. 'I'm flipping through looking for names I recognise,' I said, carefully turning the pages back and starting again in 1915. 'Sorry.'

'So Lizzy Hogg is sixteen years old, as the minister guessed,' Alec said. 'I wonder why she lives in the turret of the castle at such a tender age. Instead of with *her* own mother, whoever that might be. Especially considering that the Halliburtons have taken all their traps and gone to the continent. What?' he said again. I was not shame-faced this time. Something he had just said had snagged on my brain and laddered it.

'I don't know,' I said. I bent to my task again briefly but then asked, 'What makes you think they've taken all their traps with them?'

Alec shrugged. 'You can't travel through Europe in any style with a knapsack on your back. Is that what was bothering you?'

'I don't know,' I said again. We worked away in silence for a few minutes, except for Alec whistling the tune of that dratted song under his breath over and over again. 'You'll have to give up German ditties soon,' I said, hoping to silence him.

'We didn't give up Wagner last time.'

'More's the pity. Don't tell Hugh I said so.'

After another prolonged and thankfully more perfect silence, Alec pushed the book away and stretched out with his hands behind his head. 'I wish I knew what we were looking for,' he said. 'At least you've got some bits of gossip. I've got endless millers and maids being born, getting hitched and shuffling off. Clarksons, Murrays, Boyles, Phails, Mieks, Gilmours. I found a Hog – one G but it must be the same family. It all seems quite orderly. Nothing so salacious as the by-blows of the Halliburtons in the early years of *this* century.'

'I'm not finding any Murrays and Phails,' I said. 'There's a family of Gilmours at an outlying farm. At least, I assume Rockcliffe Farm is outlying. It sounds as if it's at the coast. Well, well, well.'

'See what I mean?' said Alec. 'I'm getting covered in ancient dust and going goggle-eyed with this old script and I haven't had a sniff of a well, well, well.'

I waited.

'What is it anyway?'

'Nessie Clarkson,' I said. 'Her one and only parent is given as our old friend the laird of Dirleton Castle.'

Alec whistled.

'I'm beginning to feel rather grubby,' I said. 'Does it have anything to do with what we're looking for, do you think? Does it have any bearing on the case?'

'It makes a nasty sort of sense of one thing,' said Alec. 'I explains why Silas and this Halliburton are such pals. I mean, they do sound like birds of a feather. I wonder if that's why Mrs Halliburton dragged him off to Italy.'

'I shouldn't imagine that would help much,' I said. 'All that sunshine and cheap wine.'

'But it must have been absolutely excruciating for her here,' Alec said. 'There are by-blows all over the bloody village. How many have we found?'

'Five.'

'And the radical vicar recording it all in his little book. I'd have fled too. Wouldn't you?'

'I wonder if they know,' I said. 'The by-blows, I mean. I wonder if they know they're – Oh my God!'

'What?' said Alec.

'Maggie Goodfellow and Paddy Watson certainly don't know, do they? And someone had better tell them.'

'Good Lord,' Alec said.

'You don't think—' I said, then had to stop to gather myself. 'I mean, you don't think Paddy Watson got wind of the fact that his sweetheart is his half-sister and then stole the parish book so she didn't find out?'

'And killed Silas so that . . . ?'

I tried but failed to make it all fit. 'We would need to go back to two separate matters happening to coincide,' I said, with a gusty sigh. 'The writers were coming to interview Mither Gollane and . . . Hang on. Something is stirring.'

'And someone else killed Silas?'

'Shush!' I said. 'Let it bubble up to the surface.'

'Like swamp gas,' Alec said. At least, however, he stopped distracting me. I concentrated very hard, reaching into my memory for something I had been told and casting about myself for something floating all around us that we had not yet pinned down. It was almost in my grasp, when Alec said, 'Aha! I've got it!'

'Go on.'

'Tell me again about Miss Goodfellow's demeanour when she came to reveal her assignation with Paddy Watson.'

'Shame-faced, reluctant, determined,' I said.

'All of which makes perfect sense apart from the determination,' Alec said. 'Why did she decide she had to give an alibi to one of however many hundred men there are in Dirleton and its environs?'

'Aha!' I said in an unconscious echo. 'Because she *does* knows he's her brother and she wanted to protect him. Of course!'

'And . . . ?' said Alec, teasing me.

'And . . . Wait, don't tell me. And . . . She knew he needed protection because there *is* a connection between the secret family history recorded in these volumes and the reason Silas died.' I grinned at him, feeling a great deal of satisfaction. 'Somehow,' I added, ruining the moment.

'Somehow,' Alec agreed, with rather a slump. 'Still, it's a red-letter day for me, beating you to the source of one of your misty notions.'

He stood and stretched, preening himself with such enjoyment that I didn't have the heart to tell him that was not what I had been scrabbling for. I was just beginning to retrace my mental steps to the start of the idea when suddenly Alec abandoned his luxurious stretch, in fact hunched over rather and, in that curious semi-crouch, drew nearer to the window and parted the lace curtains.

'Odd,' he said.

'What is?'

'How many crows does it take to make a murder?'

'How many!' I said, almost loud enough to call it shouting, for his words had helped me grasp the lost thread I had been chasing. Then the rest of his utterance hit me and once again the whole notion was gone, driven away this time by a shudder. 'What are you talking about?'

'Look,' Alec said. 'Come and see.' He shuffled to the side and beckoned me to join him. Peering out of the low window, I was treated to the arresting sight of Lizzy Hogg, dressed as ever in her ashy and indeterminate garments, chasing a flock of crows around the green. It would have been startling if accompanied by the cawing and croaking such a number of upset corvids usually give rein to, but it was rendered all the more unnerving by being completely silent. The birds flapped and settled, wheeled and broke. Lizzy Hogg waved her arms and flitted this way and that. But neither girl nor bird uttered a sound.

'She seems to be driving them towards the castle,' I said. 'Perhaps they are pets who've escaped.'

'Let's go and help,' Alec said. 'Mind and lock up tight behind you, Dandy. We have not finished with these books and I'd rather not tell the world we've got a hold of them.'

With that, he let himself out and I heard him trotting along the corridor, then the confident ring of his shoes on the bare wooden stairs.

When I arrived out on the green beside him, Lizzy Hogg had stopped flitting about like a little black butterfly and was standing with her head down while Alec tried in his kindly way to draw out of her what she had been up to. The crows, free from the annoyance of her leaps and swipes, were lazily circling and quartering, drifting gently away from the castle and towards the church. Or so I thought. When they had got themselves to the top of the manse road, they beat their wings with a great ragged flapping and settled, still silent, in a ring around the leaping stone. Finally, Lizzy let out a sound: a single moan of some great distress. She rushed off in the direction of the castle gate and, presumably, her own little turret home.

'She won't find much comfort there,' Alec said. 'Since we've pinched her precious volumes.'

'What are they doing?' I said, watching the crows. They appeared busy at some task or another, stalking around the stone like cockerels, jostling a little, and pecking frequently.

'If they were jackdaws or magpies, I'd say the tent pegs had caught their beady eyes,' Alec said. 'But they are carrion crows.'

'Oh God,' I said. 'Do you think there's blood left on the stone and they've sniffed it out?'

'Not a trace of it anywhere,' Alec said. 'The stone is bleached bare. They're not on it, anyway. They're definitely in a ring around it. Look at them, Dandy. You can see it with your own eyes.'

I had no particular desire to approach a murder of crows and discover what they had found at the leaping stone that was so entrancing them but, if they were also eating whatever they were pecking at, then it behooved Alec and me to find out what it was before every scrap was gone. Accordingly, we set off in that direction, expecting them at any minute to take fright at our approach and go flapping off. It was disturbing in the extreme that, apart from cocking their heads at us to regard us with those black pinhead eyes, they stayed put. Even the ringing of the school bell did not deflect them, nor the soft rise of the children's voices from inside as they readied themselves for freedom.

When we were close enough to see exactly what they were up to, it was with great relief that I watched two of them claim either end of their prey and indulge in a brief tug of war before they snapped it in half and each hopped backwards with its spoils.

'Ah,' I said. 'It's only worms. They must have come up to

the surface from all the water Manie was sloshing about to wash the stone.'

Alec, who was slightly ahead of me, threw an incredulous look over his shoulder, bent and shooed away the crows nearest him, then plucked at the ground himself and straightened with yet another "worm" dangling from his fingers.

'It's not a worm,' he said. 'But what *is* it?'

'String?' I said, more in hope than anything.

'Gut,' said Alec. 'Do you have a handkerchief you don't mind sacrificing? I scrubbed off book dust with mine and left it in your bedroom.'

'Gut?' I said. 'Catgut? Fishing line? The stuff that Silas tripped on? I thought you said it was gone. And why would crows want catgut so badly?'

'Guts, plural,' Alec said and held out the dangling handful to my outstretched handkerchief, letting go before I could withdraw. The children were pouring out of the school now. The sight of us checked them for a moment and then the surge continued and, at this fresh assault, the crows finally accepted that the picnic was over and flapped up from the ground with a tremendous gust of beating wings, wheeling off in the direction of the gatehouse and golf course beyond.

'Guts,' I repeated. It was not a question exactly. I stared down into my hanky and suppressed the urge to retch.

'Chicken, I think,' Alec said. He was bent almost double scrutinising the ground. 'A ring of guts laid out like a daisy chain exactly where the wire was. The tent pegs have gone too, by the way.'

'Chicken entrails,' I said, wishing I were joking but fearing that the slight wobble in my voice betrayed me.

231

'What are you doing, mister?' One of the bolder children had stopped his headlong rush for play, home or the sweet-shop and was standing close to Alec, watching him intently.

'George!' The shout came like a pistol shot and there was Miss Meek, striding towards us still in the overall she had no doubt donned to clean the blackboard and bang out the dusters. She waved little George off firmly but kindly and then stationed herself with feet spread as though to prepare for a physical onslaught. 'What *are* you doing?'

'Dealing with the second tasteless prank to take place at this spot since the outrage of the murder,' Alec said. 'Someone has strewn the innards of a chicken around the thing to attract carrion crows.'

Miss Meek looked up the green towards the castle so sharply I was surprised not to hear her neck crack. 'You are mistaken,' she said. She really did have the most remarkably bald way of speaking. 'It's not a joke and it's not meant to attract crows. It's a harmless piece of folklore that someone or other mismanaged so that the crows arrived unbidden.'

'Miss Hogg?' I said. 'She was trying to chase them away when we saw her.'

'I wouldn't have thought Lizzy would do such a thing,' Miss Meek said. 'But yes, she probably didn't like seeing all those crows at the stone.'

'Mither Gollane, perhaps,' I said.

Miss Meek's eyes flashed.

'Miss Halliburton thought the old lady might well "clean" the stone, once she herself had "washed" it,' I explained. The distinction was lost on me at the time.'

'But this "harmless piece of folklore" is a cleansing ritual?' Alec added.

'More or less,' said Miss Meek. She made a brave stab at

232

appearing nonchalant, putting both her hands in her overall pockets and letting one hip drop. 'The stone is supposed to be lucky. Someone with deep roots in Dirleton must have thought it unfortunate that a stranger met an untimely end here and has obviously tried to right matters with some sort of . . . ritual.'

'I've never heard of chicken innards being associated with good luck,' I said. 'Quite the reverse. And as for the stone, we thought it was a children's plaything. We heard that your little ones jump over it on the first day of the school year.'

'The *last* day,' said Miss Meek. 'With nettles strewn over the top to make it more of a challenge.'

'But the idea that it was tainted by Mr Esslemont's blood and that it needs to be cleansed with a ritual is all rather torrid and most unchildlike.'

'Look,' said Miss Meek. 'I don't know where you come from originally, Mrs Gilver. Clearly not Perthshire. But you must have your own old stories and traditions, wherever it is. The children still leap over the stone still because they are children, while everyone else has stopped, in these enlightened times, because they are adults. In older days, everyone would do it, at the start of the summer.'

'For luck?' I said. 'For a good harvest?'

'And Silas's death on this spot has destroyed the luck?' said Alec.

Miss Meek gave an impatient sigh. 'It's not as though anyone believes it,' she said, doing her level best to sound rather lofty at the idea. I remembered the shaking hands of the fingerprint man, though, and was unswayed by her attempt. 'But, if you must know, it's not for luck. Not exactly. It's to check that the children – these days and the adults too back in the old days – were suitable to go out into the fields and bring the harvest in.'

'Suitable?' Alec said.

The next sigh was even deeper. 'Oh very well! The tale is that only the pure can leap over the stone and that anyone in cahoots with . . . wickedness . . . will stumble. It was a test, you see.'

'Ah,' I said. 'The children are checked for devilry before they go to spoil the crops instead of helping bring them in?' I chose the word deliberately and I did not imagine the blink of surprise when she heard it.

'So, anyone who believed this old tale,' Alec said, 'would imagine that Silas, having met his death trying – presumably – to jump over the stone, was not pure. Was, in fact, in league with what you call "wickedness", in such general terms, although Mrs Gilver speaks more plainly.'

'And the sacrifice?' I said. 'The entrails of a chicken? How exactly does that bring about a new beginning with everything shipshape again?'

'Oh for heaven's sake,' said Miss Meek. 'Don't ask it to make sense! It's all complete bunkum.'

'It certainly is,' Alec said. 'The test was ill-conceived as far as poor Silas is concerned. Because the stone was booby-trapped to make him stumble. Only, the entrails suggest that not everyone knows that. It seems that someone thinks the stone did its job and sent a wicked man to his reckoning.'

'Booby-trapped?' said Miss Meek.

'Tent pegs and piano wire,' said Alec. 'He tripped and banged his head. So yes, booby-trapped.'

'Tent pegs?' said Miss Meek, faintly. Then she seemed to shake herself. 'How do you come to know all of this?'

'We have been seconded into the Dirleton Constabulary,' I said. It was not a lie, since I had not started off with a "because". If Miss Meek chose to take it as an answer to her question, that was none of my doing.

'So you're constables instead of detectives?' she said. 'Quite a come-down for you.'

She looked, if it was not too outlandish to make any sense, faintly amused. As she dipped her head and sauntered back to the school I was sure her shoulders shook with silent laughter.

'That was interesting,' Alec said, watching her go. 'Didn't you think so?'

'I am so overfed with incident that I am no longer capable of deciding,' I said. 'This case is hydra-headed.' He did not answer. I waited. Then I gave in. 'What was?'

'The tent pegs were what interested her. The piano wire should have been what tripped her up, if you'll pardon the pun.'

'And what does that tell you?'

'That the tent pegs suggested who it was,' Alec said. It chimed so perfectly with the quick succession of surprise, deflection and amusement that I was forced to concede.

'You've hit the tent peg on the head,' I said. 'If you'll pardon my pun too.'

Chapter 15

'Oh!' Miss Clarkson said, waving a duster at us. She was polishing the antlers on the mounted stag behind the reception desk. There was a curry comb at hand too, as though the poor thing's fur had been given a going-over.

'Back again?' Alec said.

'What a friend you are to the Castle Inn,' I said. 'Leaving off your sewing and baking to put in a shift as a housekeeper.'

She smirked at me in a conspiratorial way. 'I heard you're on a proper shift too. Thank you for stepping into the breach in our hour of need.' She broke off, folded her arms cosily under her scant bosom and leaned over the desk to speak confidentially. 'Given that, I don't have any hesitation in passing on this piece of evidence to you. You'll tell the captain, won't you? The sergeant? I hear the inspector's back.'

'We've yet to pin down the chain of command in any detail,' Alec said. 'What evidence?'

'Well,' said Miss Clarkson, 'I hope I'm not claiming too much in calling it that. *Perhaps* it's a clue. Perhaps it's only a titbit.'

'Why not tell us and let us decide?' I said. 'We've had a measure of experience in organising the information we're given. Lay it all out and we'll tell you.'

'That's a good idea,' Miss Clarkson said, apparently immune to sarcasm. 'Well, it's the Halliburtons, you see.' She must have been hoping for a reaction of *some* kind from the two of us, for who would hang around in a hotel where she did not actually work, reduced to the spring cleaning of a stuffed head, unless she expected her news to be of some value? Still, she could not have foreseen the sudden quivering attentiveness that took over Alec's face and I daresay mine. We were as two foxes when they hear a dog in the distance. 'They rang up,' she said.

'Where?'

'Here,' said Miss Clarkson. 'I was helping Manie with some linens. She's still not right after her shock. And the telephone bell rang and rang. I don't know where Tom was. So I came down and answered and it was Mrs Halliburton, saying she'd just got the English papers today and read the shocking news from home. And she wanted to find out if Mr Halliburton was here.'

'*Here?*' I said. 'Why would he be here?'

'They'd had a huge argument,' said Miss Clarkson. 'Mr H was determined to come home, what with everything that's going on and all the predictions.' Alec nodded, glad to hear that this man he had never met was thinking like any right-minded son of the Empire. 'And Mrs H – or so she told me – was just as determined to go to America. Or it might have been Canada, where they have a farm, I think. Or would it be a forest? In any case, he packed up a small suitcase late on Thursday and took the train to Paris, saying he meant to get himself on a boat.'

'Has anyone seen him?' I said. 'The stars would have to align rather conveniently for him to get from Florence to rural East Lothian already.'

'Or maybe it was a *week* past Thursday,' Miss Clarkson said. 'Anyway, Mrs H was livid.'

'So I imagine,' I said. 'I shouldn't like to be abandoned in Europe at the moment.'

'Oh no, but it wasn't that,' said Miss Clarkson. 'It was the hypocrisy. That's what *she* called it, not me being presumptuous. "Reeking hypocrisy," she said.'

'And what did she mean?' said Alec.

'As near as I could make out,' said Miss Clarkson, 'she didn't believe it was patriotism drawing him back here at all. He just dressed it up that way and served it to her. But what it really was, or so she said, was that he was sick to the back teeth of his business manager's . . . now what did she say? Interference, incompetence, high-handedness and complacency. She agreed with all of that. And he meant to do something about it. Which she didn't agree with at all. And of course now we know who the murdered man *was* . . .'

I shared a glance with Alec. This was not something told to a pair of special constables, drafted to punish the inspector for annoying his boss. This should have been handed to the ranking officer as soon as it was received. The thought that we were not the right recipients for the news brought another thought hard on its heels.

'Miss Clarkson,' I said, 'why did Mrs Halliburton tell all of this to you?'

'She's never had the telephone connected at the castle, so unless she sent a telegram she couldn't tell Maggie.'

'That explains why she didn't tell Miss Goodfellow,' Alec said. 'But Mrs Gilver is right. Why did she then decide to tell you?'

Miss Clarkson frowned again as though stumped by this question. 'She knows the number of the inn,' she said. 'It's probably the only number she knows off by heart. To tell the girl on the exchange.'

'But wouldn't it have made more sense for her to ask you to run and fetch Miss Goodfellow?'

'It would,' said Miss Clarkson. 'Yes, it certainly would. Oh, it's so unpleasant to have to say this—!' She stopped.

'Nevertheless,' said Alec.

'She was drunk. And angry. If you had answered she'd have told you. I think she just needed to get it off her chest.'

'Do you?' I said. 'I wouldn't have thought so. She reads in a day-old English newspaper – which got the news jolly fast, by the way – that a business associate of her husband's has been murdered in the town where she and her husband have a home, and she telephones that town to "get off her chest" the fact that her husband is more than likely on the scene, has been heard to make threatening noises about the murdered man, and might conceivably have done the deed?'

'My, you've a grand way of putting it in a nutshell,' said Miss Clarkson. 'But I didn't mean that exactly. More that she was terrified that Mr H had done it and wanted to get the worry off her chest and be told she *had* no worry because the tramp or spurned lover or whoever had confessed. Or been caught.'

'How did she take the news that the police still sought the culprit?' said Alec.

'She did quite a bit of hasty back-pedalling,' said Miss Clarkson. 'She started pooh-poohing the notion that he could have made it all the way home and rang off talking about telephoning to his favourite hotel in Paris and tracking him down there. Still though.'

'Still though,' Alec agreed. 'We have to consider it, don't we, Dandy?'

'A few questions, Miss Clarkson,' I said. 'What does Mr Halliburton look like? Might he have been your tall, thin man? Also, is he a manly man or could he be mistaken for a woman? By Miss Hogg, in the dark, from a distance? Also, if he did come back and happen to meet Silas in the middle of the night, and the meeting did happen to end in bloodshed, where would he go afterwards, if not the castle? Would Miss Goodfellow harbour him? Does he have any other family around who would take him in?'

Miss Clarkson blinked and shrank under this onslaught of questions, I was pleased to see. It took her a further moment to speak. '*Other* family?' was what she said. 'Maggie isn't family. She's his ward.'

Alec nodded. 'Quite, quite, much the best idea. I remember my maiden aunts bandying words like "natural child" and "young relation" about when I was a boy. It was excruciating.'

'But she isn't,' said Miss Clarkson. 'Who told you she was? Who's been saying that?' She was ruffled enough by this insinuation that it carried her away, along with her curry comb and her antler cloth, banging the baize door behind her.

'We need to speak to Daisy,' Alec said. I found it a surprising conclusion to draw from Miss Clarkson's evidence. 'If this Mrs Halliburton knew Silas,' he explained, 'it makes no sense that *Daisy* didn't know *Mr* H.'

'Might as well then, while we've got the bridge,' I said, slipping behind the desk and lifting the earpiece from the cradle. Before I could put the call through though, Alec cleared his throat and lifted his eyebrows, drawing my attention to something behind me. Manie Halliburton was standing in a dark corner between the door to the bar parlour and the little alcove where the hat stands and coat hooks were to be found.

'Everything all right, dear?' I said, for she seemed at least on edge, if not stricken. 'Don't worry about what Miss Clarkson said.' This was a guess, but I did not know what else might have rattled her, she who laid out corpses and took her scrubbing brush to bloodstains.

'What *did* Nessie say?' Manie asked.

'Oh,' said Alec, 'weren't you standing there this whole time?' We play a decent set of doubles after all these years and he had guessed that I wanted to find out how much of our conversation had been overheard, his and mine.

'I come up from the pit,' Manie said, with a vague gesture behind her.

I let this reference go for the moment, and instead asked, 'And what's put the wind up you?'

'No flies on you,' Manie said, returning to that signature insouciance that never quite rose to actual impertinence. 'I'm just feeling a wee bit shy, Mrs Gilver, to be honest. I need to tell you something and I don't want to.'

'Best spit it out,' Alec said. 'Or is it something you'd rather tell Mrs Gilver privately?' He sounded hopeful about his chances of escaping to the bar but Manie reassured him that it was for his ears too.

'I did something I shouldn't have done,' she said. 'I meant to be kind, keeping it quiet. But it's all gone too far now.'

'Go on,' I said, my mind reeling.

'He was married, wasn't he?' Manie said. 'Mr Esslemont. I was thinking of his wife.'

'Oh my God,' I said. 'Did he pester you?' It seemed highly unlikely, but I would not put any woman between eighteen and fifty quite beyond Silas's interest. I could not help a glance at her middle and felt a great wash of relief to see her apron wrapped twice around her waist and tied tightly, with its pocket and hem hanging straight down.

241

'Pester me how?' said Manie, as though cloaked in un-assailable innocence. 'He didn't know me. No, see what I did was I took this and that off of him when I was laying him out.'

'You took things?' I said. 'But didn't the police keep all his belongings?'

'The sergeant took his ring and his letter,' Manie said. 'And Jimmy McLean took his wallet and his watch – which I thought was nasty; as if I'd pinch a watch when no one was looking. I don't think people should be so quick to judge me and that's the truth. I do the work they won't, so they've no business looking down their noses. And especially not someone that used to steal plums over the garden wall till he was sick with them.'

'Quite, quite,' Alec said. 'But to return to your main point?'

'He was still in all his clothes when they laid him on the door and give him to me to wash and wind,' Manie said. 'I undressed him. And, like I said, I took some things away that he wouldn't have liked folk to know about. Not his wife. Not anyone.'

Not me certainly, I thought. And not Alec either, judging by the look on his face. But we cannot choose the dainty path of sheltered ignorance, whether as professional detectives or seconded constables. 'Tell us,' I said.

'He had a garment on under his shirt,' Manie said. 'Instead of a vest.'

'A garment?' I said.

'And another garment on under his trousers. Instead of his drawers.'

'You are speaking rather too cryptically, my dear,' I said. 'What kind of garment?'

'And a contraption,' Manie finished.

'Or, if you can't bring yourself to say it,' Alec put in hastily, 'show us. Or no. Don't show us but tell us where they are and we'll go and look.' I had to bite my cheeks. It was clear that, whether or not Manie could bear to say the words, Alec could not bear to hear them.

'I wouldn't know how to name the contraption,' Manie said. 'I don't know what it's called.'

I doubted that I would know what it was called either. My brain was dashing about like a mouse before the scythe, searching in vain for shelter.

'I put them down in the pit, nice and safe in a brown paper bag in case anyone should ask for them.'

'And when you say "the pit"?' I said. 'What does that mean?'

'It's there,' Manie said, pointing behind her again. 'It used to be a storage cellar but it's too damp and rat-infested for keeping most things.'

'Right,' I said. 'And how does one gain access?'

'There's a trapdoor as handy as handy,' Manie said, as though she was sharing news of a dining car on a train or a hot bath freshly drawn. 'So,' she added, sidling away, 'I'll leave you to it.' Owing to the old-fashioned volume of petticoats she wore under her striped dress, she looked rather like a cotton-tailed rabbit as she turned and fled, kicking up her hem behind her boot heels.

'Ring Daisy or brave "the pit"?' said Alec.

'Divide and conquer?' I said.

'Nice try,' said Alec. 'If I'm going down a handy trapdoor to a place called the pit to feast my eyes on Silas Esslemont's private taste in shameful undergarments, you are coming with me.'

Noticing that the natty little trapdoor rose smoothly and silently at the first gentle tug on its ring handle, I reflected ruefully on my life's path: I had never expected to descend into enough dungeons ever to become a connoisseur of their entrances.

There was electric light in this storage cellar and Alec pulled the chain hanging from the middle of the arched ceiling, before letting the trapdoor down again, sealing us off from the cloakroom.

'Would you mind checking—' I began.

He smiled and lifted it, letting a chink of light in. 'We're not trapped, Dandy. I just thought it would be an idea to have some privacy.'

'Thank you,' I said. 'I've never been all that fond of underground places. I once had a nasty experience in an icehouse.'

'And I in the trenches,' said Alec, which was a low blow and shut me up smartly. 'I don't think much of Miss Manie as an historian, do you? This is not a storage cellar.'

I looked about myself with interest – or at least with relief at having something to justify not searching out the paper bag we were here actually to find – and I could see that he was right. This little room was much older than the inn above it and the shelves around its curved walls were far too deep and widely spaced to make for the efficient packing away of bacon in salt jars or barrels of pickled fish. 'Is it a crypt?' I said. 'Those stone slots look designed to hold coffins.'

'I rather think it's a priest's hole,' Alec said. 'The shelves are bunks. Look at the end wall.'

'Golly,' I said, when I had walked beyond the dazzle of the hanging light and taken a squint. A crucifix had been carved into the stone that formed the room. It was concave but the shadows played a trick and made it appear to stand in proud relief. 'Rather sacrilegious for Silas's chemise and cami-knickers to end up here.'

'Not to mention the contraption,' Alec said.

'*Don't* mention the contraption, I beg you. Poor Silas. I think I'll give Miss Halliburton a quid tip to reward her discretion in spiriting the thing away before the police saw it. Can you imagine?'

'What we all need when we die is a Cassandra,' Alec said.

'To prophesise the date and give us a chance to put everything in order?'

'Not that Cassandra,' Alec said. 'Cassandra Austen. To burn all our letters as she did for Sister Jane. There's the bag, don't you think?'

The place was almost empty and so there was no doubt that the sturdy brown paper sack on one of the stone bunks was our quarry.

'We can't burn this if there's the slightest chance it has a bearing on the case,' I said. 'Which it might, I suppose.'

'Well, let's see what we're dealing with anyway,' said Alec. He stuffed his hands into his pockets as he spoke, however, indicating that the physical riffling through the parcel was to fall to me.

I unrolled the top of the bag and peered in. There was no lace, no ribbon, and no sheen of silk. In fact, the dreaded garments looked duller and browner than the bag holding them. I upended it and shook out a lumpy, dun-coloured roll that landed on the stone of the shelf with a dull thump.

'What on earth?' Alec said. He took his hands out of his pockets and shook loose a part of the roll, holding it up at arm's length.

'It *is* a vest,' I said. 'What's it made of?'

'I don't believe it,' Alec said. 'This, Dandy, is a cilice.'

'A what?'

'A hair shirt.'

I reached out and rubbed the hem of it, feeling the prickle of some very tough sort of animal's coat and also releasing a pungent odour. 'Goat hair?' I guessed.

'Something like that,' said Alec. 'I *really* can't believe it. Silas Esslemont wore a hair shirt? Silas Esslemont endured the mortification of the flesh?'

'It didn't work, if he did,' I said. I lifted the other garment. 'Is this a spare for when the first one's off to the laundr— Oh my God!' It was not funny, of course. It goes without saying that none of this Dirleton adventure was funny but there was something about the idea of goat-hair under-drawers that set me off. At last, I gasped, coughed my way back to solemnity again and put them down.

'And this'll be the contraption, is it?' I said, lifting the thing that had made the clunk. It was round and just the right size to fit in the palm of one's hand. The only similar thing I had ever seen was a tool, glimpsed in a shepherd's cottage once, designed to start the long and wearisome process of turning a sheep's coat into a ball of yarn. 'Is it a wool carder?' I said, miming the motion of scraping it through a heap of imaginary fluff.

'I wish it were,' said Alec. 'It's a spugna.'

'And what, pray, is a spugna?'

'Another instrument of penitential mortification,' Alec said. 'One hits oneself with it to atone for sins.'

'That's horrib— How do you know all thi— We've got to tell the pol—' I said, far too many thoughts jostling to be spoken.

'We've definitely got to tell the police,' said Alec. 'From scripture classes with a schoolmaster who was higher than year-old Stilton. And yes, it is horrible. But you see what it means, don't you?'

I always resented him wheeling out that particular gambit. 'It presumably means that Silas wasn't down here chasing pretty girls,' I said. 'And it might mean—' But Alec was shaking his head.

'The nicks,' he said. 'The little pricks and nicks all over him.'

'Ohhhhhh!' I looked at the spugna, pressed it experimentally against the palm of my other hand and held it up for Alec to see.

'But that's not all, Dandy. It means that the knife in the coffin lid was a red herring. Not even an innocent red herring that swam into our view. It was a deliberately planted red herring, put there to bamboozle us by someone who knew Silas would have these marks upon him and wanted to explain them away.'

'We need even more than ever to ring up Daisy now,' I said. 'We have to ask her what she knows about all this.' I waved a hand at the hairy undergarments and the innocent-looking little pincushion thingumajig. Alec, emboldened by finding these unwholesome items rather than satin and lace, rolled them up again, stuffed them into the paper bag and put it under his arm, cocking the other one at me. 'Shall we?'

Thankfully, there was no one at the desk when we emerged from the cloakroom alcove. Tom, visible through the door into the bar, turned slightly in our direction but it was just gone opening time and he soon reapplied himself to his task, pulling a shining tap down and sending a great gushing spout of foam into a tilted glass. Alec and I slipped out of his view unheeded.

'Pallister?' I said. 'It's Mrs Gilver. Is Miss Grant about anywhere?'

'I shall tell Mr Gilver you have rung, madam,' said Pallister reprovingly. 'And fetch Miss Grant too.'

Alec and I waited silently, ears straining hard for the approach of Tom or the return of Manie, eyes roaming casually over the familiar jumble of ashtrays, calendars, blotters and little jugs. I would never have guessed that breweries and distilleries produced as many knick-knacks as any motor-car manufacturer. Those gentlemen are not happy unless every customer grips the steering wheel with a pair of chamois gloves bearing the company name and has a hip flask in the glove box done out in the company livery.

'Hang o—' I said, just as Grant began to speak at the other end.

'What's the state of play down there this evening?' she said. 'Madam.'

'No time for that,' I told her. 'Is there any chance of getting Mrs Esslemont to the telephone?

'No need,' said Grant. 'She's in your sitting room. She was getting bored upstairs and it made a lot of running up and down for Becky so we moved her.'

'I hope the police matron doesn't spring a visit,' I said. 'That would be hard to explain.'

'We've shut the main gate and given Mac's middle boy a sixpence to run up and tell us if anyone official arrives.'

'It all sounds very cosy,' I said. 'Daisy will stay till Christmas at this rate.'

'Until the plaster's off anyway,' said Grant, chastening me. I had quite forgotten about the broken arm and the broken leg. And the widowhood, to be perfectly honest. At least, I found myself wondering why she sounded quite so glum when Grant lifted the other telephone and handed it over.

'We've got various troubling matters to discuss with you,

Daisy darling,' I said. 'And I think the best way to do it is simply to plunge in, ask everything, then all have a stiff drink. What say you?'

'I'm numb,' Daisy said. 'I feel as though I'm in a dream, so it would almost be a relief to feel something. I tried to think about being convicted of murder, being hanged even, to see if I could jolt myself into fear instead of this, but it didn't work.'

'Darling,' I said.

'Then I asked Grant to dash me over the head with a jug of cold water but she refused.'

I heard Grant, in the background, say something about velvet upholstery.

'I did love him, Dandy,' Daisy said. 'For all his faults, I never stopped loving him.'

'Rightio,' I said, an inadequate response to such an outpouring, granted, but I needed to be brisk to get through what lay ahead of me. I beckoned Alec to come near and share the earpiece. When he was comfortably huddled up beside me with his elbows on the desk, I took a deep breath . . . and chickened out. 'Let's start here,' I said. 'Tell me everything you know about these Halliburtons.'

Daisy groaned. 'I've never met them,' she said. 'Silas always maintained they were too dull for words and he wanted to spare me. See? He was very kind, in his way.'

'They don't sound dull,' I said. 'Rather too lively if anything. But go on.'

'He's known Mr for donkey's years,' Daisy said. 'They were at school together. Oh! Imagine Silas as a schoolboy. In his little shorts and cap.' I waited until she had stopped crying. 'They lost touch for a while,' she went on, presently, 'which explains why I never ran into him in the season or at our engagement party or wedding. Remember our wedding, Dandy?' She sighed. 'Then he came back into Silas's life owing to some sort of money troubles. I never really understood what exactly, only that Silas acted as . . . oh who knows . . . a guarantor? A backer for something? He was so generous. And, since it was his money, I left him to it. It made life so much more peaceful, I found.'

I daresay, I thought. If there was always plenty of money, I was sure it *did* feel nice to wash one's delicate hands of it and let one's husband do what he would. Daisy had not needed to have the dreary and mortifying conversations the rest of us endured: about shutting up our hunting boxes and doing without a chauffeur.

'But even if you never met them,' Alec said, 'you must know something about them.'

'Golf?' said Daisy vaguely. 'And I think there's a ward. And bits and bobs of philanthropy. Silas's role was never very clear. Except he did say once . . . now what was it? When the girls were small . . .' She was beginning to sound more alert and less . . . "droopy" is not a kind word to use when describing mourning. 'Ah yes,' she went on, in a livelier tone still. 'Berenice asked one of the nurserymaids to keep her pocket money and refuse all entreaties to dole it out for sweeties and picture papers, because she was saving up to buy a donkey when we went to Brighton.'

'She was the sweetest child,' I said. I remembered Berenice Esslemont's endless crusades to spare foxes from the hunt, chickens from the pot and, apparently, seaside donkeys from the drudgery of offering rides along the beach.

'It all went wrong,' Daisy continued. 'The maid spent the money on her day off. Came back roaring drunk, as I remember. Silas wanted to sack her but I said it was Bennie's fault for putting temptation in the poor girl's way and that she should have taken responsibility for herself. And I remember Silas saying that it reflected well on her that she knew her own limitations and asked for the help she needed. He said it quite befitted the daughter of an insurance broker to put herself beyond ruin, whether the threat was fire, flood, or the toffee jar in the tuck shop.'

'Yes, but what does any of this have to do with—' Alec said.

'And then,' Daisy cut in, 'I said: "Is that what you do for those blasted Halliburtons down in wherever it is? You make up for their lack of common sense?" Whereupon the strangest thing happened. Silas, easy-going Silas of all people, went quite white and asked in a strangled voice what I knew about the Halliburtons.'

'And?' I said.

'I told him I had lost my diamond-drop earrings. Or at least I had mislaid them and so I was searching all over the place and I opened the safe in his business room to see if they had ended up in there. Not as mad as it sounds because once, years earlier, he had found a string of pearls in the garden where I had taken them off because I couldn't bear the rattling while I played croquet, and he had put them in his safe as a stop gap and forgotten to tell me.'

'I meant "And what did you discover about the Halliburtons?"' I said, trying not to let any irritation show in my voice. She sounded much more like herself, remembering the happy days of croquet and small squabbles about pearls, but she still deserved gentle handling.

'I saw the deeds to their house. Is it really a castle? With a drawbridge and everything? Various other holdings too. And I found the whole thing rather rum because giving the deeds to

Silas would suggest that they were liable to bet them at poker otherwise, and that they were too broke to pay a lawyer to hold them like ordinary people do. But they seemed to have bought a school for their village, which made them sound rather worthy as well as pretty well-off, and they also owned a shop – was it a shop? – and a laundry of all things, which made them sound positively suburban and middle class. So a bit of a mystery all round. And no less mysterious after Silas practically fainted at me mentioning them.' She took a breath. 'Golly it hurts to talk.'

'You're probably doing yourself all kinds of good,' I said. 'They do say we should let out our feelings.'

'No,' said Daisy. 'I meant that I cracked a rib or two as well as my arm and my leg. But did any of that help you?'

'Not a jot,' said Alec, just as I said:

'I rather think it did, you know.'

'Did it?' Alec said taking his head away from the earpiece and staring at me.

Daisy laughed and then drew in a sharp breath. 'How do you two struggle on together?' she said. 'You never agree about anything.'

'I hope you find the next enquiry amusing,' I said. 'But I doubt it.'

'Good,' said Daisy. 'Laughing hurts even more.'

'When Silas's body was undressed to be washed and laid out,' I said, 'the woman who did it was surprised by what she found.' I waited, but Daisy was silent. It was a silence as deep and heavy as any I had ever heard and I rather thought she was letting it all in again: the bald fact of Silas being dead. It is always astonishing how many times that simple fact must reoccur to one before it sticks for good. 'He was wearing the most extraordinary undergarments, darling,' I said. 'Did you know?'

'Silas?' Daisy squawked. 'Ouch! Silas? No, you're mistaken. It must have been a prank. Gosh, if he *had* been at the regimental dinner I would say it was a practical joke. They were forever grabbing one another and putting on frocks and stockings.'

'That's exactly what I thought when the girl hinted at something strange under his suiting,' Alec said. 'But it wasn't that at all, was it, Dandy?'

I glared at him. 'Daisy dear, he was wearing a hair shirt. Like a monk does. For penance. And he'd been beating himself with a spiked pincushion thing too.'

Daisy was making the most extraordinary noises, gasping and gulping. I could not tell if she was weeping or was about to vomit. Then, at long last, she let out a hoot of laughter. 'Oh my God, Dandy, you utter horror. I can feel my bloody rib unknitting itself into two pieces again. Oh Lord, that hurts. What nonsense!'

'We saw it with our own eyes!'

'Not on Silas's body, you didn't,' Daisy said. 'Good Lord, Dandy. Have you lost your senses? I mean, I'm the last person to deny that Silas had sins to atone for. But repentant was one thing you could never call my dear sweet nightmare of a spouse. Someone is having you on.'

Chapter 16

We dismissed what Daisy said about being duped, of course. She was not here in this strange little village, where peculiar things happened on the hour every hour, including Sundays. We made our goodbyes and, even while greatly relieved to hear her sounding a little better, still we looked forward, in a most ungenerous way, to proving our point and watching her eat her words, just as soon as we had made sense of the muddle.

Cloaked in rectitude then, and since it was a beautiful evening with a promise of chops and pond pudding later, Alec was minded to take a walk in the golden light. Supper was over for the villagers, it seemed, for the children of Dirleton were out on the green with hoops and skipping ropes. Two little girls were bouncing a tennis ball each against the wall of the castle, treacherously close to Lizzy Hogg's window. Their thin black pigtails, which were doubled into loops and fastened, jounced up and down as they counted: 'Twenty-one, twenty-two, twenty-three, twenty-four . . .' before one of them tripped over a tussock and watched her ball roll away. The other girl, surely her sister, immediately stopped and waited for the wandering ball to be caught.

'How sweet,' Alec said. 'There doesn't seem to be any competition involved.'

'Donald once got to two hundred, bouncing a tennis ball against the wall of the stables,' I said. 'Teddy was so cross and jealous he darted into its path and ended the run. He had a bruise on his tummy that was perfectly round and pitch-black. Then later a red bottom from Hugh's slipper. I've never seen Hugh so angry with either of them. Even when Teddy got arrested at the end of his last term.'

'I can understand that,' said Alec. 'One wouldn't want one's child to be a spoilsport or a poor loser. Hup, there they go again.'

The pigtail sisters had regrouped and launched into the preamble of their counting game.

> *'Three witches, Three witches*
> *Marry a beggar and live in ditches*
> *Six witches, six witches*
> *Marry a laird, with all his riches*
> *Nine witches, nine witches*
> *Marry a prince with golden britches.*
> *One, two, three, four . . .'*

'One imagines Mrs Halliburton regrets marrying *her* laird,' Alec said. 'Riches or no riches.'

'That reminds me,' I said, 'what is "the usual three, six, nine"? Do you know?'

'In what context?' said Alec. 'Hang on, Dandy. Three, six, nine? What put that in your head?'

I did not want to tell him he had missed Mrs Wallace's stupendous shortbread. Instead I cast about for a plausible lie. I failed to find one. 'I can't remember,' I said. 'Someone said something or perhaps we read something.'

'We did, didn't we?' said Alec. 'Where did we come across someone going on about that series of numbers? Or no, not exactly, but . . .'

'How remarkable,' I said. It was a new experience in my detecting life accidentally to come up with an idea while merely fudging an unwelcome truth about biscuits.

'In what way?' Alec said.

'Oh, just it used to be me alone who got those annoying half notions,' I told him airily, fudging again for all I was worth. 'But you seem to have succumbed recently.'

Alec opened his mouth to query further, but then blinked and pointed, drawing my attention to the figure of Paddy Watson, who was bearing down on us from the post office cottage.

'Lovely evening,' he said, drawing near. 'Are you enjoying your stay?'

It was a peculiar opening gambit, given the purpose of our stay, and neither of us managed more than a quizzical look in response.

'I spoke to Mr Esslemont's widow today,' I said, meaning to reprimand him.

Now he cocked his head at me. 'Really?' he said. 'I thought she was in a coma.'

That set me gobbling like a goldfish that had jumped out of its bowl to die on the carpet. Thankfully, Alec stepped in before I had the chance to make chumps of us both. 'Mrs Gilver's maid held the earpiece up to Mrs Esslemont's head,' he said. 'The newest thinking from the best brain doctors is that patients in a torpor should be stimulated. Fascinating stuff. But tell me,' he went on, 'how on earth did you come to know the details of Mrs Esslemont's condition?'

'Oh,' said Mr Watson. 'Ah. Well, young McLean is a good boy and a conscientious officer but he has loose lips, I'm afraid.'

'Are you bosom pals?' I asked, for it did not seem likely. On the heels of that thought came another, though: what exactly was unlikely about a postman and a bobby being friends? The answer was just out my grasp and receding all the faster as I reached for it.

When I started paying attention again, Alec and Mr Watson were still talking about medicine – electric treatments for nervous problems, specifically – although Mr Watson seemed keen to end the discussion.

'Did you want to tell us something?' I asked him.

'I can't comment on information I'm only party to through my job,' said Mr Watson, carefully. 'It's not what postmen do.' He hesitated then. 'Of course, there are some things that postmen do but oughtn't. And that's why I wanted to talk to you. But first, can I be assured of your discretion?'

'Do you need to be?'

'Most certainly,' he said. 'I can't afford to lose my place. But I want to help you with your investigation. I want Mr Esslemont's killer caught.'

'As does everyone,' I said. 'I'm happy to agree to your terms, Mr Watson. My lips are sealed but my ears are open.'

Alec nodded, with his mouth pursed in a thoughtful manner, which made him look like a wise trout.

'Well,' said Mr Watson. 'We read postcards. We all do. It's a lot of walking, this job, and when they're right there in your hand you can't help it.'

'Good heavens,' I said. 'Is that all? Anyone who writes secrets on a postcard deserves to be the talk of the sorting office.'

Mr Watson's smile of relief lit up his rather dour face and made it almost handsome. It also made it awfully familiar, and I was reminded that, if the parish books were to be believed, we had met numerous half-sisters of his over the course of our short visit here.

'And usually no one does,' said Mr Watson. 'Write secrets, that is. Usually it's "wish you were here" or "buy bread and milk for Monday return", but these were something different.'

I thought he had paused for dramatic effect before noticing that it was the surrounding children who seemed to be troubling him.

'Let's go and sit on the bench under the tree,' I suggested. 'Away from impressionable young ears.'

When we were settled, and Alec had begun on the inevitable pipe filling, Mr Watson took up his tale.

'The postcards came to Dirleton because they had Dirleton names on and Dirleton addresses,' he said. 'I don't blame any of my colleagues for that. But the thing is the names didn't match the addresses and the addresses didn't match the names. There is a "Marmion" – the big villa on the road in – but it's Mrs Keith who lives there and this was addressed to a Mrs Souter. And then there was one for Ivy Bank, where Mr Main lives, and it was addressed to Mr Wardrop. Mr Neilson lives at Backend Holding and there was a postcard directed to Backend Holding, only addressed to Mr Peattie. And a McNeill at Lilac Cottage—'

'Which is empty,' Alec said, earning a look of some astonishment.

'Finally I had one for Miss Deathless of Monument Villa,' Watson went on, when he had recovered from the surprise of Alec's unaccountable local knowledge. 'That's when I twigged. Come.' He stood and strode off towards the leaping stone, with Alec and me in tow. We slowed when we got there, expecting him to stop, but he marched on until he stood at the cenotaph. 'Look,' he said, pointing. 'Names of fallen soldiers. Souter, Peattie, Wardrop.'

'Oh and Miss Deathless of Monument Villa!' I said, reading again the inscription on the shaft of the stone, which spoke of the "deathless memory". 'How tasteless,' I said. 'How shabby. What did you do?'

'Well, like I said, I tend to read quite a few of the postcards in my bag,' he told us. 'And I'm glad I did in this case. Because otherwise I might have delivered them to the addresses like we're supposed to. Except for Miss Deathless, I mean. But I read them, as I say.'

'And?' said Alec, to whom Mr Watson's dramatic pauses were becoming an annoyance.

'And I decided I wasn't going to be part of any such nonsense,' Mr Watson said. 'The wording varied a bit from one to another but the gist of them was all the same. "He is coming who must die". Or "One is coming who must die". They caught my eye at first because that's a very short message for a postcard. Once someone has bought the stamp they usually try to cram in as much as possible. At times the address is hard to make out with the way the message goes round and round the edge. But this was just one sentence in large script and blank white otherwise. "One is coming who must die". Nasty.'

'When *was* this?' Alec said.

'About a week before Mr Esslemont came. And died.' He added the last bit as though we might not have grasped the import.

'Four postcards for made-up people at real addresses and the fifth and last to the cenotaph?' I asked.

'No, it was five and one makes six,' said Mr Watson. 'Now, who did I forget?'

'But all saying the same thing?' I persisted.

'No indeed. The one to Miss Deathless said "by my hand". That one came up from the sack first you see and I thought it was some kind of joke. "By hand" being the opposite of stamped and sent. Do you see? I would have dismissed it as a silly prank if it hadn't been for the others.'

'And where are these postcards, Mr Watson?' Alec said. 'Would you be willing to let us see them? Or did you turn them over to someone immediately.'

'Neither,' Paddy Watson said. 'I burned them.'

'What? Why?' I exclaimed.

'Dirleton doesn't need that sort of attention,' said Watson.

'You sound very sure,' said Alec. 'As though you speak from experience.' His hint was veiled but it was definitely there.

'What sort of attention?' I asked, much more bluntly. 'The postcards hint at the murder, don't they? I'd have thought the murder itself was the thing to avoid.'

'I might have been wrong,' said Mr Watson, 'but there it is. What's done is done.'

'Indeed,' I said. 'So, in the absence of the cards themselves, what else can you tell me about them? Did the names refer to earlier residents? Is there a connection between the boys remembered on the cenotaph and the cottage residents? Sweethearts, perhaps?'

'Sweethearts?' said Mr Watson.

'There is always a lot of musing in our line,' said Alec. 'Ideas must be aired, only to be dismissed nine times out of ten. The tenth time, one airs an idea and it sticks. What were you thinking, Dandy?'

'That Silas didn't fight in the last war,' I said. 'So threats to his life sent to bereaved women, reminding them of the names of their lost loves . . .'

'Or more prosaically,' Alec said, 'someone needed to drum up some names in a hurry and copied them.'

'I think both notions sound ridiculous,' said Paddy Watson.

'Mrs Keith? She hasn't been anyone's sweetheart since Victoria was on the throne!'

'That's Mrs Gilver's notion,' Alec pointed out. 'What's the problem with mine?'

'And Lilac Cottage was never a love bower,' Mr Watson went on, ignoring him. 'The last tenant there—' He stopped dead as if someone had pulled a switch and silenced him.

'Yes, we know about her,' Alec said. 'That's still Mrs Gilver's notion though, my dear chap. And I repeat, what's wrong with mine?'

'That's all I mean to say to you,' Watson blurted out. 'I got the postcards. I've told you about them. It's your job now to work out what it all means.'

'Oh, I don't suppose that will give us too much trouble,' I said.

Paddy Watson gave a sharp nod that was almost a bow and took his leave in some haste, cleaving through the groups of children at play as he forged a path homeward.

'Well!' said Alec.

'Indeed,' I agreed. 'Jolly well spotted, darling. He pooh-poohed my idea, but it was definitely yours that bothered him, wasn't it?'

'Yes, it was me saying someone needed to come up with names and took them from the inscription.'

'But why—?' I began. 'Look, come back to the bench and sit down.'

The village children, out again for the last of the sunshine after their dinners, were busily engaged upon games of skipping and football. It still struck me, after all these years, never to see a little boy with a cricket bat. I missed the sounds of it, not at all made up for by the soft punch of boot on leather and the endless scuffling.

261

'Why,' I asked again, when we were settled, 'would that particular possibility upset Mr Watson?'

'No one likes to be made a fool of,' Alec said. He gave a rueful laugh. 'We didn't care for Daisy saying someone was having *us* on, did we?'

'That's different,' I said.

'Is it?' asked Alec. 'Let's consider it. What if there was no rhyme or reason to the names and addresses? What if they were plucked at random from the cenotaph and the post office directory?'

'For what purpose?' I said. 'To unnerve the postman? Why?'

'I think I'm beginning to see,' said Alec. 'Not to unnerve the postman. To unnerve *us*. Or bamboozle us anyway.'

'Who do you think did it?'

'Paddy Watson, of course.'

'But he wouldn't have burned them,' I said. 'He'd have shown them to us. Like Manie Halliburton showed us the peculiar lingerie.'

'No,' said Alec. 'And I know why not.' I waited. 'A postman would be the last person to show us a postcard and pretend it had been through His Majesty's mail. He knows too much about it to feel confident in the fakery.'

'Whereas Manie Halliburton knew too *little*?' I said, 'About Silas? Yes, she had no idea how ludicrous the spugna was, did she?'

'I think so,' Alec said, 'I really do think so. Because she didn't know Silas. And didn't know how well we knew him. Otherwise, she might have plumped for lingerie within the meaning of the act.'

'I'll tell you something else that has only just occurred to me too,' I said. 'I met Manie coming from laying out Silas's body and she didn't have anything in her hands.'

'Hmph,' said Alec. 'You see what this means, don't you Dandy?'

'I fear so,' I said, although my mind was reeling.

'Say it.'

'We are being fed a load of absolute nonsense. Aren't we?'

Alec nodded. 'We are being treated like a pair of fools.'

A huge wave of relief washed over me and I sat back, resting my head against the tree. 'Yes,' I said. 'Yes, we are. Daisy saw it because she hasn't been here, steeping in it. Two servings of utter bunkum.'

'Just two?' said Alec, slyly. 'What about the knife in the coffin?'

'That's three,' I agreed. 'We already worked out that the knife was a red herring. When we found the spugna. Any advance on three?' I spoke lightly, but I could feel myself getting angry.

'Of course!' Alec cried. 'Pig's blood in a stolen car and someone else's clothes? I'm more than happy to jettison the writers.'

'Although,' I said, 'something else about them is bothering me and I can't put my finger on it.'

'The crows!' Alec said, ignoring me. The floodgates were open now.

'Oh good Lord, yes!' I agreed. 'Definitely the crows. Good riddance to the crows. I shall throw my handkerchief and its dried-up contents on the fire tonight.'

'And another thing,' Alec said. 'What about the story of Mr Halliburton's return? It didn't make any sense that Mrs Halliburton would tell Nessie Clarkson, did it?'

'Nor it did,' I said. 'The theft of the parish books too. They didn't even steal the right one! Gosh, we must have pored over those things for an hour, sneezing from the dust.'

'This feels marvellous!' Alec said. 'And you know what else we can ditch? I still insist that we don't know when it happened. They changed the story about the timing, from midnight to "the witching hour".'

'Or at least they changed the story about when the witching hour is,' I said. 'What about the tent pegs?'

'Except that Silas *did* bash his head on the stone and I *found* the tent pegs. No one showed them to me.'

'No, you sat down on one,' I said. 'But consider the doctor and the police who attended Silas at the end. Not to mention anyone in the time intervening. Think about it, Alec. We went for a look as soon as we arrived. The fingerprint man was there shortly afterwards. Manie carried her bucket to the spot. We were all over the place when we found the clothes. Someone would surely have tripped before you came along, if the tent pegs had been there since the murder.'

'All right, let's shed the tent pegs from the diminishing set of real clues.'

'And that leads us to something else as well,' I said. 'Just listen to this and tell me if I've gone too far. We don't know *who* did it, obviously. We were misled about *how* it was done. We might not know *when* it was done. We certainly don't know *why* it was done. Now, with all that in mind, and if we no longer accept that he tripped over a piano wire, pegged in around the stone . . .'

'You mean . . . ?'

'I do,' I said. 'I really do.'

'Where!' Alec said. 'We don't know *where* it was done. He might well have been killed somewhere else entirely, then carried or dragged to the stone and left there.'

'I'm saying everything we've been fed about this case is utter rot.'

For a moment, we beamed at one another. I for one felt quite giddy to have got rid of so much bewildering nonsense. Then, as I was beginning to settle down, Alec's face clouded and suddenly we were no longer beaming. We were staring glumly into one another's eyes.

'Meaning that we have no clues and no suspects and nothing to go on and we're nowhere,' Alec said.

'Which does sound rather bleak,' I admitted. 'But at least we're not drowning in the red herrings that so many villagers have been more than eager to wave in front of us.'

'It was all so elaborate,' Alec said. 'The motor car, for God's sake. And where on earth did a woman like Manie Halliburton get those penitential garments?'

'Perhaps someone sent them to the laundry,' I said. 'With the little thingummy in the pocket.'

'Don't make me laugh, Dandy,' Alec said. 'Hysteria could take over quite easily.'

'Resist it,' I told him. 'What we need to do now is set about solving this thing in a sensible fashion.'

'But what do we actually know? What's left when the manure is shovelled onto the heap where it belongs?'

'We know that everyone has been lying. Going to some lengths in their lies. We need to work out why.'

Alec groaned. 'I can't,' he said. 'I know we'll have to ask ourselves that question eventually, but for now couldn't we try to establish some plain, physical facts?'

'That does sound rather lovely,' I admitted. 'Let's be quiet a minute, clear our minds, and start again.'

Alec stretched his legs out in front of him and puffed on his pipe. I lit a cigarette and made myself comfortable beside him.

The children, one by one, were leaving their playmates and going home. There was no clock and I did not hear anyone

265

call them. They responded to the sinking sun and the cooling air like little birds flying south or leaves turning brown. Only two children were actually summoned in all the time we sat there and that was the ball-bouncing pair of girls. Tom emerged from the front door of the Castle Inn and shouted to them. They protested, as children always will, but they trailed towards him and in at the pub door, pausing to let him drop a kiss onto each of their heads as they passed. He stood for another minute, looking around the empty green like a good shepherd, as though to check that all the lambs were safely gathered. Catching sight of the two of us under the shade of the tree, he raised a hand in greeting before turning away.

'Dirleton is a nice place despite everything,' I said. 'I hope we get to the bottom of this without spoiling it.'

'Let's start,' Alec said. 'Facts about the death of Silas Esslemont.'

'He misled Daisy about what he was doing and came here instead,' I began. 'His only connection to the place is a friendly stewardship he carries out for the Halliburton family.'

'No one here seems to know him, except for a rather mad old woman who thinks he is the embodiment of evil, a laundress who planted compromising objects on his body, proving that she does not know him well, and a very odd child who thinks she can herd crows. Do any of them have a motive?'

'We're off again already,' I said. 'Motives are theorising. Facts, we said.'

'He died by being hit on his head.'

'He was summoned by a letter that was found in his pocket.'

At that, we appeared to have run dry.

'We need to work out why everyone is lying,' I said.

'What we need,' said Alec, 'is an impartial, reliable, honest source of detailed local knowledge. Someone we can ask who won't simply start another round of bamboozling.'

'Constable McLean,' I said. 'He's . . .'

'What?' said Alec.

'I was going to say he isn't . . .'

'What?'

'He's like Tom. He's not . . .'

'This could get annoying, Dandy.'

'Well, we keep repeating "they",' I said. '*They* tricked us. *They're* trying to distract us. *They* threw red herrings in our path. Who? Who are we talking about? It just occurred to me that I seem to know it's not the constable nor the sergeant – I've quite come around on the sergeant – and that we both like Tom and Bella. Not just for the out-of-hours whisky and the cooking. So who is "they"?'

'Nessie Clarkson,' said Alec. 'Who told us about the telephone call from Mrs Halliburton. Paddy Watson with his postcards, obviously. Lizzy Hogg with her crows and the stolen parish books in her room. Manie Halliburton with the underwear. Maggie Goodfellow with her trumped-up alibi for Said Paddy.'

'What about the Wallaces? Or Mr Wallace anyway? He was sitting there in the church with the knife in his hands telling us he found it in the coffin lid.'

'No, not Mr Wallace,' said Alec. 'Of course not. But I definitely feel as though someone is escaping our attention.' He paused and then groaned. 'We are chumps, Dandy. What do those five have in common?

I groaned back at him. 'They are Halliburton's children, entered into the parish record as offspring of the laird of Dirleton.'

Alec sat up straight and clapped his hands. 'Suddenly it doesn't feel as if we're back at square one at all,' he said. 'We know *why*.'

'Do we?'

'It's rather simple really. Halliburton has been providing for his bastards quite generously, with cottages and jobs.'

'Cottages or *castles* and jobs.'

'Silas being the steady hand on the tiller keeping the little ship afloat.'

'Ah!' I said. 'So anyone who wants to capsize it doesn't need to get to Halliburton all the way over there in Italy.'

'Exactly.'

'They simply have to remove Silas and the whole strange little set-up will falter.'

'Now. Who would want that?'

'Mrs Halliburton,' I said. 'Or at least, I would if it were Hugh.'

'Not likely,' Alec said. 'Why then would the five half-siblings be setting up pranks and hoaxes to throw us off the scent? Why would they plunge into the middle of a murder case to protect *her* of all people?'

'But they must have done it to protect someone from suspicion,' I said. 'Nothing else makes any sense at all.'

'I've got it! Alec said. 'What if there's another one? A sixth half-sibling. If a sixth sibling killed Silas then the behaviour of the other five is explained.'

'But the motive for upsetting the apple cart disappears,' I said.

'Let's at least go back to the parish books and find out if there *is* a sixth one,' Alec said.

As we stood up, however, we saw the welcome sight of the minister and his wife out, arm in arm, for an evening stroll. 'Alec,' I said, 'come and meet Mrs Wallace. She's delightful.'

'You have a glint in your eye, Dandy. What are you plotting?'

'I'm going to face Mr Wallace with his extraordinary decision,' I said. 'If he hadn't been so "kind" as to parade Halliburton's indiscretions for all the world to see, whoever took against it – my money is still on Mrs Halliburton – might have been able to look the other way. Good grief, looking the other way is practically all some wives do from honeymoon to funeral. But I can see why having the by-blows right here and entered into the record would send her potty.'

'I think that's a bit harsh to Mr Wallace,' Alec said. 'Tracing a murder back to his door. If Eve hadn't eaten the apple and all that.'

'It was Adam who was told not to eat the apple,' I said. 'Actually.'

'Aha!' said Mr Wallace, who was just in earshot now. 'This sounds like my kind of argument. And you, dear lady, are right!'

Chapter 17

It seldom happens that Alec is forced to concede a point to me in front of witnesses. The unaccustomed fillip made me bullish and I charged Mr Wallace with his transgression rather more definitely than I otherwise might.

'Vicar,' I said, because my youth, though distant, ran through me still like a seam of quartz through rock, 'why on earth did you record the Halliburton children as plainly as all that in your record?'

'The who?' said Mr Wallace. His wife, leaning on his arm, looked up at him in some alarm.

'Manie for a start,' I said, thinking that she bore her father's name and she at least could not be denied.

'Oh . . . those . . . the . . .' said Mr Wallace. 'Plainly, you call it? I've never thought of it that way.'

'Mrs Gilver,' said his wife, 'and you must be Mr Osborne, of course. We were only going for a stroll. Why don't we turn back and talk about this at the manse? A glass of sherry, perhaps? And there are cheese straws if that's not too pedestri—'

'Nothing like a good cheese straw,' Alec said, never one to let an offer of food be rescinded.

Settled in the drawing room soon afterwards with large glasses of good sherry and a veritable platter of little pastries, Mr Wallace started again. 'I meant to be kind, as I believe

I told you last time, Mrs Gilver. But what makes you call it plain?'

'To record the parent of a natural child?' I said. 'What could be plainer?'

'Well,' Alec said, 'since you ask, Dandy, what could be plainer is to record the chap's name rather than his station. Rather a balanced kindness, Mr Wallace, if you don't mind me saying so: not to leave the mites without a name at all but to offer some shield to the scoundrel.'

'What scoundrel?' said Mr Wallace at the same time as his wife said, 'What chap?'

Alec looked at me and I looked at him and we both felt a shift. 'Halliburton,' I said. 'The laird of Dirleton Castle.'

'What?' said Mr Wallace, inhaling a few crumbs and coughing until his eyes watered; the cheese straws really were very fresh and flaky.

'And then, after he started to buy up this and that all over the village,' Alec went on, 'laird of all Dirleton. We noticed the change, didn't we Dan?'

'Halliburton,' said Mr Wallace, but blankly. 'Are you saying you think *Halliburton* is the father of all six of our little orphans?' Six indeed, I noted, and saw Alec do so too. 'You think Halliburton is Dirleton's very own Jock Tamson?' the minister went on. 'I've never met the man but one wouldn't want to think anyone could be quite so . . .'

'Careless?' Mrs Wallace suggested.

'Never met hi—?' Alec said.

I cut him off. 'We don't think so; we *know* so,' I said. 'But we thought you knew so too. And said so. Or wrote so anyway.'

'Oh!' said his wife. 'Oh my giddy aunt! Laird! *Laird*! Oh my, you thought Geoffrey was saying their father was the laird?'

'I'm lost,' I admitted.

'It's their mother,' said Mr Wallace. 'And not even their mother really. Heaven *knows* who their mothers are. But their guardian was Mrs Laird. Mrs Laird who lived at Dirleton Castle. It was my decision – taken out of kindness, as I say – to record her as their parent, so at least they had one to their name. So you see, it was anything but plain. Which is why that word surprised me.'

'Their guardian was a Mrs Laird who lived at Dirleton Castle?' Alec said.

'But this Mrs Laird didn't subsequently take over the school and the post office too,' I said. I knew we had made a mistake but still I felt compelled to defend it. 'Why did you change the entries to "Laird of Dirleton"?'

'Of course she didn't,' Mr Wallace said. 'Oh heavens, you thought . . . ? No, it's Halliburton right enough who owns so much of the property around here. Jeannie, I suppose it *does* make sense to think the children are his, actually. Doesn't it?'

'I don't understand,' I said. I glared at Alec. He did not understand either and it would have been generous of him to take a turn of saying it.

'More kindness,' said Mrs Wallace, raising her glass to her husband. 'You really are a lovely man, you know.' She turned to me. 'He did not want to record Mrs Laird's reduced circumstances in too much detail, you see. From the castle to the humblest cottage was quite a fall.'

'Halliburton kicked her out,' Mr Wallace said. 'As soon as the first child – Miss Goodfellow – was old enough to live there alone, he bought Lilac Cottage for the good woman and she moved there with the little ones.'

'Lilac Cottage?' I said. 'We've been there.'

'Oh Lord, Dandy,' said Alec. 'Didn't the neighbour say the tenant's name was Laird?'

I shook my head in sorrow at our scattiness, for he was right; she had. 'But that tenant was evicted,' I said. 'Where did he move her to after that?'

'He cut her off completely,' Mr Wallace said. 'She was thrown onto her own resources. She lives in a little hovel halfway along the back drive to Archerfield.'

'It's not much more than a shack,' Mrs Wallace added. 'But with a very pretty garden.'

Alec's jaw dropped open and, had I not been chewing the last mouthful of pastry, mine might well have done so too. 'But we thought that old woman was Mither Gollane,' he said.

'Yes,' said Mrs Wallace. 'That's right. At least, it is according to the parish books because of my dear sweet husband here, but it's caused all sorts of trouble.'

'What do you mean?' I said. 'Did Mrs Laird marry Mr Gollane after he'd been widowed?'

The Wallaces looked at one another with dancing eyes and then burst into peals of laughter. 'Oh dear,' the minister said. 'You *have* got yourselves in a muddle. "Mither Gollane" isn't a name. It's a title. Mother Gullane, in English. Mither Gollane in Scots. Mother of the parish, you see?'

I thought I began to see, faintly. 'A title given to . . . ?'

'The most prolific woman,' Mrs Wallace said. 'The most fecund of all the mothers. The luckiest, the Sarah, the old woman who lives in a shoe. She is an important character around these parts, Mrs Gilver. She is the one who oversees the leaping at the leaping stone every summer and she is handsomely rewarded.'

'And so she's of great interest to scholars of folklore, I suppose,' Alec said, glumly.

'Oh tremendous interest,' said Mrs Wallace. 'She's like the

Loch Ness Monster and the Burry Man rolled into one. Only she's a real person. Like the Dalai Lama.'

'Handsomely rewarded,' I said, which was the phrase that stuck in my mind and finally offered me a glimmer of a clue about this most tangled of cases. 'So when you recorded her wards as her children . . .'

'She overtook the last one and caused no end of fuss,' said Mr Wallace. 'I hadn't thought of that, of course. Gosh, a mere nine children wouldn't have got any woman the title this time last century.'

'Nine!' Alec and I shouted in chorus, making Mrs Wallace slop the last of her sherry onto the hearthrug. She tutted but more at the loss of a mouthful of wine than at the thought of a stain. She rubbed it half-heartedly with her toe and her husband leapt up to pour her a replacement.

'Three, six, nine!' Alec said, at a more temperate volume. 'Mither Gollane even said it to us. That she had nine children and had given birth three times. We thought of triplets briefly.'

'To be honest,' I said, 'I thought of a shortbread recipe too. And that song the children sing. "Three witches, six witches" . . .'

'I do wish they would go to the pictures on a Saturday morning and learn some different ditties,' Mrs Wallace said, strangely enough seeming more upset by this innocent matter than about any of the other more startling truths about her home village.

'They've been singing it for three hundred years,' said her husband. 'It'll take more than Casey Jones to stop them.'

'Three—' Alec said, but thankfully he saw my subtle glare, stopped speaking and hastily offered a distraction. 'We found your missing parish books, sir.'

'And we shall return them,' I added. 'Sorry it took us so long to tell you. There's just been so much incident, hasn't there, Alec?'

'A barrage,' Alec said. 'A deluge. But we'll pop them back over to you immediately. With our apologies. In fact, why don't we go and fetch them now?' He was giving me a very hard stare, one I understood perfectly.

'One question I do have,' I said as I stood and began to pull my gloves on, 'why does Mither Gollane live in the woods? Even with the loss of her tenancy, won't one of her wards take her in and give her a home?'

'That's one of the great mysteries of Dirleton,' Mrs Wallace said. 'We suspect that their tenure in their own billets hinges on them not doing so, don't we, dear? Mrs Laird displeased Mr Halliburton so thoroughly we think it made him quite vindictive. Quite manipulative actually.'

'Well, but what about her own three children then?' I said.

'Her three sons,' Mr Wallace said. 'Two of them are gone. One died in the Boer War and one died in the Great War. And both were in reserved occupations too. Farming and fishing. They could have been here still.'

Mrs Wallace must have seen my face fall, for first she squeezed my arm in understanding, then, when the squeeze was met with what I imagine must have been a very sad smile, she gave me an out-and-out hug while Alec and the minister stood around awkwardly waiting for the final goodbye.

'Right then,' Alec said when the manse door was closed behind us. He set off down the path at such a clip that gravel sprayed from under his boot heels. 'Are you all right, Dandy? Can we crack on?'

'I will not be all right until I celebrate the next Armistice

275

with both my sons,' I said. 'So we might as well "crack on" in the meantime.'

'Three hundred years,' Alec said.

'Three hundred years,' I agreed. 'Constable McLean said Dirleton hadn't had a day like Saturday for three hundred years. Said it pretty much as soon as we arrived.'

'And the other parish book that was stolen, besides the one with the five Halliburton by-blows in it, is the one from three hundred years ago.'

'If only we had knuckled down and read it through to the end we might have wrapped this case up yesterday.'

Doubt crept in as we climbed the stairs of the Castle Inn, though. 'Do you really think we'll find something of note?' I said.

'I will bet you . . . getting to regale Captain Wicks with the solution . . . that we'll find something in the new book at least,' Alec said. 'And I think I know *what* we'll find too. *Whom* we'll find. Think about what Halliburton owns, Dandy.'

'The castle, Castle View, the Castle Inn,' I said. 'East Gate Lodge, Lilac Cottage. The post office. The laundry. What am I forgetting?'

'The school.'

'Is *that* what you think, Alec? That Miss Meek is the sixth sibling?'

'I will bet you, as I said.'

'But a schoolmistress has to be of the most scrupulous respectability and rectitude. You really mean to suggest that the not-quite daughter of Mither Gollane and half-sister of Lizzy Hogg is running the Dirleton school?'

'I do and the new parish register will prove it. Anyway, if Halliburton's paying the fiddler then he gets to call the tune.'

'Supper on a tray?' I asked him, as I handed over the key

to my room and waited for him to unlock the door. 'You get started on the book and I'll see what I can procure.'

Downstairs again, I braved the public bar, where I could see Tom busy pulling a pint for one of the farmworkers who sat in a row on the high stools. He gave me a startled look as I strolled in, but gone are the days when I was too dainty to walk on sawdust or swerve to avoid a darts match. Not that there was any sawdust here.

'We're hard at it up there,' I said. 'So I wondered if we could have a bowl of soup sent up, rather than come and eat like human beings in the dining room. Sorry about the chops, mind you.'

'Bella's put them in some gravy and spices and it's all keeping warm for you in the kitchen,' he said. 'The pond pudding didn't make it.'

'Tell her she's very kind when you see her.'

'Oh, I'll see her,' said Tom. 'She's my wife, you know. And my daughters have made you some replacement pudding. They insisted you would like it and I promised I would tell you. You don't have to eat it.'

'Those two girls with the pigtails?' I said. 'What did they make?'

'Jelly with bits in,' he said. 'It's their favourite.'

I smiled. 'I shall eat it most gratefully. Bits of what?'

'Oh, fruit,' said the doting father. 'Nothing to fear. Bits of fruit.'

I became aware of a burbling little sound somewhere behind him and stepping up on my tiptoes to look over the bar I saw two little black heads peeping round the door to the back premises. Their fringes had recently been trimmed, giving them a startled look, and I thought, from the fact that each had a front tooth missing, that they must be the same age.

'Twins?' I said. They giggled and nodded. 'Thank you for making jelly. I hope there's enough for you to share it.'

'Isabel stirred it,' said one twin, the gap in her teeth making her lisp.

'And Annabel dropped in the bits,' said the other.

'But Mum had to pour the hot water in because it was hot.'

'And carry it to the cold larder because it was heavy.'

'But we made it, didn't we, Dad?'

'That's enough,' said Tom, gruff with pride. 'Go and tell your ma to warm the plates.'

Letting myself back into my bedroom a minute later, I said to Alec, 'I really *do* hope we resolve all of this without causing further harm. Dirleton has a lot to recommend it. As a place to bring up a family, I mean.' I was carrying two glasses of beer shandy, having been persuaded that this was just the thing to accompany our spice-laden supper, and so I was not looking at Alec as I spoke. It was not until I had laid my burden down that I glanced his way and saw him staring owlishly at me with the older of the two parish books spread open on his lap.

'You found something?' I said. 'In the old book? Three hundred years ago?'

'I found something and how,' he replied. 'I don't know what it is but it's something all right.' He took a draught of shandy and smacked his lips. 'We knew there were similar names, didn't we? Clarksons and Hoggs. Halliburtons, of course. But we weren't paying enough attention. Well, you might have been but I wasn't.'

'That hardly matters,' I said. 'As long as one of us got there in the end. Go ahead and dumbfound me, please.'

'Our five half-siblings discovered so far are Paddy Watson, Manie Halliburton, Lizzy Hogg, Maggie Goodfellow and Nessie Clarkson.'

'Yes,' I said. Alec's habit of spinning out his triumphs is very irritating.

'And between 1599 and 1620, right here in Dirleton, six individuals were born who had these names: Patrick Watson, Jessamine Halliburton, Elizabeth Hogg, Margaret Goodfellow, Agnes Clarkson and Marion Miek.'

'Marion Meek!' I said. 'You were right. You get to regale Captain Wicks. Your hunch was spot-on.'

'Yes,' Alec said, 'but that's not all.'

Again he availed himself of a long pause. This time I used it furiously to try to work out what he meant, what was coming. I could not have done so for a lavish pension, as I was soon to see.

'Those six people I just named died on the same day in 1649,' Alec said. 'One man and five women all died on the same day. Look, it's right here.'

I fortified myself with a mouthful of shandy and went to stand behind him, peering over his shoulder to read the entry. I was still standing there, boggling at it, when the door opened after a soft knock and the cook stood on the threshold with an enormous tray in her sturdy arms.

'Oh, supper!' I said. 'Thank you. You are kind. Just put it on the . . . And your little girls' pretty jelly too. How lovely.'

'Bella, are you in a rush?' Alec asked her. 'Or might we trouble you for some . . . ? Well, I suppose local history is what it comes down to.'

She flicked a glance at the book lying open on his lap and shrugged.

'There's a very curious entry here in this old record book,' I said. 'Six people—'

Bella gasped and took a step backwards. 'Are you at that, are you? I thought you were here to help that poor man

279

who died? Are you here grubbing about at that like all the rest of them? Does Tom know that's what you're at? Leave it. Leave it, I beg you.' She turned on her heel and banged the door shut behind her. We could hear her clogs knocking on the bare boards of the passage all the way to the top of the stairs and then rattling down them.

'What on earth?' I said. 'Should I follow her?'

'Let's not let this lovely curry go to waste,' said Alec. 'Since it cost her so dear to bring it to us. But, afterwards, it's back to Mr Wallace, I reckon. We promised to return the volumes apart from anything else.'

We were saved the trip. When the next knock came minutes later, we both thought it was Bella come back again, but when it opened we saw Mr Wallace standing there.

'I beg your pardon,' he said. 'You're at your dinner. Only, my dear wife sent me over. She's much more perspicacious than I and she saw you both twig to the fact that there was something in that dratted book. It sailed over *my* head, of course. But she's right, isn't she?'

I laid down my knife and fork – there is only so much stewed meat one can consume while theatrics go on all around – and pointed to where the volume still lay open at what was nearly its last page.

'Ah,' said Mr Wallace, when he had studied it through his reading spectacles. 'Believe it or not, I forgot it would be in this one. You'd think the date would be branded on the mind of every Dirletonite, wouldn't you?'

'The date three hundred years ago when ... what happened exactly?' I said.

'Five women and a man were executed for witchcraft,' said Mr Wallace.

'Those— Those six people were *witches*?' said Alec. Such

was his astonishment that he too laid down his fork and wiped his mouth with his napkin, giving every indication of not planning to finish his dinner.

'Of course not,' Mr Wallace said. 'They were innkeepers and maids and dairywomen. They were *accused* of witchcraft, as were so many in those torrid times. Held in the castle until they confessed and then were hanged.'

'Dirleton Castle?' I said.

'There's nothing in it,' said Mr Wallace. 'It was the usual hysterical nonsense. Silly women making up silly stories: a black dog who can change into a man and back again; carnal knowledge of mysterious strangers who turn out to be the devil. And then the church got in on it, which was hardly helpful: poking the poor things all over with hot tongs until they were too numb to yelp and then declaring that the devil's mark, which feels no pain, had been found. It was a great wickedness. A dark stain.'

'Yes indeed,' Alec said. 'Yes, of course. A very modern, very rational view of the thing. I commend you.'

'The church takes the view that if we don't give it credence then it has no power,' said Mr Wallace. 'I take the view that the little snippets of lore that have survived are harmless enough. A children's song. The stone that only the pure can leap.'

'But, still, why would anyone name six children after witches?' I said.

'Oh my dear, I know!' said Mr Wallace. 'Or I should say, I know *now*. I was new in the parish and didn't know then that the names were significant or I would never have agreed to it.'

With that, he hoisted a book under each arm and left us. We sat in silence for a minute or two after he had gone.

281

When I spoke it was with some trepidation. 'He's right, of course. It *is* harmless.'

Alec took his time before answering. 'It's all very well for him to say there's nothing in it,' he began. 'But when the very woman who took care of Halliburton's six witchy namesakes says Halliburton's agent is the devil. And when that agent dies at a stone supposed to separate the pure from the wicked, and when one of the children strews chicken entrails around the stone to cleanse it again . . .'

'It's enough to give anyone the willies,' I said. 'But you know there must be a rational explanation, don't you?'

'I know there's something bothering me that I can't put a name to. And I know what we need to do. *You* know what we need to do too, don't you?'

'Oh Lord, yes, I suppose so,' I said. 'We need to go back to Mither Gollane and ask her to explain. Even though there is nothing I want to hear less than her explanation. She's obviously mad, Alec. Even if her wards have been leaned on to disown her, one would think her own surviving child would help if he could. No one lives in a shack in the woods unless she is far too much for anyone to cope with.'

'Or unless she is truly a witch.'

'It's not funny,' I said.

'I'm not joking.'

'You are not going to succeed in frightening me.'

'I'm not trying to.'

'Alec, you *can't* be serious! There are no such things as witches.'

'There were no such things as witches three hundred years ago either, but that didn't stop people confessing and not retracting the confession even to the point of death.'

'Well, let's go and see if we can get Mither Gollane to

confess *something*,' I said. 'But I warn you, I will listen to an explanation of the names, her eviction, her alibi for the time of Silas's death and nothing more. If she starts in on black dogs and dark strangers, I'm leaving.'

'Why? If it's all nonsense and there's nothing to fear?'

I pretended I had not heard him, which is best sometimes.

Chapter 18

It was almost dark now, and the lamps in all the cottage windows glowed warmly. We caught sight of Miss Meek out in front of the schoolhouse watering her flowers and we saw the shadow of Manie Halliburton pass behind the bow window of her gate lodge. I was fearful that we would not be able to find the place in the woods where Mither Gollane had made her home, but once again there was fragrant smoke from a cooking fire and also this time the sound of voices. Alec whistled as he beat a path through the brambles and nettles to the clearing and the voices stilled before we got to the circle of light thrown off by the fire. We saw the two women, one too old to be living as she was and one too young to be dressed in black, sitting on the stump and the bucket and looking as witch-like and sinister as it was possible for anyone to look without actually riding a broomstick.

'Lizzy,' I said to the youngster. 'Mrs Laird.'

She hissed. 'Mither Gollane. Mither Gollane, I am.'

'Well, that's the question, isn't it?' said Alec. 'It looks that way, because Mr Wallace is a kind man and a bit of a fool. But you only really have three children, don't you?'

'I only really have one now,' said Mither Gollane in such a small voice that, despite everything she and her wards had done to us – setting traps and playing tricks, distracting and bamboozling and sabotaging our investigation – my heart went out to her.

'Why did Mr Halliburton choose those names?' I said. 'Such terribly unlucky names for the six little foundlings?'

'Mr Halliburton!' said Mither Gollane, with a sneer. 'That's a joke. Anyway, *I* chose the names. Good names, not unlucky ones. Important names. Names we should remember. Names just right for more Dirleton bairns who've been wronged.'

'I don't understand,' Alec said.

'Our father,' said Lizzy Hogg, 'who art in absence, Halliburton be his name.'

She spoke in a singsong voice and giggled as she did so, which made it all the more shocking. Still, it was illuminating too. 'He wouldn't give his children a name?' I said. 'He left it up to you and you exercised your right of choice as you saw fit?'

'Names of the wronged, given to the wronged,' Mither Gollane said. 'I would do it again today even with what it's cost me.'

'What do you mean?' I said. 'What did it cost you?'

'Thrown out of a castle and sent to live in a cottage I was,' she said. 'When he found out. That was all the thanks I got for bringing up his bas— for bringing up six more besides my own.'

'That does seem harsh,' I said. 'But surely you could have swallowed your pride and stayed in the cottage, instead of this.' I waved my hands around.

'Stayed?' she said, shrill enough that she disturbed the little houseful of hens who were tucked up for the night. They squawked and grumbled and eventually resettled themselves. 'He put me out of my cottage too. I had no choice but to come here, with my last, my little one. My Bess.'

She reached over and chucked Lizzy under her chin with a long fingernail. Lizzy bridled at the tickling but beamed too. 'I thought if he was going to damn me for raising witches then I would raise one.'

'You did what?' Alec said. 'You told this child she was— To pay back— That's wicked, Mrs Laird. That's dreadful.'

'She's happy,' Mither Gollane said. 'She's a sunny wee soul.'

I looked at the girl, sitting huddled by a campfire in her black rags, and thought back over all our encounters with her since we arrived here: her flittings and swoopings, her breaking into my room and dashing out again, the crows and the entrails around the stone, the parish books left strewn over her writing desk. Then I felt a jolt as sharp as if someone had slapped me.

'Wronged,' I said. 'It is too heavy a burden for a child to bear – being told they are wronged and being given someone to blame. It was too heavy for *this* little one.'

'Me?' said Lizzy Hogg. 'Is that me?'

'Of course,' Alec said. 'Oh dear.'

'Of course what?' said the old woman. 'Oh dear what?'

I knew exactly what. Mither Gollane had, inadvertently I assumed, used the very words written in place of a signature on Silas's letter summoning him to Dirleton to meet "one who is wronged". And so the poor child would be taken away and punished, no matter that it was this travesty of a mother sitting before us who had started the whole awful sequence, with her ludicrous decision to give six innocent children such blackened names.

'We're leaving now,' I said. 'We're going to the castle, Lizzy.'

'My castle? Can I come?'

'You stay here with me, my Bess,' said Mither Gollane. 'You stay away from strangers, like I taught you.'

'God forgive you,' I said.

'We will find some handwriting,' Alec said. 'And compare it with the letter.'

'What's that supposed to mean?' said Mither Gollane. 'What are you talking about? Hie! You! What handwriting? What letter?' Her voice faded as we hurried away but she was still muttering and grumbling exactly like her hens as we passed out of earshot.

'That was horrid,' I said. 'Do you really think Lizzy Hogg killed Silas?'

'I do,' Alec said. 'And yes, it was.'

'Ugh,' I said, feeling a chill, even though I was trotting to keep up with him.

'If the little turret room is open, and if we can get a sample of writing from Lizzy's desk, and if it's the same as Silas's letter, then we've got her.'

'I can't bear to think of that child in a prison,' I said.

'It'll be a hospital,' said Alec. 'Which is not much better, I grant you.'

As we emerged from the lane beside Manie's lodge cottage, we could see across the green that there was a lamp burning in the arched window of the little tower in the castle wall. 'That's a good sign,' Alec said. 'She's only visiting her mother so she probably *has* left the door open to let her slip back in. Let's hurry.'

The gate in the wall was unlocked and my heart lifted to see that the upstairs door of Lizzy's little home stood ajar too. We could see the silhouettes of moths flitting around against the lighted inside. We hurried up the steps and turned, then stopped dead in the doorway.

The room was not empty. Maggie Goodfellow sat at the desk with a pen in her hand and a pair of small spectacles on her nose.

287

'Good evening,' she said. 'Rather late to be calling.'

'If you're waiting for Lizzy,' I said. 'She is visiting your . . . guardian.'

'I know,' said Miss Goodfellow. 'I'm waiting up for her, looking out for her. This is my room, my study I suppose you would call it. Lizzy has the downstairs room, although she comes up to the castle for meals and company. And mischief.'

'*Your* room?' Alec said. 'Your desk? Your writing?'

'Lizzy doesn't write,' said Miss Goodfellow. 'She can read a little, but she prefers to have stories read aloud to her. Don't we all?'

'Doesn't write at all?' I said. 'We thought Lizzy wrote the letter summoning Mr Esslemont to Dirleton.'

Miss Goodfellow laughed. 'Lizzy could no more write a letter, address it and post it than she could fly,' she said. 'I love her. She's my sister, as I assume you know now. And I'm angry that she was used as a pawn in a silly game. But I know her limitations and she didn't write to anyone.'

'We thought, when we found the parish books in this room, that she had stolen them.'

'Oh. She did, she did,' said Miss Goodfellow. 'That was her contribution. Dreamed up without help from anyone else.'

'Contribution?' I said.

She considered us for a long, thoughtful moment, then gathered herself with a brisk sniff. 'She knew which ones to take because she's been shown them so many times, and encouraged to pore over them.' Miss Goodfellow smiled bravely and rubbed her face. 'At least she brought them to me for safe keeping and didn't destroy all that history. I assume you took them back? Quite right, of course. I would have returned them to Mr Wallace eventually. I suppose I was clutching at straws.'

'Yes, but it's still very odd to call her mischief a contribution,' I said.

'How much do you know?' Miss Goodfellow said. 'Everything? Too much? Must I give up or is there still a chance?'

'Did you kill Silas Esslemont?' Alec asked her.

She shook her head sorrowfully.

'I think you should give up,' I said. 'You could help us. We *don't* know everything, but we won't rest until we do. So. What about the *other* contributions?'

Miss Goodfellow, without moving, nevertheless seemed visibly to surrender. 'Manie's was to put those garments in the priest's hole,' she said. 'And that was her carving knife. Nessie managed to purloin the clothes while she was measuring for curtains. The name tape was a nice touch, I thought. Paddy drove in the tent pegs and thought up the postcard wheeze, as you would expect. Marion, if you can believe it, stole the car, and she had that stroke of inspiration with chicken guts. I got the blood from the butcher's shop.'

'But why?' I asked her. 'For heaven's sake, why? Tell us. We might be able to help.'

And now she did slump. When she spoke again, she sounded defeated. 'When Manie woke me up on Saturday night to say she'd heard two men fighting outside her cottage, they could have been anyone. But as soon as we saw the letter and realised who the dead one was, we knew who had killed him.'

'And decided to protect her?' Alec said.

'Her?' said Miss Goodfellow. 'Him. We decided to protect *him*. First by saying it was a woman, granted. But then we found out that Lizzy had looked out of her window downstairs and seen Marion . . . dealing with the body. Worse than that, she was *telling* people. That's when it occurred to us that there were five women who would then need alibis. So we changed tack and said it was a man. Meaning that only Paddy had to be put in the clear.'

'By means of you claiming to have spent the night with your brother,' I said.

'I made a bit of a hash of that,' Maggie said, rubbing her nose. 'But what did you think about the rest?'

'The crows, the ever-changing time of death, the knife, the phantom writers, the car crash, the news of Mr Halliburton's return, the cilice and spugna and the entrails?' I said. 'The cilice and spugna was over-egging, if I'm honest. Silas's widow laughed at the idea despite her mourning. But even that slowed us down a little.'

'I can't claim credit for the writers,' Maggie said. 'That wasn't us. So, as you can imagine, you two turning up was quite a spanner in the works in more ways than one.'

'What does that mean?' said Alec. 'Why don't you speak plainly?'

'I'll try,' she said. 'But it's all got so complicated. It was Marion's idea, of course. Paddy and Nessie and I helped work it out, and Manie was marvellous with the practical things, but Marion is very clever, far more clever than me, and she was the mastermind. She said there was no point trying to pretend it was nothing to do with us, so we had better make a chaos of clues all sort of pointing *obliquely* in our direction, but all contradicting one another. Then make sure Paddy had an alibi and we were safe as houses. You see? Only, Lizzy stole those blasted books, which pointed to us much too *baldly*. That was the first thing that went wrong. Even worse than that though, we only meant it to fool poor Captain Wicks and his men. We weren't expecting you two.'

'And yet we felt expected,' I said. 'Which was most puzzling.'

Miss Goodfellow gave a short laugh. 'When you arrived, Paddy thought Marion had added you to the plan. We *all* thought someone else had added you to the plan. Until we got together on Sunday night and realised otherwise.'

'You got together?' I said. 'To review how your stew of misdirection was coming along?'

'Not just that,' she said. 'Our— Mither Gollane needed us there to . . . It will sound very silly.'

'To cleanse the stone?' I said.

'The whole village wanted it done,' said Miss Goodfellow. 'You must have noticed how scared everyone was on Sunday, hiding in their houses.'

'Miss Goodfellow,' Alec said, sounding much brisker, surely, than he felt, 'who killed Silas Esslemont?'

'Paddy after all?' I added.

'No of course not,' she said.

'And it's not one of your sisters either?' I said. 'But it's someone you are protecting anyway?'

'Trying to. But we've made such a mess of it. I believe you when you say you won't rest until you know, but I can't be the one who does your dirty work for you. If you knew what you were digging up you wouldn't be so . . . merciless.'

'Silas was shown no mercy,' said Alec, to my great surprise.

Miss Goodfellow's face clouded briefly. 'I know murder is the worst thing anyone could do,' she said. 'That's what we're taught and that's all we ever hear. But there are acts – not even acts: habits. There are ways of *being* that feel much worse and last much longer.'

'You speak too cryptically for me, Miss Goodfellow,' I said. 'Silas Esslemont had a wife and two daughters. His murder might have taken a moment for *him* but it will last a long time for them.'

'Oh really?' she said. 'A wife and two daughters, eh? Oh well then.' Her voice was as dry as a desert and I frowned, unable to catch her meaning.

'We will find out in the end, as Mrs Gilver assured you, Miss Goodfellow,' said Alec. 'With your help or without it, we will catch him eventually. We have a great many more strings to pull on. We haven't even tried to contact Mr Halliburton yet. It strikes me as pretty likely he'd know who hates him enough to kill Silas in his stead.'

Miss Goodfellow laughed and her laugh was dry too. 'Good luck,' she said. 'If you are dead set on chasing Mr Halliburton to ground, I wish you well.'

'Let's go, Dandy,' Alec said.

'Wait!' said Miss Goodfellow, as we turned to leave. 'Don't think too badly of me. If it were my decision alone . . . But there are my brothers and sisters to think of.'

'Brother and sisters,' I said.

'Yes,' said Miss Goodfellow. 'Brother, of course. Look, let me try to explain.'

I glanced at Alec. He was ready to leave, tired of being teased and toyed with by this woman. I was minded to stay and listen. Each time she spoke, she skirted closer to the truth, I reckoned. I gestured to her to carry on.

'Our mother,' she said. 'The woman we all call our mother was terribly ill-treated. I know she says she was kicked out of the castle for our names, but it's not true. The castle was always meant for me to live in, because my mother was a lady, if you can believe anything so ridiculous. Poor Manie and Paddy were the children of servants, each sacked in disgrace for her pregnancy. So no castle for them. Nessa and Marion's mothers were office girls. We were all allotted a place in life according to our station. Wicked, isn't it?

But true. Anyway, since the castle was mine, once I was of age, our guardian was moved out to a cottage. It was years later she was kicked out of *there* for our names. She's rewritten it to make her plight sound even worse than it is. And it's bad enough, so she needn't have. In the last ten years, she's grown very peculiar, but even she couldn't have known poor Lizzy would be the way she is. The rest of us roll our eyes and make sure she's warm enough in winter, but Lizzy believes it, you see?'

'We know all that,' said Alec. 'What does it have to do with you protecting a murderer? Someone who killed a husband and a father simply because he was a proxy. An agent, Miss Goodfellow. A friend.'

'Oh, I can't bear it,' said Miss Goodfellow. 'I feel like a kitten who's played with a ball of wool and got tangled up in it like a fly in a cobweb. It's all so complicated and so ridiculous and so far beyond ever unravelling now. People made bad decisions with the best of intentions, you see. And some of it is no one's fault at all.' She paused. 'Unless we blame Gavrilo Princip, anyway.'

'Gavrilo Princip?' Alec echoed. 'Who killed Franz Ferdinand and caused the Great War? What's he got to do with this?'

I felt a cold, prickling sensation spread through me like pins and needles. As it left me, the answers came thick and fast, tumbling over one another: Mr Wallace had said that Halliburton was to Dirleton what Jock Tamson, that mythical father, was to Scotland; Miss Goodfellow had laughed so very dryly at the thought that Silas was the loving father of his girls; she said "brothers" when Paddy Watson was the only man of the six.

'Alec,' I said. 'We've been blind.'

It crashed down on me like a tidal wave: how ridiculous it was ever to believe that Silas, Silas Esslemont, philanderer of great renown, held the deeds for cottages and castles full of secret children purely to help out a friend.

'There is no such family as the Halliburtons, is there?' I asked. 'You are Silas's children.'

'There were Halliburtons,' said Miss Goodfellow. 'Back in the mists of time. It was an obvious name to pick. The name of "Esslemont" was rather too unusual to be bandied around the village.'

'But why did Silas stash all of you in the same place?' Alec said.

'Why not?' said Miss Goodfellow. 'It worked rather well. Until it didn't. Our mother was kind and seemed quite an ordinary sort of person, until she didn't.'

'Until you realised she had given you the names of witches?' I said. 'And these reprised names started garnering attention? And then what? Did some folklorist dig deep to find your father?'

Maggie Goodfellow shook her head.

'What does Silas hiding behind the name of Halliburton have to do with Gavrilo Princip?' Alec said.

We watched a fat tear roll down one of Miss Goodfellow's cheeks. 'It wasn't the names of the Dirleton witches that brought it all crashing down,' she said. 'It was the war. The last war.'

'What happened in the last war?' Alec said. He spoke so gently I could not be sure whether he sought information or whether he already knew and was enticing her to confession.

'Everyone signed up,' she said. My heart gave a lurch, but I managed to keep my attention on the present and the past, and began to see the light.

'Including two of Mither Gollane's sons,' I said. 'Two of your brothers.' It was as though a fog had been driven off

294

by a breeze and suddenly I could see quite plainly what had been right there before me all this time. Before both of us, Alec and me. 'Miss Goodfellow,' I said. 'What is the surname of the two sweet little girls, Isabel and Annabel, who made a jelly for our supper this evening?'

'Did they?' said Miss Goodfellow, sounding haunted. 'You see? Do you *see*? They are innocents. So is their mother. And if their grandmother isn't innocent exactly, at least she has suffered enough.'

'We really have been blind, Alec,' I said. 'We kept seeing Nessie and Manie there and so it never occurred to us to wonder why "Halliburton" owned the inn as well as all the cottages, the post office and castle, the school and laundry. I *did* wonder why such a friendly sort of chap refused to give his name and it bothered me to call a cook by her Christian name as though she were a maid.'

Miss Goodfellow had tears standing in her eyes but she kept her head up.

'His name – their name – is Laird, isn't it?' I said. 'The landlord of the Castle Inn is the man you consider to be your other brother, Miss Goodfellow. The only remaining son of the woman you call your mother.'

'He has never forgiven her,' Daisy said. 'He thinks his brothers wouldn't have joined up for the war if they weren't pushed out of a crowded house by all the little guests.'

'How did he find out the truth about Halliburton?' Alec said.

'From the first lot of folklorists who came to write about our mother and our names and the bad business from all those years ago.'

'So Tom Laird lured your father – your real father; Silas Esslemont – to Dirleton to pay for what had happened to his family?'

295

'He said if Silas was innocent then the letter wouldn't bring him, because he wouldn't know who "one you have wronged" *was* and he wouldn't know where to come.'

'But he did come,' I said.

'Straight to Dirleton, to our mother's camp, effectively confessing that he knew he had wronged her. Tom lay in wait beside Manie's lodge and set upon him.'

'Why now?' said Alec. 'All these years later?'

But I thought I knew. 'Because, after so much sacrifice,' I said, 'we're about to do it again.'

Maggie Goodfellow nodded and a small sob escaped her.

'How did he hope to get away with it?' Alec said.

'*He* put the names of the writers in the register,' Miss Goodfellow said. 'He meant to tell the police that an odd pair of strangers turned up and went out late at night. He was going to try to blame them for the murder.'

'Crabbie and McEwan!' I said. 'Two names plucked from the brewery and distillery trinkets in front of his eyes when he stood at the desk.'

'Without us, he would have been arrested by nightfall,' Miss Goodfellow said. 'And perhaps he should have been.'

Alec, beside me, groaned low and deep in his throat. 'Oh God, Dandy. Her last son is going to be hanged. Those little girls are going to be orphans.'

'You see? You see?' Miss Goodfellow said. 'I couldn't tell you and I couldn't not. It just goes on and on and never stops. My real mother lost to me, my father murdered, the only mother I've ever known gone mad in a hovel, my brother hating me and the rest of us, Lizzy going down such a dark road. I couldn't start another round of it, hurting those little girls, and I leapt to his aid, without thinking. By the time we recovered from the horror of it all we had already dragged him to the stone and—'

She broke off and gave that mirthless laugh again.

'Marion and I managed it between us, you see,' she said. 'So I'm not as noble as all that. I don't want to pay for my crimes either. Who would look after Lizzy if I'm in prison? And what about the children in the school? Who else could take care of them all the way Marion does? Oh God, what a mess! What a waste of all those lives. And yet *he* carried on, loved wherever he went. Hail fellow well met. Rich and safe and happy.'

'Not wherever he went,' said Alec. His voice sounded thick. 'I never cared for him. I've loathed him with a passion for seventeen years. Since your mother died, actually.'

We often say that our jaws drop but it is seldom that it happens. It happened then. My mouth fell open and I stared and stared at the woman standing before me. I did not wonder if it was true, for as soon as the thought entered my head, I knew. This was Cara Duffy's daughter. This young woman was the daughter of Alec's lost love, the cause of so much pain and loss and heartbreak, the missing child who brought the two of us together to avenge Cara's death, the very origin of Gilver and Osborne. The girl whom I had never met but who had changed my life completely.

'You knew her?' Miss Goodfellow whispered. 'I didn't even know her name. You actually knew her?'

'I knew her,' said Alec. 'Cara. And I knew her father too. Your grandfather. He left me a house in his will. I live there. You must come and visit me.'

'Cara?' said Miss Goodfellow. 'What a beautiful name. Was she— I don't even know what I'm asking. But was she?'

'She was a splendid girl,' I said. 'She should have been loved more than she was. She was a *shining* girl. You know, the first time I ever saw you I knew you looked like someone. I just couldn't think who it was.' I turned to Alec. 'Not that I've forgotten her, darling. Only, it's been a good number of years.'

Miss Goodfellow gave one more shaky sob and then there was silence. We were still standing there the three of us, when feet rattled the staircase and Lizzy Hogg burst, panting, into the room.

'Someone is abroad,' she said, her voice shrill and her cheeks hectic. 'Flitting in the moonlight.'

For one terrible moment I was sure she meant Silas, risen from his coffin and walking about. But she jabbed a finger at the window facing the green and, when we went to look, there was a cart loaded high with boxes and bundles, idling at the door of the Castle Inn. Tom Laird was just now hoisting himself up into the high seat, three dark heads behind him, shining like onyx as the moon beat down. He shook the reins and the pony took off straight over the green, the grass deadening the sound of its hooves. As we watched, the whole little family disappeared round the curve of the castle wall and was gone.

'She saw us with the parish books,' I said. 'Bella. She told him. Alec, what are we going to do?'

Miss Goodfellow sat down at her desk and put her head in her hands. 'There is lots of space in the castle,' she said. 'The girls can have a tower room each. And Bella can keep the inn if she wants to. I'll buy it for her. Unless I'm cut off without a shilling by Silas Esslemont's widow.'

'She's not that sort of woman,' I said. 'I've known her all my life and she's the last person to blame Mrs Laird, or young Mrs Laird, or you.'

'You speak as though all is lost,' Alec said. 'But there's still time. Come on, Dandy! That cart is no match for my Daimler.' He was already halfway out of the door. 'We can head them off.'

We pelted over the green and into the yard of the inn, flinging ourselves into his motor car and then, I at least, clinging on to the door handle for dear life as Alec followed the Lairds out of Dirleton. I could not watch for them. In truth, I could not keep my eyes open: he had never driven so recklessly in all the years I had known him as he did in grim pursuit of Tom Laird.

'Look out!' I said, as I felt the car tilt on a sharp bend. 'He will be caught sooner or later, Alec. It's not worth following Daisy into a coma to be the ones who catch him.'

'Good God, Dandy,' Alec said. 'What do you take me for? I'm not ruining my engine to catch a murderer. I'm trying to get to him before anyone else finds out he's running away.'

'What?'

'We can persuade him to turn himself in,' Alec said. 'All he did was fight a man and who hasn't done that, with much less excuse for it? I refuse to let Tom Laird hang for being the one who finally made Silas Esslemont pay for his—'

'Oh, Alec!' I said. 'Oh, darling.'

Alec's foot lifted a little, I think. At least the motor car stopped whining and the leaves on either side of the lane did not seem to be flashing past in quite such a blur.

'There they are,' he said.

Up ahead, the cart was slowing and now stopping, squarely in the middle of the lane. Bella and her two daughters, sitting with their backs to the driver's seat, stared back at us, their faces white in the light of our headlamps. The girls were owlish with sleep, but Bella's face was a picture of the most abject misery. I could not help thinking of all the other women and girls right across Europe who would soon be sitting on carts laden with their belongings, fleeing for their lives.

'Those poor children,' I said, thinking of all of them, mine too.

'We can't see the children,' said Alec. 'They are behind the driver's seat, out of sight. Because Tom has turned the cart around of his own volition, intending to come back and face the music. That's what I see and so I shall swear, hand on a Bible if need be.'

Epilogue

Sunday 27 August 1939

'I must say, darling, you're taking this very well.' I gave Daisy the sort of look I knew she had come to loathe in the months since Silas's death, but one I was powerless to suppress.

'This one helps,' she said, ruffling Bunty's ears. My dog had stayed by the invalid's bed for weeks and she still shot to Daisy's side whenever she visited. 'Anyway, taking what?' Daisy added. 'It's a happy occasion and I am a mere bystander.'

'Not the wedding,' I said. 'And you're right. It *is* a happy occasion. I am trying to remember that.' I looked over at Teddy, resplendent in his Royal Air Force uniform, standing beaming beside my daughter-in-law of not quite two hours in her own matching WAAF blues.

I felt my eyes fill again. Grant had been sobbing into a hanky since before the church service and Pallister had whisky on his breath. Gilverton had lost its stiff upper lip entirely, apart from Hugh, who had sung the hymns with relish and nodded off during the sermon, as though this were any Sunday. I stared at him, where he stood in conversation with my sister Mavis, searching for any sign of emotion. Giving up after a few moments, though, I turned my eyes back to Teddy and Dolly. 'They're so brave,' I said to Daisy. 'And so young.'

'Exactly,' Daisy said. 'My point in a nutshell. Compared with what our children are doing, what's a little social awkwardness?'

I glanced at Donald to see how he was faring. How drab his army dress was in comparison. But how proudly he had stood beside his little brother at the altar, and how happy he looked now, with the enormous Mallory at his side and with one fat toddler on each arm. Mallory caught my eye and mimed her exhaustion, holding up a foot to let me see her swollen ankle. I winked at her. We were both relieved that Donald was headed for the infantry and not the skies. Neither one of us would ever admit it to the other or to anyone.

'It's the secret league of women,' Daisy said, as though reading my mind. 'I am glad to know her. For one thing, I was as fond of Cara as everyone else and it's lovely to see her daughter, grown up so pretty. Can you believe Silas barely met her? Barely met any of them? Just handed them over to that strange little woman to take care of and kept himself out of the way? He didn't even pick their names!' She sniffed deeply. 'Although I've decided to believe that he went haring off down there in case one of them was in need of help, and not in case trouble was brewing for him. I spent my married life choosing what to believe and see no reason to change tack now.'

'And Silas wasn't the only one who . . .' I said, before deciding not to clothe the thought in words. 'I was a little surprised that none of their *mothers* fought to keep them.'

Daisy gave me an arch look.

'Yes, you're right,' I admitted, with a sigh. 'Of course the shameful child being whisked off and never heard of again was satisfactory all round.'

'Naturally, I shall carry on letting them live their lives down in Dirleton,' Daisy said. 'I'm not sure I can quite face knowing all of them. Miss Goodfellow is enough to be going on with, for the moment anyway.'

'But will you have to know any of them?' I said. 'Even Miss Goodfellow? Surely today is a one-off.' In fact, I had been astonished when Alec suggested bringing her along to Teddy's wedding. I had asked Daisy for her permission and been just as astonished when she leapt on the idea as her great chance to inspect one of Silas's many children.

'A one-off?' Daisy said. 'I doubt that very much. Look at him.'

I glanced over at Alec now, laughing at something Dolly was saying and turning to share the joke with Miss Goodfellow, who smiled good-naturedly enough. She was coping marvellously with what had to be an excruciating ordeal. 'What did you mean, for one thing?' I said. 'What's the other thing?'

'Well, I shall tell you but you're going to be shocked,' Daisy said. 'It might interest you to know, Dandy, that Silas and I only ever had one argument during our marriage. About all his exploits, I mean. We argued about money and the children and his mother all the time. But about the endless stream of mistresses: only one. During that fight he said something to me that cut me to the quick.'

'Should I sit down?'

'What a nasty mind!' Daisy said. 'And you so very carefully brought up! No, what he said was that perhaps if I had given him a son he wouldn't have strayed.'

'Rot!' I said. 'But very painful rot, I agree.'

'So you see I'm feeling rather smug to find out he had five *more* daughters and only one son,' Daisy said. 'I hope he's looking down – or more likely up – and seething that I found out.'

'And again, I say you're taking it all remarkably well.'

303

'It would be different if it really had been murder,' Daisy said. 'And if Tom Laird had hanged for it. Out of sheer squeamishness I might not then have been able to face Miss Goodfellow, as a representative of the six. Not in that case. I'm only human after all.'

I nodded but said nothing. As far as I knew, Daisy had never heard about Miss Meek and Miss Goodfellow dragging Silas to the leaping stone and leaving him there. All she knew was that Tom Laird goaded him into visiting, dragged him to see how his mother was living since Silas had evicted her from Lilac Cottage, and got into an understandable fist fight outside Manie Halliburton's cottage, during which Silas picked up a flower pot and tried to knock Tom out with it. Tom retaliated with another and Silas fell. Manie had put her hand on a Bible and sworn to the truth of all this. And now Tom Laird was in Saughton Prison in Edinburgh, where he would remain for many years.

Hard as I tried to abhor him for what he had done and find his punishment just, I hated to think of that friendly man who had kissed his daughters' heads, sitting in a cell. Much more cheerful to think of his wife, at the Castle Inn, busier than ever. The more lurid papers had opined that Silas crawled to the lucky stone in hopes of a miracle. The absolute gutter press preferred to believe he crawled to a cursed stone to enlist the help of the devil. And not even the most serious journalists from the very driest Scottish broadsheets were quite able to resist the six witches from the seventeenth century and the six siblings in the present day, not with Mither Gollane's shack, Lizzy Hogg's black rags, and an out-and-out castle thrown in. So Dirleton was on its way to becoming another Salem. One wondered what the rest of the village made of it, but Mrs Wallace had reported two new tea rooms and a little private hotel called Crow's Landing.

'Well, *I* don't think Miss Goodfellow will leave Dirleton Castle,' I said. 'Not as long as she's looking after her youngest sister, who is a little . . . I'm not sure of the medical term. Although she's doing rather better away from Mither Gollane's influence.'

'Oh?' said Daisy.

'Yes, that old troublemaker has been quite beaten back. Wonderful for Lizzy, but if Alec proposes to Miss Goodfellow I think she'll send him packing.'

'Proposes?' said Daisy. 'Dandy, that's abhorrent! That would practically be— And anyway, how can you have known Alec for seventeen years and still think he's the marrying sort? You are priceless.'

'He has mentioned a wife and children numerous times,' I said, haughtily. 'And he was engaged once. Not to mention several further close shaves.'

Daisy simply shook her head.

'And, if you mean to suggest that he will take Maggie Goodfellow as a mistress,' I went on, 'then *you* are the priceless one. You should have heard how he talked about Silas's doings.'

'Of course he doesn't want a mistress,' Daisy said. 'Dandy, you're a scream.'

'Well what then?' I said.

'All he's ever wanted is a family,' Daisy said. 'I think he means to *adopt* Miss Goodfellow. Which I think is rather sweet, very fitting and much less palaver. Oh, don't look at me like that,' she added. 'I'm who I've always been. Anyway, you better go and see to Hugh. He has just stalked off along the library passage, leaving your sister gaping like a goldfish.

Understandable that Mavis's conversation would make anyone flee, but he looked a little queer to me.'

'Mother?' said Donald, stopping me en route to the door. 'Is Father all right? He just gave me a terribly searching look, inspecting my uniform like a sergeant major, and then rushed off.'

Teddy, joining us, chimed in with: 'What's up with Dad? He glared at my tunic and bolted.'

'That wasn't a glare,' I said, and followed my husband.

I caught up with him not in the library but all the way along at the end of the house in his gunroom. It was dark, owing to the grille over the window and the fact that he had not switched the electric light on.

'All right?' I asked his back.

'No,' he said, still not turning. 'Are you?'

'No,' I said. I went over and leaned my head against the cloth of his coat, feeling the heave and drop of his ragged breathing as he tried to regain control.

'Let it go,' I suggested.

'Never!' said Hugh, as I had known he would when I decided to give voice to such an enormity. 'I shall never let anything go, Dandy. And nor shall you. We shall hold it all tightly together, come what may, and do it proudly.'

'That sounds perfect,' I said. 'Let's start tomorrow.'

'First thing,' said Hugh, and, right there in the gunroom, very briefly and for the only time in our lives, we wept together as one.

Facts and Fictions

The village of Dirleton in East Lothian is a real place (as are Haddington, Gullane and North Berwick) and is as charming today as Dandy found it in 1939. The church, manse, louping stane, gate lodge, castle, Castle Inn, bus stop and path to Archerfield are all still there, although there is no longer a laundry, bank, post office or school. There is a tea shop but not the same one as Alec fails to visit. The names on the cenotaph are as I have them here and some of the other off-page characters have names I found in the post office directory for that year, but none of the speaking parts are named after or based on real people. Well . . . there *were* six Dirletonites found guilty of witchcraft and executed in 1649. Their names were Agnes Clarkson, Margaret Goodfellow, Manie Halliburton, Bess Hog, Marion Miek and Patrick Watson. Their story was the spark for mine.

Acknowledgements

I would like to thank: Lisa Moylett, Zoe Apostolides, Elena Langtry and Jamie McLean at the agency; Sorcha Rose, Jo Dickinson, Jacqui Lewis, David Wardle and all at Hodder and Stoughton; my friends and family in Scotland and the US including the many booksellers, librarians, bloggers, podcasters, reviewers and fans who have cheered Dandy on for sixteen books now; my siblings at Sisters in Crime and my fellow MWA, CWA and SoA members; the other nine Criminal Minds; the coven; the fringe mob; and, while she's still here, my seventeen-year-old co-author, Rachel, who keeps one paw on the edge of my keyboard and is no end of help.

A troubled history has begun to repeat itself . . .

THE MIRROR DANCE

**Shortlisted for the Left Coast Crime's Lefty Award
for Best Historical Mystery Novel 2022**

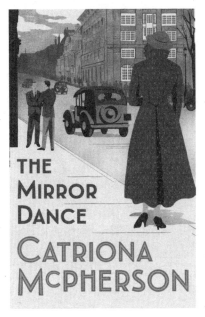

'The ever-witty McPherson has outdone herself' *SCOTTISH FIELD*

'All the wit and clever plotting fans of Christie could want'
MY WEEKLY SPECIAL

**PRAISE FOR CATRIONA MCPHERSON
AND THE *DANDY GILVER* SERIES . . .**

'A deliriously fun tale, flawlessly written' *SAGA*

'A winning heroine' *INDEPENDENT*

'Dandy Gilver deserves a damehood for increasing
the gaiety of the nation' **FRANCES BRODY**

As the NHS is born, a killer
stalks the streets of Edinburgh . . .

IN PLACE OF FEAR

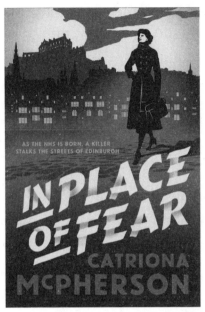

'An intriguing murder, a strong and convincing central character,
and McPherson's wonderful story-telling skills make this
a very classy mystery' **ANN CLEEVES**

'A hauntingly atmospheric weaving of social history
and layered mystery . . . McPherson's writing is compelling,
moving and memorable' **SARAH YARWOOD-LOVETT**

PRAISE FOR CATRIONA MCPHERSON . . .

'McPherson's wit has been compared to that of
P.G. Wodehouse or Nancy Mitford, and her finely researched
and choreographed narratives to the work of Agatha Christie . . .
these are the perfect reads for a night by the fire'
SCOTSMAN

'The most engaging and ingenious crime-cracker
I've met in ages' *SCOTLAND ON SUNDAY*